ALSO BY THE AUTHOR
Child of the Northern Spring
Queen of the Summer Stars

GUINEVERE

The Legend in Autumn

Persia Woolley

POSEIDON PRESS

New York   London   Toronto

Sydney   Tokyo   Singapore

POSEIDON PRESS

Simon & Schuster Building
Rockefeller Center
1230 Avenue of the Americas
New York, New York, 10020

POSEIDON PRESS is a registered trademark
of Simon & Schuster Inc.

POSEIDON PRESS colophon is a trademark
of Simon & Schuster Inc.

Designed by Karolina Harris
Manufactured in the United States of America

Library of Congress Cataloging-in-Publication Data

Woolley, Persia, date.
Guinevere: the legend in autumn/Persia Woolley.
p.   cm.
1. Guinevere, Queen (Legendary character)—Fiction.
2. Arthurian romances—Adaptations.   I. Title.
PS3573.O68G85   1991
813'.54—dc20   91-28414
                                                                CIP
ISBN: 0-671-70831-7

To the children and family who understood
that a deadline sometimes cut Christmas down to
a phone call rather than a visit; to my father,
William C. Higman; and to my high school
teacher John Chaney, whose comment "Of course
you can" led to my tackling this entire project.

Characters

HOUSE OF PENDRAGON

Arthur: *King of Logres, High King of Britain*
Guinevere of Rheged: *Arthur's wife, High Queen of Britain*

Mordred: *Arthur's son*

Igraine: *Arthur's mother, wife of Uther, High King of Britain*

Morgause ⎱ *daughters of Igraine by her first husband,*
Morgan le Fey ⎰ *Gorlois*

Cei: *Arthur's foster-brother and Seneschal of the Realm*
Bedivere: *Arthur's foster-brother and wise counselor*

HOUSE OF ORKNEY

Morgause: *widow of King Lot, half-sister of Arthur*

Gawain ⎫
Gaheris ⎪
Agravain ⎬ *sons of Morgause*
Gareth ⎪
Mordred ⎭

HOUSE OF NORTHUMBRIA

Urien: *King of Northumbria, husband of Morgan*
Morgan le Fey: *half-sister of Arthur, wife of Urien, High Priestess*
and Lady of the Lake

Uwain: *son of Morgan and Urien*

BRITTANY FACTION

Lancelot of the Lake: *Arthur's best friend and lieutenant*
Ector de Maris: *Lancelot's half-brother*

Bors
Lionel } *brothers who are cousins of Lancelot*

Belliance
Melias
Lavaine
Kanahins } *protégés of Lancelot*
Nerovens
Urr

HOUSE OF PELLINORE

Pellinore: *warlord of the Wrekin*

Lamorak: *Pellinore's eldest son in wedlock*
Perceval: *Pellinore's youngest son in wedlock*
Amide: *one of Pellinore's many illegitimate children*

OTHER MEMBERS OF THE ROUND TABLE FELLOWSHIP

Accolon of Gaul: *Morgan le Fey's lover*
Agricola: *Roman King of Demetia*

Vortipor: *arrogant nephew of Agricola*

Bagdemagus: *warlord of Dorset*
Cador: *Duke of Cornwall*

Constantine: *his son and successor*

Colgrevance: *warrior friend of Gawain's from the Continent*
Dinadin: *Tristan's best friend*
Florence: *warrior friend of Agravain*
Geraint: *King of Devon, husband of Enid*
Gingalin: *son of Gawain and Ragnell*
Griflet: *Master of the Kennel and husband of Frieda*
Ironside: *aging warrior*
Lovel: *warrior friend of Agravain*
Lucan: *Arthur's Gatekeeper and butler*

Palomides: *slave-born Arab, lover of Isolde*
Pelleas: *husband of Nimue*
Petroc: *warlord from Devon*

HOUSE OF CARBONEK

Pellam: *wounded Knig of the Waste Land*

Elaine: *his beautiful daughter, lover of Lancelot*
Galahad: *son of Elaine and Lancelot*

HOUSE OF CORNWALL

Mark: *King of Cornwall*
Isolde: *Mark's child-bride from Ireland*
Tristan: *nephew to Mark, Isolde's lover*

WOMEN OF CAMELOT

Brigit: *Irish foster-sister to Guinevere*
Brisane: *governess to Elaine of Carbonek*
Enid: *sharp-tongued lady-in-waiting, wife of Geraint*
Lynette: *daughter of Ground's Keeper in London, wife of Gareth*
Vinnie: *Roman matron in charge of ladies-in-waiting*

VARIOUS HEADS OF STATE

Anastasius: *Emperor in Constantinople*
Clovis: *King of the Franks*
Theodoric the Great: *Ostrogoth King of Italy*

OTHER CHARACTERS

Mr. and Mrs. Badger: *gardener and housekeeper at Joyous Gard*
Bercilak: *Charcoal burner and prankster who is one of the Ancient
Ones, half-civilized, half-wildman*
Cathbad: *Druid who was Guinevere's childhood teacher*
Cerdic: *Saxon leader who challenged Arthur at Mount Badon*

Cynric: *his son, kept as a peace-hostage after the Battle of
Mount Badon*

Dagonet: *Arthur's Court Jester*
Frieda: *Saxon milk-maid, wife of Griflet*

Gildas: *past suitor of Gwen, monk and student of Illtud*
The Green Man: *an Ancient God who may or may not be a figment of everyone's imagination*
Gwyn of Neath: *horsebreeder and builder of the Hall on Glastonbury's Tor*
Gwynlliw: *representative of warlords in Dorset hill-forts*
Illtud: *Prince/warrior who became a monk*
Kimmins: *crofter in the Cheviot Hills*
Maelgwn: *Guinevere's cousin, King of Gwynedd*
Merlin: *Arthur's tutor and mentor, the Mage of Britain*
Nimue: *Priestess and protégé of Merlin, wife of Pelleas*
Ragnell: *leader of nomadic Ancient Ones, lover of Gawain*
Riderich: *Arthur's bard*
Taliesin: *peasant boy who becomes a famous bard*
Wehha the Swede: *leader of East Anglian Federates*

   Wuffa: *his son*

Yder: *brother of Gwyn of Neath*

King Arthur's
Britain

ORKNEY
ISLES

Loch Ness
PICTLAND
CALEDONIA
Glen Coe
Loch Lomond
Stirling
Dumbarton • Edinburgh   Holy Isle
LOTHIAN
NORTHUMBRIA   Joyous Gard
The   Hadrian's Wall
Mote RHEGED Carlisle
Solway Firth
The
Black
Lake
Irish Sea   York

Lincoln

GWYNEDD
The Wrekin   The Fens
WELSH   Cambridge
KINGDOMS
EAST
DEMETIA   ANGLIA
Gloucester   London
Caerleon LOGRES
Glastonbury   Silchester
Winchester   Dover
DEVON Camelot
Tintagel Exeter   The Saxon Shore
CORNWALL
Castle Dore

N

0   50   100 MILES

0   50   100 KM

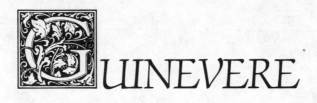

GUINEVERE

The Legend in Autumn

Preface

I love prefaces because they are the author's chance to say to the reader, "Here's what I've been thinking about for a book—if you're interested, let's explore the matter together."

In this particular case, my idea is to explore the stories of King Arthur's Camelot from a realistic point of view, looking for the character types and adventures that could have planted the seed from which the legend grew.

This business of looking for the human story behind a legendary tale is called "euhemerism," and a number of other authors have employed it over the years, from Mary Renault to Parke Godwin and Morgan Llywelyn. It has also been used by archeologists, the classic example being Schliemann's discovery of the site of Troy as a result of his treating *The Iliad* as a historical rather than fictional account of the Trojan War.

Because of my interest in the reality behind the myth, I do not write fantasy (and in spite of the covers you may find on my books, I don't write "women's romance" either). There's plenty of superstition among my characters, and more than enough love to go around, but if you are looking for a sword-and-sorcery epic, this is certainly not the book for you.

On the other hand, if you want a smashing good story filled with archetypical characters going off on great quests, following noble causes, espousing the need for honor and courtesy, and developing into a fine Fellowship—as well as engaging in duplicity, chicanery, villainy, incest, matricide, and terrible betrayals, both personal and political . . . you'll find the tales of Arthur's Round Table have been providing all this and more for hundreds of years. I know of no other single story cycle which offers a broader range of characters and endeavors, or a deeper look into the troubled heart of humanity.

This is one of the reasons I have chosen to tell the tale through the eyes of Arthur's wife, Guinevere. It seems clear that although women look at the same events as men, they see very different things. In the past men told tales that focused on who was the bloodiest, who was the bravest, and who made off with the loot (or the crown or the lady), whereas women tended to tell who did what to whom, *why* they did it, and how it will affect the rest of the tribe. I felt it was time we took a new look at this old story through the eyes of a real woman, and who better to see, know and understand the characters of the Round Table than the much-loved Queen at the heart of it?

Although it has recently been popular to make Guinevere a scapegoat for the fall of the Round Table, my research back through the literature of the Matter of Britain (as the collected stories of Arthur are called) clearly showed that whatever else was laid at Gwen's doorstep, she was always seen as the gracious and caring Queen. In the medieval stories she is sometimes referred to as "Guinevere the gay," and is credited with bringing high spirits and playfulness to the Court. At no point does Arthur consider putting her aside because she can't have children, and it is clear that there are almost as many who side with her and Lancelot as with Arthur at the end. Naturally I have built on that and (I hope) made her a lively and admirable character in her own right.

This is the last volume of a trilogy, and while each book stands alone, I'd like to summarize the first two for those who haven't read them.

The first book, *Child of the Northern Spring,* details Arthur's rise to power and Gwen's childhood. I deliberately made her a feisty northern girl who doesn't see any reason why she has to learn to wear dresses, speak Latin and go south to marry that king. By giving her a rough, tomboy background, I made sure she'd be looking at her new husband's world with fresh eyes.

In *Queen of the Summer Stars,* Gwen gradually grows into her role of queen and co-ruler with Arthur as the Round Table develops and the classic characters gather at Camelot's Court.

Now, in this book, Gwen and the rest of the cast each confront his or her moira—or fate—and, like human beings everywhere, try to do the best they can under the circumstances they find themselves in. Given the full range of characters and the scope of their dreams or disillusionments, it's a very heady mixture.

If Arthur and Guinevere lived, it would have been sometime between A.D. 450 and 550, during the era commonly referred to as the Dark Ages. This was a period of vast upheaval and great excitement, when the Roman world was being challenged—and in some cases swallowed up—by the barbarian societies that were sweeping over it. Most of Europe was in political chaos as wave after wave of Goths, Visigoths, Vandals, Alans, Franks, Angles, Saxons and various other uncivilized (literally, "non-city dwelling") peoples moved westward, each displacing the tribes in front of them. Both historically and traditionally, the only serious effort made to stop them was that mounted by the Britons, and who is to say that their leader was not a noble king named Arthur Pendragon, who seated his allies in a circle and tried to salvage some semblance of civilized behavior from the tide of barbarian anarchy that was flooding Europe.

In the end, of course, it was the barbaric Saxons who won, driving the remnants of Arthur's Britons into the Welsh mountains where they kept alive the story of their last great king in folktales for some five hundred years. When these were eventually discovered by the French bards on the Continent, they became the source for all sorts of improvising, and the Arthurian Romances were born. These stories were written for and enjoyed by a medieval Christian audience, and provide many of the tales that we think of as traditional today. (It is also this French connection that leads everyone to think of the characters as wearing shiny fourteenth-century armor and high, peaked hats with veils, though the real people would probably have been wearing mail and tunics or even togas.)

But even as the new Christian stories grew, the bards were incorporating shadows of the culture that had surrounded the original Arthur, probably without even realizing it. For instance, the old Celts were, according to the historians of Caesar's time, head-hunters. Nowhere is it actually said that Arthur and his crew indulged in that practice, but anyone who reads Malory, for instance, can't help but notice how many times one of the heroes whacks off someone's head and goes running off with it.

Then, too, fifth-century Christianity took several different forms. In Rome, the church hierarchy was based on the urban political structure—many laymen looked to a few priests who looked to their single local bishop, just as plebians looked to senators who looked to the emperor or king. But in both Britain and Ireland, where Celtic Christianity flourished, there were few cities, and the religion evolved around individual holy men who wandered the countryside, like St. Patrick. The prevalence of hermits in the Arthurian stories may well be a shadow of that Dark Age time. By the same token, the Grail Quest, which originated in British stories, reflects the individual's search for meaning rather than acceptance of Church-promoted dogma. Interestingly, the Church has never accepted the Grail story.

People often ask me how much research I do. The answer is, a lot. I've made five trips to Britain, both to explore the land and to collect books on flora and fauna. I've hiked innumerable Roman ruins, on the assumption that if I can still see them in the twentieth century, Gwen would have seen them in the sixth; stood on the remains of ancient hill-forts and tried to imagine the layout of thatched roundhouses and square, timbered halls; and mined legend, archaeology and common sense for explanations of why various characters did what they did in the legends.

There are a few oddities I'd like to clear up. For instance, the eulogy of Urien which I have given to Taliesin may, or may not, have been composed by a different bard of the same era. However, it so eloquently captures the loss felt by the followers of a well-loved warlord, I decided to include it along with excerpts from Taliesin's *Battle of the Trees* and *The Spoils of Annwn*.

Sometimes research puts the author in a quandary. For example, the Cheviot Hills of Northumbria have been famous as rounded, wind-swept grasslands for roughly a thousand years— but in the time I am writing about, they would have been covered with forest. Whenever I came up against such conflicts, I tended to go with what the modern reader would know or understand. In the same way, I have used modern place names rather than the old Roman names, simply because they are easier for the contemporary reader to follow.

In some cases I've given a complimentary nod not only to the medieval Romances of Arthur, but also to earlier sources of a particular story. The tale of Uwain is one such case. He is often called the Knight of the Lion because of having cured a lion who was bitten by an adder, after which the creature was his friend for life. Clearly lions did not inhabit Europe during the sixth century, but I used that little reference to make him a veterinarian as well as a warlord, and paid quiet homage to the first-century version of the lion story by including the detail of a thorn that Uwain removes.

Over the centuries many a bard has earned a good dinner by telling the stories of Arthur and Guinevere. I probably owe a debt to every one of them, but in particular I would like to mention those whose recent works have specifically inspired this present volume. First off is Phyllis Ann Karr, who so graphically portrayed Mordred's heartache and Cei's stoicism in her wonderful novel, *Idylls of the Queen.* I also found *The King Arthur Companion,* which she compiled with such wit and erudition, to be invaluable.

Geoffrey Ashe has been a constant source of help, information and encouragement throughout this entire project, for which I thank him most sincerely. His generosity of time and spirit in answering questions, guiding me around South Cadbury, or simply discussing the more obscure points of the legend have been particularly treasured.

The works of John and Caitlin Matthews, and Bob Stewart on the Grail, proved invaluable in my exploration of that story, and the Merlin books by Mary Stewart were my original inspiration and have been my model during the eleven years I've been working on this project.

Coming to the end of a project that has taken up so many years of one's life creates a very funny feeling. It has been a wonderful, if sometimes exhausting, experience, and I look back with much appreciation on the many people who have contributed to this work, from Shirley Kahert-Hall, who got me started with the right books back in 1982, to Dr. Ann La Barr, who has answered all kinds of questions about blood and horses this spring. To my agent, Eric Ashworth, I extend my deepest appreciation for helping me get published to begin with, and believing I could complete the whole of the trilogy when I'd only just written the first volume.

That first book was edited by Pat Capon, who extended her own faith in my work enough to recommend that Poseidon publish it. As she shaped the early Guinevere, so my second editor, Fonda Duvanel, has been my mentor, mainstay and person "without whom it could not have been done" for the second and third works. To both these fine ladies I will be forever grateful.

My love and appreciation to Parke Godwin, who, with his sharp eye and trenchant comments, has taught me more about my craft than anyone else.

And lastly, a toast to the reader . . . may you thoroughly enjoy both my Gwen and the Camelot she created.

Persia Woolley
Auburn, California
1990–1991

Prologue

Guinevere, High Queen of Britain and wife to King Arthur, sat in the shadows of the stone cell and stared into the brazier. A layer of soft gray ash blanketed the embers until a charred branch collapsed onto them and the molten heart of the coals flared up. I gasped and, shivering violently, turned to face the bed.

A spare pallet lay on the ledge cut into the rock face of the wall. Someone had thought to bring me the old down comforter that had graced Arthur's and my marriage bed for going on thirty years. I debated dragging it over to my chair—even in high summer a stone cellar holds the chill of winter, and by now both my feet and legs ached with the cold.

No mind—the dawn will bring heat enough. Heat and flames and swirling smoke around the stake. . . .

In the corner Enid knelt in prayer, her husband's heavy cloak draped over her shoulders. I watched her silently, envying her faith—there was not a single god I had not appealed to during the trial, yet now, this last night, I had no wish to commune with any of them. Whether it was fickleness on my part or theirs, I couldn't tell.

Nor do I care. It will be enough to get through tomorrow's dawn with some semblance of grace and courage—to accept my moira with the dignity expected of a Celtic queen. It is a matter of pride and honor, you see. . . .

I rose and padded across the flags, coming to stand beneath the high, narrow window. The shutters were closed against the cold, but even when they were open, I saw only a small wedge of sky. High up in the dark, a waxing moon hid behind scudding clouds.

There was a stirring beyond the door, as though a visitor had come, and my heart leapt foolishly. *Lancelot!*

No, not likely, for the big Breton lies wounded, or perhaps dead, off in the wildwood somewhere . . . my Champion, my sanity . . . and now my death. But I mustn't think of that.

"Don't see no harm in it," the guard was saying as he tugged open the door. On the wall the candle guttered in the sudden draft, its slantwise flame casting a flicker of shadows over the warrior who bent to avoid the lintel. Once inside the cell, the man straightened up and blinked uncertainly in the gloom.

"M'lady?" It was Gareth, come to bring me a steaming pitcher of spiced wine.

I couldn't help smiling—apparently he'd forgotten that I have no fondness for the grape, and very little tolerance either. Not that it would matter if I got drunk this night; any ill effects I might suffer tomorrow would end at sunrise.

"I thought perhaps you'd like some company," he said as the door went shut behind him. "But if I'm intruding, please say so."

"No, you're not intruding at all."

Dear, sweet Gareth. Long and lean, with hair the color of white gold and gray-green eyes that take in the whole world with a kind of silent wisdom. Last of Morgause's sons by Lot, he'd always been the fairest, the gentlest of her brood, and we had long been friends. I could not think of anyone more apt to share this particular night's watch, for with the end so close, I had no stomach for anything but honesty.

"How is the King?" My teeth began to chatter in spite of myself and when Gareth handed me a mug of hot wine, I clasped it gratefully in both hands and sank down on the bed. "How is he faring tonight?"

"He's devastated, M'lady. Gawain is with him, promising all manner of things if Arthur will just step in and spare your life. It was very unclear how things would be resolved when I left. . . ."

Gareth's voice trailed off and he turned aside to put a fresh branch of applewood on the brazier. I tucked my feet under me and pulled the comforter around my knees as I thought of my husband.

Pacing like a lion, no doubt. Never could handle a crisis without wearing a path through the rushes! Muttering, stamping, flailing against the fates that have brought us here—ah, my dear, could it really have been otherwise?

Is it, like my loving you, one of those things graven in the heavens above Britain which must be played out, no matter what? Is it woven into our moira—fated as surely as Tristan and Isolde's love was fated?

Or did we bring it on ourselves, blindly clinging to the old ways when the world was changing—and neither of us seeing where it was going?

"I told them I was coming to stay with you," Gareth went on, seating himself in the chair by the brazier. "If you want someone besides Enid, that is."

I glanced at my lady-in-waiting, realizing for the first time she was slumped, asleep, at the prayer bench. Not that I could blame her; it had been a long night already, and daybreak was still far off.

"I'm grateful to be thinking about something besides the morrow," I told him, resting the warm cup against my cheek. "It wasn't always like this, you know—full of dissent and division and wild accusations. Once the Companions saw themselves as family, willing to follow wherever the Pendragon led, confident and proud. . . ."

Gareth nodded. "Gawain liked to call them Men of Honor." His voice lifted with an echo of the enthusiasm that used to fill our days. "Why, when I first came to the Fellowship, I was awed to be among such heroes. Of course, I looked on them as any youngster would, seeing a world of demigods instead of a bunch of eccentric hooligans."

Eccentric hooligans! The term brought a rueful snort, and I wondered if Gareth truly thought all the Companions fell into that category. Arthur had used the term himself, once, but only in reference to the wildman Gwyn, not the entire Fellowship.

Yet maybe it wasn't that far off the mark—hadn't the Round Table begun simply as a gathering of ragtag warriors come to see who had survived the summer campaigning and who had not?

That was at Caerleon, and Merlin had lain his prophecy on us, promising that all who joined Arthur's Cause would find immortality and fame eternal. He foretold a brotherhood like none other, full of adventure and glory—and afterward the fighting men flocked to us as though we had the elixir of life itself.

But Arthur wanted more. In a world overrun by barbarians, where even the Emperor had left Rome in favor of living in Constantinople, my husband was determined to salvage some semblance of just and civilized behavior in Britain. Originally Merlin's dream, it had become Arthur's Cause. So we'd built the Round Table into a political forum, a Fellowship of majesty and grace, where client kings put aside blood-feuds and agreed to settle their disputes around the council table rather than on the battlefield.

Eventually even the old Celtic warlords had come to heel under the Banner of the Red Dragon. There'd been enough unity of purpose to stop the Saxons who threatened to overrun the whole of Britain, and make them Federates under our rule. We'd done it all, and done it well, in the first ten years of our reign, and built the fortress of Camelot besides.

Still, by its very nature, the Fellowship was full of disparate factions. Even among the Companions, the handpicked cavalry that Arthur himself led, there was a startling diversity, eccentric and otherwise. Men of courage, of vision, of wild commitment to their different causes, they were as likely to go haring off after their personal dreams as a hawk is likely to stoop on a dove. . . .

"But special, M'lady," Gareth was saying. "Even the most difficult of them was special."

"Special indeed," I whispered, taking another sip of wine. The steam that rose from the cup danced before my eyes, and in it I saw the past with the bleary cheer of one unused to imbibing. "Splendid people for splendid times, weren't they? Do you remember the midsummer tournament at Camelot? . . ."

1

Midsummer

t was a year of wonders that took us from the simple pleasures of a British spring to foreign realms and thoughts that made my head swim. And it ended with the realization that nothing would ever be the same again.

The winter had been mild, and when the soft green haze of spring began to hover in the branches of the oakwoods, anemone and primrose burst into bloom like stars flung by the handfuls into the leafy loam. By the time the cuckoo was rending the night with its call, whole drifts of bluebells carpeted the rides between the trees, and thrushes filled the day with their buoyant, life-loving song. And as May stole into our hearts, a trio of hedge sparrows flitted gaily through my garden, though they were more often heard than seen. I was sure I'd never known a more beautiful time in all my twenty-six years.

The exuberance of the season filled our household. The youngest pages took to putting frogs down each other's backs, while the squires stared, moony-eyed and hopeful, at my maids-in-waiting, who often as not stared back. Even the warriors felt the change in the air, turning restlessly from sword practice to dreams of victory and great renown.

I stood in the kitchen doorway, watching Arthur and Lancelot complete their early-morning rounds of the fortress. Matching stride for stride they crossed the courtyard, heads bent in conversation as they discussed the plans for the day.

Arthur—ruddy and solid and bronzed from years in the saddle, wearing his long brown hair pulled back at the nape of his neck.

His cheeks were clean shaven as any Roman, but his mustaches grew full and drooping in the Celtic fashion, and he moved with the natural assurance of a man born to be a leader.

And next to him Lancelot—lithe and lean, black hair cropped in the pageboy fashion of the Picts. Set wide above high cheekbones, his blue eyes sparkled like the waters off the Cornish coast, sometimes bright and playful, sometimes deep and sad. But it was the mouth that fascinated me, for an overabundance of teeth lent his lips a full and sensual look quite at odds with his otherwise ascetic air.

Night and day, body and spirit—no two men more different, or more complementary. Surely there was never another more fit to be High King than Arthur, nor ever a lieutenant of better mettle and loyalty than Lance. What woman would not love them both? Or feel honored to be loved by either?

Arthur came through the doorway, pausing to lift the milk pitcher from my hand and downing the whole of it before taking his place at the kitchen table between his foster brothers, Cei and Bedivere. Even when they were growing up in an obscure court in the heart of Wales—long before anyone dreamed of the High Kingship of Britain—the three of them had been a team, with Arthur spawning the ideas, Cei and Bedivere finding ways to make them happen. Now my husband greeted them jovially, wiping his mustaches with the back of his hand.

"Lance and I were just discussing how short-tempered and touchy the warriors are getting," he began.

"It's the wages of peace," Cei grumbled, looking up from a cup of cider. "Fighting men without wars feel cheated of a chance for glory."

"Then what do you say to hosting a tournament?" Arthur continued, good-naturedly ignoring the interruption. "Maybe make it part of the next Round Table meeting?"

Bedivere nodded thoughtfully. Bedivere—craggy and silent, he was as even tempered as Cei was sharp. Arthur's best friend since childhood and his lieutenant in the early years, he was a man who gave full measure of his love and devotion, never stinting, never regretting. After he'd lost his hand in the High King's service, he became our diplomat and adviser, helping to train the boys in swordplay and sometimes entertaining us with the harp.

Yet he never looked on Lancelot—the one who replaced him at Arthur's side—with bitterness or rancor.

"Admirable idea," he opined, using the gauntlet and hook that replaced his hand to offer the platter of fresh bannocks to Lance. "Give them a chance to turn boasting into action."

"And if you opened it to everyone in the realm, we could recruit the best of the newcomers into the Companions," Cei added, his sourness beginning to give way to enthusiasm. As Seneschal of the realm he not only collected taxes and screened the new applicants for the cavalry, he also kept the royal larder stocked and presented the lavish feasts for which we were growing famous. "I'd like to see it begin on midsummer's eve; hold the peasant games at night and the warrior's exhibitions during the day. Might be quite a festival."

Thus it was decided, and every messenger carrying word of the Round Table meeting delivered the news that jousts and drills and examples of fine riding would be featured, and any who wished to compete would be considered for placement in the cavalry. Naturally those who were already Champions to the client kings were welcome, but afterward would return to their overlords. That arrangement assured us of having excellent warriors living throughout the whole of Britain, available should there be a major crisis, yet not swelling our own ranks beyond the level of feasibility. Any one king can only feed so many military mouths. It was a good system, and as Lance noted, it bound the smaller leaders to us, and added to the sense of Fellowship in the councils.

So we set about making plans for the most splendid gathering ever. Cei took charge of the feasts while Lance organized the tournament and Arthur and Bedivere laid out the political agenda. For years Arthur had been trying to establish a code of law that would apply to all Britons, although many of the client kings shied away from it, fearing it would curb their autonomy. Still, he'd be bringing the subject up again this year.

In the Hall I unlocked the trunks and hampers and cupboards under the loft so that my ladies-in-waiting could sort through our treasure trove, picking the best of silver and pewter, ivory and glass to grace the curved trestles we'd put in a circle. And I opened the cedarwood chests which held the precious pennants, personally shaking them out while the smell of pennyroyal made me wrinkle my nose as I checked for moth holes.

The lengths of heavy wool—red and ochre, blue and green, black and purple and maroon—all were covered with silk embroidery as rich and handsome as the tapestry of the Red Dragon which hangs beyond the dais at the end of the Hall. Worked in bright colors and gay designs, each bore the name of a Round Table member, and when they were brushed and sponged and hung over the backs of chairs, they became a badge of honor unique to the Round Table.

As usual the plump little matron Vinnie took umbrage at my wardrobe. "What's the point of being High Queen if you don't remember to dress up now and then?" she nattered. "The people expect to see you all decked out and fancy once in a while."

It was a battle we'd waged, lovingly, since the days when she was my governess in Rheged. Having grown up a tomboy in that wild, northern region, clothes and fripperies were the last thing on my mind. So I was more than happy to leave the matter to her, confident that she'd create something suitable out of bits of lace and scraps of Damascus brocade left over from the days when trade flowed freely throughout the Empire.

On the day our festivities were to begin, I delivered myself to Vinnie and Elyzabel, content that they would clothe my long, lanky frame in regal robes and turn my haystack hair into something approximating a royal coiffeur.

While Elyzabel coaxed my side locks into waves and looped several long braids up on the top of my head, I reached for the ancient torc of queenhood and admired it once again. A twisted rope of gold shaped to fit the neck, it had wonderful pop-eyed creatures worked into the rounded knobs that protected each end. How many adventures had they participated in? How many monarchs, both good and bad, had they observed? They gave this symbol of free-born majesty both humor and elegance, and I smiled at them once more, blessing the memory of Arthur's mother, who had given it to me as a wedding present.

Vinnie was just settling Mama's coronet on my head when a trumpet call from our gates announced our guests' arrival.

"Drat, they're here already!" I exclaimed, slipping the torc around my neck and jumping to my feet.

"But the crown's not pinned down!" Vinnie wailed.

"I'll manage," I shot back, one hand holding the golden circlet firmly in place as I bolted for the door.

The week to come would see me constantly at our guests' disposal, feeding and entertaining them, and looking after their every need. I'd have to balance the claims of old friends, new allies, jilted lovers, recent widows, jealous rivals and whomever else the world saw fit to bring to our doorstep. So I climbed up the narrow stairs to the lookout tower atop the Hall, determined to have an early look at them before the formalities began. It would give me a chance to assess who of the Fellowship was coming, who not, and what the mood was likely to be.

"Splendid sight, M'lady," the young sentry commented when I emerged through the hole in the floor.

"Indeed it is," I answered, perching on the windowsill and gazing out over it all.

Below the four-tiered walls of Camelot's hill, the land spreads out like a rumpled coverlet, dotted here and there with fields and pastures, except to the east, where a series of close, lumpy hills are flanked by tracts of forest. The view to the south and west stretches long and far, a patchwork of peaceful farms and occasional belts of wildwood, while to the north lie the marsh and mire of the Somerset Levels, and the odd, flat lake that laps around Glastonbury's Tor.

Closer by, the trees along the Cam river grow dense and shady, while directly below us a small, ferny brook makes its way between steep banks. Here the woods and meadows were alive with camps. Arthur had set up extra tents around the list since the inn at the village was no doubt packed, and large as our new fortress was, we couldn't possibly sleep all the nobles who would attend.

The sound of laughter and good-natured banter drifted up from beneath the trees, and I thought of the midsummer frolic that would fill the twilight of the night to come.

The first of our royal guests were making their way through the thick double gates of our topmost wall. Urien of Northumbria was in the van, the black raven on his banner fluttering over the warband that followed close behind. Next came the white boar of Duke Cador, but I searched in vain for the grizzled old warrior who had been the first to rally to Arthur's Cause, some fifteen years ago. It appeared he would not be joining us, for it was his son, Constantine, who led their men.

Beyond them Geraint rode with his wife, Enid. They both wore the Roman dress of the south and seemed to be in fine spirits, as though marriage much agreed with them. Enid had been one of my ladies at Court, and this would be our first visit since she had left us three years back, so I was looking forward to a private chat.

Next came Pellinore of the Wrekin—dear old Pelli, rough and raucous as they come. He was but one of many warlords whose people had preferred to leave their dying towns and move to the nearest hill-fort after the Legions left. Once the man had been obsessed with a naïve quest for the perfect woman; now he took great delight in raising his late-in-life son, Perceval.

The tot rode in front of his father, baby legs splayed across the saddle. Pelli steadied him fondly in the crook of one arm while he lifted the other in salute to the guards at the gate. His bearskin cape came open with the gesture, revealing the enameled hilt of the Welsh dagger he wore instead of a Roman sword.

I glanced beyond him, wondering if his son Lamorak was here. If so, it would be the first time the fellow had returned to Court since his encounter with Morgause. When I couldn't see either him or Gawain of Orkney, I heaved a sigh of relief—the bad blood between them constantly threatened to unsettle the Round Table.

By now so many people were streaming up the cobbled drive, it was hard to make out individuals. I caught a quick glimpse of Pelleas and Nimue and determined once more that Gawain's banner was nowhere to be seen before the contingents from farther away pressed forward.

These I recognized by sound rather than sight—an Irishman strummed his traveling harp as he led a batch of immigrants from Fergus's new settlements around Dumbarton. A handful of Caledonians followed, marching to the skirl of bagpipes while the silvery notes of their flutes announced a small group of dark, sly Picts. After that came the Cumbri, those northern Celts of Wales and Rheged whose singing rang out boldly as they advanced.

Music and color and excitement swirled around them all, and I knew Arthur would be pleased. He wanted our distant allies as well as client kings to come to Camelot and take back news of all the great things we were accomplishing.

"I don't really care *what* they talk about," he'd said. "It doesn't matter whether it's our feasts or Taliesin's songs, or the fact that Bedivere is still a splendid warrior, one-handed or not—as long as they're impressed enough to tell their people what they've seen. The desire to share our glory is the best way I know of to get them to join the Cause."

Looking down on them now, I was confident they would go home full of wonder, for we had planned this occasion carefully, starting with the Round Table council—which would conclude with a twilight procession to the midsummer meadow, complete with village girls flinging garlands of flowers upon the Champions —and ending with the tournament days and final feasting. There was no way they would forget this occasion.

When Urien and his retinue reached the forecourt of the Hall, I turned and dashed back down the steps.

On the loft landing I paused before the big bronze mirror. Long and lean, with masses of apricot hair and a face more interesting than pretty, I was hardly the picture of a beautiful queen. But I wore the torc of royalty with dignity and grace, and though I'd never be as regal as Arthur's mother, Igraine, or as lovely as Mama had been, I had the respect of my husband, the love of my people, and the tender concern of Lancelot.

So I smiled at the image in the mirror and gave her the old Roman thumbs up sign, then gathered my skirts and rushed down the main staircase.

Halfway to the bottom I felt the golden circlet on my head begin to slip forward. My hands were full of the heavy robes of state and I was in too much of a hurry to stop, so I tilted my head to one side and by the time I reached the bottom step the crown was riding rakishly over one eyebrow.

Lance was just coming to join Arthur at the door, and he stifled a laugh at the sight of me.

"That will never do, M'lady," he admonished, stepping forward to adjust the circlet. I grinned up at him, grateful for his help.

"Thought you weren't going to make it this time," Arthur noted as I took my place beside him. He gave me one of his droll sidewise glances, both knowing and amused.

"Gawain and Mordred aren't among them," I whispered breathlessly, tugging my garments into place. "Pelli's here, sure as rain, though I didn't see Lamorak, or Cador of Cornwall, either. But an Irish group has come, as have some Picts."

Arthur acknowledged my news as the double doors of the Hall were thrown open and the two of us marched forward to meet our guests.

The entire area between the steps to the Hall and the end of the barn had filled with strapping men and sleek horses. There was much milling about and greeting of old acquaintances as the leaders dismounted, and after Arthur and I welcomed them, my husband stepped into the crowd.

The men who had brought ladies with them came forward to avoid the press and I was just greeting Enid when Arthur hailed me above the din.

"You'll never guess what Gwyn has brought you as a gift!"

The mob parted and when I realized Arthur was standing next to a carriage, I let out a yip of delight. It was one of those two-wheel contraptions such as the Welsh nobles use. Agricola had let me ride in his when we were in Demetia, and the last time we visited, he'd taught me how to manage the horses. The very notion of owning one of my own was scandalously exciting.

"It's beautiful, is it not?" Gwyn announced pointing to the ribbons twined along the tongue and the bells attached to the back rim. Even the spokes of the wheels had been stained bright colors, and an embroidered shawl covered the cushions on the bench. "I bring it especially for you," the little man allowed, "but think I better keep it at my horse farm lest Your Highness forget all about matters of state in favor of gallivanting about the countryside."

He cocked an eyebrow in amusement and cast me a sly look. Gwyn of Neath—impish, gnarled and brown as a beechnut, our wily neighbor carried the air of the Otherworld about him. I personally suspected he was related to the Old Gods, but that wouldn't keep me from accepting his gift.

"May I have the honor?" he asked, gesturing for me to board the conveyance. I paused a moment, staring up at those black, glittering eyes and wondered just how far he was to be trusted. More than one fairy king has been known to kidnap a mortal woman.

"Surely you're not afraid, M'lady?" he challenged. "The great queens of the past didn't flinch at anything, remember?"

My pride rose to his bait like the trout to a May-fly. Lifting my chin with a laugh, I climbed into the carriage and sat down on the bench.

No sooner had I done so than he let out a roar, and cracking his whip above the suddenly rearing horses, wheeled them around and headed toward the staging area beyond the gates. A number of the townspeople who were to lead our procession in the evening had followed the visiting royalty up to Camelot, clustering near the gateway to talk with Dagonet, who was organizing the details of the parade. As the slewing carriage bore down on them, flower girls, musicians and acrobats fled in all directions, shrieking in surprise and fear.

I yelled at Gwyn to stop but he was intent on urging the horses on, howling like a man possessed as he sent the animals careening along the narrow track that curves up from the base of our hill. Looking back, I caught a glimpse of Arthur vaulting onto a horse's back while the rest of the Companions stood gaping in astonishment.

Obviously the fey Welshman didn't care that he was interrupting a Round Table meeting; nor had he any interest in my carefully planned procession. There was nothing for it but to hang on for dear life, so I clutched my crown with one hand and the rim of the carriage with the other as we dashed down the steep track and veered off toward town.

Merrymakers and shopkeepers scrambled out of our way when we went clattering through the village. Some raised their fists and swore while others hollered encouragement, but through it all Gwyn gleefully continued to snap his whip in the air. A flock of geese scattered in terror as we rounded the corner and headed for the bonfire meadow.

Arthur and the Companions were in hot pursuit, the pounding of their horses' hooves shaking the ground behind us. I glanced again at Gwyn, hoping desperately that this was just a high-spirited prank, not the beginning of disaster.

The little man looked over at me, shrewd and laughing as always. "Nay, M'lady, I mean you no harm. But it will do your husband good to rescue you for once. Too often that Breton, Lancelot, gets all the credit."

I could barely catch my breath, let alone laugh out loud, so I settled for shaking my head in mock reproof. He was right, of course. Lance had come to my aid so many times, he'd been named the Queen's Champion years ago. Perhaps Gwyn was simply giving Arthur an equal chance to play the hero.

The wind was tugging at my hair, making a mess of Vinnie's coiffure. Finally I slid the crown over my wrist for safekeeping and shook my tresses free. They streamed out behind me as I clutched the front panel of the carriage for balance. White-knuckled or no, I was loving every moment of it.

The horses fairly flew over the ground, and when we reached the clearing where the bonfire was lain, we made a sweeping circuit of the green before the little man brought his steeds to a snorting, plunging halt.

"That, Your Highness, should satisfy your need for adventure for a while," Gwyn announced. "Mind you don't try driving like that when you use it, though, for it's a magical cart that requires a firm hand."

"I'll remember," I assured him breathlessly. "Only sober transportation, unless you're with me."

With another wink and dimple, Gwyn darted around to help me out of the carriage as Arthur galloped up. The Welshman presented me to my husband with a courtly bow, then turned to his horses and calmly led them away while Arthur and I stared at each other, speechless.

"Are you all right?" he demanded, concern vying with relief.

"Absolutely," I responded, nonchalantly planting the crown atop my head. "Scared witless, but fine. Though I'm afraid Gwyn's prank has turned our stately procession into a shambles."

By now most of the Companions were racing full tilt across the meadow, still not knowing I had been safely deposited. The rest of the guests, along with the townspeople and members of the procession, were hurrying up on foot.

Arthur shook his head in bemusement and stared after the master of Glastonbury Tor. "Eccentric hooligan. . . ." he muttered good-naturedly.

It was clear that by the time we rounded everyone up again and trekked back to Camelot, we'd have lost most of the afternoon, so Arthur suggested we put off the council meeting until the end of the tournament, and move right into the midsummer celebration.

I nodded in cheerful agreement and slipped my arm through his. In spite of the lost pomp and pageantry, it was a wonderful way to begin the festivities.

Later, when everyone was fed and the fire lit, Dagonet drew out his elder pipe and began to play a lively tune. The Scottish contingent brought forth their bagpipes, and even the Picts joined in with their flutes as a circle formed and the dancing began.

Arthur and I led the first round, but when the musicians paused, the High King called Lancelot over. "You know how I hate to dance," he apologized, twirling me toward the Breton.

Lance's arms went around me, steadied me for a moment, then dropped to his sides. It was always like that—our coming together, yet having to stand apart.

Arthur admonished us to dance our shoes to tatters, then went off to discuss the northern situation with Urien. I turned to look after him, too used to it to be hurt, too aware of Lance to be sorry.

"What's M'lady's pleasure tonight? Dancing? Games of chance by the fire? Strolling in the birch grove?" The Breton spoke in the deep, low tone that still sends shivers down my spine, and the warmth of his closeness surrounded me. I looked up at him, seeing the dark brows, the broad cheekbones, the eyes that crinkled as he smiled. I let my gaze linger on his lips a minute too long and felt the old desire waken.

"Dancing!" I said quickly, deciding it was unwise to risk the privacy of the woods.

So dance we did, as we had on countless nights before. Skipping, spinning, hopping to a gleeful tune, we capered under the stars like the Celts of old . . . sometimes whirling away with others, yet always returning to each other, drawn together as irresistibly as iron filings to a lodestone.

When we first discovered the love that flowed between us, I naturally assumed that we would bed, Celtic queens having the right to a personal as well as public life. But Lance saw that as a betrayal of Arthur's trust—though later, as our passion grew, he begged me to come away with him and be his wife in fact, if not in law. That was a far more difficult choice than simply bedding, for I love my husband, too, and could not imagine abandoning him and my people. Still, I might have done so when the secret of Mordred came to light, had not the boy been suddenly cast on my doorstep, half-orphaned, frightened and desperately in need of family. So I had vowed to raise the child as my own . . . and that was the end of running away with Lancelot.

But not the end of loving.

It was Lance who had run, traveling the length and breadth of Britain in search of . . . peace? forgetting? a new lady? No, never that. Always he swore he would love only me—it was, he said, this very love which brought him back to Camelot. Back to my side and Arthur's. So the three of us resumed our work as a team, as though Lance had never left—friends and comrades, each devoted to the other in our different ways. Lance and I never spoke of what might have been, but rested content in the knowledge of the love that would always be between us.

Now we danced the night away until the early dawn began to lighten the eastern sky. Arthur suggested that Lance drive me and the carriage back to Camelot while he paced beside us on his stallion. I leaned back among the cushions, delightfully, dizzyingly exhausted, content to watch the two men chatting quietly beside me, their profiles crisp and clear against the silvering sky. The rest of the revelers fell in behind, singing softly as they escorted their monarchs home after a night of celebration.

Surely there was never a realm more blessed, a people more cheerful and content, a king and court more deservedly honored. I thanked the Gods that had given us such a splendid moira . . . never guessing how fragile it would all turn out to be.

2

The Tournament

ur guests slept late after the night of carousing, but by noon everyone had gathered at the water meadow by the stream, where the flatness of the land provided the best field for horse- and sword-play.

The greensward was surrounded by the pavilions of various Round Table Champions, each with his own standard stuck in the turf beside his tent flap. Nestled between them, and spreading into the woods beyond, were the peddlers' stalls. Some were little more than blankets laid on the ground and covered with items for trade or barter; others were lean-tos, hastily constructed around the base of a tree or propped against a similar hut for support. Here one could find spurs and bridles and pieces of tack or decoration, remedies for lameness, colic, coughs, witches' knots in mane or tail and anything else a horseman might need to keep his animal healthy. Horse blankets, curry-combs and variations on the canvas and wooden loops we call stirrups abounded, while at one end of the list the Royal Smith set up his forge at Arthur's behest. Here the people could get tools mended, horses shod or weapons sharpened, all at our expense.

Cei had built a reviewing stand with bright awnings and gay bunting. Once the majority of the Court had arrived, Arthur and I walked slowly toward it down the length of the field with pages, heralds and Irish wolfhounds in attendance.

These last were my pleasure, for Arthur preferred the great snarling black brutes Gwyn bred and trained for him for war. But I'd lived with Irish wolfhounds since childhood and even brought a pup to Arthur as a wedding present. We were now well into our second generation of gentle giants—like many large dogs, they don't live long—and I continued the tradition of naming them for Roman heroes. It amused my husband, who was fond of reminding me how suspicious I used to be of Roman ways. But the names seemed appropriate for the large, stately animals, and it was the gray-coated Claudius that paced beside me now, his massive, scruffy head under my right hand.

When we were all settled and Claudius was lying by my feet, Arthur signaled for the tournament to begin.

The trumpeter, so necessary in battle for conveying the commander's wishes to hard-pressed warriors, gave the notes of assembly a lively, playful air.

Two by two the standard-bearers of the nobles came forth, bridles jingling, pennants lifting in the freshening breeze as they paced the length of the meadow to present us with a formal salute before trotting briskly to their positions at the edges of the turf. The flags were almost as colorful as the pennants we hang from the backs of the chairs in the Hall, and when they were all in place they formed a bright, impressive ring.

Another trumpet flourish announced the entrance of the High King's standard as Bedivere and his squire rode onto the grass. The Banner of the Red Dragon was unfurled in all its glory, and the boy who held it concentrated on keeping the pole steady as they cantered to the center of the turf. The two riders came to an abrupt and solemn halt, then pivoted their horses slowly in place. The flags of the client kings dipped respectfully; it was a rippling progression that made me think of field poppies bowing before the wind.

After completing the maneuver, the one-handed Champion advanced to the reviewing stand where Arthur and I sat, and gave us a proud salute.

Slowly and majestically Arthur and I returned the greeting, and once Bedivere dismounted and brought the Banner to its place beside us, Arthur declared the tournament open.

When Lancelot led the cavalry out for a display of precision riding, a gasp went up from the crowd. This was the first year we'd been able to mount all the Companions on the black horses specially bred by Gwyn, and they made a most impressive sight. Each man carried his own colors on his shield, naturally, but Arthur and I had presented a pair of golden rondels set with red enamel to each Companion, to grace the headstall of his bridle. The handsome bosses gleamed rich and elegant against the satiny-black horses' heads.

Going through their drills, wheeling and turning and regrouping in close quarters and at high speed, the Companions were a wonder to behold. I had no doubt the more distant tribes would be inspired by the stories of Arthur's mounted warriors and decide to make treaties with us instead of war.

When the cavalry work was over, Lance came to take his usual place beside the High King, along with Lynette, who sat by me. Lynette—more urchin from the streets of London than noble of either Celt or Roman lineage, she was the youngest of my maids-in-waiting, and the most mischievous as well.

"Move over, you big scamp," she admonished the wolfhound as she plunked herself down on the stool and scanned the crowd. Peasants and townspeople and visiting nobles milled around the tents, found places to sit on the sidelines, and even—in the case of the more adventurous youngsters—climbed into the surrounding trees for a better view. As the field cleared and preparations for the individual trials of skill were being made, Lynette suddenly reached across and tugged Arthur's sleeve.

"Your Highness, my cousin holds a small fortlet by a river ford —nothing fancy, just a fortified steading, really. But ever since her father died last winter, the local warlord has been pestering her for marriage. With only a few farmhands to protect her, she's asked me to find a Champion to put the fellow in his place. Do you think, with so many warriors here for the tournament . . ."

The girl's voice trailed off hopefully and Arthur shrugged. "You're free to ask whomever you wish," he told her. "Got the best in the realm to choose from, I'd say."

The ancient call to battle, sounded on silver-rimmed aurochs' horns, was booming and rippling around the glade. There is no other sound like it, and every Celt knows in his blood it is the signal of life and death. Although this was only a tournament and test of skill, each of the contenders who hoped to prove his prowess before the King raised his head expectantly at the sound.

Like the nobles, these warriors came in all shapes and sizes— young and hopeful, mature and confident, some with rich trappings and fancy mounts, others dressed in sturdy homespun and riding country nags. One freckle-faced lad made his way from group to group, offering his service as a squire to anyone who would accept him. A cadre of southern dandies hooted in derision and sent him packing, but later I saw him talking earnestly with Pellinore, who gave him a jovial clap on the back and sent him over to see to his armor.

Lynette was carefully scanning the group, looking for a likely Champion. At last she turned away, dissatisfied. "If only Gawain were here," she murmured. "He'd help me in a minute, I know."

The gamin was probably right, for Arthur's nephew had recently taken a vow to protect all women and was still full of enthusiasm over the idea. He was also one of the most famous warriors in the land; his absence at the tournament meant the field was open to all comers, and there was much speculation as to who would win the prizes of the day.

The contests began easily enough, with Cei carefully pitting men of equal skill against each other. Lance's cousin Bors, as blond as Lance was dark, was a fierce and showy swordsman, well matched with Gaheris of the Stag's Head, while Bors's more taciturn brother, Lionel, fought ably against the sly and wiry Dinadan of Cornwall.

Gradually, as the less familiar names were called out, there was more room for unexpected surprises, and when the herald announced that Lancelot's protégé, Beaumains, would take the field, a stir of excitement went through the crowd. Beaumains had been at Lance's steading in Northumbria for the last year or more, and no one knew he had returned until this very afternoon.

"He's developed so well at Joyous Gard," Lance explained proudly, "I thought it was time to introduce him to the rest of the warriors. I have no doubt he'll qualify for the Companions."

Certainly the young man who took the field was a far cry from the boy Lance had found wandering on the Road several years back. Although he was still tall and willowy, he no longer had the half-starved look of a waif, and while that youngster was unfamiliar with more than the rudiments of horsemanship, this lad had an excellent seat.

There's always a group of old men who gather to gossip around a forge, but this afternoon they moved away from the fire, their interest piqued by this Fair Unknown. Even the Smith laid down his hammer and came forward to watch.

Beaumains rode onto the field carrying an unmarked shield and wearing an old Saxon helmet, which gave him an air of mystery. The audience murmured curiously, trying to place him among the many squires at Camelot. That he was introduced as Lance's student spoke well of him, but they would withhold judgment until they saw what he could do. The boy acquitted himself handsomely, and by the time he had unhorsed two opponents, the crowd was shouting its approval.

It was only when he stepped forward to receive his prize that he took off his helm. The pale blond hair tumbled down to his shoulders and a murmur of recognition ran through the gathering. Arthur smiled broadly, delighted that the youth who had earned his first year's keep in our kitchen should so excel.

Lance was equally pleased. "I couldn't ask for a better student. Whoever that lad's family is, they can be proud of him."

Arthur leaned over the edge of the reviewing stand and bestowed the prize of a golden bracelet on the young man. It was a gesture that both congratulated him on his victory and brought him up to the level of warrior fit to receive gifts from his overlord. Even Lynette greeted him warmly, surprised to see him after so many months.

"Thank you, Your Highness." Beaumains spoke calmly and clearly as he slid the bracelet onto his wrist. "But since there are no wars to fight, I need to prove my prowess some other way. I beg you give me a mission that will let me show the world what I can do."

Arthur looked puzzled for a moment, but remembering Lynette's request, I suggested the boy go to the rescue of her cousin in the Welsh Marches.

When he heard what the problem was, Lance's pupil began to beam. "I'll not only rid the lady of this warlord's pestering, I promise to send him back to swear allegiance to you as well."

"Will you now?" Arthur mused, stroking his mustaches as he sized up the lad.

I turned to Lynette, thinking the girl would be glad of the offer, but instead she was scowling ferociously.

"My cousin needs a *Champion*, not an untried boy," the girl declared. "A hero proven in battle and able to strike terror into the blackguard's heart."

"What's this? Beaumains isn't good enough for you?" Arthur was both bemused and surprised that the lass should be so picky.

"I'm sure he'll become a fine warrior, someday," Lynette hedged, rounding on him with an air of practicality. "But right now he's only the boy I worked with in the kitchen—a brave fellow, and quick to boot—but not very impressive. You have to admit that, M'lord . . . not nearly as impressive as Gawain or Lancelot, for instance."

My husband's eyes flashed with amusement. "Well, Gawain isn't here, but you're welcome to ask Lance to be your Champion."

"Not my Champion, my cousin's," Lynette responded, then ducked her head at the realization she was correcting the High King.

"My dear," Lancelot put in, "you could not find a more upright and honorable fellow to take up your cause."

Beaumains flushed at the praise, but he looked steadily at Lynette. "Who was it who put out the fire when the coals spilled out of the oven at Martinmas?" he asked.

"Yes, I know it was you . . . I said you were quick."

"And who netted the mad dog when it came foaming and frothing into the kitchen garden?"

"So you're brave and fearless too. . . . I never said you weren't, Beaumains. All I said was you aren't very impressive."

The new warrior snorted indignantly. "I dare you to come along with me, and see how impressive I can be. I bet you'd turn tail at the first sight of a bandit."

"Would not!" Lynette hurled back at him, stamping her foot emphatically.

"Then it's settled," Arthur announced firmly, before the two youngsters got into a free-for-all. "Beaumains will undertake to relieve your cousin of her problem, and you'll go along to show him the way—and observe his behavior."

The youth bowed deeply before us, and the audience cheered happily, but Lynette turned to me with a look of pure horror.

"You mean that's really what's going to happen?"

"So it would seem," I answered, giving her hand a pat. "I'm sure you'll find him more impressive than you think."

But the girl just stared after him, obviously not convinced.

Cei took Lance's place next to Arthur when the Breton rode onto the field and challenged all comers, only to discover no one would come forth.

"Everyone knows he's invincible," the Seneschal muttered and I fetched him a sharp look. Over the years he'd proved a genius at ferreting out hard-to-find items, and his loyalty to Arthur was beyond question, but his acid tongue and frequent moodiness were often wearing. "No point in going against a man who can't be bested," he complained.

When Lance had to retire for lack of takers, Cei suddenly climbed down from the dais and called for the crowd's attention. Standing in the middle of the list, he challenged the King of Devon to swordplay on foot.

A buzz of excitement went up, for Geraint had a reputation as a fine warrior as well as a military genius, and his skill with the blade far exceeded Cei's. But instead of picking up the challenge, the southern king tactfully declined.

"I came to be entertained, good Seneschal, not to draw my sword," he said good-naturedly.

Cei frowned at the answer, and turning suddenly, demanded that Beaumains take the Devon king's place. "Wouldn't want the scullery boy to go into battle against that fellow up north only to find he's not experienced enough," he explained.

Concerned, I glanced at Arthur. It was Cei who had derisively named the lad Beaumains—"Fair Hands"—when the boy declined to give us his family name. Many a man, young or old, has cut his ties with the past because of personal misfortune, and we made it a policy to respect such people's privacy; Arthur was one for judging people by their present conduct, not past circumstances. Still, Cei had looked on the lad with scorn, and I was worried that he would take out his anger at Geraint's rebuff on the boy.

I had misread the Seneschal, however. He fought both bravely and with courtesy, for all that he received a thorough drubbing. Next to the lithe young man, it was clear the Seneschal's years as Court gourmet had thickened his waist and slowed his arm. But he took his defeat with good grace, and even congratulated Beaumains on his prowess afterward.

So the first day of the tournament was clearly Beaumains's.

On the second it was Pellinore who took the prize. The warlord of the Wrekin came at his opponents like a whirlwind, long hair flying and great voice howling savagely. Despite the fact that his myriad of grown children had made him a grandfather many times over, he managed to unhorse everyone who rode against him, including Bors. When the fierce blond Breton graciously saluted him as victor, the crowd gave them both an ovation.

Pellinore had stood in my father's place at the Bride Blessing before Arthur and I were wed, so he was counted as my kin and I took a special pleasure in presenting him with a large gold and enameled brooch from our treasure.

Rough and rugged as ever, he beamed up at me as I put it in his hand. "I'll wear it till the day I die, M'Lady," the massive man assured me.

"Me too," piped up Perceval, who had wriggled away from the grasp of the freckle-face squire and trotted to his father's side.

"We both of us thank you," Pellinore announced as the tot, suddenly turned shy, wrapped his arms around his father's leg, half hiding behind it. After giving me a formal bow, the warlord of the Wrekin turned to walk back to his tent. He shortened his stride to match that of the toddler, and I smiled fondly to see the youngster hopping along at his father's side, tiny hand engulfed in Pellinore's huge one. We would do well to have several generations of Pelli's sons among the Companions.

Arthur was about to signal the closing ceremony of the day when an unannounced rider galloped onto the green. He wore a jerkin covered with what looked like dragon's scales, and on his head was a long white veil which hung down his back and fluttered at the sides of his face. A fine black cape streamed out behind him, its hem and shoulders covered with rich golden embroidery worked in mysterious patterns. He carried a black shield, and the horse he rode was white, with fine lines and a delicate head. But most amazing of all was the turbaned servant who ran, stripped to the waist, next to the mount as Saxon warriors are said to do. The fellow was sweating, having run for who knows how many miles, and the afternoon sun glinted off his shiny skin . . . which was purple-black!

"What on earth . . ." Arthur exclaimed as Lance's hand dropped to his sword hilt.

The rider reined in so abruptly that his beautiful steed came to a crouching halt, haunches bunched and tail sweeping the ground behind.

"Arthur Pendragon, High King of Britain," the stranger called out, "I bring you greetings from the Emperor of the East, as well as a present from the King of the Franks."

The man swung off his horse and tossing the reins to his servant, made his way toward us as the audience held its breath, fascinated by such a spectacle.

"Is that you, Palomides?" my husband asked, bounding to his feet.

"Aye, M'lord, just returned from Byzantium."

Palomides, the Arab knight—dark-skinned, shining-eyed, he was the silent courtier. Born into slavery in the Mediterranean, he'd been brought to Britain as a boy and was freed when his owner died. Arthur took an interest in him because of his idea for stirrups and his fine horsemanship. With his exotic look and shy—almost introverted—ways, he'd caught many a lass's notice, but he gave his heart only to Isolde, the beautiful Queen of Cornwall. It was to forget that unrequited love that he'd gone back to Arabia, searching for some sense of home and family.

Now his dark countenance was lit by a flashing smile and he dropped to one knee as Arthur strode across the green to meet him. The Arab stared long and steadily at his King. It was a look I had seen often before—that of a warrior pledging his trust in his warlord. It held hope and love, fidelity and joy in equal measure and Arthur responded in kind, for the bond between a fighting man and his leader must be strong enough to overcome even the fear of death itself.

"Well come home, my friend," the High King cried, pulling the Champion to his feet and clapping him heartily on the back, all the while telling him how glad we were to see him again. "But enough—get yourself to the baths, and when you've soaked away the grime of the Road, come join us at the feast so that everyone can hear of your travels."

News of Palomides's arrival spread through the Round Table like excitement through a beehive when a new patch of flowers has been found. The tournament was all but forgotten as everyone rushed to dress for dinner, eager to take their place in the Hall before the Arab began to recount his adventures.

It seemed incredible that one of our own had been to places most of us knew only in song and legend . . . and had lived to come back to tell us about it!

3

Palomides

hen Arthur and I arrived at the Hall for the feast we found Palomides surrounded by a gathering of kings and warriors, proudly displaying a fair-sized falcon that perched on his wrist.

"In the East many nobles use these birds for hunting. It is a fine sport, and this is a magnificent specimen," he explained.

The raptor glared at us with the fierce, untamed look of its kind, and even after it was hooded and moved to a wooden perch, it never lost its air of wildness. I was sorry to see such a creature of freedom restrained and tethered under my roof, hemmed in by the press and push of humanity.

As the Fellowship dispersed to find their seats, Palomides's dark glance moved slowly around the room, drinking in the light and color and faces of the Round Table. "Ah, M'lady, it is just as I used to conjure from memory," he sighed. "Though I don't recall the lamps."

I assured him they were new. Last winter Cei had fitted the curved table segments with wrought-iron poles from which to hang oil lamps. The Smith had hammered out the shape of each member's own device so that Bors's bowl of light was held in a net suspended from the beak of a pelican, and Gawain's by the talons of a golden eagle. There was much debate as to whether Arthur's should take the form of the dragon of High Kingship or the bear, which was his personal totem. At length we decided on the bear, for Arthur said the dragon represented all Britons, but at the Round Table he was but one voice among many.

The lamps cast a steady light and were themselves quite beautiful, being fashioned from bowls and vases of silver or clay, old Roman goblets or even handsome shells. Caught in their nets like miniature moons suspended beside each guest, the light of their floating wicks played on white napery, dark jewels and plush fur, as well as the seamed faces of older warriors and the hopeful countenances of lads such as Beaumains. Across the circle from me, Nimue and Pelleas were surrounded by their own nimbus, which came as much from their love as from the lamplight.

Closer at hand my own lamp, carved from translucent stone by some Imperial artist, pooled its light on the embroidery of my sleeve and spilled over onto Lancelot. On those occasions when a special guest took the lieutenant's place beside Arthur, the Breton, being my Champion, would sit next to me.

He was watching Palomides like a child delighted by the return of a best friend. "It's good to have our philosopher back," he noted. I smiled to myself—Lance most appreciated the Arab's spiritual side, whereas Arthur had dubbed him "the leopard" for his deadly fighting skills. I wondered which of those aspects Palomides himself felt more at home with.

Cei had done a fine job with the menu and a steady stream of servants came and went between the trestles, bearing trenchers of meat and fish, bowls of fruit and flagons of the Roman wine the Seneschal always managed to provide. There were ducks and partridges, hare and venison, special dishes of eels in sauces with pepper and lovage—in short, all the unusual and remarkable things that Cei loved to present.

After everyone was fed, the children took finger bowls and towels around to the guests while servants cleared the tables and we all settled back against cushions and soft sheepskins. At my feet Claudius stretched contentedly, then cocked his head, prick-eared, when the Court Fool bounded into the open space in the center of the Round Table.

An acrobat by training, Dagonet leapt and capered in his brightly colored clothes, pirouetting gaily around the circle of our guests, drawing in their attention like a weaver gathering the warp of a loom through his hands. At last he came to a stop before Palomides and, with an exaggerated bow, bade the traveler tell us of the worlds he'd found in his journeying.

The Arab rose slowly and moved out into the center of the circle. As he did so, the black-skinned servant, who had been standing behind his chair, came forward to crouch in front of the trestle, never taking his eyes from his master.

"Ah, the Empire of the East is a world beyond imagining," Palomides began, his voice filling the Hall. "There are cities to take your breath away—rich and splendid in history, squalid and teeming along the Red Sea or burning white and baking under the eye of the sun. There are deserts that take weeks—sometimes months—to cross; vast seas of sand, scoured by the hot wind with only here and there a palm-shaded oasis to sustain life. And space, Your Highness . . . space such as you can't imagine, here on your lush green island. But then, my people couldn't believe that I lived in a land where it rains every third day and water bubbles freely out of the ground."

"So you found your family?" Lance broke in.

Palomides shook his head, suddenly saddened. "Not close relatives, only the tribe we had come from. But I get ahead of myself."

He paused and held out his goblet, and the turbaned servant leapt to his side. Here, within the structure of normal life, the man seemed even more exotic than out in the sunshine—like the falcon held prisoner on a perch—and many of our guests made the sign against evil at his appearance. He filled his master's cup, then sank down at the base of one of the carved wooden pillars that holds up the loft and sat cross-legged as Palomides began his tale.

The Arab had taken passage for Constantinople on a merchant ship from Topsham, sailing through the Pillars of Hercules and along the coast of the Middle Sea, stopping at Narbonne and Marseilles for trade and provisions.

"Marseilles's where I first heard about Theodoric, the Goth who now rules Italy. He's an odd one, Your Highness—came to power by killing the old king before him, but has given the Empire more than a decade of peace since."

"The Empire?" Arthur queried. "Are you saying there is a barbarian who preserves the concept of the Empire, rather than destroying it in order to set up his own separate kingdom?"

"Aye. This Theodoric is not the typical unwashed savage,"

Palomides concurred. "He's a civilized sort who spent his childhood as a political hostage in the Court at Constantinople. So he pays homage to the Emperor in the East and has kept the Roman government of Italy intact—honors the Senators and that sort of thing. They say his army is made up entirely of Goths like himself but he gives them no power in governing."

The warriors in our Hall were beginning to fidget, having little interest in politics so far from home. With the mention of the army they quieted down again, however, no doubt curious about their eastern counterparts.

"Theodoric is trying to rule a country of two separate peoples," the Arab noted, elaborating on tales he'd heard of great waves of Goths pouring over the mountains into Italy, trundling along with all their earthly goods piled in huge, lumbering wagons, driving their flocks before them. Most of them had settled into peaceful farming, taking over deserted villas or clearing new land. Still, it must have been shocking to see a whole nation of foreigners swarming over the land like locusts.

That is one of the advantages to living on an island—at least the Saxons and Angles and Jutes who keep invading our shores come only in scattered boatloads. And most of those have sworn fealty and become Federates under our rule, for all that they are aliens on our shore.

"Theodoric has separate laws for the Goths and the Romans, each based on their own historic codes," Palomides continued. "But he's compiled them all in a collection called the Edictum. He holds it's for the good of all his subjects, whether barbarian or Roman, Catholic or Aryan, Pagan or Jew."

By now other guests at the Round Table had begun to shift about and I tried to catch Arthur's attention before a dissertation on legal matters put everyone to sleep. But examples of other people's laws were exactly what Britain's High King wanted to hear, and he wasn't about to be distracted. "Were you able to get a copy?"

"No." Palomides shook his head. "But while I was in Ravenna I met a Roman noble who is an adviser to Theodoric—Boethius, his name is. He promised to keep watch in the bazaar for whatever manuscripts might be useful for you. And he himself has worked on such matters."

The Arab paused to drink from his goblet and I spoke up quickly. "Did you get to Constantinople?"

"Ah, M'lady, indeed. It is truly even more exciting than Rome, now that the Eternal City is in decline . . . greatest center of learning and art and commerce there is."

He went on to describe the fabled city that sits on a spit of land between two seas, with a natural harbor for those traders who come by boat instead of caravan. The bazaar is a crossroads of goods from all over the world—oranges and bronzeware from India; shining silks and beautiful gilded platters from Persia; leather and black goat-hair capes from Spain, cotton and papyrus from Egypt and linens from Panopolis. There was, he said, even a display of British wool at one of the stalls! And perfumes, wonderful perfumes. On a warm day they filled the city with their fragrance, though sometimes the stench of the tanneries overwhelmed them.

"Did you see the Emperor Anastasius?" Arthur inquired.

"No, M'lord, I'm afraid not," Palomides turned suddenly serious. "It seems the Emperor is very old. . . ."

"But what of the letter we wrote to him? Did you deliver it?"

"Not exactly. I tried, Your Highness, but they are all very strict about being Christians, those eastern nobles, and no one would see me because I am an infidel who represents the Pagan king of a small and insignificant island."

"Hmmph," Arthur snorted, clearly disconcerted. He picked up his wineglass and began to swirl the contents of it, still watching the Arab.

"But I saw the most amazing buildings in the city, M'lady," Palomides went on, turning eagerly to me. "They build them with domes—roofs like inverted bowls that create great open, airy spaces beneath their arch. The Royal Palace has terraced levels all the way down to the shore, and the Hippodrome is immense —the longest arena you could imagine—where they hold chariot races and circuses. Circuses with jugglers and acrobats, trained lions and dancing bears!"

The traveler turned back to the Companions with a quick smile. "Noisy, colorful, riotous affairs, full of pageantry and politics—you can't separate one from the other in that city. It's a place of constant contrasts, of private gardens filled with lemon blossoms—and stinking streets full of rabble; of the dank, sea-wrack dregs of a harbor overlooked by opulent houses where mosaic pictures cover the walls. Not chunks of murky stone, such as our villa floors have, but bits of brilliant glass, backed by gold, that shimmer with color. They are amazing, those mosaics . . . changing hues and casts as the sunlight changes, so that they are always subtly different."

Palomides paused and lifting his head, let his gaze probe the high shadows where our ridgepole holds up the roof. Awed by the visions his words had called up, we all sat silently waiting for him to continue. In the hush I could hear the rustle of feathers where a stray sparrow, or perhaps a pair of doves, had perched in the rafters for the night. Compared with the great places he told of, Camelot now seemed small and rustic.

"From Constantinople I traveled down the Incense Route along the edge of the desert, looking for my relatives," the Arab said presently, bringing his attention back to the Fellowship. He described the Bedouins he met, the Shrine of the Three Goddesses at Mecca and his eventually finding the tribe his family had come from. "They live outside the southern gates of Jerusalem, and guard the Holy City from attack."

"Jerusalem? You were in Jerusalem?" Griflet's voice reflected his awe, and the other Christians in the audience leaned forward eagerly. Palomides turned aside to whisper something to the turbaned servant, then smiled directly at Griflet.

"Indeed, I reached Jerusalem in September, in time for the great fair. Crowded, stinking, filled with masses and masses of people . . . it's unbelievable. Yet in spite of that, the city is amazing—full of churches and convents, monasteries and hostels for travelers. The church of Golgotha, with its great bronze chandelier, was packed with pilgrims. You've never seen so many pilgrims, from Spain and Greece, Antioch and Alexandria, Constantinople—even from Rome herself. Everywhere you hear different tongues, yet the place is filled with piety, and the love of Christ pours over the land. It takes your breath away to see what can be done, all in the name of the one God."

Palomides's eyes shone at the memory, and I wondered suddenly if the man had decided to convert. Back before the Empire collapsed, when every Briton was also a Roman citizen, they say most people were Christian. But in the century since the Legions left, the Old Gods have come back and now one finds most every kind of religion at Court—followers of both Celtic and Roman gods, and those like Lionel and his brother Bors who practice the rites of the soldiers' god, Mithra . . . as well as the different kinds of Christians.

I'd known a number of people born to that faith, like my foster sister Brigit, who went to live in a convent, or the Roman matron Vinnie. And some at Court, such as Griflet's wife, Frieda, became Christians as adults. Even Lance was fascinated by their mixture of mysticism and miracle, stopping to visit with any old hermit and sometimes staying in deserted chapels to pray the afternoon away. Still, it made me uneasy.

Not that I had anything against the White Christ himself. Indeed, as Brigit had explained it, he was a sort of archdruid, able to commune directly with the Father God. Nor did I mind the holy men like the teaching monk, Illtud—he was a loving person who was both practical and caring. It was the Roman Christians I found distasteful, with their belief that all other gods were evil and their followers blasphemers. The very notion sent a chill down my spine, and I was glad when Palomides began talking about his family.

"It was among the tents of the Ghassanid that I found an old man who had known my grandfather—remembered the day he and my father, who was only a lad, were captured and dragged away by slavers. I suppose my parents met later. . . ."

Palomides's voice dropped as he withdrew into some quiet, private place within himself. I wondered how much he remembered of his own days as a slave.

The turbaned servant had come to Palomides's side, a small trunk hoisted on one shoulder. The lamplight rippled on the muscles of his arms when he placed the coffer at Palomides's feet. The Arab stared at it absently, as though it contained the relics of his quest. Finally he turned and lifted his gaze to us, his face composed in a soft smile.

"So my mission was finished, for there was no one close enough for me to call family. I traveled on a bit more before deciding to return to Britain. But I bring with me not only this fine, adventurous fellow from Ethiopia"—he gestured to his servant as the man opened the trunk—"but also a few small gifts."

Excitement crackled through the Hall as the servant reached into the treasure box. He lifted a glass vial with gold thread twined about its neck and Palomides carefully bestowed it on me. Lance used his dagger to break the wax seal, and the fragrance of roses filled the air when I removed the stopper. I thanked the Arab for his gift but made a mental note to give the perfume to Vinnie; roses are fine for pretty women and fancy, but I prefer the clean, cheerful scent of lavender and never use any other.

There was an exquisitely painted icon for Lancelot, and a dagger from Damascus which was put aside for Gawain's return. The Hall buzzed with *oohs* and *aahs* as one exotic gift followed another, but when Palomides personally lifted a bundle wrapped in sheepskin and advanced toward Arthur, the whole Fellowship went quiet.

"From the last stop on my journey, the Court of Clovis, King of the Franks, I bring you a ceremonial Gift of State." Carefully pulling the covering back, the Arab disclosed a gilt-and-silver helmet, conical in shape and covered with ornate designs and metalwork. "He would have you know it's the best *spangenhelm* in his treasury."

Arthur rose to accept the present. "May it be worn only in show, and never in opposition to the Frankish leader," my husband announced, lifting the thing high so that all might see it. A gasp of amazement went up from the Fellowship.

At last, with a smile, Arthur turned back to Palomides. "It would seem, dear friend, that you have traveled the world for us, and we are grateful that you have brought so much back with you."

The Arab bowed his head and reaching for his goblet, turned slowly to address the whole of the Round Table.

"It has been a fine adventure, and I'm very glad I went. But the most important thing I found came not from the treasuries of kings, or even the history of my own people. It is the discovery that 'home' lies within my own heart—not out there, someplace else." He paused once more, his dark eyes shining. Slowly he raised his goblet. "By blood I am neither Celt nor Roman, but I am British to the core, and my heart belongs here, with Arthur and the Champions of the Round Table."

He gestured gravely to the circle, toasting his fellow warriors, then drained the cup. A brilliant smile swept across his features. "It is good to be home."

"Hear, hear!" cried Lance as kings and warlords leapt to their feet, clapping and stamping their approval. The Companions rushed forward to lift Palomides onto their shoulders while the rest of the Round Table members applauded loudly when he was paraded around the circle. There was much hugging and back-pounding among friends, and even the Picts and Caledonians, who sat in the corners of the Hall, joined in the celebration.

Carried on the great upsurge of camaraderie, my heart lifted with joy—full of wonder about the lands across the sea, and the happy conviction that we were achieving something just as remarkable here at home. My eyes filled with tears that prismed the sights of the Hall as Dagonet led a cheer for all of us.

It is one of my favorite memories, from the days of our innocence.

4

Working Monarchs

or all the pomp and pageantry we invested in the Round Table, its basic function—beside providing Arthur with a platform for his political concepts—was to be a council for exchanging news, settling disputes and assuring ourselves that Britain's borders were intact.

This year there were precious few disputes among the members, the different kingdoms were keeping the Roman Roads clear and safe, and the Saxon Federates had stayed behind the agreed-upon boundaries.

"Quiet as a cat at a mousehole," Bagdemagus noted succinctly. Ruddy-faced and pugnacious, the Dorset warlord had been chosen to represent the brotherhood of Britons whose line of hill-forts kept the South Saxons from moving west. Though he spoke in Latin, he and his kind were contemptuous of fancy ways, and he delivered his report in solid, practical terms.

"Ever since you beat 'em at Mount Badon, Your Highness, those Federates have kept their heads down; from South Hampton to Winchester, they're minding their own business. Never hear a word about their dead leader, Cerdic, or anyone thinking to rally around his son. You still keeping that boy hostage up in Wales?"

"Cynric?" Arthur nodded. "Being fostered by Cei's father—the same man who raised Bedivere and me. What about the coastal waters? No more landings along the Saxon Shore?"

"The usual immigrants," Bagdemagus replied. "Though two long boats were reported, making for the Isle of Wight."

"That is a natural landing place for them," Geraint of Devon noted, his elegant manners and aristocratic airs in sharp contrast to the warlord's ways. "I'm happy enough to see them settle there, if it means they no longer raid and plunder the settlements along our rivers. Particularly," he added, "those on the river Exe."

There was a round of laughter at that, since Geraint was fiercely protective of his holdings, and took great pride in his efforts to revive the Roman city of Exeter.

"With the Saxons contained, the trade at my wharves in Topsham has flourished," he announced. "The freighter Palomides took was but the first of many." In the last year three vessels filled with tin had sailed for the eastern markets, and two Byzantine merchant ships had put ashore, bringing fine pottery and silk, as well as many amphorae of wine.

"The best to be had," Geraint assured us. "Even Cei would approve." This brought more laughter because the Seneschal was famous for his discriminating tastes where wine was concerned.

"In fact," the debonair king added graciously, "we'd be happy to share it with any of you who care to come visit Exeter. My Queen and I will make you most welcome—though you must leave your arms at the city gate."

A skitter of surprise rattled around the Table at such a notion, but before anyone could question it, Arthur requested the news of Cornwall.

King Mark of Cornwall had never joined the Fellowship, so it was Duke Constantine who kept us apprised of what happened in the western country. Trade with the Irish was flourishing, Queen Isolde was still the loveliest lady in Britain, and churches were springing up everywhere. Mark himself was a devout Christian, and it appeared that his people were emulating their monarch.

Nor was this the only place such activity was noted. Agricola Longhand, the fine old Roman widower whom Arthur had made King of Demetia after he helped put down an Irish incursion in that southern Welsh kingdom, allowed that the Irish were now sending holy men, not warriors, across the Irish Sea. "Perhaps they like the climate here better," he suggested with a smile.

There was no representative from Carbonek as their king, Pellam, had been struck down by a blow from his own sword years back, and the wound in his thigh would not heal. His kingdom had become a Waste Land, suffering from plague and drought and terrible pestilence as a result. It reminded us all how closely the fate of the land is tied to the fate of the king—only a vigorous, healthy monarch can assure a healthy, vigorous land.

One of the neighboring warlords reported that things in Carbonek were little changed: Pellam's Pagan subjects prayed daily for the Old Gods to take him and give them a new ruler, while the Christians beseeched their deity to make him well, since Pellam was a convert to their faith. Meanwhile the land lay fallow and unused.

Next came news of the various other leaders in Wales. Those in the central mountains were generally warlords more concerned with cattle raids than matters of state, or peaceful men who counted on their steep mountains to keep their marauding neighbors at bay. In either case, they tended to be self-reliant and suspicious of anything that might limit their own power. The Courts along the coast were much more cosmopolitan, and many of those kings, such as my cousin Maelgwn in Gwynedd, maintained elaborate households and traded frequently with the Byzantine ships that came from beyond the Middle Sea.

Maelgwn was not at the Round Table, having gone to live in a monastery, but a regent reported in his stead. I tried to keep from glaring at the man; it was not his fault his king was so despicable.

Finally it was Urien's turn to speak. Urien—the Raven King of Northumbria, fierce old warrior and proud monarch. Once he had hoped to become High King himself, and led a rebellion against Arthur at the beginning of my husband's reign. Yet after he surrendered, there was never a better ally.

His own lands were prospering, Urien said, save for an occasional border problem with the rambunctious chieftains from the Caledonian Forest to the north. The Saxons along his eastern shore were quiet, but he was having problems with continual flooding at his capital of York—many of the low-lying buildings were no longer usable, and the river trade was not what it had been in the days of the Empire. I dismissed these as no more than the usual complaints, but leaned forward eagerly when he came to speak of my own land of Rheged.

"As Regent in Your Majesty's place," he began, nodding in my direction, "I'm pleased to report that the threat of murrain encountered by the farmers in the Kendal area has passed. The peasants made sure to build more and larger Beltane fires than usual on the hills this last May Day, and so far the plague has not struck again."

I nodded and sent an appreciative prayer to Brigantia, thanking the Goddess for saving the rest of the land. Murrain can bring on famine and pestilence faster than anything else.

"The ironworkers of Furness have sent the High King a new coat of chain mail as repayment of their debt from three years past," Urien went on, "and all is well in the rest of Lakeland."

I watched the crusty fellow closely and wondered what he was not telling us. Although his own land was quite sizable, Urien had coveted Rheged since I was a child, and clearly enjoyed acting in my place. He would not be the first regent to shade the truth so as to keep the real monarch from hearing tales of unrest, unfair taxation or anything else that might indicate the people were not happy with his tenure.

I also noticed he had made no mention of his wife, Morgan le Fey, and wondered if he even knew what the High Priestess was doing in her Sanctuary at the Black Lake. There was no love lost between them and I thought it possible he preferred to ignore the woman rather than keep track of her. Such an attitude smacked of the arrogant belief that if he scorned her, she would no longer be dangerous. I, myself, knew better.

Eventually everyone had their say, and the men began asking Palomides about the strange armor he brought back. From there the discussion moved to the weapons and tactics he'd learned of in the East, and before long they all trekked down to the stables to inspect his remarkable Arabian stallion, which he said had more intelligence and stamina than any other creature he'd ever ridden.

I intended to find Enid for a chat, but an overbearing matron from Cornwall swooped down on me, determined that I should accept her daughter as one of my ladies-in-waiting. I've never found the arrangement to be practical—most such girls are more intent on finding husbands among the Companions than helping me with the distaff side of running a court. But just as we bound the parents to us by making their sons squires, there were times when my accepting the girls couldn't be avoided. In this case, when the woman began extolling the Christian virtues of her child, I suggested that perhaps she would be happier in the Cornish Court, where bishops and priests abounded.

"But Queen Isolde is so . . ." The woman searched for a word that would convey her disdain without being outright treasonous, then shrugged eloquently. "Well, there was that problem with Tristan."

I sighed inwardly, thinking that the whole world was bent on punishing the child-bride for having once sought a life of her own by running away with her lover. That Isolde eventually went back to King Mark and had been an exemplary consort ever since was usually forgotten.

In the end I agreed to take in the girl, and told the mother to have her report to Vinnie, who had charge of the care and chaperoning of such youngsters.

Nimue had come to my side during the conversation, and she shook her head in bemusement. Nimue—the doire whom Merlin had found when she was still a young girl overseeing a holy well. She had become not only his apprentice but the great love of the Magician's older years, and when he was no longer able to guide and protect Arthur's reign, it was Nimue who took his place, becoming both adviser to Arthur and good friend to me.

"I sometimes wonder how you manage," she grinned. "Just keeping track of who wants what—and why—requires the skill of a professional juggler."

"Indeed," I answered ruefully. "Any queen worth her salt is worn out by the end of the day. But," I added under my breath, "there's news I haven't heard that needs discussing."

"Urien made no mention of the Lady of the Lake," the doire responded in equally hushed tones.

I nodded, glad to know I was not the only one concerned about what Arthur's half sister might be up to. Ever since she had tried to kill my husband in her attempt to put her lover, Accolon, on the throne, I was suspicious if she lay silent too long. Accolon might be dead, but it seemed unlikely Morgan's dreams were.

Sliding my arm through Nimue's, I gestured toward the stairs and asked the doire to help me check Camelot's pharmacia. Even before she answered, we were headed up to the loft.

The herbs and simples for healing are kept in a closet beyond

Arthur's and my bedroom, well away from the busy areas of the Hall. Once I unlocked the wicker cupboard and we began sorting through jars and packets, the doire and I were able to talk quite openly.

"There hasn't been much news of Morgan since she tried to seduce Lancelot into helping her unseat Arthur," I noted. "That was several years back, but I can't believe she's abandoned the idea."

"Probably not abandoned," Nimue agreed, holding up a vial of rosemary oil. "But getting rid of a popular king is hard and nasty work. And Morgan's ambitions are split; on the one hand she wants the power of the throne, and on the other she's determined to make worship of the Old Gods dominant throughout the land. But there are some who no longer trust her as a spiritual leader."

My eyebrows went up and Nimue put down the vial with a nod. "The Lady of the Lake is losing credence among the druids. Her insistence on giving the Goddess supremacy over all the other Gods does not sit well with our Pagan priests. So perhaps your sister-in-law is too busy trying to consolidate her own base of power to be plotting against you."

"Perhaps," I agreed, unconvinced.

The doire reached over and put her hand on my arm. "Have no fear, Gwen—I will let you know if there's any indication Arthur is in jeopardy again. Now, tell me, how is Albion's Queen doing?"

Her use of the ancient name for Britain brought a smile, and I assured her I was quite well.

"And the royal marriage?" she prompted.

"The most solid in Britain," I assured her. Ours had been a political union to begin with, though I'd grown to love Arthur early on. And he'd come to love me, too, in his way; his distress when he thought I might leave once I learned about Mordred was proof of that. But after eleven years together I was as much a part of Arthur's world as the sunrise, and even more taken for granted. So we laughed and argued and worked to make the Round Table a success, like parents struggling to raise a child, but never seemed to touch in more than flesh.

"What of Lancelot?" Nimue continued, her great, dark eyes scanning my soul. She was the only person, other than Isolde, to whom I could speak freely about the Breton.

"Ah, with Lance it is the opposite. We are just as close as ever, he is just as adamant about not going to bed, and I suppose we will spend the rest of our lives like that." I gave her a rueful grin. "But I'd be lost if he wasn't here, beside me."

Nimue's gaze shifted to some space between now and the future, and I thought her eyes widened briefly. Then she was bending over a tray of packets, her slim fingers riffling quickly through them. At last she wrinkled her nose and pushing the herbs away, declared that she'd send her husband home alone after the Round Table while she stayed on to help process the simples for our medicine cupboard. With that we went to join the rest of the folk in the Hall, but I wondered what she had seen that made her think she should remain at Camelot.

The feast that night was typical of our best hospitality, and afterward our own bard, Riderich, gave over the Harper's Stool to the visiting storytellers of other monarchs. Before long the Hall rang with the ancient tales of glory and bravery, of famous heroes and the Gods who guided them. Most of the performers told their stories in the time-honored way, accompanying the well-loved words with runs of notes or an occasional chord, until Riderich's pupil, Taliesin, set his small Irish harp on his knee. Then the sounds became melodies as he poured forth songs every bit as charming as any that Tristan himself might have sung.

We listened, enthralled, for among Celts there is no force more powerful for invoking peace or pride than music. When the magic of the young man's playing died away, Urien's bard, Talhaern, rose to his feet and requested that we allow Taliesin to come study with him. Considering that Talhaern was called the Father of Inspiration, it was a fine compliment. I wondered if he knew how many people thought Taliesin was a changeling child, more fey than mortal, and that he was sometimes taken with fits, when strange words poured from his mouth. But perhaps that wouldn't matter, all storytellers being somewhat mad, and the look of joy on Taliesin's face was marvelous to behold, for he was convinced he was destined to sing songs powerful enough to make the very Gods weep.

Next morning I was up early, seeing to the foods that would be put out for those of our guests who wished to eat before leaving on their journey home. As I headed for the henhouse to collect the eggs, I caught sight of Enid walking slowly along the parapet above our wall. Dropping my basket by the hutch, I went bounding up the stairs to join the new Queen of Devon. But I stopped cold when I saw the expression on her face.

Enid—dark and pert, with a quick wit and fearless tongue; the girl who'd married the most eligible bachelor king in Britain. That Geraint was a brilliant military leader and she well known for looking askance at brash warriors made for much speculation about their match. But that wouldn't account for the misery that surrounded her now. I lifted my skirts and ran along the parapet toward her.

"Enid, whatever is the matter?"

She looked up at my voice, then half turned away until I caught hold of her shoulders and the words came pouring out. "Oh, M'lady, I don't know what to do. Geraint and I can't seem to get pregnant, and it's not for want of trying."

Her brown eyes were shining with tears, and we stared at each other without reserve, two women suddenly sharing a similar sorrow. She leaned her head against my shoulder and I put my arms around her as she began to sob.

There was no need to speak of the confusion and hurt barrenness brings forth; the soul-searching and recriminations, anger and fear and silent, desperate bargaining with the Gods—I'd known them all myself. So I held her close while her pain overflowed in weeping.

"What is Geraint's reaction?" I asked when the crest of her tears had passed. Enid might not be my daughter, but I would certainly speak to her husband if he was adding to the problem.

"It doesn't seem to upset him, M'lady, though I'm sure he feels it in the normal sense of missing being a father."

She was silent for a bit, and I thought of Arthur. My inability to produce offspring hadn't bothered him at all, for he had little interest in children and all his time was consumed with the Cause.

"It feels as though there's a big hole in the center of my life that nothing else can fill." Enid didn't try to cover the despair in her voice. "How can I fill the emptiness, M'lady?"

"Take in a child," I told her firmly. "One in need, as Mordred was in need."

She sniffed loudly and fumbled for her handkerchief. "Does he know?" I searched her face, wondering how much *she* knew.

"About his mother's death and all," she went on. "We heard, even in Devon, that Morgause met an unseemly end."

Unseemly end? The miserable woman deserved everything that came to her, whether she was Arthur's other half sister or not. But of course I couldn't say that out loud, so . . .

I shook my head and chose my words carefully. "I don't think he's heard. Bedivere threatened to personally thrash anyone who breathed a word of it at Court, and the boy's never brought the subject up. Gawain looks after his little brother some; took him north to Edinburgh on this trip to meet with the Picts. But mostly I oversee his everyday life."

"Has it met your need, M'lady?" Enid inquired hesitantly.

"Aye, that it has." I brushed the last of the tears from her cheeks and smiled. "We spend our mornings together. I give him riding lessons, or take him on errands, and then we study Latin. His mother had him tutored in both reading and writing, before she died, and this arrangement seems to please everyone—though he's far fonder of the reading than I am."

"As I recall," my erstwhile lady-in-waiting said, giving me a droll look, "you'd rather tell a tale yourself than pick over some old scroll. Maybe, like Bedivere, your second calling is to be a bard."

"With my voice?" I grinned, horrified at the notion of trying to sing anything. Since neither Arthur nor I could carry a tune, we made it Court policy to keep our mouths shut and not assault the household's ears. "No need to invite a palace revolt," I concluded.

Before we climbed down the stairs and returned to the Hall, Enid paused to take my hand in gratitude. "Thank you, M'lady," she said softly.

The court in front of the Hall was filling with horses and squires waiting for their nobles to leave, so I hurried inside to the rest of the guests and Enid went to find Geraint.

Later, when the two of them came to say their formal good-byes, I gave the new Queen a special hug. For a moment she drew in her lower lip as though to keep from crying, then, with a toss of her head, turned to smile at her husband. Brave, stubborn, fighting to keep self-pity away—I nodded my approval, confident she was becoming a Queen worthy of the title.

Arthur and I stood on the steps of the Hall, waving as the last of the Fellowship departed. Among them were Beaumains and Lynette, riding through the gates together. The new warrior was clearly pleased to be off on an adventure, though the girl was still dubious about it all.

"At least the little baggage will keep him on his toes," Arthur allowed with amusement.

That night, as we were getting ready for bed, Arthur and I went over the high points of the gathering just past. He was generally pleased with the results, though he'd put aside discussion of the law code, thinking it best to wait until he had a chance to see the Edictum Palomides had mentioned.

"And what of Beaumains?" I asked, taking the pins from my hair. "Aren't you afraid Cei's right—that he's too inexperienced for the task he's taken on?"

Arthur shrugged. "If Lance says Beaumains can hold his own out in the big world, then he can hold his own."

There was a pause as he tugged off a boot and I began to comb out my hair. Thick and wavy, it is the color of red gold honey and is my best feature—and my one concession to vanity. I wash it regularly, and brush it thoroughly every night. Now I leaned over and drew the ivory comb through the length of it.

Once, as a child, I'd seen my father comb out Mama's hair, letting it tumble across his hands and piling it playfully around her shoulders. It was a deep copper red, like the color of her sorrel mare, Featherfoot. I remembered everything about Mama as being beautiful—her hair, her face, her charm and laughter—even her dedication to her people, for she took sick and died while nursing the hundreds who flocked to our Hall in search of succor during a year of famine and plague.

But most of all I remembered her relationship with my father—tender, loving, and sometimes touched with an air of romance that made them both glow with happiness. Peering at my husband through the veil of my hair, I wished just once he'd drop his guard enough to let a little romance into our lives.

"There's other men I'm more concerned about than Beaumains," he noted, putting his boots in the cupboard by the window.

"Oh? Anyone in particular?"

Arthur chewed on the ends of his mustache. "Geraint, for one.

Did you notice that he didn't take part in the tournament, even though Cei challenged him? Some of the men say that new wife of his is sapping him of the will to fight, what with her disdain for military matters."

"That's ridiculous," I responded. "Just because Enid encourages him to find other solutions to problems besides drawing a sword doesn't mean the man's become a coward."

"No, of course not. And Geraint was one of the heroes of Mount Badon, so it's not a question of his bravery." He stretched lazily, then taking a nightshirt off the peg, began to chuckle. "No one can fault Pellinore's courage! I haven't seen such a fiery display since the last time Gawain got swept up in battle-lust! But I'm going to have to talk to Gawain again, when he gets home— remind him there's no call for his continual jibes and threats against the men of the Wrekin. Pelli killed his father in battle, in fair combat. This vendetta he's carrying is not only bad for morale, it's the reason Lamorak didn't come to the tournament—he fears one of those Orcadians will stab him in the back."

Arthur's tone was full of resignation, and the straw in the mattress rustled as he sat on the edge of the bed. But some instinct made me ask, "Anything else of concern?"

There was a long pause, and when I'd finished plaiting my hair, I turned to look at him directly. My husband was resting his chin on his hands, elbows on his knees, while he frowned off into space.

"Constantine says his father's dying. Cador was the first, Gwen —the very first to recognize me after Merlin declared I should be King—and I've never gone to battle without him. It won't feel right, not having the old Duke of Cornwall at my side. Not that Constantine isn't a worthy successor, but I'll miss the father. . . . Aye, I'll miss the father."

I was stunned by such an admission of feeling and rising from my stool, came to stand before my husband without a word. When he looked up, there was sorrow and bafflement in his eyes. Every king learns to live with the grief of warriors dying—men, both young and old, who gave their lives in the effort to fulfill their lord's orders. But this was different and, I suspected, closer to the mortality we all share—debilitation, simply from living so long.

I bent over and planted a kiss on Arthur's forehead.

"Here now, enough gloomy thoughts," my husband announced, running his hands up my thighs. "We've a good tournament behind us, a bed with fresh sheets, and time enough to savor both."

As he pulled me down onto the mattress, I wrapped him in my arms, trying to comfort with my body the uneasiness of his spirit. There was no way of knowing whether I succeeded or not, for my husband had retreated behind his usual wall of banter, and when our loving was done, he simply went to sleep.

But I lay long awake, thinking of the things I had found most important at this meeting of the Round Table: of Palomides's trip and Enid's sorrow, and Arthur's own two half sisters: Morgan, weaving dark plots beside the Black Lake, and Morgause, whose shadow reached even from her grave to obscure our sun. These were matters of the heart and soul, yet they shaped our future every bit as much as cavalry maneuvers or politics, and I was sorry that my husband and I were never likely to speak of them.

Looking at his profile while he slept, I wondered if I would ever find a way to breach the isolation of the man known as Arthur Pendragon.

5

Nemesis

hose bloody Picts!"

Gawain was howling like a hurricane when he burst into the room Arthur and I use as an office, two days after the last guest had left.

Gawain—Morgause's firstborn son, arrogant and stocky, with massive shoulders and a temper that matched his flaming hair. He was the perfect picture of the ancient Celt, even to the scars that furrowed his arms and creased his boyish face. And, like most Celts, he would cry over a lovers' ballad one minute and be ready to bring down heaven because he'd missed a tournament the next.

"I swear they use treaties and the promise of them to drag out everything! You'll die of old age if you wait for their councils to make a declaration, and they can tie things up for months, no matter what the agreed-upon date. If only you'd let me take care of them *my* way, I would have been back in time."

Arthur looked up from the long table, giving his nephew a sardonic smile. "If I left our diplomatic relations up to you, we'd have another war on our hands within a week."

It was said with such good humor, Gawain couldn't help but laugh in response.

"Still," Arthur went on, "it's just as well you weren't here for the jousting—gave the others a chance to claim the prize. Pellinore quite outdid himself this time."

The Prince of Orkney tensed at the mention of his enemy's name, and his face froze. Arthur held his gaze like a man staring down a half-wild animal, controlling it by sheer force of will.

"I tell you this because you'll hear it soon enough anyhow, and you and I must reach an accord about your denunciations of Pellinore and his clan."

Gawain's hands had balled into fists and his face flushed crimson. Slowly and deliberately, Arthur rose behind the table while his nephew glared at him.

"When your father joined Urien's rebellion against me at the beginning of my reign, he knew he could die—it is always a possibility in war. But such a death is honorable, and is no cause for starting blood feuds. Yea Gods, if every man who killed another in combat was held for murder, I'd have no fighting men left! I made a point of honoring all who surrendered—Urien of Northumbria and yourself particularly. As one of my best warriors, I named you the King's Champion, and as my sister's son you are next in line to stand for the throne. I value you and your brothers and need you at my side—that should be clear. But I also need the men of the Wrekin, and I want your word you'll make no more threats against them."

For a long minute the two men leaned toward each other, staring in hard, unblinking silence across the table as though across a grave. When Gawain finally spoke, his words rumbled out of his chest while the rest of him remained motionless, all his physical strength channeled into controlling his rage.

"And what of the fact that it was Pelli's son who was in my mother's bed the night that she was killed? If it hadn't been for Lamorak, she would still be alive. Have you forgotten that, Uncle?"

Arthur's response was just as taut and to the point. "As Queen of the Orkneys, Morgause was free to bed whomever she chose. That it was the son of her husband's death-dealer was unfortunate, but I lay that to her lack of judgment, not to Pelli and his kin."

He spoke with the dispassion of a ruler who must be above the tangle of family loves and hates. From his voice one would never guess that he had detested Morgause; had forbidden her to come to his kingdom of Logres, just as he now forbade Morgan le Fey to do so. They were sound decisions, made by a man who found himself betrayed by the women of his blood. But what they cost him in personal terms, one could not even guess.

I wondered suddenly if it was this need to distance himself from them that kept his heart hidden from all others as well.

The Prince of Orkney might be volatile but he wasn't stupid and although he grumbled a bit more, in the end he backed down and agreed to put an end to the tormenting of Pellinore and his son.

Arthur straightened up with a sigh of relief. "I can't tell you how glad I am to hear it," he said, his voice full of affection once more. "I count you and your brother Gaheris among the best of the Round Table Fellowship, and would be loath to lose either of you."

No mention was made of Agravain, the brother who sobbed and howled in his cell on the Orkney Isles, tormented by memories no human should know. Perhaps, in some unspoken way, his very name had been stricken from the family roll, for matricide, like incest, is despised by all.

"And Mordred?" I asked. "Does he know his mother is dead, and at whose hand?" I suspected Gawain might have used this trip to Edinburgh to enlighten his younger brother as to Morgause's fate.

"Yes, M'lady—I showed him her grave—a soft, shady spot, with a view over the Firth. Mordred will soon be old enough to be a squire, so he's old enough to hear the truth. We sat together in the quiet of the grove, and I told him straight out that it was Agravain who beheaded her in a wild, bloody rage when he found her abed with Lamorak. The boy took it bravely, as befits a chieftain's son."

There was a pause, and I wondered if Gawain had also told Mordred who his father was—if he knew. But the redhead made no further comment, and Arthur turned the conversation back to the tournament.

The story of Beaumains's besting Cei brought a gleeful laugh from the Orcadian. "Who would have guessed that scrawny fellow would turn out so well? Wish I could have been here to congratulate him."

"I'm afraid he's left already—went off on a mission to prove his worth." Arthur came out from behind the table and clapped Gawain on the back. "We should be getting down to the practice field. I want Lance to hear your news about the Picts."

"Aye," the Orcadian responded cheerfully, falling into step beside his king. As changeable as the Scottish weather, he had already forgotten the blackness of his recent rage. At the door he turned back to me. "If you've a mind to go on with Mordred's lessons in the morning, I think the lad would like that."

I thanked him with a grin, deeply pleased I could continue teaching the boy who had become the child of my heart, if not my loins.

Mordred, the enigma—the boy who favored neither his Orcadian brothers nor his ruddy, voluptuous mother, but like his Aunt Morgan had black hair, beautiful features, and an intensity of spirit that set the very air around him crackling. By the look of him one would never guess his true parentage, and often while I sat next to his bed when he was feverish, or made his tunics, or cheered him on in his first attempts at swordsmanship, I prayed that his nature, in the end, would reflect his father's side of the family. At least he had his father's eyes, for unlike Morgan's eerie green ones, his were a soft, warm brown.

One could see the questions of all mankind reflected in those eyes; eyes that filled with concern at the sight of a wounded animal, or flashed with excitement when he grappled with a new idea. No doubt all mothers take delight in seeing the world anew through their children's eyes, but this was the first I'd known of it, and the experience filled me with joy.

The boy was overflowing with news about the trip to Edinburgh and during our first morning together regaled me with descriptions of the town that had grown up around the gray fortress perched atop its steep outcropping of rock.

"And a natural mote," he explained, drawing a rough map on his tablet. "More like a swamp, really—but it makes it that much harder for enemies to reach the ramparts. Gawain says such tactics of placement are half the battle won."

I listened and nodded, waiting for some mention of his mother, but Mordred carefully avoided the subject, and before long we were back to our regular studies as though he'd never been away.

He picked up his favorite scroll, an ancient copy of *The Iliad* from Merlin's library. It was tattered and worn, but Mordred loved the tale of the Trojan War, so we pored over it frequently, with me explaining what Cathbad had taught me of the Greek endeavor while Mordred corrected my Latin and tried to improve my syntax.

He looked up suddenly, a scowl darkening his face. "Who do you think was the bravest, M'lady . . . Hector or Achilles?"

"Well, Hector understood that he was facing a warrior beloved by the Gods," I suggested. "And it takes tremendous courage to go against supernatural forces."

"And Hector was defending his home, which would add to his courage," Mordred mused, absently stroking his upper lip where the shadow of a mustache was forming. "Gawain says a man will fight twice as hard for his own piece of turf as for conquest." The boy glanced up at me, then shifted his gaze to some far distance. "It always seems unfair that the Gods caused Hector's death."

Like Gawain, Mordred had a soft spot for the underdog, and I smiled at him. "Just think how the course of history would have changed, if Hector and the Trojans had won! Why, Aeneas wouldn't have fled to Italy, and his grandson Brutus might never have reached our shores. We would have been born Ancient Ones, not Celts, if the Gods hadn't taken a hand in things."

Mordred rounded on me suddenly, his eyes bright with curiosity. "Is it true that Gawain once lived with the Ancient Ones? The other pages say so, and when I asked him, he didn't deny it."

"Then he must have, for no honorable Celt lies," I answered firmly. "The Prydn were a band of Ancient Ones—nomads who followed their reindeer from pasture to pasture, never clearing land or using iron or staying long in one place. It was when their paths crossed ours in Scotland that your brother fell in love with their Queen. But that was quite a bit ago, my dear—quite a bit."

I thought of the tempestuous affair that had burned so fiercely over that whole winter. Swaggering with pride, the King's Champion had presented his love at Court, boasting of her prowess as leader of the nomads. But the courtiers made fun of the half-wild girl dressed in bad-smelling skins, and she turned on them with scorn and hatred when she saw their hypocrisy. In the end, Gawain could no more leave Arthur and the Companions than she could desert her people, and they parted with pain and anger and slashing hurt.

He never found another to love as he'd loved the homely

Ragnell, and I doubted that she'd ever given her heart so completely to anyone else. The scars of their encounter ran deep—
Gawain's cheek still bore the mark of her nails, where she had
raked him on their last encounter—and for a long while after
that the Orcadian had used women without conscience. It was
only recently that he'd come to espouse the notion of defending
and protecting them.

"What did he tell you about the Prydn?" I prompted.

"That they are the firstborn of the Gods, and live outside with
nature and the seasons, distrusting man-made houses with closed
roofs and paned windows." Mordred turned those luminous eyes
on me. "Can they really make magic?"

"So it is said. There are many kinds of power that we in our
snug houses have lost touch with," I answered, thinking as much
of Merlin in his cave as Ragnell living among the Hollow Hills.

"Aunt Morgan makes the most powerful magic of all, because
she's High Priestess of the Goddess." Mordred's voice filled with
family pride. "Gawain says she made Arthur High King because
he's our kin, and she gave him Excalibur as proof of the Goddess's
blessing. Someday he's going to take me to meet her, at the Black
Lake."

I nodded silently, thinking it best not to get involved in *that*
rats' nest. No doubt someday he'd meet her, but for now I had no
desire to explain to the youngster that even though Morgan had
helped put Arthur on the throne, she had also tried to take his
life. And I knew the High King would be furious if the boy asked
leave to go see her; Morgan le Fey was Arthur's nemesis as surely
as Gawain was Pelli's.

"Maybe," I cautioned Mordred, "your visiting the Lady of the
Lake can wait for a while. At least we don't need to bring it up
to the King at the moment."

The lad searched my face as though seeking the answer to some
unexpressed query. But finally he acquiesced, and we turned our
attention back to the Trojan War and those tales of ancient
families whose moiras had been twisted into tragedy by the Gods.

*In my tomboy youth I had been deeply envious of that Helen who
was so beautiful men went to war over her. Fortunately beauty is not
a requirement for being a good monarch, or I'd be serving my people
as a stable hand. Yet oddly, the only women I've ever been jealous of*

were named Helen—well, Elaine, *actually*—but each was beautiful in her own way, and both were deeply enamored of Lance.

The first was a girl from Astolat, who died in a boating accident. But the other, Elaine of Carbonek, was very much alive, and if she was only a thorn in my side then, she was shortly to become a dagger at my heart.

6

Discovery

n a ripe, golden day in late summer, Lance and I rode over to Glastonbury to see if the people at the apple orchard needed more kegs for the cider they would be pressing for us. Already the harvesting was under way, with farmers and neighbors and villagers all working together to gather the grain. At the end of one field a group of rowdy rooks rose flapping into the sky above an elm spinney, as cheerful and noisy as the workers below. I watched the children scrambling among the weeds at the edge of the tilled land, cutting the stout green grasses and twisting them into bindings with which to tie the sheaves, and when they saw me, they waved merrily and called out my name.

I smiled and waved back. Autumn is my favorite season and with the harvest under way, the time of crisping morns and frosty nights could not be far away.

Beneath me my filly tossed her head and nickered. The foal of the beautiful but flighty mare Arthur had given me as a wedding present, she was a rich copper chestnut with flaxen mane and tail, and I'd named her Etain for her beauty. Gwyn had bred and trained her at his stable near Glastonbury and swore she was more reliable than her high-strung mother.

This was the first time we'd been out on the Road together, and she was full of energy, pulling against the bit and prancing sideways with excitement. I suspected she loved to run free as much as I did, and before long I challenged Lance to a race.

"Best wait till you're more familiar with your animal," he cautioned.

"Can't think of a better way to get acquainted," I countered, bridling at his reasonableness. But his point was well taken, so I dropped the subject.

"Palomides has been telling me about his trip," the Breton said as we trotted along side-by-side. "He met the most extraordinary people—fire-worshiping Zoroastrians and eunuch priests of the Goddess Cybele, as well as Jews and Egyptians and the Bedouin shamans. But the ones he found most impressive were the Christians. On the street corners of Arles they were arguing Pelagius's concepts of free will against Bishop Augustine's doctrine of divine grace! And they have monasteries devoted to translating the philosophers of all ages: libraries full of *ideas*, Gwen, not just chronicles of conquests and wars. Of course, not all monasteries are devoted to learning. He stayed at one in the Syrian desert that had grown up beside a pillar sixty feet tall, built by a Christian who was seeking God."

I cocked one eyebrow skeptically, wondering why on earth anyone would make such a thing, and was promptly told he was a hermit named Simon who wanted to discipline his flesh and get away from people at the same time, so he lived his life on the tiny platform atop that column, without shelter from sun or wind, night or cold. Ironically the people assumed he must be pure and holy, so they called him a saint and flocked to the base of his pillar by the thousands. From all across the desert, whole tribes swarmed to see him, drawn by curiosity but converted by the awe this man of God inspired.

I wondered what could drive a person to set himself so far apart from the warmth of human contact, and tried to imagine what he was like, red-eyed and dried up like a raisin, with matted beard and hair, smelling to high heaven as he railed at the world below. "Maybe he'd never had a bath, even when he was young," I suggested. "They say you don't miss what you've never known."

Lance paid no heed to my flippancy, being intent on his subject. "The holiest Christians go off into the desert, much like the druids make a retreat to the wildwood and live by their wits with only the Gods' guidance. Sometimes, Gwen, I think that civilization clouds our sight, so that we lose our ability to see The Divine. Those strange, crazy hermits may be nearer to God than we know."

I cast him a dubious look. As far as I was concerned, life was here to be lived and I couldn't understand why anyone would make it more complicated than need be. So I teased him about spending too much time philosophizing with Palomides, and warned that so much thinking was likely to make him soft in the head.

"I can't help it," he answered gravely. "It's the only way I know to come at the world. If I can't define it mentally, I don't know what it is." Then he turned and gave me a dazzling smile that was full of bemusement as well as love. "We can't all be as intrepid as you."

"Intrepid, my foot," I sputtered, wondering what any of this had to do with anything important. And then suddenly we were laughing together at the ludicrousness of taking ourselves so seriously.

If Lance was my Champion and protector, making me feel cherished and loved and even beautiful, it was I who lifted his spirits and kept him from dwelling too much on the dark, mystical side of things.

By midmorning we'd reached the Causeway to Glastonbury, and the horses' hooves drummed hollowly on the ancient logs that had been pounded into the reedy swamp long before the Legions came. The day was pleasant and without wind, so the waters of the lake lay unruffled, smooth as a sheet of Roman glass. For years the Celts have called the hill that rises out of the lake Ynys Witrin—Glass Island—though others know it as Avalon—the Isle of Apples—because its orchards are so fine. In either case, it earns its name.

We talked with the cider man, then met with Gwyn, who came down from his fortlet on the top of the Tor to join us for lunch at a dockside tavern where we chatted amiably while the water birds rose and fell in great gathering flocks along the edges of the lake. When it was time to go, Lance went for the horses, and I told Gwyn how pleased I was with Etain. The little man beamed with pride.

But when the Breton brought our mounts around, Etain's ears were laid half-back, and her eyes white-rimmed with nervousness. Lance was frowning sharply and handed the restive animal over to me with the curt announcement that we must leave immediately. Gwyn cocked his head to one side and extended his hand in farewell, but Lancelot gave him only a mute nod in return.

We rode toward home in silence, and my efforts at starting a conversation met with nothing but gloomy preoccupation on the Breton's part. At last I gave up trying to draw him out, for he seemed to be struggling with more than some obscure question of philosophy.

When we came to a small ford, he abruptly turned off onto the streamside path and without a word led the way to the edge of a meadow. Tying the horses to a willow clump, he came round and raised his arms to help me dismount.

Startled, I looked down on him. All those years our never bedding had been his decision, not mine, yet now he stood, reaching up to me in evident appeal, and my heart quickened at the notion that he'd changed his mind.

When I leaned out over the space between us, he grasped me firmly around the waist and lifted me in a wide, gentle arc. I was light as thistledown in his arms, buoyed by the strength and safety of his presence, and even after my feet touched the ground, he kept one arm around me as we made our way through the willows toward the waterside.

"There's something I must tell you—something very painful." His voice had gone rough and I pulled away slightly, trying to see his face, but he turned his head away abruptly. "Don't look at me —not just yet, or I'll never find the words."

So we walked together, arms around each other's waist, with my head resting on his shoulder. The quiet murmur of the stream filled the silence as we approached a flat rock that nosed out over the water. Willow branches trailed down into a pool, making a kind of grotto around us, and an iridescent dragonfly coursed back and forth above the water. Surely, I told myself, nothing dreadful could happen in such a lovely place.

We sat down, leaning against each other like children, and I nestled beside him as he began absently stroking my hair. It was a long time before he spoke, his voice very soft and distant.

"When I left you after Mordred came, I made you promise that if you ever needed me, you'd send word. And that I would come, wherever you were, whenever you called. Do you remember?"

I nodded silently, recalling our parting and the great aching loss that had settled over me once he was gone.

"I went everywhere . . . down to Canterbury and along the Saxon Shore, over to Cornwall, up to the kingdoms of Wales . . . but I couldn't escape you. Morning or night, you were the first thing I thought of, the last I prayed for. Even in my dreams you were with me. Then I went to Carbonek, to see how the ailing King of the Waste Land was faring. . . ."

I stiffened as the pert, pretty face of Elaine rose to memory. "No doubt Pellam's conniving red-headed daughter made you more than welcome," I said, sitting upright as my own hateful jealousy came awake.

Lance turned suddenly, staring at me so intently all thoughts of Elaine vanished. He cradled my face between his palms and spoke in little more than a whisper.

"I thought it was the message I'd been waiting for, that you'd finally sent for me . . . been drinking too much, and when her governess, Brisane, handed me a scarf that smelled of lavender and said, 'M'lady's waiting' . . . it seemed the answer to all my prayers. I didn't even stop to wonder why you'd be at Carbonek. Without candle or rush-light, or even a moon beyond the casement. . . . Oh Gwen, I didn't know how much was dream, how much was real. . . ."

His eyes filled with anguish and we stared at each other in silence as the meaning of his words sunk in. Lance, who would not share my bed as a matter of "honor," had been tricked into a liaison by the one woman I already envied.

Pain and understanding, anger and compassion rushed through me. Lance was a man like any other, with all the needs of any Champion, and I had no right to demand fidelity from him . . . I who romped comfortably enough with Arthur any night of the year.

But it hurt that the girl had been Elaine. She was all the things I was not—young and beautiful, and supremely confident that all men would love her, if only because she looked so luscious.

"Cheeky little creature," I snapped, "always up to some charming game, as though her desires were at the center of everyone else's thoughts. She'd been trying to trap you in a romance ever since you first met—and to think she should have succeeded by playing on your love for me. . . ."

My anger was rising, focusing on the girl who had been so smugly convinced that Lance would someday be her mate. The deception she had played on him was played on me as well, and I hated her for it. I gulped and looked away. Over the reeds at the water's edge the dragonfly darted and hovered, a shimmering illusion, now here, now gone.

"Well, no great damage done," I said at last with a great, deep sigh, as though I could expel both my outrage and hurt in that one long breath. "You're back here now, and that night's fling need not be repeated . . . unless you wish."

"Of course I don't wish!" Indignation rasped Lance's voice. "In the morning, when I realized what had happened, I was infuriated. I told her that I never wanted to see her or her scheming, treacherous governess again. I'd have run that meddling old woman through, if she'd crossed my path."

He swallowed hard, then went on.

"But it seems that's not the end of it. The groom at the stables just now passed on the rumor that Elaine is coming to Camelot . . . with a child she claims is my son."

The words were spoken quietly, but they cut through me like a searing, slicing knife. The old, aching void of barrenness opened up again—bleak and empty, full of despair and the bitter knowledge that I could never achieve what every milkmaid and scullery girl found so exceptionally easy. Not only had that chit of a girl bedded the man I could not, she'd given him a child as well. A child . . . the very gift of life and immortality which I could never give Arthur or Lance or anyone else.

The air had gone out of my lungs and I stared, stupefied, at the dragonfly that had come to rest on the edge of the rock. It had lost all its color, like a world gone dead.

Gradually realization seeped through me. It spread through my body like a giant, throbbing bruise until even my fingers and toes ached with the pain of it. Jumping to my feet, I let out a wail and began to run blindly toward the horses.

"Gwen!" Lance's cry reached me as I tugged Etain's reins free and swung up into the saddle. "Gwen, wait!"

But the filly took her cue from my wordless scream, pivoting to head across the meadow toward the broken woods beyond. I leaned forward, keeping enough pressure on the bit so that she was still within my power, but urging her on as much as possible.

After the first few strides she lengthened out, growing more confident by the second.

Behind us, Lance's horse was pounding to catch up, so I gave Etain's ribs a solid whack with my heels, and she summoned up an extra burst of speed as we entered the trees.

It was not the first time I'd tried to outrun my fate. When Bedivere confirmed that Mordred was indeed Arthur's son, I had bolted from the knowledge, racing into the wind of an oncoming storm.

But that was down a clear Roman Road. Now I was trying to guide an inexperienced animal through an ever-darkening wood. Hazel withes whipped my arms as Etain swerved wildly to avoid the most obvious thickets, and I barely ducked in time to miss a low-hanging branch. The trunks of huge trees raced past as she bolted through the forest, and I wondered fleetingly how soon before we'd crash headlong into one of them. At last I gave up trying to guide her, and letting her have her head, twined my hands in her flaxen mane and crouched forward along her neck.

Instinctively the filly plunged toward the openings where golden sunlight denoted space between high arching oak and ash. We plunged dizzyingly from shadow to light and on again, and the blood that pounded in my ears drowned out all thoughts of jealousy and betrayal, irony and woeful lack. The whole of my world had narrowed down to simply trying to survive.

Suddenly the land fell away and I caught a glimpse of soft, rolling pastures beyond a stone wall. Etain was going too fast to stop, so with a tightening of knees and thighs, I set the filly to the barrier, praying she had more sense than her scatter-brained mother.

She took the wall at full speed, collecting and launching into the air as though she'd grown wings. Even her landing was graceful, without stumble or hesitation, and when I shifted my weight and gathered up the reins again, the young mare slowed to a trot, tossing her head and arching her neck proudly.

A great wave of relief and affection washed over me—I was still alive more because of her good instincts than my own, and I patted her withers gratefully.

Behind us Lance's warhorse cleared the wall with practiced ease. By the time we'd crossed the pasture he'd caught up and we rode side-by-side in measured silence.

Whatever else that horrendous ride had produced, my panic had subsided, leaving me able to think calmly once more—though I still couldn't bring myself to look at him, lest the rage that was building in me toward Elaine should be channeled directly at him instead.

The air between us turned as brittle as glass on the verge of shattering. With each breath the wall of silence rose higher, like the crystal tower the peasants claim Nimue erected around Merlin. It hid not the death of a body, as the old stories say, but my withdrawal from love, and I paid no heed to the young, childish voice that begged me to relent before I imprisoned both of us in icy bitterness.

Lance watched me anxiously, and I didn't have to see them to know his eyes were pleading for forgiveness. Understanding I could give; forgiveness was beyond my grasp. At last, when he dismounted to open the pasture gate at the Road, I faced him with a cold smile.

"Not bad for her first time out," I said, patting Etain's neck and refusing to acknowledge the cause for my flight.

The Breton's response was formal, accepting the distance that I was putting between us, but his voice was more ragged than the pursuit would warrant. "You might have been killed, M'lady."

"Oh, lots of things might have happened that didn't," I flung back, lifting my chin defiantly. There was no way I would admit to anyone—not the Gods nor Arthur, nor even Lance himself—how terribly deep the hurt had gone.

So we rode back to Camelot in silence while I laid layer upon layer of pride across the wound before Elaine could arrive at Court and take Lancelot away from me.

7

Other Women's Sons

t seems there's something worrying at you, M'lady," Elyzabel said, concern making her unusually bold. I had chosen her to take Enid's place as my maid and confidante in part because her broad northern accent reminded me of my childhood in Rheged, and her older years gave her advice an added weight. "I'm more than willing to listen," she offered.

We had ridden out to do some harvesting of our own, this being the best time to gather devil's bit and the roots of marsh mallows. On the way home we went to gather some of the barbed teazles our weavers use for fulling, but as we approached the tall, dried plants, we found them surrounded by a charm of goldfinches. Perched on the spiky seedpods, the pretty little birds were busily extracting hidden seeds, fluttering and trilling among themselves without taking any notice of us. I stared at them in silence, wishing I could pick my way through my own thorny situation as blithely.

"If you want to talk about it, that is," Elyzabel continued, and I looked over at her. Seeing the friendship and concern on her face, I was tempted to pour out the whole story of Elaine's trickery. But caution stilled my tongue. What if the rumor wasn't true? Maybe Elaine wasn't on her way to Court. Maybe she hadn't even conceived, in which case there was no reason to mention the sordid little affair to anyone. Certainly I didn't want to expose Lancelot to unnecessary embarrassment if it could be avoided.

So the words stuck in my throat, and I ended by shaking my head mutely. I would go on struggling with the devils of jealousy and rage by myself.

To the rest of the world I was always the busy Queen—quick, competent, unruffled by the daily squalls of a High Court. Even Arthur saw me so, and I doubted he noted the new edge to my voice. He even seemed oblivious to my tossing and turning as night after sleepless night went by. But then, my husband would sleep through anything that didn't threaten his Britain.

Only Lance, keeping himself as distant from me as I was from him, could guess at the chaos inside—the unshed tears, the long, heart-broken pleadings with the Gods, the wild swings between rage and sorrow.

The thought of Elaine filled me with silent curses—at the girl, at Lancelot, and finally at the Gods. I turned the subject first this way and then that, trying to find a way to accept it graciously, but the very possibility of her bearing him a son opened too many taunts from the past.

At least he had told me as soon as he heard the news, so it wasn't really like finding out about Mordred. I had had *no* warning about that, for Arthur had kept the wretched secret of his fatherhood hidden from all save Bedivere and Merlin. So I'd blundered into that discovery all unknowing, and been devastated by Morgause's gloating revelation.

It had never occurred to me that Arthur might have a child by someone else—or that that someone might be his own half sister. He hadn't known who she was at the time, though Morgause had been fully aware when she lured him, young and bedazzled by his triumph at the Great Battle, into her incestuous bed. He discovered soon after, and she'd made sure he knew when Mordred was born, holding the secret of his paternity over Arthur like a sword balanced precariously over his head. And when Mordred was coming up to his eleventh birthday, she brought him to Court so that he could serve Arthur along with his brothers Gawain and Gaheris and Agravain.

Mordred's existence did much to explain Arthur's hatred of Morgause, but there would never be any way to know what her plans had been for the boy; it was barely a day later that Agravain had cut off his mother's head. Arthur's family never did anything by half measures.

Morgause's death relieved us of worrying about her plots and schemes. But it also left Mordred a half orphan—full orphan in the eyes of the world, who assumed King Lot had fathered him on the eve of the Great Battle. Poor hapless child, born into a skein of bitter conniving that was none of his making—I could not let him be cast away so cruelly.

So I had insisted we take the boy in. As yet no one had guessed his relationship to Arthur, and I had no idea how much Mordred himself knew. Like his mother's death, it was not something we spoke of. That's where the matter rested and might well remain, for Arthur was not likely to acknowledge the lad on his own.

But Lancelot's son was a different matter. Whereas Arthur's paternity was silent, Lance's would probably be trumpeted throughout the realm. And while I could have a hand in raising Mordred, there was neither reason nor likelihood that Elaine would let me anywhere near her child. In all probability she'd try to take the Breton back to Carbonek, and I told myself that that was better than having the two of them stay here. Lance was a natural father—the sort of man who stops to swing a toddler up on his shoulder or console a child with a scraped knee, a broken toy, a lost kite. How often I'd seen him walking down to the barn, surrounded by a gaggle of children all full of questions or riddles or just the pleasure of being near their idol—only Bedivere was as beloved by the youngsters. So I could not believe he would turn aside from one of his own.

But neither was I willing to let him go without a struggle. What had happened could not be undone, but I prayed the Gods would spare us a public scene; with any luck I could intervene, could meet the girl privately and try to deflect the demands I felt sure she'd make on Lancelot.

But whether by accident or design, my nemesis arrived at Court while the entire household was assembled for dinner.

Lucan the Gatekeeper marched importantly into the center of the circle, round face beaming, and trumpeted, "Elaine of Carbonek asks that you grant entrance to her and her son, Galahad."

A gasp of surprise went through the assemblage and I froze, stung by fire and ice. Arthur, who was gnawing on a drumstick, shot me an inquiring glance. Putting the best face on it that I could, I smiled at my husband and told the Gatekeeper to show her in.

Elaine glided across the Hall like a wraith floating above the ground. In spite of coming from the poverty-stricken Waste Land,

---

she was handsomely arrayed, wearing a pale green mantle of softest wool. Where the hood fell back, her red hair tumbled in ringlets and curls down over her ample bosom. A sizable bundle of blankets filled her arms, and she held it tenderly for fear of waking the child within. Once she was clearly the center of attention, she paused, ingenuously staring down at her offspring's face. The sanctity of young motherhood surrounded her and the babe like a nimbus, and when she had basked fully in its aura, she lifted a soft and limpid gaze to Lancelot.

In spite of all my effort, a gut-wrenching anger leapt up behind my mask of royal dignity. The girl, however, chose not to acknowledge my presence, either in word or look. Turning slowly to Arthur, she curtsied deeply, her expression radiating sublime happiness.

"Your Highness. I bring you a new warrior, who will be raised to serve you as well as his father has."

Arthur smiled indulgently at the young beauty. "And who might his father be?"

"Why, I thought the whole world knew." Elaine dimpled demurely. "It's Lancelot of the Lake."

"Lance!"

Arthur's surprise ricocheted around the Hall, and all eyes turned to the Breton, who flushed furiously. "By the Horned One," my husband swore, "what a wonderful surprise. Why didn't you tell us?"

My heart plummeted as Lancelot rose to his feet. He'd gone very pale and looked only at Arthur, not me or Elaine. "Because I didn't know. I have not seen this lady for two full years, M'lord, and she sent me no word."

"Well, no matter. The news has finally arrived." Arthur banged his fist on the table and leaning back in his carved chair, grinned happily at his lieutenant. "Splendid news. Absolutely splendid. About time you settled down and started a family."

Lance gulped, and a hundred words of denial crowded my throat, but I kept my jaws clenched though my face burned scarlet. Gawain, who had guffawed the loudest at the news, now led a cheer for the new father, and the men clapped and stamped their approval.

"You must help arrange the wedding," Arthur announced,

turning to me. His voice and manner were so expansive, you'd think parenthood was a state he much desired. "We'll make it a royal occasion. And," he went on, beaming again at the girl, "if your father is still too ill to travel, I'll take his place at the Bride Blessing. That is, if you wish."

"Oh, yes, Your Highness." Elaine's response was breathless with pleasure, and she sent him a flutter of appreciative smiles.

The fury in me slipped its leash, and I leapt to my feet without thought or volition. One of the pages jumped forward to pull my chair back and I mumbled some hasty excuse before I stormed through the kitchen door. The Hall had gone abruptly silent, but the force of my anger drove me out into the night without regard to protocol. If I must be drawn and quartered emotionally, it didn't have to be in public.

I started down toward the stables, instinctively heading for the hay-sweet security of Featherfoot's stall. Originally my mother's mare, she'd been the gentle companion of my whole life, nickering and nudging and simply letting me cry against her neck many times in our years together. But the laughter of stablehands gathered in the tack room caused me to veer away from that haven, and I retreated to the garden instead.

Whatever the response to my abrupt departure, the merriment in the Hall had resumed, the glad gabble of congratulations murmuring behind me. No doubt the precious beauty from Carbonek was handing Galahad to his father. Mentally I saw the child waking to stare, sleepy-eyed and curious, at Lance . . . could see the great Champion drinking in the warm innocence of young life, enraptured by the miracle of his own offspring. When the toddler laughed and reached toward the sparkle of Lance's eyes, how could he fail to smile in return?

In the tree above me a thrush burst into song, casting its net of magic against the stars, and my heart welled with the ache of my own inadequacy, the sorrow of impossible dreams. Not only would I never know such a moment with a child of my own, now I was about to lose Lance to one who did.

Sinking down on the marble bench, I stared up into the night, waiting for the blessed release of tears. Yet anguish closed my throat and neither sound nor tear came forth. Stifled, choked off, unable to lessen the misery with weeping, I sat still as a statue in the starlight, without even the moon for company.

Gradually the sounds of the Hall fell to a soft mutter as I plunged into the black night within. Lost, alone, cut off from the cheerful embrace of my Court because of a love I couldn't have and a barrenness I couldn't change, I shivered in misery and barely realized that Lance was speaking from behind me.

"Is that you, Gwen? I thought you'd retired to your chamber."

I began to tremble as the hoarse-whispered words reached me, cringing before the news I was so sure he'd bring.

He came to stand in front of me, a darker form amid the shadows. We stared at each other through the blackness, each knowing full well the other's distress, yet unable to bridge the chasm of circumstance. A terrifying void gaped between us and I scrambled to my feet, flinging out a screen of words in a desperate effort to retain some semblance of pride. Better that I give voice to the inevitable than that I wait for him to.

"What are you doing here, Sir? Have you not got a family to look after? A babe who comes complete with cozy wife to warm your hearth and rock the cradle. What a pretty scene it makes—how cleverly it all works out! I can see the years passing, with a new bairn every fall, until the Hall at Carbonek rings with the laughter of generations to come. How very nice for all concerned . . . even your poor wretched father-in-law, King Pellam. Poor man, lying on his bed of pain, neither brave enough to end his life nor strong enough to get well. Looks like they all found a savior in one night's work, my dear. Lancelot of the Lake, providing Elaine with love and protection the rest of her life, and a great brood of children as well. Giving the old invalid a powerful son-in-law to keep his enemies at bay. Who knows, you could even become the King of Carbonek eventually, and bring the Waste Land back to life, as well."

When I stumbled to a halt, gasping for breath, Lance spoke up, doggedly trying to ignore the venom of my attack. "I have told Arthur I will not wed the girl. I explained that the child was the result of a trick, and I will not saddle all of us with a loveless marriage."

He reached out to me, as though by taking me in his arms he could undo the disaster that had come from that earlier embrace, could erase the twisted bitterness inside me.

"Don't you touch me," I hissed, striking out blindly in the dark. My hand stung suddenly as it crashed against his cheek.

There was a moment's silence while I stared at him, aghast at what I had done. But the misery too long held silent had not yet run itself out, and the words continued to pour forth. "Just go away. Take your accursed honor and get out! I can't stand the sight of you and your cunning lady—so go—*now*—this moment!"

Even in the shadows I could see him tremble, fists clenched, eyes glittering with tears. Suddenly, with a great, heartbroken sob, he spun on his heel and bolted from the garden. A long, piercing scream trailed behind him and when I threw myself down on the bench, the golden circlet fell from my head with a small metallic clatter.

"M'lady? What is it, M'lady?" Nimue bent over me, trying to gather me into her arms as Arthur and Cei came stamping down the garden walk. The torchlight flickered over their frowning faces.

"Are you all right?" Cei asked, his hand moving to his dagger.

I nodded mutely, unable to meet any of their eyes.

"Then who screamed?" Arthur demanded.

"Lancelot," I whispered. "He was distraught. . . ."

"Shush now," Nimue insisted, beginning to rock me as though I was a frightened child while she spoke to the King. "I'll fix her a sedative and take her upstairs, M'lord. She's much too unstrung to stay here shivering in the night air."

"Yes, of course—by all means," Arthur agreed, glancing toward the wall of the fortress. "Someone look to Lance—he's probably in his chambers." My husband looked back at me. "You're sure, lass, 'twas no one here but the Breton? No enemy in ambush?"

Only I who love him, I thought bleakly as I shook my head.

Nimue had me on my feet by then and, having stooped to retrieve the circlet, guided me carefully through the Hall and up the stairs. I wondered vaguely where Elaine was, but didn't have the strength left to deal with her. Tomorrow would be soon enough for that.

It was well past noon before I woke, making up in dreamless slumber for the week of sleepless nights just past. But wakefulness brought memory and a deep, gravid despair. In my misery I had brought about the very thing I feared most—Lance's departure. I groaned aloud.

Nimue came over and peered down at me anxiously.

"He's gone, hasn't he?" I whispered.

"So it seems." She nodded and sat down beside me. "His horse is still in the stable, and his clothes are all hanging in their closet. But the man himself is nowhere to be found. At daybreak a sentry discovered a rope hanging from the parapet—they think Lance used it to lower himself over the wall."

"And Elaine?"

"Wailing tragically that her life is ruined. She thinks that you sent Lance away out of jealous spite."

"Arthur? What does he think?"

Nimue sighed, then gave me a wan smile. "The High King had already heard Lance's declaration that he would never marry the girl. Between death and desertion and the old tradition of temporary marriages, there's many a Celtic princess who's raised a royal son by herself, so Arthur isn't much concerned about that. He is concerned about having his lieutenant turn up missing, however, and has sent out search parties to comb the woods."

I sat up in bed and took the doire's hand, regret making my voice small. "Elaine's right, you know. It wasn't done to spite her, but I did drive him away."

"You, or life, or his own moira." Nimue shrugged eloquently. "We all play out our different fates, Gwen, and his lies between him and his gods just as much as between him and you."

No doubt she meant it as a kind of consolation, but it brought to mind the vision I had once had of Lancelot as a priest—stiff and rigid and bound by a hundred Christian strictures that I neither understood nor trusted. The very memory made me shudder.

"I will ask the Old Gods for help in finding him," the doire promised. "But right now we must get you up and dressed. There's a whole Court downstairs, wondering what really happened last night."

I gaped at her, horror-struck at the notion of facing the household. "Not yet," I pleaded, clutching at the covers and trying to pull them up to my chin. "I can't possibly see anyone today."

"Of course you can." Nimue's words echoed down through the whole of my life. She might have been Mama or Vinnie or my childhood love, Kevin, all trying to impart to me the first law of royalty—you do what has to be done, no matter the personal cost.

"After all, you are their Queen," she added.

I stared at her blankly, wondering if she knew how little I cared, at this moment, about being a monarch.

"Everyone knows how fond both you and Arthur are of Lancelot, and as your Champion they understand there's a special bond between you," she went on patiently. "But if you don't go downstairs, the whole Court will be buzzing with rumors tomorrow, wondering if Elaine has taken the proper measure of things. Oh, I know, by tradition a queen has a right to her own lover, and maybe, if Lance were anyone else, it wouldn't matter. But he's the King's lieutenant; closest in fact, if not in blood, to the King himself. So rumor breeds speculation, and speculation breeds fear —fear that you aren't loyal to Arthur, fear that you are too distraught to govern, fear that the throne is in danger. You know how quickly that sort of thing spreads."

She was right, of course, so I sighed wearily and clambered out of bed while she collected jewels and torc, dress and girtle. Not only must I make an appearance, it seemed it must be a regal one.

Somehow I got through the rest of the day, listening to everyone's concern but keeping my mouth shut. Then suddenly, after dinner, Elaine of Carbonek advanced upon me across the Hall. Her lovely eyes were brimming with tears and her voice was hoarse from crying.

"Wretched woman," she hissed. "You're just jealous because Lancelot loves me instead of you." Everyone in the Hall went silent, and she turned to them in appeal. "She cannot tolerate the idea that he doesn't want to be her Champion anymore . . . always at her beck and call, as if he were one of her wolfhounds."

Vinnie bore down on the girl like an indignant whirlwind. "You can't talk to the Queen that way," she admonished, trying to lead her away.

"Of course I can," the beauty declared, shaking off the caution. "I'll show the whole world how cruel she is, how haughty and selfish and only thinking of her own pleasure. Why, if you only knew what Lancelot told me. . . ."

"Enough!" I declared, rising from my chair. "You are clearly too distraught to realize what you're saying. I order you back to Carbonek until you can come to grips with reality."

That apparently reached through the girl's hysteria, for her attitude of righteous denunciation began to melt. And instead of appealing to the audience who watched us, fascinated, Elaine focused only on me.

"You have the power to banish me, M'lady . . . but we both know that it is unfair. If it weren't for you, Lancelot and I would be living together, raising our son together. I would be here to greet him each time he returns. His son would bring him the joy of parenthood . . . a joy those who never know it can't understand. To deny both father and son that pleasure, to stand between Lance and his moira, is cruel and vicious and unfair." Her voice deepened with conviction, and she pulled herself up to face me as staunchly as possible. "Whatever misery befalls the Breton is on your head, unfair, ungracious, and ungentle Queen!"

With one last glare of defiance, Elaine turned and stalked out, leaving me both shaken and speechless.

Vinnie trotted after her, hoping to soothe the young mother. Whether she succeeded or not I never learned, for the Maid of Carbonek left Court at next light, still complaining of me and swearing to wait her whole life long for Lance to return to her.

Poor Elaine—for all that she lacked the magical talents of Morgan le Fey, she'd become as adept at self-delusion as the High Priestess, and like her, had only herself to blame for her fate.

And yet, if she hadn't played such a wretched trick on the Breton, I could have commiserated with the girl. . . . There was no way to forget Lancelot, once he'd come into your life.

8

Aftermath

laine's sudden departure from the Hall broke the spell of silence that had gripped the household. There was a rustling of comment as people turned to their companions, everyone having something to say about what had just happened.

My face had gone crimson and I stood there shaking with anger and embarrassment. Not only had the girl insulted me as Queen, some of her barbs were perilously close to the mark. I stood naked before my courtiers, knowing of no way to retrieve the situation.

"The Maid of Carbonek is obviously mistaken," Arthur announced, his voice bullying the room into silence. "One can understand her being upset, if she expected Lancelot to greet her with joy and approval. But it's quite unfair to blame my Queen for the Champion's decision."

There was a general muttering of agreement, and I sank back down on my chair, grateful for Arthur's help. Dagonet leapt forward, making some amusing comment on the nature of love, and before long he had everyone laughing. True to his duty as a jester, he drew the audience's attention to lighter matters.

But when Arthur and I were in our chambers that night, we prepared for bed in silence. The sting of humiliation Elaine's words had brought was fading, but the shadow of her accusations lay between us. Suddenly I wanted to tell him she had been wrong. . . . I hadn't tried to keep her and Lance apart, hadn't sent him away for loving her. Hadn't meant to send him away at all. It was the presence of the child which had shattered me, making me say things I didn't mean. I wanted my husband to know that.

Dragging the comb through my hair, I said as casually as I could, "I'd like to talk."

"Talk?" He sounded as though it was an appalling idea. "Whatever for?"

"Well," I hedged, turning to face him, "just so that we understand each other."

"Yea Gods, Gwen. We've been married for more than a decade now. What is there to understand?" He turned away, intent on hanging his tunic on the peg. Clearly he wasn't going to make it easy.

"I mean about Lancelot and me, and the things Elaine said."

There was an instant when Arthur froze; a moment when, reaching up to the hook, his whole body went taut as a warrior's does at the first shock of a mortal blow. I saw it in the muscles of his shoulders, the power of his forearms extended toward something not yet grasped. And then it was gone. With a snort he completed the motion and began to speak, still with his back to me.

"Hmmph! Pretty little thing, Elaine, but I'd say she's a bit unstable. A girl like that can cause a man all sorts of woe. Lance was right in not wanting to marry her. Now, don't you worry about it. She'll be well enough cared for at Carbonek."

Somehow he'd taken the conversation away from my intent, and I watched, confused, as he came to the foot of the bed and bent to rummage in the wicker chest for a clean nightshirt. Never once did our eyes meet.

"That's not what's bothering me," I declared, doggedly plowing toward the truth. This time, I thought, this time he's not going to deflect me, and I'll bring the matter into the open. "It's about my relationship with Lance. . . ."

Suddenly I didn't know where to begin, how to put into words the years of love and denial, of tenderness and appreciation and sharing with each other the things I couldn't share with Arthur himself. Without that as a background, how could he possibly understand that I could love and need Lance as well as him. "It goes back a long way. . . ."

My husband pulled the nightshirt over his head and, still without looking at me, went to the basin and began splashing about like a duck landing on a pond.

I stared at him in disbelief, anger flickering beneath my confusion and sorrow.

"Listen to me, damn it. I'm your wife and I'm trying to tell you something important!"

"I am listening," he declared, his words muffled by the towel as he rubbed his face dry.

"No, you're not. You're avoiding me, as usual." Frustration and exhaustion stifled my voice and, throwing down my comb, I stalked to the window. The silence crackled with unsaid words. He came to stand behind me, and when he spoke again, his manner was calm and reasonable.

"You want to tell me you weren't trying to break up a love-match. Well, I know that. The whole Court knows that. Or that you and Lance are . . ." Reaching out, he put his hands on my shoulders as his voice dipped. ". . . are very close. Well, I know that, too. I knew someone would come for you, eventually. I just didn't know it would be him. Even though you would not leave me, still I knew I could lose you. That *I* could lose you, even though you stayed. I suppose he gives you things I don't have time to—don't know how to. Poems and philosophies and such."

For a moment the silence returned, soft and aching this time. His grip had grown stronger, holding me firmly so that I could not turn to face him and see the sorrow I heard in his words. Then his hands relaxed and his voice strengthened.

"The Court know that as well, and they'll make of it what they choose to. I choose to be glad my lieutenant and my wife are such good friends—there'd be hell to pay if you were enemies, considering how closely I work with both of you! And as far as what happened in the garden last night . . . I don't want to hear about it. It's none of my business, and when he comes back—in a day or a week, or whenever—I won't let him tell me, either."

Arthur's hands were sliding down my arms and came to rest, gently clasped, across my belly. "We may live in the public eye, my dear, but at least we can respect a bit of privacy among ourselves."

I sighed and leaned my head back against his chest, knowing that this was as close as he'd ever let me come to talking about it. Whatever grief or conflict either of us felt would remain resolutely hidden. Still, just as Lance and I controlled our passion by focusing on Arthur, Arthur and I could give each other solace by focusing on Lance.

"What if he doesn't come back?" I whispered.

"Oh, he will. You'll see." Arthur's tone steadied into his usual confidence. "Once he's had a chance to adjust to the shock of parenthood—bound to unsettle a man, learning about it that way —then he'll be back. And if we haven't heard from him by the end of a week, we'll start making inquiries. He's probably gone up to Joyous Gard. Now, come on, Lady"—he dipped his head to whisper into my ear—"my feet are getting cold and it's time for bed."

And so the subject was dropped. Thinking about it later, I didn't know if I was glad or sorry, but Arthur obviously saw the matter as settled.

Lancelot didn't come back that week, or the next, and everyone began to be concerned. We made queries throughout the area, and when he wasn't found close by, Cei organized a broader search. In his typically thorough way, the Seneschal sectioned off areas of the map and designated a different Companion to cover each. Lance's cousins, Bors and Lionel, and his half brother, Ector de Maris, led search parties of their own. Yet the Breton was nowhere to be found, and as the search broadened, our men began bumping into Geraint's in Devon, Pellinore's in the Welsh Marches. Even the messenger who was dispatched to Warkworth returned from Joyous Gard with word that no one had seen him there.

All my life my hasty tongue had gotten me into trouble, and this time it had wounded one I loved. A small, merciless voice in my head reminded me of it constantly. The only respite was during my morning rides, racing Etain along the local tracks or running pell-mell down the Roman Road that leads to Ilchester, with the wind whipping through my hair, banishing all thoughts. If Mordred wondered why we spent more time in the saddle than at the scrolls, he didn't mention it, and while it gave me a chance to get better acquainted with my fiery little filly, it no doubt improved my stepson's seat as well.

But if the days were hard, the nights were worse. When the

Hall was snugged down and silent, despair overtook me. Not only did I miss Lance's presence—his conversation, his laughter, his assurance that I could do anything—I feared for his safety, seeing him alone and hurt or ill, set on by bandits or bleeding to death in some accident, with no one near to give him aid. Only sleep could blot out such fears, but all too often it was riddled with nightmares.

These were strange, ambivalent dreams, more full of dread than action, and often focusing on a holy man who materialized out of the mists. Druid or priest, I couldn't tell, but the eerie silence that surrounded him was like the pall of death, and I fled from it with the same terror I used to flee from the nightmare of Arthur dying in battle. Sometimes I woke drenched in sweat, heart pounding and covers tangled, and would wrap my arms around Arthur, clinging to my husband for dear life.

It was Arthur who asked Nimue to use her Sight in an effort to locate the lieutenant. The doire found nothing, even after conjuring up the most powerful of the Old Gods, Cernunnos, the trampling, snorting, antlered god of the woods who is consort to the Goddess.

"But did you tell Him to bring Lancelot back?" I asked.

"Tell Him?" she queried, bemused by my arrogance. "One doesn't command the Gods, Gwen. One can only ask their help, not tell them what to do." I hung my head, ashamed that my distress had made me so rude. "I do have something for you, however," the doire went on with a forgiving smile. "A small spell to use yourself, when the moon is new."

So she gave me a special set of words, and from then on I watched the phases of the Goddess's orb impatiently, carefully repeating the incantation when the new moon glimmered, pale and shining, in the western sky. I always added my own prayer as well, pleading with the Gods to return my love safely, for I could not imagine facing the rest of my life without him.

Arthur was equally concerned, and as the weeks passed we both poured all our energy into ruling the realm. With autumn full upon us we started to receive reports on the harvest. When the tally of grain milled and meat smoked, fish salted and apples stored began to take shape, we could see who had a surplus of things and who was in need. The actual trade arrangements would be left up to the local leaders, but we were able to tell each emissary how things stood in the other regions.

Yet I noticed that whenever a new envoy arrived with report in hand, the first question Arthur put to him was, "Have you any word of Lancelot? Heard any stories about the Champion from Brittany?"

Invariably the response was a shake of the head. After a time I came to dread the answer, for Lance was the most admired member of the Round Table, and stories of his adventures flew across the realm like swallows coming home for summer. If no one was talking about his exploits, it must be because there weren't any. I lived with the secret conviction that Elaine had been right, and if Lance died, his passing would be on my head.

Finally, in early October, Gawain suggested we contact the Ancient Ones.

"For all that they avoid people and cities, there's precious little that goes on among mortals they don't know of, M'lady," the Prince of Orkney allowed. "The Prydn came to admire Lancelot during the winter they stayed at Stirling, and word of his reputation spread among all the tribes. If anyone can tell us where he is, they can. Whether they will or not . . ." He shrugged eloquently, doubt clouding his countenance. "Still, I am willing to ask."

The graciousness of his offer was touching, for Gawain had avoided the Little People ever since his parting from Ragnell. Even now I noticed that he had not mentioned her by name.

We drew a message in picture form on the face of a wax tablet and carefully closed the wooden cover before taking it to a special spring in the wildwood. There he heaped a small pile of stones over it, poked a sprig of rowan berries into the rocks at the top, and quietly walked away, confident the Ancient Ones would find it shortly.

But when the Orcadian went back a week later, the rowan had been replaced by a cluster of holly leaves, and the wax face of the tablet was blank.

"Blank? What do you mean, blank?" I demanded as he handed it to me.

"See for yourself, M'lady. The wax has been smoothed out, and the cover replaced. I have no idea what it means."

The ambiguity of the response terrified me. It could mean Lance was safe in the Ancient Ones' care, or equally signify that he had died. I've always believed I could face anything, as long as I knew what it was; but this was unknowing at its worst, and I wanted to run, screaming, out of the Hall.

Slowly, grimly, I faced the fact that there would be no word, either from the Ancient Ones or from the commoners. And for the first time in my life there was nothing I could do—High Queen or no, I was powerless to wring news out of the depths of silence. I might never know whether Lancelot was alive or dead.

We stayed at Camelot that winter, leading the rituals and looking after the welfare of our people. On the last night of October, the terrible night of Samhain, both Pagans and Christians huddled together around our fire. It is the time when Gods and ghosts are known to stalk the land while the ancient sidhe, spirits from before the time of man, steal the souls of careless mortals. Mindful of the danger, our household took pains to be safely indoors before the sun had set and the gate between this world and the Other swung open. And next morning we began the rejoicing of survival when Arthur sacrificed the white bullock with Lionel, the Mithraite, in attendance.

Then, just as winter closed the Roads, a Christian priest from the Continent made his way to Camelot. He was a mild-mannered man of middle years, gone mostly bald, who bowed when he presented Arthur with a scroll on the laws of King Theodoric.

"It's only a condensation and not a complete rendering, Your Highness," Father Baldwin noted apologetically. "But Boethius thought you'd be happy with anything that gave you some idea of what they cover."

Arthur opened the scroll, which appeared to be old and much used already, and carefully scrutinized the Latin phrases of its beginning lines. From the expression on his face, it was more than satisfactory.

With a broad smile, my husband invited the clergyman to winter over with us. "The Queen will find a room for you," he added nonchalantly, then, remembering that I did not get on well with clerics, gave me one of his "this is important" looks.

I watched the new priest suspiciously, sure that he would reflect the Church's attitude that women were second-class citizens. But Baldwin proved to be a gentle soul, prone to self-effacement rather than paternalistic scorn, and before long I grew comfortable with his presence.

With a resident priest to hand, we celebrated Christmas in the Hall that year, combining it with the holiday for calling the sun back from its winter wanderings. All the household and many of the Champions, whether Pagan or Christian, came to hear Mass, and both Arthur and I knelt through the service. At the end Bors spoke up, asking the Christian Father God to protect his cousin, Lancelot. It seemed that Bors was beginning to put his faith in Father Baldwin's religion.

During the dark winter months Arthur pored over the legal scroll, discussing various points with Baldwin and Bedivere or the Companions who lounged around the fire when the weather was bad.

"Did you notice that Gawain now supports my idea of a legal system?" Arthur asked. He moved restlessly about the room as I snuggled under the comforter. "Don't know why, for sure," he mused.

"Maybe he sees it as a matter of honor," I quipped.

"Maybe. At least the Companions have accepted the idea of justice based on evidence and testimony rather than Trial by Combat. With any luck, they'll never again have to put their lives at stake in order to prove someone else's guilt or innocence."

I thought of my own ordeal, when Morgan made the people believe I had tried to poison Arthur. Lance had saved my life by risking his own in Trial by Combat. It was then I realized the Lady of the Lake would use any means to get rid of me, though it had taken my husband a greater time to recognize his sister's treachery. Only Lance had seen it clearly and tried to protect us.

At the thought, fear and panic rose up again. Oh Lord, if only I knew that he was safe. . . .

Arthur gave me a perfunctory glance as he came to bed. Something on my face must have shown my thoughts, for when he slipped between the sheets, he slid his arm around my shoulders and pulled me to him.

"You're still worrying about the Breton, aren't you, lass?"

"Aye," I whispered miserably.

"Me too—me too," he admitted, patting my shoulder in com-miseration. "But we'll find him—no matter how long it takes, we'll find him and bring him home. In the meantime, you go ahead and cry for both of us."

Such unexpected tenderness weakened my resolve, and a long sigh went through me, followed by wave after wave of gusty sobs. Finally, at last, the tears broke loose and I wept long and hard in my husband's arms. It was one of the dearest moments Arthur and I ever shared, and I've always remembered it with gratitude and love.

As the gray, bleak winter came to an end, Father Baldwin baptized Bors. I thought Palomides might convert as well, but the Arab seemed to be struggling with larger questions and was not ready to declare his acceptance of Christ as the only path to the Godhead. He came to see me one afternoon, however, hopefully suggesting that Lance had gone off on some spiritual journey of his own. "We often talked about the need to leave the lures of the world in order to find God."

I remembered the story of Saint Simon on his high pillar, and the holy man in my dreams. It was not a fate I would wish on anyone.

When the snow melted and the Roads were cleared for travel, a great rangy beast of a man appeared at our gate. He carried a red shield and was clad in an armored jerkin, half chain mail, half metal scales. From the way he moved, I guessed he was well past a warrior's prime, and his stoutness came from age, not muscle. Still, he made a fierce impression as he stood demanding entrance in the name of Beaumains.

The sentry was uncertain what reply to make, but Mordred and I were just returning from our morning ride, so we led the new-comer up to the Hall.

"Smells like a stablehand," Cook commented as the fellow splashed about at the water trough, trying to make himself pre-sentable to the King. I nodded in agreement and left Mordred to tidy him up while I went to find Arthur. The two of us had barely taken our places on the dais before Mordred brought the lout into the Hall.

The man stared about in gape-mouthed wonder, his eyes moving from the lions that were carved on the arms of our chairs to the Red Dragon that climbed the wall behind us. Finally, with a massive sigh, he let his gaze drop to the two of us.

"Your Highnesses," he rumbled, going stiffly down on one knee. "The young warrior who bested me at the ford made me swear to come to Camelot and offer service to you—else he will hunt me down and lop off my head. He said he was only a kitchen lad at your Court, but in truth, if your sculleries fight like that, I'd hate to face a Champion of the Round Table."

Arthur managed to keep a straight face, though I could see he was as surprised by the tale as the fellow was humble in telling it.

"We commend your courage in coming here," the High King intoned. "If you would stay with us, Bedivere will find a place for you among the warriors. Er . . . do you have a name?"

"When my jerkin was new, my wife called me Ironside," the man answered with a sigh. "The good woman's dead these many years, and my armor is more rust than shine, but I'd be pleased to spend some time with your men. Just make sure to tell that young one that I've honored my oath, and he can put away his sword."

So Mordred took Ironside to find Bedivere and Arthur raised an eyebrow in my direction. "It looks as though Beaumains is coming into his own," he mused.

"Who is this fellow everyone talks about?" Mordred asked the next day when we were seated at the long table, practicing our writing.

"You remember—the boy Lance found on the Road." But Mordred swore he'd never met him, and when we figured it up, either Beaumains or Mordred had been gone when the other was at Court. "I'm sure you'll like him," I concluded, thinking it would be good for my stepson to begin making friends among the younger warriors and not always be tagging around after his older brothers.

As the great cycle of the seasons came round to spring, my spirit rose with it. The marsh of the Somerset Levels turned green and whispered with the stirring of tadpole and newt; warblers and voles played out their busy lives amid the reeds and willow-banks, while enormous flocks of water birds came to nest on the lake. At Camelot we were busy packing, for as soon as the May Day rites of Beltane were over, we would be starting on a summer journey to the kingdoms along the south coast of Wales.

"We might hold another tournament," Bedivere suggested. "Stories of last year's event have traveled throughout Britain, and everyone wants to try their luck at the next one."

We were standing at the table in the kitchen where Cook had put out cider and bannocks for those who wanted a last bite before we moved out onto the Road. Arthur finished off his beaker before nodding in assent. "The amphitheater at Caerleon's a good place for it, and if we plan for the first of August, we'll celebrate Lammas with the Fellowship as well. You and Cei can stay at Caerleon to arrange things while I go visit the neighboring Kings," he added, giving me a smile. "Keep you from racing all over creation in Agricola's carriage."

I wrinkled my nose in response. Arthur had talked me out of taking my own carriage on this trip, on the grounds that it would be unseemly unless we rode together, and he needed the independence that his warhorse would bring. Now he was even blocking my use of the King of Demetia's vehicle.

"After all, I need you in one piece," he teased, wiping his mustache with the back of his hand. "The people would never forgive me if I got careless with their Queen."

It was on that jesting note we left Camelot.

The high mood maintained throughout our trip. Birds of all kinds flitted through the woods that flanked the broad Roman Road, while the Banner of the Red Dragon rippled proudly in the breeze. Behind us the entourage of courtiers and household spread out like a bright, spangled ribbon of gaiety. Many of my ladies-in-waiting were escorted by Arthur's Companions, while the older matrons, such as Vinnie, rode in a trundling wagon and gossiped among themselves.

Even the artisans came with us, for Smith and Bard, Kennel Master and Cook, would all be needed over the summer. Frieda and Griflet had charge of the wolfhounds, while the warriors ranged back and forth along the length of our party. At the rear Gwyn and his brother, Yder, rode next to the new black horses they'd be taking to Illtud's stables.

I personally was delighted to be on the move again. Camelot was fine, but something in my soul needed to be out and roving.

Bedivere rode between us, taking pride in pointing out the new signs of prosperity—here the fields of a deserted villa being reclaimed by a peasant family, there a copse of hazels well managed by forest folk. Even the livestock looked healthy and well fed; stolid cows, thick-fleeced sheep and sleek horses all raised their heads to watch us go by.

Bedivere cast an appraising eye over Etain. "How do you like your new filly? You know Gwyn's mighty proud of having bred and trained her for you."

"Well he should be," I confirmed. "Her mouth is gentle and her heart immense. And she loves to race," I added, looking at Arthur.

"Really?" My husband gave me one of his droll, sidelong glances. "Seems to me we haven't had a good run since Featherfoot got too old to keep up."

"It's been awhile," I agreed, surreptitiously gathering in the reins and shifting my balance slightly.

His reply was still bantering, even as he collected his own steed. "Too long, I think. Don't know if this old fellow still has the wind for it."

"Which old fellow?" I challenged, eyeing the gray at my husband's temples.

"The four-legged one," he exploded. "To the next milestone!"

And then we were away, pounding down the soft verge beside the pavement, daring each other on and grinning like children with never a care in the world. Even the horses loved it; the stallion running with his neck outstretched, great hooves scattering divots of grass behind and the young filly racing to keep a nose ahead, nostrils flared and tail lifted in the high-plumed style of the Welsh Mountain ponies. No one felt like stopping when the milestone slipped past, so we followed the Road over the crest of the hill, pulling up only when we came to a rocky ford.

"Clears the head," Arthur opined as we waited, winded and happy, for the rest of the caravan to catch up.

And the heart, I thought, nodding in agreement. For the first time in months I was racing exuberantly toward the future. Apparently even the season of despair must give way to the passage of time, and though the loss of Lance would always leave a void, I was both pleased and happy to be alive again, at last.

9

Caerleon

y teacher, Cathbad, used to say there might be times when our moiras crossed and recrossed those of the others that shaped our lives . . . all at once, and each without knowing. That summer at Caerleon was one such time.

Like most Roman cities, Caerleon is built on high ground near the banks of a river, with a massive fortress at its heart. Once Legionnaires had marched through the gates and down the paved Roads, past the taverns and shops, baths and amphitheater that cluster outside the walls of the fort. Now the inhabitants speak more Celtic than Latin, while thatched round-houses and the huts of newcomers sprawl higgledy-piggledy in the shadow of the fortress walls.

Yet even during the Time of Troubles, after the Legions had left and tyrants ruled the land, the people looked at the ruins of their Imperial buildings and remembered grander days. So when Merlin declared that Arthur Pendragon would be the king to heal the wounds left by so much civil strife, the natives of Caerleon took him to their heart. It was here he was crowned, here we had held the first Round Table—albeit inadvertently—and here we had come again to celebrate Lammas and hold a tournament. No matter that we made Camelot our headquarters; Caerleon knew itself to be the High King's city, and turned out to meet us with cheers and joy as we crossed the bridge over the river Usk.

Among the attributes of the town—besides a fine amphitheater and three working baths—was the basilica of the fort itself. I have never seen another building as impressive; made of stone, it is hundreds of feet long, with a semicircular apse at the end of the nave and colonnaded aisles along each side. Here huge columns lift the central roof several stories high, and under the lofty ceiling clerestory windows let in great shafts of sunshine, making the long nave remarkably light and airy. It is a magnificent place in which to hold the Round Table, so Cei and I set about turning the nave into our Hall.

We were not the only ones preparing for the occasion. Townspeople shook out buntings and draped them on walls, baskets of blooming flowers were hung from the eaves or sprang up on gate posts, and even the dancing bear was brought out.

Arthur and I stayed in the praetorium of the fort, which was comfortable enough. Since there was no garden to attend to, I often walked down to the river before the day properly began. It gave me some chance to feel the earth under my feet, the green leaves against my skin, the song of birds within my heart. On one such morning my path crossed that of the bearkeeper taking his big, shaggy charge to the amphitheater.

"He needs a bit of freedom, just like anyone else," the man said as I fell in with him, being careful to keep him between me and the animal. The trainer gave me a sharp-eyed, sidelong appraisal, no doubt as cautious of me as I was of his bear. Apparently satisfied that I wouldn't upset his pet's routine, he invited me to join them in the amphitheater. "Gots his likes and dislikes, like anyone else, but mostly he's good-natured, as long as he gets plenty of exercise," he noted fondly.

In the entrance passage leading to the arena we passed the niche where a small statue of Nemesis, Goddess of Fate, stands. It reminded me of Elaine's declaration that whatever befell Lancelot must be on my conscience. I shivered as though a curse had been laid on me, and cast the Goddess a small prayer in the Breton's behalf, then hurried after the trainer, who had already entered the arena.

Once inside the building he unclasped the chain from his animal's collar. The bear swung its head back and forth, snuffling the air, then began to shamble about the arena. It found a particular sandy patch in the early sunshine, turned a somersault, and began wriggling on its back like a horse rolling after it's been unsaddled, all four legs in the air. It grabbed hold of its own hindfeet and, rocking back and forth, pulled itself to a half-sitting position. Resting on its tailbone, front paws holding the splayed feet apart, it peered at us raffishly over the broad expanse of exposed tummy. I couldn't help but laugh at its clowning, and it nodded its head up and down as if to encourage my mirth. It was pleasant to think that even the bear enjoyed our presence here.

During the next weeks we sent out invitations to the Fellowship and proclamations about the tournament. There was housing to organize, a menu to construct and entertainment to arrange. And it all needed to be in place by mid-July, when the High King would return from his state visits.

Arthur and his men hastened on their rounds, stopping first to see Illtud at the monastery at Llantwit. I was sorry not to be along for that, for I liked the warrior prince who had become a monk and turned his estate into a monastery. He admired Arthur's military acumen, and recognizing our cavalry's constant need for fresh, well-trained horses, had set up stables for training our remounts.

On this visit he and Gwyn would decide which of the horses to train for battle, which to geld for riding, and which to trade off for domestic use. I smiled at the notion of the Christian holy man and the fey horse breeder working so closely together.

Later the royal party went to the hill-fort at Dinas Powys, where they hunted waterfowl with the scruffy warlord, Poulentis, admired the man's new pigs and drank great quantities of honey brew in the small, drystone building he called his Hall. By comparison, when they were in Demetia they ate off elegant pewter plates and spoke Latin with the wise old aristocrat, Agricola. It was here that Gawain left the party, going off to look for a hermit who was said to be living in a rocky cove among the shoreline cliffs. Such interest on the redhead's part surprised me, and even bemused Arthur.

"It seems that philosophy is taking up more and more of my nephew's time," he noted. In fact, Gawain had not returned with the King's party, though he would certainly arrive in time for the Lammas gathering. After last year it was unlikely he'd miss this tournament.

As the time for the festival approached, people of all sorts poured into Caerleon. Peasants and farmers came from far and near to observe Lammas; client kings and their Champions came to take part in the Round Table and tournament; and a fine assortment of mimes and acrobats, sword swallowers and jugglers, came to perform on every corner.

Two days before the Round Table convened, Gwyn and Yder accompanied me in a stroll through town. We stopped to admire an enterprising young fellow who had found a selection of masks among the ruins of a theater and was putting on a small performance all by himself—one minute as a coquette, the next minute as a tyrant, depending on which mask he held before his face. I laughed heartily at his jesting and made a mental note to have Cook send round a picnic supper for his efforts.

A little girl, whose mother was hawking flowers, came sidling up to me and thrust a bouquet into my hands before disappearing in a fit of giggles behind her mother's skirts. I thanked them both for the gift, noting that field poppies are one of my favorite flowers.

In the Square a crowd was gathering to watch the dancing bear. The keeper had slipped a muzzle of stout leather over its nose and kept tight hold of the creature's chain, for the people crowded around it in awe and delight. They regarded the bear's presence as a kind of talisman binding them even more closely to Arthur.

"So this is your husband's namesake," Gwyn teased, referring to the similarity between Arthur's name and the Celtic word for bear. "Seems as though it could give the King some lessons in dancing."

I laughed, knowing Arthur would have been amused as well. The animal was standing upright, looking remarkably like a giant man with a big head, sloping shoulders and long, pudgy torso. The keeper piped a lilting tune and went prancing about the Square while the bear followed after on its short, stubby legs, jouncing along in an oddly disjointed fashion, as though it were indeed dancing.

Both the song and the laughter of the crowd were infectious, and the bear commenced nodding its head in time with the music. When it paused to look directly at me, I wondered if it remembered the morning in the arena. Without thinking, I held out my bouquet of flowers as a gift.

Quick as lightning the paw swung round, scimitar claws slashing through the fabric of my sleeve before they hooked the posies from my hand. The force of the animal's thrust gave me a glancing blow and sent me sprawling on the paving stones as a hideous scream broke the air.

Although he was no more than half the bear's height, Yder went swarming up its back, dagger in hand, filling the air with howls of rage. Clinging to its shoulders, the little man plunged his dagger over and over into the ruff of fur and fat protecting the creature's nape.

The bear shook itself violently, ripping the chain from its keeper's hands. After a moment of shocked silence the crowd began to roar, and while half the people scrambled to get away, the other half converged on Yder and the bruin, some trying to pull the wild Welshman from their mascot, some attacking the animal in Yder's behalf.

Blood spurted everywhere, over both me and the stones, and I watched with horror as the mass of flailing arms and legs and claws seemed to sway endlessly back and forth. Screams and grunts and a long, shivering groan came out of the scuffling mass before it finally sank to the ground from its own sheer weight.

Suddenly there was silence, and I pulled myself to my feet while the tangle of people began to disengage. Here was a scraped arm, there a bloody nose, but aside from Yder and the bear, all others seemed to be more dazed than wounded.

Without a word Gwyn dragged his brother free of the inert animal as the trainer knelt beside his dying pet. A lake of blood was spreading over the paving stones, and a great, deep sob rose in my throat. I had no more meant to cause the death of the bear than I had meant to drive Lance to his, and a sense of bitter, futile destiny hemmed me all around. Hordes of curious townsfolk had gathered, staring helplessly at their mascot and murmuring in consternation.

Yder lay gasping for breath in his brother's arms, and I made my way to him. He was covered with blood, though it was impossible to tell if it were his or the bear's.

I knelt shakily by my would-be rescuer and took his hand in my own. The little man's eyes were glazing over, and I was afraid he, too, had met his end on my account.

With great effort he focused on my face and wheezed out a declaration. "Now that Lancelot's gone, I'd like to take his place, M'lady."

The idea came as such a surprise, it caught me speechless, and Yder lost consciousness before I could reply.

"He's always had a romantic streak," Gwyn explained with a shrug. "Yder's dreamed of becoming your Champion since he first met you—probably the only one at Court glad to see Lancelot go."

I stared at the two men in amazement, thinking them both mad beyond measure. "I swear I had no idea. . . ." I stammered.

"Oh, that's all right, Your Highness. Everyone knows the Breton is your favorite and as the best warrior in the land, most suited to be your protector. What you don't realize is how many men would like to claim that honor themselves." Gwyn gave me an impish grin, then turned his attention to his brother. "Yder's more scared than hurt—a couple of days doctoring will see him well again."

By now Elyzabel had made her way to me, her festive dress as splattered with mud and blood as mine was. She insisted on checking my arm which, miraculously, had not even been scratched when the bear's claws slashed the sleeve. "We'd best be getting on, M'lady," she suggested, offering me her arm. "At the least your hair needs recombing, and a rest wouldn't do you a bit of harm, either."

I nodded, glad for her support as I rose to my feet and we made our way to the praetorium. Both she and Gwyn proved to be good nurses; I stayed quiet all the rest of the day, and Yder was back on his feet by the next evening. He moved stiffly, like one favoring sore ribs, and would not likely take part in the tournament, but he seemed to have suffered no permanent damage.

Since Lance's departure I had made a habit of inviting a different warrior to sit beside me each night. So on Yder's first night back he was seated next to me in order that the Court see I was grateful for his valor on my behalf. In truth I felt more compassion for the bear than the man, but we chatted amiably enough and I was relieved to find that since his habitual shyness had returned, he made no further effort to pursue his suit to become my Champion.

This year we had decided to hold the Round Table meeting first, then the tournament and finally, on the last night, a Grand

Feast to go with the Lammas rites. Watching the members of the
Fellowship take their places for the Council, I noted that Enid
and Geraint seemed as comfortable and happy together as before,
though there were no signs of pregnancy, either past or present.
Ironside was quite smitten with the dark-haired queen, however,
and solemnly handed her a nosegay as he passed their segment of
the Round Table. It was such a quaint thing for the old reprobate
to do, I couldn't help smiling. For all his gruesome history at the
river ford, there was a sentimental streak underneath his bluster.

Agricola arrived with his long-faced, pasty-skinned nephew at
his elbow, and Bagdemagus marched proudly to his seat, announcing to anyone who would listen that the men of Dorset had
asked him to be their permanent liaison with the High Court. I
wasn't surprised that Nimue and Pelleas hadn't come; the doire
and her husband were more than happy living on his remote, if
sizable, holdings and since she'd spent so long with us last fall, it
was unlikely we'd see her again unless Arthur were in danger.

Much more peculiar was the fact that neither Pellinore nor
Lamorak were in attendance. This was the first Round Table Pelli
had ever missed, and all through the day I found myself glancing
toward the door, expecting to see the big warlord of the Wrekin
come bursting in.

Most of this year's news was peaceful—there were more immigrants than usual crossing the North Sea and settling along Northumbria's coast, and up beyond the Wall Caw's son, Hueil, was
making life difficult for his neighbors, but when had that not
been the case? Everyone agreed that it seemed we finally had
achieved a stable peace, and there was much toasting and self-
congratulations among the Fellowship.

Arthur brought up his studies of the Edictum, but refrained
from arguing outright that we needed some such laws of our own,
and before long attention turned to questions of trade. The Picts
readily agreed to send us their fine heather beer in return for
cuttlebones from the eastern shores and salt to be carted up from
Droitwich. And the Scots bartered barrels of herring in exchange
for a supply of fine buckles and harness wares from the Irish
jeweler at the Mote in Rheged. I had known the artisan when I
was a child, and had watched, fascinated, as he crafted a blue
enameled brooch for my birthday. Years later Arthur and I com-

missioned him to make the gold-and-red rondels for the Companions, and by now his reputation had spread throughout Britain. It
was certainly well earned.

In the late afternoon, when the Council was over, I was suddenly confronted by Agricola's nephew, Vortipor, who haughtily
announced that his quarters weren't up to his usual standards.

"You're welcome to go camp in the meadows like the rest of
the warriors," I noted with ill-concealed irritation. "We thought
you would want to be with your uncle in the praetorium, but tent
space can surely be arranged by the edge of the woods."

"Of course I should be near my uncle," the noble replied,
contriving to look down his long, skinny nose at me. "But both
he and I are used to having our own private suites, and the little
room you've given me hardly qualifies as a suite."

"No, I don't suppose it does," I agreed absently, refusing to
take his complaint seriously. I turned away as Enid joined me,
and dismissed the courtier with a shrug. "Well, you have our
permission to move whenever you wish."

"I don't like that fellow," the Queen of Devon declared as
Vortipor moved away.

"Oh, he's just a poor relative trying to use his uncle's position
for his own betterment," I commented, thinking the man more
of a nuisance than a threat.

"But you never know what sort of trouble they can cause behind your back." Her comment was so pointed, I stopped to take
a closer look at her. Although she seemed far more at ease with
herself and life than during our last talk, there was the pinched
look of strain.

"Did you follow my advice about the child?" I asked.

"No. Geraint wants one of his own blood, or none. But I've
started a school of sorts at Court, and help to teach the youngsters
whenever I find time. It does help, some." She gave me a clear
and honest smile, the sort that comes from looking life squarely
in the eye and accepting what you see. "Odd how things never
come out the way you expect, isn't it?"

"Very odd," I agreed, and we both laughed ruefully.

"The stupidest thing of all is what's happening among Geraint's
warriors. Here they sit in our Hall, feeding at our board and
drinking our wine, riding the best horses, wearing the best clothes

. . . and all simply to be on hand if we need them. But is that enough? No. Do they enjoy being with their families, in peace and safety? No. Do they look for other things to occupy their time? No. They demand new weapons and then go looking for new people to use them on. Recently they've taken to blaming *me* for the lack of wars, claiming that before I came, there was always enough battle and booty to go around. Good heavens, you'd think they'd appreciate the fact that Arthur's truces and Geraint's diplomacy make all that killing unnecessary now. It's ridiculous, I tell you."

I agreed with her wholeheartedly, remembering Cei's comment about the wages of peace.

Enid suddenly changed the subject, giving me a quick smile. "Geraint has taken quite an interest in this law code Arthur talks about. I think he'd like to borrow the scroll when the High King no longer needs it."

"Borrow?" my husband exclaimed when I mentioned it that night. "Poor old thing is almost in tatters as it is. Perhaps I can find a cleric to make a copy for him. He mentioned to me how restless his men are—several have even implied he's lost his nerve. I just hope he doesn't do something foolish, simply to prove them wrong. By the way, have you heard anything about the men of the Wrekin?"

"No. . . ." I shook my head slowly. "Do you suppose Pelli still distrusts Gawain?"

"I doubt it—the Prince of Orkney gave me his word last year, remember?" Arthur sat on the edge of the bed and stared out the window at the quarter moon before getting between the sheets. "Pelli's probably too busy chasing down a new woman. I'm more worried about Agricola. He's having trouble with that nephew of his; seems that Vortipor is agitating to make kingship hereditary rather than elective. It looks as though he'll try to take the throne as soon as Agricola's gone, without waiting for the people's acclamation."

"But that's tyranny!" I finished plaiting my braid and came over to the bed. "Surely the people will insist on their right to decide who's king!"

"Hard to say." Arthur punched his pillow, and yawning loudly, turned away. "Certainly *I* don't favor the notion."

Even though I couldn't see his face, I suddenly knew it reflected his distaste for his own son. For a moment I wanted to rail at him, to berate him about the distance he kept between Mordred and himself, for I was sure if he gave the lad a chance, he'd find him as charming and eager to please as I did. But with a Court full of guests, now was not the time. So I shuttered the lantern and got into bed with a sigh.

Tomorrow promised to be a very busy day.

10

Gareth

sst, M'lady. Are you alone?"

The sibilant whisper filled the henhouse, and I whirled in surprise. It seemed to have come from the shadows beyond the nesting boxes. A pile of empty hemp bags looked awfully lumpy, and I eyed them with suspicion. "Is that you, Lynette?"

"Yes ma'am," the girl avowed, poking her gamin face out where I could see it. "Beaumains wants to keep our presence a secret, but I came on ahead. I told him you'd hide me for a bit."

"Oh, you did, did you?" I lifted an eyebrow and she giggled.

"But of course. Can't be no harm in it, and I said you were always one to appreciate a surprise." She scrambled to her feet and instinctively reached for the basket I was holding, then realized she couldn't carry it into the kitchen without being seen. "I wouldn't want to spoil his fun, seeing that he did such a splendid job on old Ironside."

"Ah yes, the stout fellow who showed up at Camelot."

"Then he did follow Beaumains's orders!" Lynette's eyes fairly danced with satisfaction, and she gave a little hop of glee. The story was going to come bubbling out of her whether or no, so I sat down on an overturned barrel and suggested she tell me about it.

"Well, M'lady," she began, her voice going solemn, "Ironside had set his tent up beside the stream and was challenging everyone who wanted to cross the ford. He'd taken the shields from the men he'd bested and hung them up in the branches of a staghead oak—there must have been more than a score of them, making a ghostly clatter when the wind blew. We could hear the sound of them through the mist, and I made sure to keep close behind Beaumains. As we got closer, there was such a foul stench, it made me gag." Like a Master Bard recounting terrors of the past, the girl was re-creating her own horror in a torrent of words. A shiver slid down my back. "Then, as we came around a stand of alders and approached the ford, I saw two things at once . . . the dead and rotting body of a warrior hanging from the bottom branch of that oak, and the ogre below, who growled his challenge at Beaumains like a boar—all grunts and snarls."

Lynette went thumping about the henhouse, stirring up straw dust and causing the hens much consternation as she mimicked Ironside's ferocity.

"When Beaumains called him to account, the fellow's face grew as red as his shield. The old toad started swaggering and boasting, but Beaumains didn't say a word—just drew his sword and waited for his opponent to quit flustering and put up a defense." Lynette jumped back in imitation of Beaumains, squaring her shoulders and holding an imaginary sword with two hands. "There was a parry, and a thrust"—crouching and weaving, she waited for the opening, then swung the weapon up over her head —"and a whack that took my breath away."

The imaginary weapon came down with a sidewise sweep which was so forceful, it spun her around and sent the remaining hens squawking into the yard. When her dizzying spin was completed, she clasped her hands together under her chin and gave me a wicked grin. "It was that fast; he knocked out that old warlord before you could say 'Jack-in-the-Pulpit'! Beaumains is going to be the best Champion of the Round Table, you wait and see."

I laughed at the sheer exuberance of the girl. "Then you're pleased with the job he did? There was nothing you could fault him for, after all?"

Lynette ducked her head and smiled to herself. "Only that he can never find his way—if I hadn't been watching the landmarks, we would have ended up in Cornwall instead of the Welsh Marches."

"Sounds as though he'd be wise to keep you with him, just to get to where he's going," I teased. "And was your cousin pleased with his performance?"

"Pleased!" The urchin's whole body registered indignation, and she made an unladylike grimace. "The little hussy threw herself into his arms the first time they met. But I fixed that—put a dose of powder in his nettle beer."

The girl was immensely proud of her solution, but I was non-plussed. "You did what?"

For a long moment those mischievous eyes studied mine before she decided to explain. "When I came to be with you at Court, my mother gave me a packet of powder and told me a pinch of it works wonders in cooling a man off; she thought I might need it among all those randy warriors. But I put it to better use, keeping Beaumains out of my cousin's bed." There was an awkward pause, then she added, "It's only temporary, you understand, so I had to give him a lecture on the proper behavior of a Round Table Champion. It seems to have worked, for we stayed with my cousin upward of the last ten months, and there aren't any stray babies waiting to be born."

Shaking my head in amusement, I inquired when Beaumains planned to make his presence known.

"This afternoon, at the tournament," she answered promptly. "Since he asked for this adventure before the assembled Fellow-ship, he wants to return victorious before them all as well."

I grinned at her explanation. Clearly our Fair Unknown had a flair for theatrics as well as battle, so I agreed not to divulge their secret until the lad himself put in an appearance.

Before the tournament began, Arthur took part in the cere-mony for new squires. These were the boys who, after years of being errand-running and tack-mending pages, would now offi-cially become apprentice helpers to full-fledged warriors. They stood at attention, their sponsors behind them, prepared to pledge their loyalty directly to the High King.

Mordred was the last in line, standing in front of Bedivere. I had made my stepson a splendid new tunic—he outgrew his old ones at a horrendous rate—and had sewn the badge of King Lot's house on the sleeve, since there would surely be talk if I'd given him the High King's badge. Still, I held my breath when Arthur came to a stop in front of him.

The Pendragon's eyes flicked from the badge to Bedivere's face.

Solemnly the one-handed lieutenant reached out and rested his good hand on Mordred's shoulder. "I have the honor to present the youngest son of the House of Lot," the craggy lieutenant said. "He will someday be a fine warrior, and an honor to his father."

Arthur swallowed drily and dropped his gaze to the boy. For a long moment they stared at each other, eye-to-eye, and I marveled that the rest of the world didn't see what was so obvious to me—the same fine, level gaze that marked them as father and son.

"Are you ready to give me your promise?" Arthur asked.

Mordred's answer was clear and he spoke his oath calmly and well. Arthur heard him out, nodded abruptly, and without another word turned and strode to the reviewing stand where I was seated. I let out my breath but continued to watch Mordred, wondering how much he understood of what had just transpired. But there was nothing in his face except pride in his new status; one would guess he had no idea how closely he was tied to the King who tried so hard to ignore him.

Once the new squires and their mentors had moved off the field, Arthur gave the trumpeter the signal to begin the tournament. Our different guests brought forth their flags, and when Bedivere cantered onto the field, it was Mordred who rode next to him, carrying the Red Dragon into the center of the arena. Slowly they wheeled to allow the other pennants to be lowered in salute. When the maneuver was complete, Bedivere and Mordred brought the Banner to our box and saluted Arthur in the name of the people.

"Why don't you join us?" I suggested as Bedivere fixed the standard in its place behind Arthur.

So it was that he and Mordred were seated beside us through the day, watching as both Champions and contenders displayed their best skills. Dinadan, being light on his feet and wiry, put on a fine show of swordsmanship against the more powerful but slower Gaheris; Sagramore, always a sturdy man but like a bull— slow to build up momentum and equally hard to stop—caught some interest in the new grip he used on his lance; and Palomides clearly out-performed everyone else on horseback, both known and new. But by midafternoon it was clear that Gawain had excelled in all the disciplines and should receive the prize. Until, that is, an unknown opponent entered the arena to bring the redhead a challenge.

The newcomer was well equipped and graceful in action, and I soon realized it was Beaumains. The two men battled for some time, both on horseback and on foot, and when Gawain lost his balance, the Fair Unknown was on him in an instant, sitting astride his chest and pinning his arms to the ground.

"Yield," he cried, "yield in the name of Morgause, Queen of the Orkney Isles!"

There was a gasp of confusion in the audience and some small scuffling between the combatants, then Gawain was struggling to his feet as the newcomer took off his helmet. The sun glinted off his flaxen hair and a roar of remembrance went up from the audience. The blond youth had grown into full manhood during the last year, and I smiled proudly at him.

"By the Gods!" Mordred suddenly cried beside us, leaping to his feet. "It's Gareth! My brother we thought was drowned." The lad vaulted over the railing and started across the sand, still crying out his brother's name.

Beaumains looked up abruptly when he heard Mordred's voice, then rushed forward, opening his arms to the new squire and taking him into a bear hug as the audience murmured curiously.

Gawain, stunned by the realization he'd been fighting his own kin, gaped at the two of them until they turned to include him in a joyful, back-pounding embrace. Tears of happiness streamed down all three faces.

I thought of Morgause, weeping as she told me that Gareth had been lost at sea, somewhere near the Old Man of Hoy. Yet here he was, fully alive and well. For all that I bore the woman no love, I was sorry she had gone to her grave grieving for a son who was, in fact, not dead . . . until I remembered it was Gareth himself who had refused to divulge his background. Perhaps he'd feigned his death as a means of escaping from his mother. If so, it spoke volumes about the power she wielded over her children. For a moment my gaze rested on Mordred, and I wondered again what she'd told him and what not.

Altogether it was a fitting climax to a fine tournament, and everyone was full of excitement when we gathered to celebrate the rites of Lammas that night.

I've always liked the August festival. It's the most cheerful of the four high holy days—happier than Samhain, less frenzied than Beltane, and certainly more fun than Imbolc, which introduces the dreary month of February. Everyone participated, bringing offerings of bread baked from the first milling of this year's crop to be piled on a table in the courtyard.

There were fresh oat bannocks and coarse barley loaves, hard-crusted horse bread of who-knows-what mixture, and the fine wheat biscuits from our own ovens. I'd watched as Cook shook her head over them that morning, decrying the dimples in the crust that showed where the kitchen sprites had danced on the rising dough. "Good Neighbors, we call them. Pesky imps is more like it!" she'd muttered, quickly making the sign against evil lest the spirits take offense at her too-hasty words. Still and all, the golden pillows were light and lovely, and a worthy present for the Gods of harvest.

When all the bread had been arranged, Father Baldwin put aside whatever qualms he had about leading a Pagan ceremony, and not only blessed the fruits of the year's labors, but thanked all of the local Gods as well as his own. I listened to his grace and thought that if all clerics were as big-hearted as he was, I would welcome them more gladly.

Once the bread was broken and the blessed wine shared around with everyone in attendance, the Fellowship moved into the basilica. The Round Table had been set up with the chairs and pennants, curved trestles and glowing lamps laid out in their circle. It was full of color and high cheer, and goodwill all around. Lynette sat beside me while Gareth occupied Gawain's place next to Arthur, and there was much banter and retelling of the youngster's adventure. But afterward, when people were wandering from one group to another, the lad came to join Lynette, and I broached the subject of his reported death.

"That was not premeditated, M'lady." The blond warrior swirled the wine in his goblet and stared down at the maelstrom in the middle. "Some years back, just before my thirteenth birthday, I was in a boat that broke up on the high seas near the great rock they call the Old Man of Hoy. But by the luck of the Gods a fisherman found me more dead than alive, clinging to some floating debris well out in the Pentland Firth. He and his wife nursed me back to life, and when I realized no one knew I was royal born, I seized the chance to shape my life myself. With older brothers like Gawain and Gaheris and Agravain, I knew I would walk in their shadow if I didn't prove myself on my own terms."

He grinned across me to Arthur. "The older ones had left when I was so young, they didn't recognize me when I arrived at Court; I was just another country boy hoping to find a place as a squire. Between Lancelot's training me in weaponry and your sending me on that quest, I had both the tools and the opportunity I was seeking. I owe a great debt to both of you." Gareth's happiness was evident, but at the mention of Lance a frown crossed his brow. "I haven't seen the Queen's Champion since I arrived. Surely he's not elsewhere when you're holding a tournament here?"

I caught my breath, realizing he had not heard of his mentor's disappearance.

"Lancelot has been gone almost a year," Arthur responded slowly. "We've looked everywhere we could think of—Joyous Gard, Cornwall, Wales—even sent letters of inquiry back to Brittany, where the rest of his family lives. But no one has seen him."

"Did you ask the Lady of the Lake?" Gareth was looking back and forth between Arthur and me. "He grew up at her Sanctuary, after all. It wouldn't be unreasonable for him to return there."

Apparently the young man didn't know his aunt was bent on usurping the throne, or that she'd attempted to enlist Lance in her plans. For a moment I considered telling him, but he had moved on to another point.

"The High Priestess is famous for being the most powerful healer in Britain. If he was wounded or ill, she would be the natural person for him to turn to. Let me go to the Black Lake and see," he pleaded. "Besides, I haven't seen my aunt for years, and I'd rather that she hear I'm alive again directly from me than from some stranger."

Gareth's optimism was so contagious, the hope that Lance might still be alive began to quicken in me. "By all means, go," I told him, unclasping my brooch and putting it in his palm. It shimmered like the changing hues of the sea when I closed Gareth's fingers over it. "Take this as surety of our confidence in you."

"Your Highness!" His exclamation was one of hurt as well as surprise. "I have no need of such gifts. Lancelot has been my mentor, my friend—indeed, closer than the father I barely knew. If I can serve you both on the same quest, it is my good fortune, not a matter for payment."

I smiled at his indignation, but pointed out there might be expenses to defray, and in the end he kept the brooch. It was the one from the Mote, the one I'd watched being made, but no matter how fond I was of it, it was more important to find Lancelot.

Arthur signaled to the Jester, Dagonet, who soon had the Hall quiet and attentive so that the High King could honor Gareth for his past exploits and explain why he was leaving us again so soon.

"It is my pleasure," the new Champion answered, his eyes shining with an inner fire. "What more could one ask of life than to serve the best king in the world, and prove one's mettle by helping to redress the wrongs in his kingdom, or coming to the aid of fellow Companions? Surely, it is the highest honor." He gestured broadly around the Table, as though in invitation. "Everyone," he averred, "should have a chance to go on such quests—it's good for the soul as well as the body."

*　　*　　*

Those were prophetic words, my friend. Prophetic, indeed.

I looked across the gloom of my cell at the tall, blond warrior who was sharing this last night with me and smiled at the memory. "Little did any of us realize what such an idea would lead to."

"Aye, M'lady." He sighed, and seeing how low the fire burned in the brazier, rose to put another piece of wood on the coals and stretch the muscles that grew cramped from sitting so long in the cold. "Back then, we were just discovering what we were capable of. And if our eyes were blind, it was with the wonder of all the things that could be."

"Perhaps innocence is always full of wonder," I murmured, letting him empty the last of the wine into my goblet.

And goodness knows, we were nothing if not innocent, that summer in Caerleon, though the shadows of dark knowledge were filling the woods around us, drawing closer in the flesh as well as spirit.

11

Pellinore

ews of Gareth's trip was the talk of the household, and the next morning, even before our guests had left, Mordred brought the subject up, asking to go to the Sanctuary with his brother. "He could take me as his squire, so I could see Aunt Morgan without having to ask the King's permission."

It was a point well taken, and I admired the cleverness of it. He watched me closely, with an aching hopefulness, and I frowned before answering. "Yes . . . well, perhaps this is not the best time. We'll be heading north ourselves, with the whole Court—going to Carlisle for the winter, you know. I'm sure Bedivere needs you to help with those arrangements."

Mordred's disappointment was so naked, I had to look away. How many times past had I denied him such a visit? The High Priestess used people without mercy, and the fact that he was her nephew would not keep her from exploiting the boy's innocence. I was not ready to expose him to such danger and preferred to have him angry with me rather than shattered by her. So he went off to his afternoon lessons with the aggrieved expression of the young who don't understand why their requests cannot be met, and I wondered, for the hundredth time, how to untangle the web of hatred and resentment within Arthur's family.

The problem was that it went back so far—back to when Igraine was the wife of Gorlois, Duke of Cornwall. He had been a widower and far older than she, having already raised that same Cador who now wasted away in Cornwall. But he was a good and thoughtful husband in the way older men can be, and Igraine had borne him two daughters—lively Morgause and dark, secretive Morgan. The trouble began when the beautiful young Duchess caught the fancy of Uther Pendragon, a man of unruly tempers who was newly chosen High King. Gorlois went to war to protect his wife, and was killed on a night raid against the King's camp at the same time Uther lay in Igraine's bed, having gained entrance to Tintagel in the guise of the Duke. The people credit Merlin's magic with bringing that about, in order to ensure that Britain's greatest king would be conceived under the most propitious of stars. Certainly the result was a hasty marriage between the widowed Duchess and the High King . . . and the birth of Arthur.

But the daughters of Gorlois were convinced that Uther had killed their father, and they hated him with such a deep and unflagging passion that Igraine had to send them away shortly after the wedding. So both Morgause and Morgan grew into womanhood blaming Uther for not only the loss of their father, but their mother as well.

When I came south to marry Arthur, Igraine took me under her wing, smoothing out my tomboy roughness and letting me take the place of the daughters she hadn't raised to womanhood. On her deathbed Arthur's mother told me the story of those days at Tintagel; of how she had honored the Duke Gorlois and feared Uther's passion and had tried to avoid the moira which, nonetheless, had made her High Queen of Britain.

That was privy information that I had shared with no one— not Arthur, nor Nimue, nor either of my sisters-in-law. But I used to wonder how much of the daughters' bitterness toward Uther—and their fear of being displaced again—shaped their feelings for his son.

Morgause's seduction of Arthur in an effort to gain power over him through the presence of his child, and Morgan's swings from staunchest advocate to treacherous plotter were, perhaps, more understandable when one knew their family history. Still, it did not make them any easier to live with . . . and I could think of no way to explain these things to fourteen-year-old Mordred. So by the time we led our party out onto the Road they call Watling Street, Gareth had left on his new quest and Mordred was still with us.

The Road makes its way up the long, rumpled swath of land that marks the boundary between two worlds. To the east spread the soft, fertile midlands dotted with Roman villas, while in the west the wild Welsh mountains rise, home of the old Celts who call themselves the Cumbri. The Marches that separate these two lands are strange and fey, full of blue mists and green woods, and hills that rise like islands out of time. Many of them are crowned by ancient hill-forts now in the hands of warlords such as Pellinore of the Wrekin. But even where one can't see the terraced earthworks of bank and ditch crowning the highest points, there is the feeling of being watched by eyes both human and otherwise.

The Roman Road drives straight as an ash-pole through verdant forests and the ruins of whole towns. Cycles of life and death shimmer on the air like a warp of light stretched on the loom of Forever, and I rode through it remembering it was the route down which Arthur and I came on our way to Sarum to be wed.

How the people loved us then, dropping hoe and fishnet to become part of the procession that escorted their young King to his nuptials. We had ridden to our destiny—right into the heart of spring on a wave of high spirits—with half the population following after.

I glanced over at my husband and Bedivere, who were conversing as they rode side by side. All of us were broader now, made more solid by the years. Even the farmers who paused in the autumn plowing to wave, or the travelers on the Road who moved to one side to let the King's party pass, had lost the lean and hungry look of our youth. Here, as on the Road to Caerleon, the peace and plenty that favored our reign spilled its richness over all.

We camped in fields and meadows, stayed at such inns and roadhouses as we found, and whenever possible visited the warlords in their hill-forts. That's where I began to hear the stories.

". . . walks through the woods at night, with all the animals following after," the daughter of a tavern owner whispered to Lynette, who listened raptly, mouth half open in amazement. "And green—he's all over green; skin, hair, clothes . . . even his horse is green."

"What's this?" I inquired, pausing to smile encouragingly at the girl.

She crossed herself hastily and bobbed a kind of curtsy. "Beggin' pardon, Your Highness, but I was just reporting what my uncle's brother-in-law saw. Up in the north it was, in a wild, fearsome place. They say he's wreaking all sorts of havoc, and getting bolder with every visit."

"And who is 'he'?"

"Some claim it's the Old One—the Green Man of Eld come back again."

I've noticed that dragons and giants and shadows of the Old Gods always appear a great distance away, never close enough to be confronted. "But not nearby?" I queried.

The child shook her mop of curls, turning with a delicious shiver to Lynette. "Not yet, at any rate," she whispered.

What a pity, I thought, wishing it were possible to get within sighting distance of such a thing. Yet when I mentioned it to Arthur, he burst out laughing.

"Don't talk to me about foolhardy Celts," he teased. "Who ever heard of a queen wanting to go twist the tail of some old deity?"

I wasn't exactly interested in riling the creature, just seeing it, but Arthur had a point, so I shrugged and forgot all about the subject until we reached Wroxeter.

Once a hub of Roman activity, the city has stood empty for generations, its buildings decaying and towers unmanned. In the past travelers skirted its walls, fearful of the haunts of plague and pestilence they enclosed. But Arthur led our party right through the sagging gates and made camp in the shelter of the basilica's wall. And after a communal meal of trout from the nearby Severn, Arthur and I walked away from the campfire, climbing to a perch on the deserted ramparts as twilight descended.

"What do you think about building a lodge here, lass?" my husband asked. "Maelgwn forfeited all this land as reparation for kidnapping you, and it would make a fine retreat from the world."

I snorted scornfully and looked about the ghostly place. Ravens nested in broken walls, wooden signboards hung askew and what doors were left creaked on rusty hinges, making it a setting more fitting for the Green Man than a human court.

But more importantly, the city had belonged to my cousin, Maelgwn.

Maelgwn—the King of Gwynedd, who kidnapped and raped me barely five years after Arthur and I married. Maelgwn, whose ravaging of my body left me sick to the point of death and barren forever after. The terrible memory still made my stomach turn.

After Lance had rescued me, Maelgwn took shelter in the monastery at Bangor. It was a clever move, effectively placing him beyond vengeance by either Arthur or Lance. Yet in spite of the years gone by and the silence of the man, his very name filled me with dread, and I wanted no part of his property.

"Can't we put our lodge somewhere else?" I inquired. "There's my holdings at Carlisle, or out at Appleby. Surely we could build a retreat there, closer to my own people. Why, I remember a waterfall by the Eden River . . ."

Arthur shrugged. "Rheged's too far from Camelot for what I have in mind. But we'll see; if you don't fancy Wroxeter, maybe someplace else will catch your eye." It was clear he had no notion of how much the encounter with Maelgwn still disturbed me.

Suddenly a voice cut through the dusk, making me jump.

"Your Highness?"

"Over here," my husband answered, standing up to peer at the figure that moved toward us. Silhouetted in the fire's glow was the biggest man in the realm, outside of Pellinore. "Lamorak, is that you?"

"Aye," came the response. "From the number of fires, I reckoned it had to be the royal party. I can't tell you how glad I am you're here!"

There was something more than simple hospitality in his voice, so we scrambled down from our perch, falling into pace beside him as we all moved back toward camp. "Have you any word of my father?" he asked.

"No. Isn't he at the Wrekin?"

Lamorak shook his head. "Pellinore left for the tournament in early July, and we've had neither news nor message since. Some of the returning Champions came through last week, but they said they hadn't seen him at Caerleon. It's made for much uneasiness at the fort, and I was hoping you might know his whereabouts."

Both Arthur and I shook our heads.

"There's been talk about the Green Man recently," Lamorak went on cautiously.

"Nearby?"

"No—farther north. But they say he's huge, and invincible. Very polite, in a roguish way, and fond of issuing deadly challenges . . . and you know how my father loves a challenge." Lamorak was keeping his voice casual, but in the fire's glow I saw his fingers move as he made the sign against evil. "Of course, that's all just hearsay from the peasants. Still, I'd be obliged if you'd come to the Wrekin tomorrow, just to reassure my people that life is going on as usual and Britain's not being overrun by demons and such."

So the next morning we headed for the Wrekin, that long, whalelike ridge that rises up out of the forest so unexpectedly. The broad path climbs through woods of oak and holly, birch and yew, and when we paused partway up the trail, a wild, cackling laugh suddenly split the air. I shivered in spite of seeing the green woodpecker flit away, and Arthur gave me an amused look.

But by the time we reached the massive walls of the fort atop the ridge, an eerie, chilling wail welled out to greet us. The cries of keening women ricocheted from Hall to barn as Lamorak came to meet us at the gate, his face haggard and eyes red.

"It's my father," he said flatly, as the tears ran down his cheeks. "Yesterday a hurdle maker was gathering hazel rods in the forest by Wenlock Edge when he stumbled on the body . . . or what was left of it."

I gasped aloud and reached out to steady myself against Arthur, appalled at the idea that such a bulwark of the realm was gone.

"He must have died shortly after leaving home," Lamorak went on. "What with the warm summer months, only the cape was recognizable—that and the brooch you gave him at his last tournament, Your Highness."

His words echoed in my head: "I'll wear it till the day I die." The memory shook me like a wind.

"So he wasn't robbed," Arthur noted, absently helping me sit down. "At least we can assume it wasn't foul play."

"Not quite." Lamorak shook his head. "From the slashes in his cape, I'd say he was stabbed in the back. And his big bay stallion has not been seen; someone must have ridden it away, or it would have returned to the stable. They weren't that far from home."

"And his wife?" I asked, trying to remember her name. "How's Tallia taking it?"

"Ah, Tallia died several years back, M'lady, during childbirth. My father remarried soon after—a young girl I think you never met, who is a distant relative of King Pellam's in Carbonek. She's half out of her mind with grief, sobbing and wailing and swearing she'll take her son, Perceval, back to Wales. She's never made friends here and has no wish to stay."

I nodded slowly, hoping that Elaine and King Pellam would take the new widow in—otherwise she and the tyke could be lost, forced to become beggars, or live half wild among the outlaws and other forest peoples.

When we went into the Hall I tried to talk with her, to ease her grief and suggest that she join our household, at least temporarily. But she grew even more distraught, declaring that it was Arthur and the Round Table that had killed her husband with the lure of honor and glory. In the end we left her there, and once we paid our respects to the dead, returned to the caravan waiting for us at Wroxeter.

"At least it can't be blamed on the Green Man," Arthur noted sourly. "The Gods don't use daggers in the back, so it must have been a flesh-and-blood enemy." Startled, I remembered the Orcadians' hatred for the men of the Wrekin. And glancing at Arthur, I saw his jaw set grimly. "I will not tolerate blood-feuds in the Round Table!"

But when the news was shared, Gawain and Gaheris both swore they'd had nothing to do with Pellinore's death, and considering the importance Gawain put on honor these days, I thought it unlikely he'd kill an enemy so treacherously. It was also implausible that sweet-natured Gareth would have done such a thing, and Mordred, who was too young to be truly suspect, had been at Court during the time when Pelli died. Agravain, the only other member of the Orkney faction, was still held captive in the northern isles, struggling with the memory of killing his own mother.

"Perhaps," Bedivere suggested, "we'll never know who killed Pellinore. And I for one would rather remember the vitality and enthusiasm of his life, and not dwell on the bitterness of his end."

As usual, Bedivere's advice was both excellent and well taken.

We laid over at Chester while Arthur met with Maelgwn's regent, reviewing the readiness of the warriors, seeing to the state of the crops, and settling whatever disputes needed his attention. The city itself is one of my favorites, but the fact that it belonged to my cousin made me glad to leave, and we arrived at Carlisle well before Samhain.

As a child I had not cared much for Rheged's only city, preferring the lakeside steadings and mountain enclaves. But years of living in the comfort of the south had made me more appreciative of the Roman trading center at the western end of Hadrian's Wall. The big old house on the riverbank is quite comfortable, the aqueduct to the fountain in the Square still functions and the constant stream of traders, moving not only north and south over the big stone bridge but also east and west along the Wall, means that both news and merchants give the town a lively air. It was here we would spend the winter, and I settled into our house with the additional gladness of being close to my own people once more.

On a rainy evening shortly after Samhain, Gareth returned from his trip to the Sanctuary. He was soaked to the skin and came into the Hall, teeth chattering and long hair dripping, just after the evening meal. I took one look at him and ordered that he get dry and warm while Cook scurried off to fix him a steaming bowl of brose.

The young warrior sank to his knees in front of me, however, and humbly bowed his head.

"Your Highness, I have failed to find Lancelot." When he looked up at me, I could have sworn there were tears as well as raindrops coursing down his face, and I put my hand on his shoulder in commiseration. "I cannot keep your brooch when the cause was not met," he went on, putting the blue pin from the Mote into my hand. I tried to insist it was well earned, but he wouldn't hear of it. "There is a matter of honor involved, Your Highness," he said, sounding very much like Gawain.

"Ah well," Arthur sighed, "the Breton will show up sooner or later."

"But there is other, much better news," Gareth went on, gratefully taking the foaming bowl Cook offered him and sitting down before the hearth. The warmth of the fire made his wet clothes steam, wreathing him in mists, but his eyes were full of excitement and he took no notice. A fine smile spread across his face. "My brother Agravain now lives at the Sanctuary, and Aunt Morgan's rescuing him from the terrors of his past."

Agravain—the dark and handsome son of King Lot. He was cunning and devious where Gawain was open; lazy and self-centered where Gaheris was hard working; cruel and arrogant where Gareth was sincerity itself. And though Gareth was clearly delighted by the news, I stared at him and wondered if he had any idea how vicious his older sibling was. What with living at Joyous Gard with Lancelot, he'd not been at Court when Morgause died, not seen the horror up close.

Arthur gave Gareth a piercing look and began chewing on the ends of his mustache. "So Agravain is with Morgan? And she's cured him of his fits and rages?"

"Indeed, M'lord," the young man beamed. "I spent several evenings with him, and outside of an occasional nervous outburst, he seems perfectly sane again."

"I've had no word he'd left the Orkneys. How long has he been at the Sanctuary?" Gawain asked with a scowl. He at least seemed to realize this might be a mixed blessing.

"Came a few weeks back. Some druids found him wandering in the Marches, lost and frightened, and out of his wits. Who knows how long he'd been that way before they brought him to the Black Lake?"

Arthur and I exchanged glances, both no doubt thinking of Pellinore, but neither of us spoke.

"Agravain knew neither his own name nor his past," Gareth marveled, "but if he'd come on foot the length of Scotland, hiding from the Picts and living by his wits in the wildwood, it's no wonder he'd turned raving. The High Priestess has restored his mind as well as his body, and one would never guess the agonies he's known. I don't wonder the people worship her or call her the greatest healer in the land."

I bit my lip and looked at my lap, wondering what Arthur was making of the news. But instead of the anger I expected from him, he clamped his mouth shut and stared into the fire.

A chill ran through me and I pulled my scarf tighter around my shoulders. The loss of hope for Lancelot was a deep, quiet ache, but the arrival of Agravain brought quick, sharp fear. It was entirely possible Morgan would try to turn him against us—or even tempt him to usurp the throne.

After her attempt on his life, Arthur had forbidden her to leave the Sanctuary without our permission, thereby hoping to isolate her among the mountains and dales of the Lake District. Yet even from a distance she had managed to draw the most untrustworthy of the Orcadians to her Sanctuary. I began to wonder which was worse: watching her traveling freely through the land, stirring up trouble among the peasants, or having to worry what kind of treachery she was conjuring in her lair, hidden away beside the Black Lake.

Slowly and surely I felt the woman's presence grow stronger, and prayed that she would do nothing to spoil our return to Rheged. It was my first visit home in many years, and I wanted so much to enjoy a country winter, back among the people of my own land.

12

Rheged

ergus had been a big, red-headed Irishman when he had given his daughter, Brigit, to my father as a peace-hostage, back when both she and I were youngsters. He was balding and paunchy now, with a weathered face well creased with laugh lines, and he surveyed the Irish wolfhounds that lounged by our fire with paternal pride.

"Descendants of the pup I gave you as a wedding present? Think of that!"

Arthur grinned in response, and began to tell the man how famous the first wardog, Cabal, had become. "Bravest bitch I ever owned: quick to learn, and wonderfully loyal—saved my life during the Saxon wars."

The Irishman beamed at the notion of having contributed to his High King's safety, and hooking his thumbs into the top of his breeches, leaned back against the sheepskin of his chair, thoroughly enjoying the visit. To a man who lived in a wattle and daub roundhouse, our solid Roman building with heated floors and muraled walls must have seemed the height of luxury.

The dog breeder was not our only guest that winter. Rough-dressed men from beyond the Wall swaggered in, led by chieftains in plaid kilts and shaggy fur capes. A Pictish envoy, his body covered with tattoos, made the trip down from the Highlands, and any number of merchants, peddlars and occasional holy men came to pay their respects at the big house in Carlisle.

"I've been thinking," my husband would say casually to each guest as they sat over mugs of ale while the fire blazed. "Been reading this Edictum of Theodoric's, and it seems to me we should have something like it—laws that a man can count on wherever he lives in Britain. Oh, nothing to do with taxes, mind—each lord needs to settle those among his people—but about keeping the peace, establishing justice. . . ."

And our guests, depending on their nature, would nod vaguely or question pointedly or sometimes offer suggestions as to what all it should contain. After so many years of trying to implement the idea, it was gratifying to get some positive reactions.

"I'll civilize them yet," my husband allowed one night, reaching for me under the down comforter. "If I can tame Rheged's most famous tomboy, I ought to be able to convert its men."

"Don't you go counting on my tameness," I shot back. "This country's been led by more than one independent queen." And then we were tussling and teasing like newlyweds until our coupling was complete and we lay in a heap of exhaustion. There might be whole worlds of emotions I couldn't share with my husband, but our bedding was always a pleasure.

When the weather was nice we sallied forth from Carlisle, visiting the towns and steadings that I'd grown up in. Being so far north, Rheged had missed the devastation the south suffered before Arthur quelled the Saxon uprisings at the battle of Mount Badon. The Lakes with their steep falls and hidden valleys, Pennine towns such as Appleby and Kirkby Thor, even the farms around Carlisle, had all prospered during those years.

A steady stream of travelers crossed the great stone bridge over the Eden, carrying made goods and messages to the fractious kingdoms beyond the Wall, returning with news and pelts and occasionally a fine golden torc accepted as barter along the way. The town thrived as a center of trade and hosted a weekly market where farmers brought their goods as well. There was even a cathedral, and the little Roman matron, Vinnie, immediately made the Bishop's acquaintance.

"He's a fine man," she informed me, "who would be glad to have you grace his congregation." So on a bright Sunday morning Vinnie and I and many of my ladies-in-waiting all went to Mass together. "You should invite him to Court," the matron prompted afterward, and made a point of hustling me up to meet the Christian patriarch.

"Well," he announced, looking me slowly up and down as though I were a fish of dubious freshness, "it's not often we get a Pagan of your stature in our humble church."

Considering that the building was originally the fort's basilica, I had a hard time thinking of it as humble. Still, I was about to ask him to join us for dinner when he spoke again, disdain dripping from his voice. "Of course, the one I look forward to meeting is your husband."

"Perhaps he'll come to call on you sometime," I snapped, gathering up my skirts and flouncing away. I could see no reason to ask anyone that rude to share my table. Nor would I change my mind, even though Arthur suggested such an invitation would give the Bishop and Father Baldwin a chance to get better acquainted.

I did send for the Bishop when Vinnie was dying, however, and he not only gave her last rites, but arranged for a Christian burial as well. We all stood saddened beside the marble coffin when she was interred in the Roman cemetery outside of town, and I found a large stone pinecone to put by the grave.

Vinnie's wasn't the only death that year. Shortly after the midwinter festival a messenger from Wales brought word that Sir Ector had died. Father of Cei, foster father of Arthur and Bedivere, he'd served his kings loyally, even taking in the young Saxon hostage, Cynric. I thought of how well he'd shaped the boys in his care and hoped the son of Cerdic had benefited from his guidance as well.

Arthur and Cei and Bedivere all went to Bala Lake for the funeral, leaving Gawain with me in Rheged. "It is the least I can do, when he gave me such a childhood," my husband said, a catch coming into his voice. "Besides, Cerdic caused me enough grief at Mount Badon. Geraint may say the Saxons are quiet around Winchester, but I intend to keep a close rein on Cynric —we can't afford to let him slip away when there's more than enough of his father's old allies who could raise an army against me if they had someone to rally them."

While they were gone, I wondered what it would be like to live with the offspring of our sworn enemy in the household— like a warbler hatching a cuckoo chick, we might find out too late what a threat he was. The very notion sent a prickling down

my spine, and I had to remind myself that I knew several Saxons
—the Kennel Master's wife, Frieda, among them—who were
loyal, friendly and industrious.

The men returned within a fortnight, a young blond squire
riding between them.

"Your Highness," Cynric said, bowing stiffly to me. In the
seven years he'd been with Ector he'd taken up our tongue, and
now spoke with only a slight German accent. "I am honored to
be a guest at your Court."

It was a pretty speech, and I smiled at the newcomer, thinking
that Ector had accomplished far more than we'd expected. The
lad was comely, with an open face and an air of quiet self-
possession. At least, I decided, wait and see how he fits in before
you condemn out of hand. It's one thing to be cautious about
Saxons and quite another to see enemies where there may not be
any.

"I'm Mordred," my stepson said, suddenly stepping forward to
greet the lad. For a moment the two boys eyed each other, like
young dogs deciding whether to play or fight. Then Mordred
grinned. "I, too, was born far away, but the High King's Court
has become my home . . . I hope you'll find it such yourself."

Cynric's reserve melted just a bit, though he continued to study
me gravely and certainly was uneasy with Arthur. That was natural enough, however, considering that the boy was a hostage.

The northern spring is still as crisp and beautiful as I remembered from childhood, and when lilies-of-the-valley carpeted the
feet of oaks, I found myself thinking often of Lancelot and wishing he were here to share it with me. And there was never a new
moon went by that I didn't make the prayer Nimue had given
me, wishing fervently that it would bring the Breton back to me.

As soon as the Roads opened following the thaw, Arthur and
Gawain went out along the Wall to solidify alliances, while I
took a small contingent of warriors through Rheged to see that
Urien was doing a suitable job as my regent.

"Just wish he lived closer," Eirwyn told me. The man was one
of the country barons who governed his dale in the age-old manner of the Cumbri, and he squinted out over his holdings as we
stood by the gate in the drystone wall. The steep sides of the
mountains that hemmed in the valley were casting long shadows

upon the lake where an osprey dove for a fish and rose in a shower of water, his catch dangling from one claw. It was a sight dear to my heart, in a world as remote and cut off from the rest of Britain as my past was from my present. "Makes it very awkward having Urien all the way in York when we want to hold a Council here," the Baron added thoughtfully.

"But he's fair and honorable? You've no complaints on that score?"

"None at all," Eirwyn answered. "He's as good a monarch as we could ask for—unless we had you back, of course." I caught the twinkle in the old man's eye and laughed with pleasure at the compliment. There was no way I would consider leaving Arthur to come rule Rheged, but it was nice to know I was wanted.

We stopped at Galava, staying in the Roman fort at the end of Windermere's water, and the people crowded along the path to bid me welcome. I paid my respects to the Standing Stones at Castlerigg and told Mordred of having brought Gawain to see them, back when we were both children and the red-headed Orcadian was visiting with his father, King Lot. And at Patterdale I stood under the tree that guards Saint Patrick's Well and offered a prayer for Kevin for old-time's sake.

Kevin—childhood's companion and my first love. The Irish lad had run away when it was clear my moira lay in a royal marriage. For years I waited his return, praying to any Gods who would listen to keep him safe. Kevin—with the black hair and blue eyes. He and Lancelot looked so much alike that even Arthur had been fooled when Kevin came to Camelot, wearing the robes of a Christian priest, a few years back.

I paused, and added Lancelot to my prayer as I tied a cluster of buttercups to the branches already thick with votive ribbons and small gifts. For all the things which had changed since I'd run free across the meadow at Patterdale, here I was again, standing by a holy well, asking the Gods to protect a love gone missing.

"M'lady, look at the ducks we've snared." Mordred's voice broke my reverie, and I turned to see him and Cynric loping along the path.

In the months since the Saxon had arrived, he'd held himself aloof, shunned by the British squires and ignored by the men. But gradually a cautious friendship grew up between my dark-haired stepson and the towheaded hostage, and when they had asked to come on this trip together, I was pleased to bring them both. Released from lessons and full of youthful exuberance, they treated the sojourn as a holiday—sprinting across the meadows, climbing trees, playing pranks on each other and occasionally on me. Now they came pelting up, each brandishing a brace of mallards.

"Cynric's a real expert at snaring," Mordred exclaimed, and the blond boy ducked his head diffidently.

"Learned the tricks of it at Lake Bala," he said, obviously pleased by the praise.

"Ought to be a nice surprise for Cook," I allowed, taking their arms and heading back to the steading. Thus they escorted me through the trees, laughing and jesting as we went, and when the meadow opened up and the roundhouse was in sight, they pulled away to race ahead. I sighed happily, glad that the two youngsters who were most alone at Court should have found companionship in each other.

Even before Beltane, Arthur decided to move on to York in order to confer with Urien about the new barbarians said to be landing along the upper coast of Northumbria.

When he was riding proudly at the head of his warriors, or sitting majestically among the Fellowship at the Round Table, Urien was still a figure to command respect. But in his own den, surrounded by the remains of the old Imperial City, the Raven King of Northumbria showed the mark of his years. I looked at him in the torchlight of the Hall and realized that, like Cador, he had grown old in the service of Arthur.

It had been a long life and full. In the early years he'd contented himself with cattle raiding and harassing the borders of Rheged. If he wasn't out marauding, he was hunting or wenching, or drinking, like any Celtic warlord. Not even marriage to Morgan had changed that, and when she turned her attentions to the Old Ways and became a priestess at the Sanctuary, he hardly noticed her absence.

It was their son, Uwain, who had been caught in the breach, raised by servants and doing the best he could to bridge the gap between his parents.

"Glad to see you," Urien growled, coming to meet us at the

gate of the Roman fort. "I've been making some plans for fortifying the north—thought we ought to go over them."

So Arthur ended up being closeted with the old man for hours on end, going over maps, discussing options, examining the reports that warned of trouble. My ladies and I spent our time exploring the shops and stalls among the crooked little streets they call snickelways, and one afternoon Urien put a barge at our disposal so we could take a picnic down the river to a lovely meadow where the local Bishop had his manor.

It was this same Bishop I was expected to entertain when Urien held a feast for us at the end of our stay. It was not a task I relished, but since Urien had no queen in residence, it fell to me to act as hostess.

The Bishop of York was more polished than the one at Carlisle, but he carried a smugness that came of thinking himself exceptionally holy. And that night at dinner he made a point of talking specifically with Arthur and pretending I didn't exist. It was a trait that infuriated me.

"The wisest thing the King of the Franks ever did was to become a Catholic," the cleric announced. "Best way to bind a diversity of people together is through a common belief."

I smiled inwardly, thinking that was exactly what we had done with the Round Table.

"With the sanction of the Church behind him, Clovis has gained immense respect in what's left of the Empire," the Bishop went on, casting Arthur a sly look. "Even the Emperor of Constantinople recognizes him."

Palomides choked and hastily put down his wine goblet, no doubt remembering that Anastasius would not see him because Arthur wasn't Christian.

"But I thought the Frankish kings were Pagan shamans . . ." I said quickly, wracking my brain for everything I knew about the rulers of the barbarians across the Channel, ". . . that their lives are proscribed by holy rites, and their hair hangs down to their ankles because if they cut it, they will break faith with the Goddess."

"Ah, there's no accounting for the odd beliefs of heathens," the Bishop replied smoothly. "But whatever they used to do, that's all in the past. I met Clovis and found both him and his wife to be excellent Christians. In fact"—the holy man paused to look specifically at me—"it was Clotilda who showed her husband the true faith after they were married. It's amazing the influence a good woman can wield."

I squelched a tart response and glared fiercely at the water in my goblet until the unsaid words were well past. Slowly but surely I was learning to control my tongue.

"In some ways you have much in common," the Bishop continued, unrelenting in his courtship of Arthur. "Both of you are trying to forge a united country out of disparate tribes, holding them together by the strength of your personalities. And both have inherited as much Roman as local culture and customs. Of course, he's not a philosopher like Theodoric, and laws aren't of much interest to him, but Clovis is a name to go down in history, mark my words."

I sniffed, and dismissed the Bishop's statements as so much propaganda. From what I remembered, this Clovis was little better than a cutthroat bandit—an opportunist who, like Agamemnon or Caesar, would use anything or anyone to further his own ends. I reminded myself, however, that it wouldn't hurt to keep apprised of what he was doing.

The rest of the feast went well enough, but the next day, just before we left for London, Urien asked for a chance to see me alone. When he led the way to a terrace overlooking the fine old city, I glanced at him surreptitiously, wondering if he'd had news of Morgan le Fey.

"It's about my son," he began awkwardly.

"Uwain?" I sat down on a marble bench. "Have you heard from him recently?"

"No." Urien's voice was harsh and stiff, but he sagged noticeably and took a seat himself. "I was hoping you might have. It's hard not to feel bitter, M'lady, when your only son is banished for something he didn't do."

"I know . . . I know." I spoke gently, wondering how to tell him that I, too, felt Arthur's action had been unfair. There was no evidence that Uwain had been involved in Morgan's plot to capture the throne, yet Arthur had sent the boy from Court simply because he was her son.

"As a man gets old"—the admission was hard-wrung and difficult—"well, he starts wanting to have the next generation beside him. If Uwain were back here with me, he could handle things in York while I'm in the north. As it is, not even knowing where he is . . ."

"I'll send word if I hear anything," I assured him, and made a mental note to mention it to Arthur when the time seemed right.

Urien nodded silently, and I ventured a query of my own. "Is there news of the High Priestess?"

For a moment the old man straightened, and a kind of resolute fire leapt to his eyes. His jaw tightened and he instinctively shifted his hand to his sword hilt.

"The High Priestess remains at her Sanctuary next to the Black Lake, M'lady. She has not applied for permission to travel through the rest of Rheged, and I have not encouraged it. But if that changes, I shall certainly let you know."

He got slowly to his feet, and, giving me a curt nod, stalked away. Watching him leave, I wondered how long Morgan would be content to stay at the Sanctuary now that she had brought Agravain to her lair.

As soon as we reached the Imperial Palace in London, Arthur began making arrangements to visit the Frankish king in Paris.

"Now who's being a foolhardy Celt?" I stormed when he told me. "Those people are savages. What if they decide to hold you for ransom, or kill you outright?"

"Gwen, I'll never have a better chance," my husband replied, slipping into the "I'm being patient" mode he often used when I raised too-hasty questions. "Bors has arranged everything through his contacts in Brittany; my safe-passage has been sworn to; and with everything calm here in Britain, now's the time to go."

"What if the boat sinks?" I flung myself across the room, propelled as much by amazement as fear. "Everyone knows how chancy the Channel is. Any crossing can start out easy and calm, but storms come up so quickly . . . what if you drown?"

"Then you'd become Guinevere the First of Logres. Can't say the client kings would elect you High King in my place, but they could do worse," he teased, carefully wrapping Excalibur in its beaver-skin case. "Don't fret so, my dear. I've come through far worse than this on my own home turf—nothing's going to happen to me now. Besides, I'm taking Gawain along as bodyguard and heir apparent. Do him good to get acquainted with the people of the Continent."

In the end, of course, I stood on the dock below London's bridge, waving my scarf and wishing them all well. Bedivere was beside me and he gave a good-natured chuckle as the boat came even with the signal tower and, rounding the bend, was lost from sight. "You weren't really surprised he decided to do such a thing, were you?" he asked.

"No, I suppose not." I stared up at the craggy lieutenant and shook my head in wonder. Nothing that Arthur did could deeply surprise either of us anymore.

* * *

Ah, my King, how many times you put yourself at risk, all in the name of your Cause. And yes, I know you would say it has all been worth it, for we've ruled long and well over a united Britain. But now, on this night before my death, I wonder which of us is in more jeopardy. . . .

13

Stonehenge

ith Arthur gone, I held Court at London, seeing to local matters and adjudicating disputes between unruly neighbors or contentious shopkeepers. It was while I was thus occupied that Lucan the Gatekeeper came to tell me a chieftain with a Swedish accent was demanding an audience.

"Wearing a wolfskin slung over one shoulder?" It was a likely guess, as Wehha of East Anglia was the only Swede we knew.

"That's him." Lucan nodded emphatically, his round face suddenly serious. "Do you want to have Bedivere with you before I let him in? The man is most peculiar, you know."

I laughed and assured Lucan there was no need for such precautions. We'd been dealing with Wehha for years, and I found his stilted Latin and affectation of Roman more amusing than imposing. But he'd more than proved his loyalty to Arthur at the battle of Mount Badon, so while he might be eccentric, I doubted he'd be treacherous.

When Lucan announced the arrival of Wehha and his son, Wuffa, of East Anglia, everyone in the Hall turned to stare at the door.

The Swede had brought his entire entourage with him and was traveling with full panoply. The first to come through the door was a steward holding aloft a strange metal staff with ribbons and feathers fixed to its top. "Good as any Roman standard," Wehha had explained proudly the first time we saw the thing. Next came a solemn lieutenant carrying the oddly shaped whetstone the barbarian used as a scepter. Smooth and oblong, its tapered ends

Persia Woolley

bore the faces of Gods and ancestors carved into the stone, and the man who held it inclined it first to this side, then to that, like a priest blessing the faithful. Our courtiers nodded respectfully as the fellow passed, then turned back to the door expectantly. The steward, who had come to a stop before my chair, stepped to one side and thumped his standard three times on the floor. Only then did Wehha strut into the room.

The man was as big and rangy as I remembered, with masses of blond hair and quick blue eyes. At his side strode a younger version of himself; more lean and aloof, but with a similar arrogance. It took me a minute to realize this was Wehha's son grown into manhood—the last time I'd seen Wuffa, he was still a lad.

As they crossed the room, a scowl began to darken Wehha's features. When he came to a stop in front of Arthur's empty chair, I could see the trouble coming. For a man who didn't even allow his women in the mead-hall, paying respect to a High Queen was bound to be difficult.

"I came to treat with Arthur Pendragon," the Swede declared. "Where is he?"

Making my voice as cordial as possible, I explained Arthur was visiting other monarchs on the Continent.

"Not here?" The words echoed like thunder as the barbarian turned to scrutinize every corner of the room.

"I would be happy to treat with you," I offered.

"I do not discuss matters of state with women." Wehha's terrible Latin made the scornful comment almost funny. "When King Arthur returns, tell him I extend an invitation for him to visit my holdings."

With that the man turned and marched from the room, as indignant as though he was the one who'd been insulted. I watched him go, half amused at his pretensions, half outraged by his lack of respect. The son was less precipitous in leaving, however, and while the father might be bombastic in the extreme, Wuffa was a study in insolence. He stared at me with the brazen look of a man sizing up a woman for his bed. My hackles began to rise and my hands doubled into fists as I got slowly to my feet.

The young warrior raked me with his eyes one last time before he backed down and turned to follow his father. I stood there

143

glaring at his back, thinking I'd have to put the randy pup in his place once Arthur returned.

When our business was concluded in London, I took the household back to the fortress above Cadbury, stopping by the villa at Cunetio. The excess of daughters who sought to be ladies-in-waiting lived here, since there was simply no way to have all of them at Camelot at one time, and I intended to tell them that, with the death of Vinnie, they would have to return to their families. But the majority of them begged to follow me home, and in the end I accepted their requests with a certain chagrin—without Vinnie, I would have to look after them myself.

We spent the first week at Camelot sorting out which trunk belonged to whom, finding enough box-beds to sleep them all, and rounding up every available mattress. Some of these were not in the best of condition, and I made a note to collect extra barley straw for new stuffing come harvest time. At least, I thought gratefully, I can pass my summer in simple tasks, with nothing more demanding than trying to find ways to keep my ladies occupied and overseeing the workers when harvest time arrived. With any luck, Arthur would return to find a rested wife and well-provisioned headquarters.

So I was hardly expecting news of great note when Lynette found me pulling up weeds in the little garden that had become my private retreat. "There's a druid asking for an audience," she reported. "He says his name is Cathbad, and he won't talk to anyone but you."

The name came from far back in the past, and I rocked back on my heels. "I expected all druids to be old and crabbed," the gamin went on. "But this one looks to be in his prime and right handsome, too."

I nodded my agreement and brushing the dirt from my hands, walked thoughtfully toward the Hall. In some ways I put no more trust in druids than I did in Christian priests, and for all that Cathbad had been my tutor in Rheged, I wondered what brought him to Camelot. Years ago he'd gone to serve the Lady at her Sanctuary by the Black Lake, and I'd never been sure but what the High Priestess had turned him against me.

Cathbad was standing at the far end of the room, scrutinizing the tapestry of the Red Dragon. His back was still straight, his hair still thick, and when he slowly turned to study the architecture of our Hall, his face was full of the same intense curiosity with which he used to dissect flowers or examine a new insect with his students. A rush of nostalgic fondness swept over me.

"Well come, friend," I called. He brought his gaze down from the roof beams and after carefully appraising me, gave me a smile touched with paternal pride. When he held out his arms in invitation, I ran to him, kneeling to receive a blessing. "It's been a very long time."

"That it has," he answered, laying his hands gently atop by head. "But you're the royal one here, so I suggest you get back on your feet, Missy."

The use of my family nickname was equally dear, and by the time we sat down for tea, we'd slipped into the old teacher-pupil roles. It was then, over a cup of peppermint brew, that he came to the reason for his visit: Morgan le Fey intended to hold a ceremony at Stonehenge on midsummer's morn for the purpose of purifying Agravain.

"What!" I exclaimed, suddenly pulled back to being High Queen. "Morgan is coming to Logres? Right into the heart of Arthur's kingdom—when Arthur's banished her on pain of death? Surely you are mistaken."

"I'm afraid not. She seems to think she can act with impunity since her brother's across the Channel." Cathbad looked down into his tea and inhaled its fragrance. "I myself was sent to carry the word to other druids, to the doires who keep the sacred wells, and to such of the peasantry as would like to attend."

I stared at the man, aghast, my head spinning with a dozen questions. "What about Agravain? What's she going to do to him?"

"Morgan believes the rite she's devising will both purge him of his guilt for slaying his mother and bring the Goddess's blessings on us all."

"How?" Stories from the days of heroes and glory, when Celts and Gods lived side by side, have been passed down for generations. I had heard them as a child, and come too close to seeing my own father offered up not to be aware of the possibility it might happen again. "Is she planning to use him as a human sacrifice?"

"I don't think so," Cathbad observed. "I don't know why she is doing this, but it could be simply to help the man. He is her nephew, after all."

I nodded, still puzzling over the matter, and asked the druid why he had come to tell me about it. He stared out one of the windows, and his expression became ineffably sad.

"Morgan le Fey has been a devout leader, a woman of enormous conviction . . . but in the last half-dozen years there's been a change. At the Sanctuary all prayers are directed to the Great Mother . . . not only are the male Gods no longer honored, their names are never spoken aloud. As a consequence men are no longer included in the ceremonies. Morgan claims that in the old times only the Priestess and her nine acolytes were accepted as holy, and she's determined to reinstate that regime." Cathbad sighed and looked back at me. "She's become fanatic on the subject and has lost many of her supporters as a result. Oh, the commoners will continue to revere her, but the major families no longer send their most promising children to be trained at her Academy."

He paused, and I thought of the fine schooling Lancelot had received at the Sanctuary. It was there he had learned the arts of science and history, medicine and war, and all the other things that made him invaluable as Arthur's lieutenant.

"Perhaps it's Morgan's fear of the Christian Father God that makes her so difficult," Cathbad continued. "She tolerates no discussion, allows no dissent . . . particularly if it comes from a man. She's even organizing a crusade to make it mandatory that all people worship the Goddess. *All* people," he repeated slowly, "regardless of their own desires."

We had heard rumor of this before, though without the support of the High King, she would have little success. "You know Arthur won't allow that," I interrupted. "Of all the things my husband holds dear, the right of every man to choose the Gods by whom he lives—and dies—is one of the most important."

"*That* is why I am seeking asylum with you and the King," the druid said slowly, as though it hurt even to put the idea into words. "There is no longer a place for me at the Black Lake, but I understand that all holy people are welcome here."

I searched my mentor's face, wondering if this was some sort of trick on Morgan's part to embroil Arthur in a religious war. But Cathbad returned my gaze, his eyes full of the sorrow of seeing all that he had dedicated his life to become corrupted. There was no way I could doubt his sincerity, and I smiled as I put my hand on his sleeve. "Of course you can stay here—at least until you have a chance to talk to Arthur."

He bent his head and his voice was soft and humble. "I knew there were reasons why the people call you the most gracious of queens."

"I had the best of teachers," I quipped, refusing to let the scene become sentimental. He raised his head with a laugh, and I saw the flash of humor make his eyes lively again.

So I set about finding quarters for the druid as well, though my mind played constantly with the question of the ceremony. What was the Lady planning? What role would Agravain have? And how would the people respond? Finally I decided to attend the midsummer rite in secret and see for myself what my sister-in-law was up to.

"I don't like it, Gwen," Bedivere stated flatly when I confided what I meant to do. "Don't like it at all. Who knows what kind of plots she's hatching about you and Arthur? And she can be very persuasive—if you're discovered, she could whip the crowd into a frenzy against you."

His point was well taken, but with my lanky build and plain face, I'd been mistaken for a man more than once when I wore breeches and covered my hair with a cap. And since this was a matter that had to be attended to, the one-handed lieutenant finally gave in, agreeing to provide me with a hooded peasant's cloak if I promised to let Griflet come too. The Kennel Master has saved my life once before and, since he was not one of the better-known Companions, would not be likely to be recognized.

"But you must take a vow of silence," Bedivere warned him after he agreed to accompany me.

Griflet looked at me with great solemnity. "For the Queen's safety, I will not even tell my wife," he promised. Considering how close he and Frieda were, it struck me as a remarkably dear pledge.

News of the ceremony was sweeping through the countryside and soon became the talk of the household. Mordred immediately asked permission to take Cynric to the event.

"For all that you've become friends, the Saxon is still a hostage, and as such cannot leave the Court," I told him hastily, looking for an excuse to keep the two of them from Stonehenge; even an accidental penetration of my disguise could mean my life. "Arthur left him specifically in Bedivere's care. I will not go against that wish."

My stepson accepted my decision, but gave me one of his odd, unfathomable looks. Like his father and his Aunt Morgan, Mordred could drop an impenetrable mask across his feelings whenever he wanted to keep the world at bay. It seemed to be a family trait.

My foster sister, Brigit, had recently moved to the convent at Amesbury, which was quite close to Stonehenge, so I let it be known that I was going to visit her and would be away from Camelot for several days. Griflet and I left early in the morning, without fanfare or fuss, and had exchanged our courtly clothes for raggedy peasant costumes well before noon.

We let my old mare Featherfoot set the pace, and by the time we reached Amesbury we were just another pair of tired and dusty pilgrims among so many. It was evening when Griflet left the horses at a stables and we joined the flow of people making their way to the Standing Stones.

The Gods have left circles of upright stones all over Britain, but none are more sacred than the one known as Stonehenge. The huge, rough pillars stand three times the height of a man, and those that form the outer ring are topped by equally large lintels which bind them together to make an enormous circle. The Greeks assumed it was a temple to their sun god, Apollo, but we Britons know it as the Giant's Dance, and have no thought that it was the work of one God alone: even the most powerful of deities could not have erected such a structure without help.

In his youth Merlin had been commissioned to replace several of the stones that had fallen, and he made the place a monument to past Celtic heroes. But by the time the Magician had completed the task, his own father lay dead and buried beneath the Altar Stone. Years later Arthur's father was buried there as well, making it a kind of crypt for High Kings. Someday Arthur himself would be interred within the inner Sanctuary.

As we rounded the last gentle rise, the ragged stones came into view, looming stark above us against the evening sky. The majesty of the scene was breathtaking, but I stopped dead still at the sight of the whole panorama, for the entire circle of Stonehenge was ringed by campfires. Hundreds, perhaps thousands, of pilgrims were gathered around communal pots, sharing bowls of bubbling stew and filling the twilight with the sounds of laughter and dancing. It was a far bigger gathering than I had expected, and a chill of apprehension ran across my shoulders.

Pulling my hood well forward so that it hid my face, I trailed along beside Griflet, letting him do the talking for both of us. He greeted everyone affably, occasionally mentioning that we were brothers come up from the country to celebrate midsummer's dawn and see what miracle the Lady would perform. His story was readily accepted since everyone else had come for the same reasons.

There was much speculation as to what was going to happen, and quick glances flitted frequently toward the torchbearers Morgan had stationed at every arch of the outer circle. Whether they were there to keep the rabble out or to hold unspeakable powers within, they would stand in stony silence throughout the night. Some of our companions made the sign against evil, while others nodded reverently toward the Sanctuary, but I noticed that none made the sign of the cross. Perhaps the Christians had no desire to confront Morgan in her terrible rite.

Neither Griflet nor I wanted to join the revelry that would go on all night long, so we spread our bedrolls within the shadow of one of the monoliths and got what sleep we could.

In the coldest hour just before dawn we were wakened by a deep, somber tolling, as of a massive bell. Everyone began to run toward the great stones and as Griflet and I scrambled to our feet, the crowd surged past, carrying us with it. Somehow we became separated, and I found myself in the front row of observers, who were swept into the inner circle. The torchbearers had regrouped around the central precinct to keep the audience from advancing too close. They were big men, perhaps part of the cadre of bodyguards Morgan took everywhere, and my neighbors jostled for position in order to stare around them, trying to see through the horseshoe of rough pillars that surround the Altar Stone.

A pair of flambeaux had been placed at either end of the altar, and in the center of their light a dwarf was slowly and rhythmically swinging a two-handed hammer against a gong that stood taller than he was.

The sight made me shiver. Morgan's lieutenant had the powerful upper body of a smith, broad-shouldered and bull-necked, but his legs were so short that he only came up as high as the average man's ribs. Grim and determined, he accompanied the Lady of the Lake everywhere, and some said he loved her with a deep, if hopeless, passion.

When all the faithful had gathered, the dwarf let the last note of the gong fade out into the night. In spite of his size, he had an immense voice and shortly announced the arrival of Morgan le Fey, High Priestess of the Goddess and Lady of the Lake. The crowd hushed, straining forward to see, and murmured in wonder when my sister-in-law swept out of the shadows and leapt onto the flat table of the Altar Stone.

Always beautiful and petite, she stood still as a statue while the torchlight flickered over her long white robe. The wild, night-black cloud of hair that surrounded her face was unbound like a girl's, and a massive golden torc ringed her neck. Slowly she turned to address the whole circle, her arms extended in the traditional blessing, and once she had commanded all attention, she raised her hands to the starry sky in silent salute to the Goddess. As the sleeves of her gown fell back, I saw the golden serpent she had twined around one arm, and the flash of heavy enameled armbands on the other.

Standing there, taut as a bowstring, the High Priestess waited for the coming of the deity. I thought of the single purpose that binds priest and monarch together: both must be willing to offer their life as a bridge between the Gods and their people. In return we expect both loyalty and cooperation, readily given. Here the crowd responded fully, sending wave after wave of respect and love toward the Lady. At last she brought her arms down with a grand, sweeping gesture and, after calling the Goddess from every quarter of the horizon, began her prayers.

Morgan's voice was pure magic, swooping and soaring on the

air around us, reaching from the heights of heaven to the depths of earth as she called forth the Mother. Spellbound, the crowd followed her ritual as she paced about the altar, now sprinkling it with water from a special caldron, now flinging bits of incense into the embers of a thurible. For more than an hour she purified the holy precinct, built up walls of mystic protection, and prepared for the coming of the dawn.

As the eastern sky lightened, the giant stones seemed to coalesce into faint, pale mists that took silent shape in the darkness. Above them the great lintels hung in space, suspended between silvering heaven and darkling earth. We mortals in the middle drew together within their arc, trembling with hope and fear.

The High Priestess moved into a dance, turning in a slow, pulsing pattern to a music only she could hear. Her green eyes glazed as the trance took hold, guiding her feet, moving her faster and faster. She gave herself over to it until she became a whirling, spinning dervish, skin dripping with sweat and wild hair whipping out in strands like a head full of snakes.

"Send us Your blessing, O Matrix of Life," she panted. "Extend to us Your compassion, Your power, Your forgiveness!" She tossed her head back and forth, surrendering totally to the force of the Great One, and her voice grew in power as both body and spirit built to a crescendo. "Forgive Your son, Your poor blemished son who, in a moment of despair, took the life of her who bore him. Purge him of the Furies, make him whole and clean and new again. Raise him up, O Mother, raise him as You raise the sun!"

With a great sob she flung herself flat on the Altar Stone, her arms outstretched toward the entrance of the Hanging Stones. All eyes followed her gesture. There to the east, silhouetted against the midsummer sun that peeked over the horizon, the Heel Stone stood pointing like a black finger to heaven. Slowly, inexorably, the blinding silver disk lifted skyward, casting the long shadow of the outlier straight toward the High Priestess. An immense silence surrounded us as though the whole world held its breath while we waited, watching the shadow shrink as the sun climbed. And then the miracle occurred—uncoiling himself from the dark earth at the base of the Heel Stone, a man came slowly erect until he, too, stood black against the glory of flooding light.

"Agravain!" Morgan cried, and the crowd let out a long-drawn sigh as high overhead a lark began to sing. "Come forth and meet your brothers, who embrace you once again and forgive you the death of their mother."

Morgause's son paced slowly along the Avenue from Heel Stone to Altar, and the murmur that welled up from the assemblage grew into a chant.

"Agravain, Agravain!" they called, all attention riveted on the penitent. In that moment I cast a surreptitious glance at the High Priestess, and ice poured through my veins. Gareth, Gaheris and Mordred had joined her on the Altar Stone.

I stifled a cry of disbelief. Had I not expressly forbidden the boy to come? Or had he thought only Cynric was denied? How long had Mordred and his brothers been with Morgan, and what had she revealed to them? The prospect of the crowd hearing of Arthur's having lain with his sister brought tears to my eyes and pain to my stomach . . . incest is the most ancient of taboos, and who knew what punishment the people might demand?

By now Agravain had reached the Altar and knelt with abject humility before his siblings. Gareth reached out to him first, and between the two of them he and Mordred lifted the penitent to his feet. Bathed in the light of a new day, it was clear that all three faces were wet with tears.

When they came together in a familial embrace, a roar went up from the congregation. Relief and joy poured from every throat, swelling to a cry of triumph that filled the air. People were falling to their knees in grateful homage to the Goddess and I sank down as well, bowing my head forward until the hood completely covered my face. I dared not look up for fear one of the Orcadians would recognize me, so I waited, staring at the dark earth, sick with fear of what Morgan was about to unleash.

The crowd grew calmer, then silent with expectation, and Morgan sent a declaration ringing out over our heads.

"Would that your Queen were here! As your High Priestess I represent the Gods, but Gwenhwyvaer"—she let the ancient form of my name hang on the air—"Gwenhwyvaer represents you, the people. She should be here for you. She was invited, but chose not to come."

The crowd began to mutter, and my stomach tied itself in

knots. In my concern for Arthur I had not foreseen that Morgan would use this as an excuse to turn the people against me.

The voices around me were growing ugly, and I hunkered down farther, until my forehead touched my knees. I had heard the dreadful rumble of the mob when my father almost died, heard them crying for his life, knew the blood-lust mobs could feel.

Finally the wave of discontent crested and as it began to ebb, the Lady signaled for silence.

"At least we are fortunate to have the scions of the House of Lot before us. All, that is, save one."

Now she will lay bare the truth, I thought, feeling my gorge rise.

"And he, Gawain of the Bright Hair, heir apparent for the High King's position—he is off confronting the barbarians in France!"

A fine shout of approval spun above me as I lay, fists clenched and body drenched with sweat. I couldn't believe Morgan was calling the crowd's attention to Gawain, not Mordred. What possible reason could she have to meander through simple things when Mordred was her greatest weapon?

I swallowed hard against the bile in my throat. Was it possible she didn't know of Mordred's paternity? Or was she playing a longer, more vicious game, wherein she would set up the son to challenge the father later on?

Finally, when the congregation had had their fill of applauding the sons of Lot, the crowd began to stir restlessly, wanting to disperse. So Morgan gave them a final blessing and sent them on their way.

The people began to mill around me, but I lay crumpled in a heap, wrung out and exhausted by what might have been. Griflet came to my side almost immediately and dragged me, weak and wobbly, to my feet. "Told you to leave off that wineskin," he bellowed as he slung my arm over his shoulder. "What sort of fellow are you, getting drunk at a holy celebration? Why, if you weren't my brother . . ."

I hung my head and let him carry me along, staggering now and then as though I'd been trampled physically as well as mentally, and when we got the horses from the stable, Griflet insisted we go directly to Brigit's convent.

"Lord help us, what have you been doing to yourself?" my foster sister cried when she saw me. "Queen or no Queen, you can't be any use to anyone when you're this unstrung." With a flurry of efficiency she had me undressed and put to bed immediately, and told Griflet I was not to consider traveling until the next day.

So I lay back on the pillows in the guest bed, grateful for the familiar, gentle bossing of the woman who was the closest thing I had to mother or sister. How many times she'd come to my aid—whether bandaging up childhood cuts or keeping me alive during my illness after the rape, it was Brigit who had always known what to do and done it well.

Once I was settled and my foster sister sat down beside me, I related the whole adventure, though without mentioning that Mordred was Arthur's son.

When I finished, Brigit's face folded into a frown. "Morgan has always resented you—at least since the moment you married Arthur. How it must have rankled to see her mother favor you above either of her own daughters! Oh," she added when I started to protest, "I know they had been estranged for years, and you did nothing to cause the rift. But what with her anger over that and the fact that if it hadn't been for Arthur, her own husband might have become High King, Morgan no doubt still thinks she has ample reason to wish you ill."

The Irish girl looked down at me and softly shook her head. "Between your own willfulness and the moira the Gods gave you, it seems you'll always be tempting fate."

I managed a grin of sorts, wondering if she'd forgotten that as a Christian she wasn't supposed to believe in the Old Gods. A wisp of bright red hair had strayed from under her veil, and I reached up to brush it back, teasing that she was forever seeing boggarts and hobgoblins lurking in the shadows.

"Be that as it may," she answered, hastily crossing herself, "we both know how cunning Morgan can be. I want you to promise that if things get too difficult—or unsafe—at Camelot, you'll come stay with me, wherever I happen to be."

"Of course," I assured her, never dreaming it would come to pass. "But only if you will promise the same, and let us shelter you if you need it."

So we made the pact, and when I was ready the next day, parted with a fond hug.

"Don't forget," she admonished as I swung into the saddle, "to give my best to Arthur when he returns. You know I pray for his well-being daily."

I smiled down at the freckled face and dancing green eyes, thinking how lucky I was to have such a close friend. And on the way home I made a little prayer of my own to the White Christ —after all, it couldn't hurt to ask both the known and unknown deities to send my husband home safe and sound.

14

Distant Kings

ust as you said, his hair hangs all the way to his ankles." Arthur paused to give me one of his side-wise looks.

"No . . ." I shook my head in amazement, and he burst out laughing.

"Well, maybe not quite *that* long. But you were right about Clovis being a scoundrel. Tyrant, assassin, opportunist, bully—and sly. Very, very sly. And to top it off, he loves practical jokes!"

Arthur stretched contentedly. The boat from the Continent had barely made it across the Channel before the autumn gales set in, sending the men riding hard from Dover to Camelot as the weather darkened. They arrived at the Hall just before the evening meal, and now, after a good night's rest, my husband and I were catching up on the news before getting out of bed.

I glanced at Arthur, glad that the trip had been such a success. He'd returned happy as a boy with a creel full of fish, overflowing witn news and comments and ideas.

"Those Franks started out as a bunch of nomads—just another tribe of barbarians who became Federates of Rome, taking shelter on the Empire's border in return for fighting off invading Goths. But after the enemy had been chased over the Pyrenees, one way or another Clovis got rid of the other Federate leaders. Now he's set himself up as king of a sizable territory."

"And the Emperor didn't stop him?"

"By that time Theodoric had taken over Italy, so there wasn't anyone closer than Constantinople who might have reined him

"Indeed, lass." The High King of Britain stared at his hands, suddenly at a loss for words. Some inner struggle went on before he admitted, "Not only met with him, I apologized for having sent him away—maybe unfairly—after Morgan's attempt on my life. The lad has grown into a full-fledged man . . . and he was gracious about forgiving me."

"Oh, love, I'm so glad!" I threw myself across the bed, wrapping my arms around his shoulders from behind. "Truly, it was a fine, upright thing to do . . . and I'm proud of you."

"Thought you might be," he grumbled, then broke my embrace as he got to his feet. Relief in getting through the ordeal was plain in his voice. "And you can be proud of him, too. The boy you set to work caring for the horses has become famous as an animal doctor. One hears stories everywhere about his deeds—they even say he took a thorn from the paw of a lion and the beast follows him around like a pet."

"A lion!" The trip was sounding more and more interesting, and I began to regret I hadn't gone along. "Did you see it?"

"Um-hm." Arthur reached for his breeches. "The only lion I saw was the one painted on his shield. But then, you know how stories like that spring up."

I sighed and climbed out of bed myself, secretly sorry the lion wasn't real. Uwain deserved something special to make up for the injustice we had dealt him, and a pet lion would have been just the thing.

The Hall was overflowing for dinner that night, full of the good cheer that comes of greeting comrades home. Arthur reported on his stay in Paris—a hodgepodge place of brick and stone perched on a pair of islands in a river called the Seine—and the precarious balance of power between Clovis the Frank and King Theodoric in Italy. The Frankish leader continually threatened to grab off adjoining territories while the Goth sat in his splendid capital in Ravenna and checked his every move. And both were recognized by Anastasius while we were not.

"If you ask me," Arthur concluded, "the Emperor in Constantinople is using each to keep the other in line. So far it's worked to our advantage: Clovis is too distracted by Theodoric to harry the men of Brittany."

"Thank goodness," Bors interrupted. The colorful blond Breton flexed his muscles as he reached for another chunk of venison. "If that weren't the case, I'd be home defending my father's borders instead of enjoying a place at the Round Table. By the way, has anyone heard anything about Lancelot while we were gone?"

The question dropped like a stone through water, and I felt the scab of forgetfulness ripped off the old wound. After two years there was still no word, and hope of finding the missing Champion alive had grown dim.

There was a general murmur of demuring, and Bors's brother, Lionel, spoke up in his slow, deliberate way. "I think I shall go south to look for him. No one's checked that area yet."

Although there was nothing to draw Lance to the south, I had to admire the mulish sense to the man's logic. But having made that declaration, he lapsed back into his customary silence, and a pall began to settle over the Hall.

"It's important not to take those Continental bastards too lightly," Gawain said quickly, shifting attention back to the European trip. "They may claim to be the heirs of Rome, but they've naught in the way of honor."

"Ha!" Arthur chided his nephew affectionately. "Between their honor and your hotheadedness, we almost had a war on our hands!"

There followed an account of Gawain's encounter with an envoy from Rome, in which the Orcadian tweaked the beard of an upstart diplomat. The warriors cheered their favorite as the story spun out, full of pride that one of their own had shown the effete remnants of the dying Empire what a real Briton could do.

"Took all the skill I had to smooth it over," Arthur whispered to me. "Heaven help us if the Orcadians ever slip the rein I keep on them."

I studied my husband, wondering what he would think of the news about Agravain and the Lady. So far I had not mentioned it to anyone, not wanting my own presence at Stonehenge exposed. Now I debated how to tell him what had happened, and when.

But Gareth brought the subject up that night, pleased and proud to recount how his sibling had been forgiven not only by the family but also by the Goddess. "Pledged himself to serve the

Great Mother for the rest of his days," Morgause's son averred. "He would like to return to his place in the Fellowship, Your Highness, if you'll have him. And as his brother, I do humbly beg you consider his request."

Arthur's face was a study in conflict, mirroring his rage at Morgan's defying his edict against her coming to Logres, then his recognition that the Companions would be glad to see Agravain reinstated. In the end he bowed to Gareth's gentle urging, suggesting that the culprit need only ask our forgiveness for having broken the peace. But the next day, when Arthur and I bent to the tasks of ruling the realm, I brought up the question of the man's involvement in Pellinore's death.

"It would be as hard to prove as the stories about the Green Man," my husband countered, pushing back from the long table spread with maps and reports. "Agravain claims amnesia, and there's no more than circumstantial evidence linking him to the murder. Just because he was in the area isn't sufficient reason to bring him to trial, though I grant you, he bears close watching in the future."

I snorted at the understatement, thinking that Arthur's concepts of justice might prove to be a double-edged sword if a likely felon was let free in the name of fairness. At least, I told myself, it should protect the innocent from being found guilty of unwarranted charges.

Arthur had brought home several new warriors from Brittany, making sleeping space harder than ever to come by. I blessed the fact I'd made extra mattresses, converted a portion of the guest rooms to a woman's dormitory, and even accepted Griflet and Frieda's offer to share the Kennel Master's quarters. It was Bors and his brother who bunked with them, fitting right in with the homey domesticity of the little house. Frieda was pregnant again, growing riper with each month, still chasing her energetic twins even as she made ready for the new bairn. Once I'd yearned deeply for a such a state; but now I watched my favorite Saxon with gladness for her pleasure rather than envy at my own lack. Time seemed to have drawn the sting from that sorrow.

Toward the end of April, when the rooks took to tumbling in the cloud-racked skies, Mordred and I strolled along the wooden platform that tops the great wall of Camelot. Since he'd become a squire, the morning lessons had come to an end, replaced by hours of sword practice, cavalry drills and the learning of battle tactics. What little time he had to spare was generally spent with the other squires or, more likely, with the towheaded hostage, Cynric. Looking at him as we turned to lean against the parapet, I realized he was well-nigh as tall as I was and taking on the cast of a man.

"It's as though he holds some kind of grudge against me for an offense I can't even remember," Arthur's son said softly. "Oh, I know he recognizes me as kin—Mama always said he must do that—but it's clear that of all his nephews, I am the one he wants least contact with." When he turned to face me, his brown eyes were full of doubt and confusion, and I caught my breath in fear of the question that was bound to follow. "Do you know why that should be, M'lady? Or if there's any way I can make amends?"

I held his gaze for a long minute, feeling my heart break with his innocence. *Damn it, Arthur, why did you always punish him for your own guilty conscience?* Anguish at the nakedness of the boy's pain, and the sure, dreadful knowledge that I would keep his father's secret at the expense of the lad's right to an answer, brought tears to my eyes, and I turned away with an oath. "Drat this wind, it blows dust in your eyes even on a clear day."

Mordred was immediately all concern, bringing out a handkerchief and offering to find the offending particle. I dabbed at my eyes, trying to say it was nothing while I struggled for composure. "Perhaps," I offered, "you should ask the King himself."

"Mmmh. . . ." The response was leaden with the knowledge it would do no good, and he turned back to the parapet with a sigh. The mask of unconcern settled over his features again, and I wondered if he'd seen through my ruse. At least it was clear he had no idea of the blood-tie between them. Then suddenly he was scowling, bent forward in concentration.

"There's riders down there." He pointed off toward the track that leads from the Roman Road to Camelot. "See, M'lady— coming on at a real clip. Too many to be Royal Messengers, but too fast for normal travelers."

I followed his gesture, picking out the tiny group that moved toward us at a canter. Without a banner to announce them, it was impossible to tell where they hailed from, but as they broke from cover at the foot of our hill, I caught sight of Lionel's insignia on one of the shields.

"Quick," I told my stepson, "go tell the King that Cei and Lionel are returning from the south." The two of them had headed off for Cornwall not two weeks back, hoping to see if King Mark knew anything of Lance's whereabouts. Considering the speed at which they approached, it was likely they were returning with news of import.

The two Companions burst into the Hall without even pausing to wash off the dirt and grime of the Road before reporting to their King. Lucan rushed forward to relieve them of their swords, but they brushed past him, hustling a third member forward between them. A long black veil swathed the small frame of the newcomer, and when they all three knelt before us, a woman's hand lifted the garment aside, and I saw her tear-stained face.

"Enid!" My exclamation filled the Hall as I leaned forward. "What on earth . . . ?"

"It's Geraint, Your Highness." Cei's normally caustic tone was tempered by the importance of his news. "The King of Devon has fallen in a battle against the Saxons."

Arthur stiffened beside me, and I saw Enid sway at the pronouncement. But she gripped Lionel's arm for support and spoke out firmly, determined to recount her husband's death with all the respect that was due him.

"He kept the peace for eight long years, and served Your Majesty's Cause well and faithfully. Never mind that the northerners chided him as having grown weak and womanly; he shrugged off such comments for the hollow posturing they were. But M'lord, when our spies reported Saxon longboats being beached— dragged ashore by armed men in mail, not moving up a river, waiting while their occupants pillaged some small steading— that's when Geraint donned his buckler and called for his house-guard. There was such fire in his voice, no one could doubt his bravery."

Enid could not go on, and she crumpled against Lionel. It was Cei who spoke up, his words rising over her quiet sobs.

"We'd arrived the day before, and when the news came, I tried to get him to wait for reinforcements from Bagdemagus and the men of Dorset. But Geraint was intent on engaging the enemy before they could establish a beachhead and hoped that if he took them by surprise, it could be kept to a skirmish rather than a pitched battle."

So Geraint and his warband swooped down on the invaders, and all through the afternoon the battle raged, now in the surf, now on the strand. Time and again the elegant King set upon the barbarians until the foam of the ocean turned red and the blood of the enemy ran down the flanks of the British horses. But neither could rout the other, and at dusk the two sides drew apart, retiring to makeshift camps at different ends of the beach. Cei was relieved, for he felt confident the morning would bring fresh warriors from Dorset.

A ghostly fog began to roll in, shrouding the shore like a damp, thick fleece. The men eyed it nervously, wondering what it hid, until a terrible voice boomed forth from its heart. "They say the King of Devon is only fit to stay at home with his head pillowed in his wife's lap," it jeered.

Geraint, who was taking off his armor, turned in rage at the words. Slipping on his bull-hide vest, he grabbed up shield and sword and called for a fresh horse. The light of battle flared on his brow, as though the Morrigan, great Goddess of blood-lust and death, had descended on him. He leapt to his mount and rallied his men, then with a bloody yell, charged into the dank, unholy mist.

A number of his warriors followed, but once inside that devil's brew, they could not tell friend from foe, and those that could staggered back to the safety of higher ground. Yet the sounds of terrible conflict came rumbling and screeching from the blanket of white, and many claimed the battle lasted well into the night. It seemed as though the very souls of Saxon determination and British defense were struggling for the future of Albion.

Cei paused in his story and swallowed hard. "When dawn came and the fog lifted, the entire beach was littered with the dead."

Invader and defender alike lay twisted in the grip of death, washed by the incoming tide, eyes vacant and staring. Tiny crabs nibbled at the edges of open wounds while the scavenging gulls screamed overhead. Even the barbarians wept to see the price of bravery, and before the remnants of Geraint's warband could claim his body, the enemy had seized it and laid it in state upon the proudest of their ships. "Hail to the bravest of foes, the most honorable of warriors," they chanted, paying him the greatest homage of their kind. With all solemnity they rowed the vessel across the water to a nearby headland.

"There they built a pyre, as is their fashion, and consigned the King of Devon to its flames, assuring him immortality in their legends as well as ours." Cei looked slowly around the circle of warriors and household that had gathered in the Hall. Tears streamed down his face and theirs, but when he turned back to Arthur, his voice was full of tragic triumph.

"A man who braves the mist of the unknown is a man of rare courage, Your Highness. In his death he brought further honor and renown to the Round Table, and we are fortunate to have called him comrade."

Arthur bowed his head in grief and a long wail of mourning filled the Hall. Through brimming eyes I watched the new widow, thinking it a cruel moira which brought about such needless death; if he had only waited till morning, the story would have been quite different. It struck me as ironic that the sensible, Romanized Geraint had been goaded into a foolish encounter in defense of that most Celtic of virtues, personal pride.

Later we held a ceremony of our own for the dead King, and I found a place for Enid to stay, since she had no desire to return to Exeter.

Arthur and Bedivere called a Council to determine who should take Geraint's place, and Bagdemagus of Dorset put forth Gwyn-lliw, a wily old warlord in command of one of the hill-forts in Dorset. He seemed a good enough choice, and Arthur was pleased when he agreed to take over the defense of Devon.

"But only after I've made sure there's not a single invading warrior left," Arthur announced bitterly. So by early summer he'd gone off to reinstate order along the south shore, leaving Bedivere and Gawain with me at Camelot.

The loss of Geraint lay like a pall upon the Court, and no one felt it more cruelly than Enid. I watched helplessly as she struggled to make sense of a senseless loss. "He was such a good monarch," she would say, as though debating with invisible forces. "Far better than creatures such as Mark in Cornwall or that new Vortipor that's taken over Agricola's throne. A man who cared about his people, who loved life and beauty and shared that love with noble and peasant alike. Why? Why should a king like that go to his death when toads and tyrants sit smug upon their satin cushions? I ask you, where is the fairness in that, M'lady? Where is it?"

I listened to her railing, offered what comfort I could, and was more than delighted when she asked to take over Vinnie's job of looking after my ladies-in-waiting. Since the girls came, got married and left to form their own households with alarming regularity, I barely got to know their names before they were off on a new life. Now I could turn them over to Enid and not have to think about them again.

As summer deepened, she began to find succor in daily talks with Father Baldwin. The priest was gentle and kindly, letting her rage at the moira which had struck down her husband in his prime, and reassuring her that the love of the White Christ cherished his spirit even after death. Perhaps I should not have been surprised when Enid asked to be baptized, though I worried her newfound religion would dull her quick wits with platitudes and silence the tongue that kept gods and men alike on their toes. On the last point I need not have feared, for Christian or Pagan, Enid would never be one to tiptoe around sleeping dogs.

Word from the south said that the invaders had melted away like the fog they came out of, though whether they had gone back across the North Sea or were being hidden and cared for by Federate farmers, no one could say. So Arthur decided to make a methodical search of all steadings from Winchester to the sea, insisting that individual landholders swear fealty to him and reassuring himself we were doing everything we could to keep the Federates under control. As a result, he probably would not be home for several more months.

It was dull news and predictable, given Arthur's distrust of the Saxons. News from the north was far more interesting, for the Green Man was said to have been sighted again.

"You'd think they'd go away and leave the poor thing alone," Enid commented. "It's probably just some poor demented scoundrel driven to madness by the ways of the world."

"Mad, maybe," Bedivere agreed. "But not necessarily a scoundrel. More than one just man has taken to the woods that way, managing to live on berries and clothed in animal skins."

"Be that as it may," Gawain mused as he methodically stropped his dagger along a leather belt. "These sightings could be the Master of the Fields come forth again. One never knows . . ."

I shot the Orcadian a quick glance. Always a cautious man where the Gods were concerned, he made the sign against evil before going on. "What say I take a party and go settle this problem once and for all?"

"And leave Camelot undefended?" Bedivere lifted an eyebrow of inquiry. "With Arthur off in the south, you're in charge of the warriors here at home."

Gawain flushed, embarrassed at having forgotten his first duty. "Well, someone should look into it," he muttered.

Bors had been twisting the ends of his elaborate mustaches, and he spoke up eagerly. "I'm not bound to stay here . . . I could go up through the Marches and have a look, and still be back by the time Arthur returns. And if this creature is all that they say, it will give me a chance to prove the power of Christ over Pagan fiends."

There was a murmur of assent, and Lionel suggested that he accompany his brother. "Been years since we've gone adventuring together," he opined.

Clearly both men were in need of something to do besides lounge around at Court, so after provisioning them with dried foods and jerky and a leather tent, Bedivere and I stood at the top of the cobbled drive and waved them on their way.

There was something childishly stirring about the cheerfulness with which they went in search of the supernatural, like boys on a lark. It was touching and amusing at the same time, and I looked up at the one-handed lieutenant and grinned.

That was, of course, before we came to know about the Green Man firsthand, and I was intensely curious as to what they would bring home.

15

Prayers

omeone once said that prayers are simply dreams grown older, and perhaps they were right. When we were young, Merlin's dream of a Britain grown strong and whole under a just king had filled us with fearless enthusiasm. Now that energy had been tempered by time and the knowledge that a man can die in a skirmish as easily as in a battle. Geraint's death brought home how fragile we all are, so I prayed daily that Arthur's work among the Federates would end well and he'd be home soon.

I prayed for others, too: for Lance, in whatever lands he wandered; for Mordred, who did not even know the shadow that stalked him; and for Bors and Lionel, trying to trap the supernatural with a fine bravado. All the Old Gods—Brigantia and Cernunnos, Mabon and even the Horse Goddess, Epona—were hounded by my entreaties that summer.

Then, as autumn netted the land in gold and the bracken turned copper on the hills, my prayers were answered.

"Make way—make way for the King's men!" The sentries rushed to swing the massive gates open and sent a page flying up the hill to me. He found me in the kitchen, wrapping cheeses in waxed linen for winter storage.

"Quick, M'lady. It's Bors and Lionel returned, with a litter between them and a wild man strapped to it. Raving, he is, like some ferocious beast."

I dropped what I was doing and ran to the steps of the Hall, wiping my hands on my apron. People were pouring out of every door—ladies from the spinning room, grooms from the stables.

Even Cook was close on my heels. We ran down the drive to where the curious formed a knot around the newcomers. The little crowd jostled this way and that, then parted as the Bretons' squires pushed them back. A ragtag entourage emerged from the press.

Bors and Lionel advanced up the steep incline. They kept the horse between them moving at a steady pace, constantly checking the travois that trailed behind them. Lamorak of the Wrekin walked beside it, his hand resting on his sword hilt while his eyes scanned the crowd. I wondered if he worried that Gawain and his brothers would attack him even in the King's stronghold.

"A fiend. They've caught a fiend," one of the more excitable pages cried. "Maybe it's the Green Man."

"But it t'ain't green at all," argued his companion. "Just dirty and bleeding."

"Watch out!" someone warned as the bundle on the litter thrashed about. "He could break his bounds."

Fear and amazement silenced the onlookers, and many among them made whatever holy sign their Gods gave them for safety. By the time I reached the little party, everyone else had stepped back in awe, waiting to see what would happen.

"Lamorak found him in Clun Forest," Bors announced, halting his horse and swinging out of the saddle. He took my arm and murmured softly, "It's a terrible sight, M'lady. Mayhap you want to wait until we get him cleaned up a bit."

But I brushed past him, drawn toward the creature by a force I did not question. The smell was rank—not only was he dirty and unkempt, festering sores oozed on one leg and gruesome bruises covered his arms. The triangular face was slashed across, swollen and furrowed with dried blood. Groaning deliriously, he moved his head constantly from side to side, and when he opened his eyes, they focused on nothing at all. But the blueness of them blinded me.

"Lance . . . oh, Lancelot, what happened to you?" My knees went weak and Bors tightened his grip on my arm.

"Most likely a bear," my escort said. "Seems to have been some time back, for he was in this state when Lamorak chanced on him during a hunt. We met them on the Road. This was the only way he could be transported, he's raving that bad."

Tears of joy and anguish poured down my cheeks, and I

reached toward the pitiful shape that struggled at the brink of death, only to have Bors pull me back sharply.

"He's out of his head, M'lady, and might harm you. We need to take him to the stables and put him in a box stall until he's well enough—or worn out enough—to let us see to his wounds."

They were words well chosen, but I flung them aside. "Nonsense. This is the finest warrior of the realm, the Queen's own Champion. Do you think Arthur would countenance his being kept in a barn?" I drew myself up fully and looked from Bors to Lionel and Lamorak. "Take him into the Hall. We'll build up a fire and care for him there."

The men hesitated for a fraction of a moment, and Gawain, who was just arriving from the lower pasture, stepped to my side. "You heard Her Majesty," he thundered, glaring with particular severity at Lamorak.

So we struggled into the Hall, where I ordered a clean pallet be found and laid out on one of the trestle tables close by the hearth.

"Cook's going to find it in the way," Lynette ventured.

"She'll manage," I snapped, unable to think of anything but Lance. He was almost as big as Lamorak, and strong as well, so it took all the men present to restrain him as they lifted him onto his new bed and pulled the broad leather straps tight.

"The surgeon is with Arthur in the south," Gawain reminded me. "We'll need to find another healer."

I opened my mouth to order Morgan le Fey be brought, but closed it hastily in frustration—if only her damnable scheming hadn't made her an enemy!

Nimue came to mind next, but she'd gone with Arthur also, determined that the people should know that the successor of Merlin still guarded the Pendragon's reign.

"Brigit," I said decisively, looking about for Griflet. "My sister in the convent. She's a fine medic and must be sent for at once." Then, remembering that a member of a holy house was no longer subject to royal authority, I amended the command. "Ask her, for the love she bears her God, to get permission to attend this man."

Griflet nodded and ran out of the room. I could count on his being on the Road within the half hour.

"Where's Palomides?" The Arab had often assisted the surgeon on the battlefield, and I was sure he had brought back powders and unguents from the East that could help us now. When he came to my side, I asked for something to make Lancelot sleep, and before long he returned with a syrup that was heavy with the smell of poppies.

"Opium," he explained, looking dubiously at Lance, who still groaned and occasionally strained against the straps that held him secure. "But it should be swallowed. . . ."

I tore a strip of linen from my shift and twisting it into a wick, sopped up as much of the syrup as it would hold, then turned and perching on the edge of the table, leaned over Lancelot.

Under the matted beard his lips were cracked and dry, and his eyes glazed with fever, but drop by drop I coaxed the sedative between his lips. Half the time he turned away, so that the liquid trickled into his beard, but I simply gave him more, confident that sooner or later it would take effect. Time ceased to have any meaning as I sat there, determined to keep my love from death.

When his breathing steadied to that of sleep, I bathed his wounds myself, soaking the dirt and pus from the raw skin, applying the leeches when Lynette brought them from the pond. The filthy rags that clung to his body were cut away, each sore addressed, each bruise salved. It was a long and difficult process that seemed to last forever but I focused on one small patch at a time, working tirelessly until that one was taken care of, then moving on to the next. Days and nights could have passed, for all I knew.

Finally, when he was made as clean and comfortable as I could manage, I ordered my carved chair be brought from the dais and set beside his bed. Weary to the bone, I sank into it. Enid wanted me to go upstairs to sleep, but I waved her away, too tired even to speak. When Cook pressed a cup of broth into my hands, I took it blindly and sipped the steaming nourishment as my mind wandered.

Just so I had seen Mama, in the days before her death, tending the sick and dying who had come to our Hall for succor the year that plague and famine struck. Worn to a wraith, she had given every last ounce of energy—and finally life itself—to the people who needed her. She had many patients while I had only one, but I would pour as much of myself into keeping that one alive as she had in trying to save all who counted on her. Her actions were fueled by the pact between monarch and subject, whereas mine came from personal love as well as duty. Yet we both drew on a depth of strength rarely tapped, and I drifted into a doze with her last words whispering in memory: "Once you know what you have to do, you just do it."

How long that vigil lasted, I have no idea. Trancelike, I moved between waking and sleeping, barely noticing if it was day or night. Bedivere saw to managing the Court, Gawain handled the men, sending them on to hunt or help the locals with the harvest, and between them Enid and Cook kept the women busy. Lamorak, I was told later, began the return trip to the Wrekin as soon as he'd seen Lance safely home.

Whereas in the past I prayed only in the evening, now I sent constant petitions to every God I'd ever heard of, from Cybele of Syria to Wodan of the Swedes, pleading for Lance's life.

Let him live, oh please let him live, I begged. It doesn't matter about me—he needn't love me anymore, needn't even remember me, if it comes to that. Just let him live. I'll stay away from him, if he wishes, and ask nothing more than foregiveness for having been so unfairly cruel. He can go off to Elaine and the babe at Carbonek, if that's his will. . . . I'll not stand between him and his moira again. Just let him live. Dear God, let him live.

The litany went round and round in my head as Lance's fever mounted and his delirium deepened. Brigit arrived just before the crisis, bringing her knowledge along with a satchel full of salves and powders. She checked him over with crisp efficiency and allowed that I had done an admirable job of caring for him so far.

"Now it is truly up to God," she added, putting her hand over mine. "You might try praying to the Christ."

It was the only time she ever coaxed me toward her faith, and I looked at her hopelessly as I answered. "I already have—and to his Mother, too."

"I might have known," she whispered, giving my fingers a reassuring squeeze.

The fever broke that night, and by morning the delirium was gone. I left him in the Irish girl's capable hands and threw myself across my bed, too exhausted even to undress. I suppose it was Enid who did that for me, for I awoke at noon the next day, safe under the down comforter and well rested.

It was still a while before Lancelot regained consciousness. I sat beside him, sometimes doing handiwork, sometimes just remembering the hours he'd sat by me when I was recuperating from the rape. A tie to sanity, he'd been, as I wandered through nightmare dreams. Now it was my turn to be the same for him.

Life in the Hall went on all around us, making space for the sick bed and the Queen like the waters of a river eddying around a stone. Cook did indeed grumble about having him so close to her cooking area, but I noticed she'd pause now and then to look at him, shaking her head in amazement that he still lived. And on a fine, Indian-summer afternoon she bustled in from the kitchen, smelling of fresh air and new-mown hay.

"The farmers brought him a corn dolly to give him strength," she announced, climbing on a stool and hanging the charm from one of the pot hooks on the wall. I nodded my thanks, staring at the age-old symbol of completed harvest. Everyone, from Pagan peasant to Christian nun, was rallying to Lance's side, each bringing his or her own bit of energy to the great pool that kept him alive. It occurred to me that in their own ways, they loved him as much as I did.

It was then I felt his eyes on me, soft as a caress along the cheek. And when I turned toward him, his blue gaze never faltered, but drank in my presence with quiet solemnity.

Oh Glory, I thought suddenly, what if he hates me for all the things I said before he left? The idea stilled my heart, and I stared back at him, hardly daring to breathe.

The faintest of smiles crept first to his eyes, then to the full, rich mouth half hidden in his beard. Without a word he extended his hand and I grasped it in my own, drawing it in under my chin and pressing my lips to our intertwined fingers. Neither of us spoke, or looked aside, but let the years of fear and separation melt away in that long, silent gaze. Worlds of terror and bereavement slipped away, and the bright, dazzling knowledge of the love neither could forswear rose up between us. A single tear dropped from my cheek.

"Now that's a good sign," Brigit said cheerfully, coming to stand between us and the rest of the Hall. She was bringing me a cup of soup, but bent instead to lift Lance's head from the pillow and raised the cup to his lips. "Let's get some nourishment into you, Sir."

He drank a little before leaning back and closing his eyes again. But as he drifted back to sleep, his hand found mine again, and we sat together through the evening that way.

So began the long convalescence. The sores healed slowly, the raking from the bear's claws left only moderate scars, and a plaster of comfrey root helped the broken ribs knit whole as time progressed. At first he was content just to lie wakeful, staring into the fire or watching me while I spoke of little things—the boar Dinadan had brought in from the forest, the news that Arthur would be returning soon, the story of Gareth's encounter with Ironside.

As the days passed, he grew restless to sit up, and before long I found his bed surrounded by friends and Companions, each bringing news of the years since he'd been gone. I still sat beside him as the shadows of night closed down, and came to share a private moment or two when I first woke, but for the most part life was moving back to normal. And by the time Arthur arrived, Lance was able to move about, albeit gingerly.

"Best sight I've seen in years," my husband exclaimed, striding across the room to where Lance stood with the help of a cane. "I can't tell you how splendid it is for all of us."

"No less so for me, M'lord," the lieutenant answered, trying to go down on one knee.

"No you don't," Arthur burst out, catching him midway. "Half-starved or not, you're still too big for me to lift comfortably." For a moment I thought he would clap his friend on the back, but the Breton's evident weakness stayed his arm, so he slung it around Lance's shoulders instead. "Now, come join me at the table and tell me where all you've been."

It was a subject no one else had broached, and when I took my place beside Arthur, I was of two minds about it. Curiosity prodded me to find out what he'd done, where he'd gone, what he remembered. But the sheer pleasure of having him home, and the fear that he might recall I was to blame for his misadventures, made me hope he would keep silent.

As it was, Lance simply shook his head. "I started off in search of something—maybe my soul, maybe the meaning of life; after so long a time, I cannot remember clearly. Since I had no way to get to Egypt, where such a search can be conducted in the desert, I did the next best thing—went into the wildwood. It is almost as dangerous, and certainly as remote from humankind. But whatever spiritual lessons I set out to learn, before long the mere question of survival took precedence. Perhaps I grew sick, or crazed, or both. The very notion of coming face-to-face with another human terrified me, and I moved further into the forest, sleeping in caves and coming out only at night. From there on I don't recall much, until the bear. She was a huge, angry sow who thought me too near her cubs and swiped me heavily along one side. Before I could recover my balance, she dragged me into an all but fatal embrace. . . ." He shuddered and gave me a lopsided smile. "Definitely not as friendly as the dancing bear at Caerleon."

A twinge of regret went through me, and I realized he had no way of knowing that poor animal was dead.

"I . . . I don't remember much after that," Lance concluded, "until I came to, here in Camelot, and thought at first I'd attained the heaven Christians tell about."

"And well come you are, friend," Arthur noted, raising his drinking horn in a toast. "To the pair of fine Companions who found their cousin when they went in search of adventure in the name of the Round Table. To the Fellowship, made whole again by the return of my lieutenant. To the peace in the south, with new administrators overseeing the Federates. And to the years ahead—may we all continue to grow and prosper."

Everyone drank to that, though I quaffed water rather than the wine Cei was sharing all around. It was a fitting end to a long, harrowing ordeal, and a fine beginning to a new life, not only for Lance and me, but for the Fellowship as a whole.

16

Mosaic

'*ve never seen the famous glass mosaics that Palomides spoke of, never gaped at pictures floating in the air or shimmering with gold. But I have lived with rainbows, and gasped at the fire that leaps into being when a field of winter weeds turns from white frost to blazing prism as the sun touches it . . . and when I remember the years after Arthur's return from France and Lance's having been found alive, it is like standing in the heart of all those colors, and more.*

In the spring after Arthur's visit to Clovis, Bedivere left for the Continent to represent us at that Court and to keep an eye on the safety of Brittany's borders.

"He's always been my best diplomat," Arthur noted as the one-handed Champion waved good-bye from the deck of the ship casting off from London's busy wharf.

And outside of Merlin, your most trusted friend, I thought. Certainly we were in need of such an envoy, for Gawain's set-to with the Roman ambassador had left us with a ragged reputation on the Continent.

"Mordred's rather at loose ends since Bedivere left," Lance commented a week or so later.

We were in the garden of the Imperial Palace, where I was trying to espalier a pear tree against the remnant of a south-facing wall. I had honored my promise to the Gods, letting Lance set the distance between us. He was quieter and even more thoughtful than before his disappearance, but the underlying trust and understanding between us was still there. I could not ask for a dearer friend or a more faithful Champion, and although the love still burned, we were careful not to let the fever rise.

"I thought maybe Arthur would take a hand in Mordred's training," Lance added.

"So did I." I stepped back and squinted at our work, then sighed. "It's an unlikely dream, you know . . . hoping that Arthur will ever accept the boy."

"Maybe that's understandable, given the circumstances." As always, Lance spoke discreetly. Although Arthur had confided the secret of Mordred's parentage to his lieutenant, the dark-haired Breton never mentioned it directly.

I nodded, remembering Arthur's comment the first time I chided him about not taking a more active interest in his son: "Ah, lass, don't ask me to be all things to all people, and I'll not ask it of you." To fault the finest King in the Western world for not being a good father might well be considered unreasonable.

"Perhaps I can fill the gap," Lance suggested. "Since Gareth's on his way to becoming a Champion, I'm in need of a new squire. Mordred has as much promise as his brother—maybe more—and it would be a pity to let his education slip to the point where he couldn't stand at the High King's side."

Thus Lancelot became the mentor of my stepson. Watching him help the lad refine a stroke, hone his blade or check the tack for his horse, I couldn't help wondering if Lance dreamed of the day when his own son, Galahad, would be old enough for such instruction.

At the end of the Round Table meeting in London, Lynette and Gareth married. Nimue was there to perform the Bride's Blessing, just as she had blessed me before my wedding to Arthur, and Cathbad, who was now part of our household, performed the ceremony. We threw the gates of the Imperial Palace open to all who would come, as the groom was a favorite among the Fellowship, and since Lynette's father was the Grounds Keeper at the Palace, everyone in London fancied himself a friend of the bride.

I stood by the fountain, greeting our guests and thinking with pride that under our rule London had gone from a decaying ruin to a thriving British center. Although Arthur refused to let Saxon boats use the harbor, fearing they would bring arms and sedition, the barbarians who lived in the City and nearby villages were peaceable enough. Many turned out for the wedding, and when the circle dance started, all joined in, regardless of their backgrounds. In the center the gamin bride ducked her head as Gareth bent to kiss her, and squealed with delight when he picked her up and carried her into their private chambers. Some things, it occurred to me, never change.

We wintered over in the City, in part because Arthur wanted to complete the repairwork on Caesar's Tower that tops a knoll in the far corner of the city walls. I had hoped he would let it be; once before, when he was shoring up the walls of the thing, a skull had been unearthed, and immediately the Druids claimed it was that of the Old God Bran. They still looked askance at what they considered a desecration of their relic, and chided us for the irreverence. But Arthur wanted to make the Tower secure, and considering that it commanded both the riverfront and the hinterlands beyond the fort's wall, I couldn't blame him.

With the coming of spring we decided to fulfill our promise to visit Wehha at his holdings in East Anglia. Lancelot was anxious to get back to Joyous Gard to see how it had fared during his time in the forests, so Arthur gave him a fine new stallion named Invictus, and we waved him on his way up Ermine Street, while we turned to ride east toward Colchester.

Mordred and Cynric came with us, and even though Arthur and I had mastered the rudiments of the Saxon tongue, we promoted the peace-hostage to the rank of interpreter.

Outside of Colchester we stopped at Gosbeck, where the yearly fair was in progress. Here in East Anglia the Saxons were able to land their goods, and the market was full of items from the Continent as well as those things from the Mediterranean which had been carted overland from the wharves at London.

Not only the goods but also the venders were of every description, which made for a colorful scene. The blond Swedes and fair-skinned Angles displayed their gorgeous goldwork pieces. A swarthy Greek touted his selection of olive oil and dried figs to northern residents who hadn't the vaguest concept of the sunny lands they came from, while someone else presented a selection of Egyptian bronzeware decorated with blue enamel. We ourselves caused something of a stir as Palomides and his turbaned squire strolled by, the hooded falcon perched on the Companion's gauntlet.

I watched Mordred and Cynric, the one so dark and the other

so blond, moving among the stalls—now flirting with a wench, now joking between themselves. With any luck, I thought suddenly, this could be the face of the future, when Saxon and Celt put aside their fears and see each other as brothers.

Later we climbed the steep road to Colchester's fort, marveling at the ruins of a huge Roman temple, and ate our oysters in the shadow of some Caesar's statue.

"Makes you wonder, doesn't it?" Arthur mused, staring at the weathered face. "Merlin once told me Claudius was a stammering, limping scholar who had little intention of becoming Emperor. Yet they made him a God in Colchester."

I caught the wry look on my husband's face. "I wouldn't want to be an Empress if divinity came with it," I allowed, and we both laughed.

Compared with Colchester, Wehha's stronghold was small and primitive. Like most of the immigrants who came across the North Sea in shallow, open boats, his people brought little with them but their hopes for the future. And like other such leaders, Wehha had worked his way up a river till he found a place totally removed from both Roman city and British farm. I've noticed that whether they were carved from the clay lowlands in the south or set, as Wehha's was, on a sandy heath smelling of salt marsh and tidal flat, the barbarian settlements were always wrapped in isolation and self-sufficiency. Perhaps there's something in the Teutonic soul that needs such circumstances to make them feel at home.

The sentry atop the stockade had seen us coming from a distance, and when we arrived at the gate, it was Wuffa, Wehha's arrogant son, who greeted us.

"My father is dying," he announced once we were inside the heavy wooden wall. "It would please him to see you."

Arthur nodded and swung down from his horse as Wuffa turned away, never even acknowledging my presence. For a moment I thought I would be forced to join the women in their separate quarters, but I slid my arm through Arthur's and, holding my head high, accompanied him to the Hall in spite of Wuffa's scowl. Wehha might relegate his women to the kitchen, but I was High Queen of Britain, and intended to pay the Swede the respect he was due on his deathbed.

A hush fell as we crossed the compound. Stablehands and sculleries stared at me as though I were a ghost. Even the guards standing at attention beside the Hall's main door blinked at the notion of a woman walking next to the High King. But when we stood before Wehha, the dying Swede turned his tired eyes on me, and I caught the echo of a smile in them.

"The British Queen honors me," he whispered before turning his attention to Arthur.

The robust figure was barely discernible under a heap of furs and blankets. His once-florid face now looked like a death's-head skull, for it was the wasting sickness that was claiming him. When he reached out a palsied hand, the fingers were little more than knobby sticks. Yet his presence was still commanding, and for all that he was surrounded by servants and doctors plying him with possets and fussing at his pillows, one still knew he was a powerful leader.

"I have told Wuffa he must always support the Pendragon," the dying man affirmed. Arthur had to lean close to hear his words, and while they spoke, I looked about the Hall.

The wooden walls were hung with banners and shields, a large bearskin and numerous pelts of wolves. Firelight gleamed off the fine wood and glinted on the spears that were stacked neatly by the door, being ready to hand if the warriors had need. The hounds that slept around the hearth were sleek and healthy, and another, probably Wehha's favorite, lay near his bed, head resting on paws, eyes never moving from his master's face. In all the steading this was the creature which would grieve the most when the man's spirit left him behind.

Near the bed, on a stand where it served as a tabletop, was the large silver tray from Constantinople that Arthur had given Wehha in recognition of his loyalty to us. I was glad that, if he couldn't die in battle, at least the Swede was surrounded by the warmth of caring retainers and the treasures he'd collected.

Wehha's energy was ebbing so we didn't stay long, and after leaving the compound, rode along the river path in subdued silence. As the Deben flows toward its estuary, it runs beneath a bluff, and Arthur gestured to the windswept height. "That's where he wants to be buried. They will lay him out in the ship that brought him across the North Sea and build a barrow over it so that future generations will remember that he founded his dynasty here."

Even now I find it a touching thought, though Wehha's ridge was a bleak place from which to confront eternity. At the time it made me glad I was born a Briton and would not be buried on a lonely shore in a land not even my own. No matter where they scatter my ashes, I will be home in Albion.

We spent a summer with Mark and Isolde of Cornwall, staying at Castle Dore, which nestles above one of those jewellike bays along the Cornish coast.

Isolde of Cornwall, daughter of the Queen of Ireland and wife to the jealous, aging King Mark. Beautiful, willful—she and her lover, Tristan, had turned their kingdom upside down with their grand romance. It would not have mattered had Mark not been a fanatical Christian, unwilling to allow his child-bride the freedom to her bed that any other Celtic queen was given.

Yet for all that I once thought her nothing more than a spoiled darling, I had grown to like Isolde when she and Tristan fled Cornwall and sought sanctuary with Arthur and me in Logres. During that time we'd become close friends and exchanged many confidences. Eventually, when Mark threatened to make war on Arthur if she didn't return, Isolde had ended the relationship with Tristan and returned to her duties as Queen of Cornwall. Over the years any number of warriors—including Palomides—had developed hopeless passions for her, but after she gave up Tristan, she never looked at another man. Whether it was out of loyalty to Mark or Tris, I never asked.

"It's passable," she said, referring to her life at present. "I've been studying the healing arts for some time now—Mark grows cranky as his years add up, and this gives me something to do that doesn't make him jealous. Then, too, there's plenty of trade with my people in Ireland, which means visitors and envoys of all kinds. And sometimes travelers bring me news from the Continent." Her lovely violet eyes returned my gaze with candor. "I have heard that Tristan married a Breton girl who is also named Isolde. If so, I wish them well and hope they have many children."

It was a gentle comment, made by a woman grown wise in her years, and I smiled at my friend.

"But what of you and Lancelot?" she asked, smiling in return. "How does the other famous pair of the day?"

"The same as ever. Close, without touching. He's been gone recently, acting as envoy for us among the northern tribes. The chieftains beyond the Wall respect him; they call him the Man of Honor."

One dark brow lifted gracefully, and Isolde shook her head. "I have never really understood what all this fuss over honor is about . . . which was, no doubt, part of the problem with Tris."

"No doubt," I concurred. It was their lack of honor that had so shocked the world. Swept up in a "fated love," they had stooped to all forms of lying and duplicity in order to continue meeting, never honestly admitting the affair that everyone else tittered over. Until they ran away together, that is.

"No two people should love each other the way we did," she said softly. "And it's good that he's in Brittany. I'm not sure I could go on being Cornwall's Queen if he were closer."

The admission came from some deep, central part of her and was doubly poignant because I knew how thoroughly she had been trained to consider the needs of her people first. No queen leaves her throne except under the direst of circumstances—or when the country's security demands it.

"I notice there's quite a contingent of young men with white shields in your entourage." Isolde changed the subject gracefully, turning to look out at the men preparing for a display of horsemanship. "Isn't that something new?"

"The Queen's Men," I responded. "Made up of warriors who have vowed to serve me until such time as war crops up. It began with the youngsters who followed Lance about everywhere, and when he took Mordred as his squire, they became a sort of informal cadre with Gareth and Mordred at their head."

"They make a pretty sight," the Irish beauty mused.

And a gay one, with their bright colored pennants flying as high as their youthful spirits. When Mordred became a fullfledged warrior and member of the Round Table, it was the Queen's Men who cheered him loudest and toasted him longest. Lance was as proud to sponsor him as he had been in sponsoring Gareth, and even Arthur took part in the festivities, clapping the new warrior on the back and announcing we were lucky to have such fine swordsmen at our command. Mordred beamed with pleasure, taking in the much-deserved attention like a thirsty plant drinking in dew. *It was the high point of his young life, that precious moment when dream and reality almost came together. If only it hadn't been so short-lived.*

"M'lady, I need your advice," Mordred ventured as we rode to Wells to fill our kegs with the holy water that bubbles out of the ground. Such water was indispensable for use in preparing medicines. "Now that I have become one of the Companions, I would like to find some way to better serve the King . . . some special cause, or quest. Do you know what he might like best?"

What was I to say? I, who knew Arthur would never allow him close, never even admit to their blood-tie? I looked at Mordred and realized for the first time that he was a grown man seeking to make his way in an adult's world.

"Perhaps," I said cautiously, "you can be most helpful politically. That is, take an interest in his plans for the Round Table, help him coordinate the new law, or act as envoy to outlying allies. Why, with your friendship with Cynric, you'd be a natural to advise His Highness on the Saxon Federates. There is no one who takes a special interest in their problems or represents their needs at Court. Maybe you can fill that niche." At the time it seemed a stroke of inspiration, and I was well pleased to have come up with it.

The doire who guarded the sacred waters was very busy that day. Not only did the royal party fill the enclosure of her precinct, there was a gathering of locals milling about outside the temple grounds.

"The Witch," somebody whispered. "The Witch of Wookey has come to confer with the doire."

A shiver ran down my spine. Years ago I had heard of the hag who lived in the cave known as Wookey Hole. I had even thought of visiting her in my effort to cure my barrenness, though Gwyn had cautioned against it, saying she was known to be as much inspired by evil as by good.

We waited with the rest of the supplicants, listening to local gossip and speculation about the witch. "Has the Sight," someone said. "Casts the evil eye," reported another. "Doesn't take kindly to being slighted," a third volunteered. Finally, about the time I was thinking we should leave and come back another day, the door of the temple swung open and a crabbed crone sidled onto the porch of the holy house. The goat at her side paused and surveyed the gathering with its strange, hypnotic eyes.

"What's this?" the Witch croaked, blinking in the sunlight. She peered about the glade as her fingers curled around the crystal ball which hung from her belt. "Royal visitors as well as commons? The Pendragon's Queen, no less—a lady too proud to visit the Witch of Wookey, back when she wanted children."

I stared at her in amazement, wondering how she knew. Without a word she marched straight up to me.

"There's not much I don't know, my proud one," she cackled, scanning my face with white-webbed eyes. "This old granny still has a trick or two up her sleeve."

With that she turned and stumped away, the crowd parting silently to let her through. Some covered their eyes, while others bowed before her. I just stood there, involuntarily making the sign against evil.

"What was that all about?" Mordred inquired.

"A minor problem, from back before you came to Court," I answered, shrugging off the encounter. "Nothing to concern us now."

We waited our turn with the doire, then hurried back to Camelot, for Palomides was leaving to go settle in Northumbria and I didn't want to miss bidding him farewell. At the time, he was hoping to capture and train his own hawks there, though that was a project that never came to fruition.

Nor was the Arab the only one to leave. Ector de Maris returned to live on the Continent for good, while both Lionel and Bors divided their time between Camelot and Brittany. At one point my wry friend Dinadan accompanied them to Brittany, in order to visit Tristan at Howell's court.

Bedivere returned to Camelot after Clovis died, bringing me a lovely knee-length tunic of crimson silk which was a gift of Queen Ingunde, consort to Clovis's son, Chlotar. There was also a remarkable collar of filigreed and granulated gold for Arthur and a fine set of the glass claw-beakers still being made in the Rhineland despite the collapse of the Empire. Since the Britons have no knowledge of how to make glass themselves, these were a fine, rare gift.

My foster sister, Brigit, left the convent in Amesbury to start a holy house of her own in the Chiltern Hills, near London. Bedivere, who had once hoped to marry the Irish girl, escorted her and her sisters to their new home, and stayed to make sure they were settled in and safe before coming back to us.

A sense of adventure filled our Hall during those days. Camelot had become a hub for travelers passing from north to south, east to west. News of happenings far or near was brought to our doorstep almost as quickly by our guests as by the Royal Messengers. And if there was a challenge to be found, the men could count on hearing it first at Camelot.

Ever since Gareth had made his name by besting Ironside, the rest of the Companions had been busy devising quests of their own. Off they went, alone or in groups of two or three, sometimes on a definite mission, sometimes simply looking for wrongs to right, injustices to redress.

"It's becoming an occupational hazard," Arthur commented one night at bedtime. "Thank goodness they don't all take a notion to leave at once!"

"Well, it really isn't doing any harm," I responded, removing the pins from my hair. "And Dagonet's foray into Cornwall gave us all a good laugh."

Our Jester had gone to visit his cousin at Castle Dore, and while he was there, had composed a very unflattering song about King Mark. The old goat heard it and Dagonet was forced to leave rapidly with Gaheris, who traveled with him, guarding his flank.

"Not," the Jester assured us, "because the work was of poor quality, but because its content was too truthful."

Arthur laughed and agreed that it had added a certain spice to Dagonet's report on the southern shore. "At least things are quiet politically. God help me if the Saxons decided to make trouble when half my men are gone."

But the Saxons stayed quiet, as did Morgan le Fey. Cathbad, who retained his good standing with the rest of the druids, kept a sharp ear out for any word that the Lady of the Lake was preparing to leave the Sanctuary. So far there were not even any rumors to that effect. I myself kept an eye on Agravain, fearing that he might be acting as a spy for Morgan. But the behavior of Morgause's most handsome son was above reproach, and he stayed close to Camelot, except when he occasionally sallied forth on minor quests of his own. These were invariably resolved quickly —Agravain being a deadly fighter—and never lasted long enough to include a trip to the Black Lake.

As the time of peace and plenty spun out, Lance left us more and more often, following some adventure or going to his retreat at Joyous Gard. There he worked in his garden, attending to the orchard or overseeing the kitchen crops, and patrolled the Northumbrian coast for Arthur.

"Urien has done a fine job overall, but he's getting old and stiff and can use the help," the big Breton explained. "Then, too, it's a good way to keep my men and horses in trim."

Lance and I never spoke of the summer when Tristan and Isolde, and all my ladies and I, joined him at Joyous Gard for a season of laughter and gaiety and nothing more pressing than the discovery of love. Sometimes I wondered if it had truly happened, or if it was only the half-remembered dream of a Queen so busy with matters of state she'd lost touch with the earth itself. Either way I did not dwell on it.

In those golden years each man contributed his own color to the Round Table mosaic. Gareth became a father twice over. Gaheris came into his own, proving to be the most stable of the Orcadians. Bors continued to build a reputation as a fierce and colorful warrior; Christian or not, he was known for showing no mercy, and I cannot recall his ever being bested. Cei, on the other hand, was forever getting beaten; even though he'd grown solid through the middle, he regularly went off looking for glory —and generally came out the loser.

Once, when we were holding Court at Caerleon, the Seneschal decided to check on reports of a bandit band and stumbled onto three of Vortipor's men instead. Cei's haughty manner angered them thoroughly, and the warriors responded in kind. Their shouting match escalated to the drawing of swords, and Arthur's foster brother had to make a hasty retreat, galloping headlong into the yard of a roadhouse and bolting for the pub just ahead of his pursuers.

"Lance and I happened to be staying there, as we'd been checking the horses at Llantwit," Mordred reported. "We'd just set up the chess board by the fire, and you can imagine how surprised we were to see the Seneschal come pelting into the tavern as though the Sidhe were chasing him. We ordered more ale and settled down to an evening exchanging news. When the ruffians came to the door, they saw the odds had grown more even, so they went away."

Both Cei and Mordred assumed Vortipor's men had returned to their own camp, but the next morning Lance got up very early and taking up Cei's shield and helmet, went down to the stable and stole his horse as well. He'd been riding less than a mile before the threesome broke cover, thinking they would finish off the Seneschal for good. Much to their surprise, the man they took for Cei taught them a quick lesson and left them all with sore heads and bruised ribs. Later the Seneschal rode home astride Invictus, wearing Lance's armor. Naturally no one accosted him, thinking him to be the Breton.

"And that," Mordred concluded happily, "is why the Seneschal is currying Lance's stallion in the stable right now."

The tale amused everyone, but none enjoyed it more than Father Baldwin. The priest had grown quite fond of Cei—they shared a passion for good wines and sometimes talked until late into the night over a glass of the best from our cellar. "Do the Seneschal a world of good to relax and not take himself so seriously," the holy man allowed, wiping tears of laughter from his eyes. "And I'm sure it does him good to know that, in spite of his sharp tongue, he has friends willing to risk their lives in his behalf."

During that time an odd friendship developed between Cathbad the Druid and Father Baldwin, for when he wasn't imbibing with Cei, the cleric was fond of philosophizing with my old teacher. Perhaps all truly holy men have a natural bond.

I would see them, sitting like cats in a pool of sunlight on any spring day, discussing the age-old questions of Existence. Baldwin would grow more and more excited as he developed some point, while Cathbad made a steeple of his fingers and leaned back in his chair, eyes closed. I could have told the priest that the druid wasn't asleep, that he was simply mulling over what he was hearing, but the cleric was so interested in his own ideas, he wouldn't have stopped to listen to me. Nine times out of ten, Baldwin would suddenly stop and stare suspiciously at the druid, horrified at the idea the man had nodded off in the middle of his argument.

Only then would Cathbad move, opening his eyes and sitting upright. "You're quite right, sir, as far as you go. . . ." he would declare, and poor Baldwin, startled out of his wits, would sink back wordlessly while Cathbad picked up the theme exactly where Baldwin had left it. I sometimes wondered just who was playing with whom.

There were major achievements and minor during that time. Mordred had not only learned the Saxon language from Cynric, he'd taught the hostage to read and write, so the two of them became our resident scholars. Between them they collected a vast number of riddles—Saxons are inordinately fond of wordplay—so there was many an evening spent round the fire with Cynric reciting the complicated descriptions and everyone else trying to guess their meaning. I was glad to see it, for now that he had reached manhood, the towhead clearly chafed at being held in captivity, no matter how comfortable it was. At least this gave him some way to participate in our communal lives.

Of greater import was the adoption of the legal code. Slowly, over a long time, Arthur had generated enough enthusiasm among the client kings and warlords to make work on an actual code the next logical step.

"It's finally coming to fruition," he told me gleefully after the Round Table Council in which Urien allowed he would at least study the code. "We'll give them laws they can count on, rights they can be sure of. Oh, Merlin would be proud of this day, Gwen —proud indeed!"

Interestingly, Gawain was as excited about the idea as Arthur. "No more local tyrants," he allowed, "but a code of honor throughout the realm—what a fine notion that is!"

I watched the redhead with amusement. As a boy he'd seemed destined to grow into the wildest of Celtic warlords. Yet now he was a man of courtesy, sworn to protect the weak—particularly if they were women—and uphold law and order.

For all his brusque ways I was dearly fond of him and wished he would find a wife to round out the personal side of his life; someone to settle down with, as he had once thought to settle down with the Prydn Queen, Ragnell. But in his typically complex way, once the bitterness of the parting between himself and the leader of that small nomadic tribe was past, Gawain kept all other women at a distance. Rescue them, protect them, treat them with respect, yes. But let them get inside his guard . . . not likely.

* * *

Until, that is, the Green Man came to prominence again. Suddenly the Prince of Orkney's moira tightened around him as honor and courage and the love of his life all came together at once. It is a frightful, devastating thing to see that on which you've based your whole life be tested—I know, I speak from experience. In the end, of course, all you can do is face down your fears as best you can . . . as I shall at dawn, as Gawain did in the Perilous Chapel. And be grateful for the prayers of others. Heaven knows, we all prayed for the redhead when he went to meet the Old God's challenge.

17

The Green Man

t was in the very heart of autumn, after the harvest was in and the swineherds were shaking acorns and beechnuts down for their charges. The beekeeper was wrapping his skeps in straw for the winter and I was mixing the last of the summer's honey into a pickling brew for hams when the messenger arrived requesting an immediate audience.

I joined Arthur in the Hall, but he insisted that everyone, including the Companions, be present to hear the news, so I surveyed the stranger while we waited.

Most of the Royal Messengers were young and agile, full of energy and knowledgeable about all the ways to travel quickly across the land, whether through the swampy marsh of the Somerset Levels or across the rugged spine of the Pennines. This man looked to be in his midyears, however, but hardy and capable of riding hard for long stretches. From the look of him, he'd come straight through, stopping only to get fresh mounts along the way. Whatever he had to relate must be important.

When everyone was assembled, the messenger raised a tankard of ale in salute to us. "Your Hall is justly famous for its warmth and hospitality. It seems a pity to bring such harrowing news into this peaceful setting."

"Harrowing?" Gawain asked, reaching for the ale pitcher.

"Indeed," the man responded, covertly making the sign against evil. "The Green Man has been seen again."

It had been some time since we'd had reports of the creature, and Arthur sent me a sidelong glance. "What do they say of him now?"

"That he's a monster, Your Highness." The man's voice dropped and he glanced about apprehensively. "The churchmen claim he's the horned devil, but there's many who think he's the Old One of the land—Master of the Wilds and all the animals thereof. He's not only green, M'lord, leaves and branches sprout in his beard, out of his ears, even from his loins. Of course, I haven't seen him in person, but those that have say he is a most awful giant. And he's now challenging men to combat with his terrible ax."

"Ax?" Surprise ruffled the room, for like the bow and arrow, axes are considered working tools and would never be used by an honorable warrior.

"Aye," the messenger went on. "A huge ax for felling trees— only he uses it to fell mortals. The blade is bigger than two handspans and shimmers as green as the rest of the apparition. He never misses with it, and you can hear him sharpening it anytime the wind comes down from the Perilous Chapel. I tell you, Your Highness, whether this creature is fey or demon, he is terrorizing all who go near the Wirral."

The man licked his lips drily, and I signaled a page to give him more ale. The boy picked up the pitcher next to Gawain, after the Orcadian refilled his own drinking horn.

"So you've talked with people who've actually seen him?" I asked. The messenger nodded before taking another draft, then ran his tongue over his mustaches and continued.

"For most, only their headless corpses tell the tale. But there was one, a burly little charcoal burner who lives and works in the wildwood. I was at the annual fair at Beeston Rock—that enormous, jagged chunk of mountain that rises out of the flat lands near Chester. It's an easy landmark to find, which makes it a natural place for a market. This year everyone was talking about the Green Man—how he stalks through the forest and people flee from him in terror lest he challenge them to the Head Game. That's his favorite pastime, they say: the game where he offers to trade blows."

The messenger swallowed hard as a clammy sweat beaded his forehead. Arthur leaned forward, encouraging the man to continue, and Gawain sent the page to refill the pitcher with ale.

"Well, while everyone else was talking about how invincible

the Green Man is, this little collier came up to me. Small and weathered, he had the look of the Ancient Ones. Pointing to the Dragon badge on my sleeve, he asked if I was King Arthur's man. When I told him I was a member of the Royal Messengers, he went down on his knees and begged me to bring his story to you."

It seems the Green Man had accosted the collier in the heart of the woods, demanding that they play his game. The little man pointed out he carried no sword of his own, but the giant insisted, allowing that each would strike the other as hard as he could, with the mortal being allowed to deliver the first blow. He even loaned the trembling man his ax. Because the human was so short, the Green Man knelt down and bared his neck, as though for execution. Naturally the collier was used to chopping trees, so he hefted the brutal blade and brought it down clean and true on the Green Man's neck . . . whereupon the giant's head flew off and rolled across the ground, coming to rest at the foot of a birch tree.

But instead of falling dead on the spot, the headless cadaver hopped after it and, picking up the grisly thing, tucked it under his arm and announced he expected his opponent to allow him his return blow at his own chapel on New Year's Day. The collier was horrified at the prospect and begging the ogre for mercy, asked to be released from the dreadful game. After some thought, the Green Man decided to let him live on the condition that King Arthur's own Champion would agree to take his place.

"Gawain of the Round Table is much touted for his bravery," the Green Man roared. "Let us see how much is boasting in the safety of the Hall, and how much is honest courage."

"And that," the messenger concluded, "is why I rode straight here, thinking you should know of the giant's challenge. He swore to be at the Perilous Chapel on New Year's Day to see if the Prince of Orkney is brave enough to take the collier's place. If so, the King's Champion may come armed, but must not use his weapons for his own defense until after the Green Man has delivered the stroke meant for the charcoal burner."

"Now, wait a minute," Arthur exclaimed. "If this creature has ado with my men, let him come to Camelot and deliver his challenge in person."

There was a murmur of assent, but Gawain leapt to his feet,

his face flushed and eyes bright with excitement. "This is a personal challenge to me, M'lord, and I intend to meet it."

Gawain had been quenching a mighty thirst and hadn't stopped to think of the full scope of the challenge.

Arthur gave him a worried look and suggested that perhaps a party of Companions might look into it. There was an immediate clamor of men volunteering to go, for the story had a strange allure. It was the sort of adventure that bards would tell of for generations to come, and as Arthur once said, there never was a Celt who could resist the promise of fame and eternal glory. No doubt that's why so many wanted to accompany Gawain.

But the Orcadian drained his drinking horn, then looked around the circle and shook his head. "I go alone, without even a squire," he announced.

"Alone?" Arthur voiced his dismay, while the rest of us stared at the redhead in disbelief.

"Yes, alone. I will stay with you through next week while we celebrate Samhain, then go off in search of the Green Man's Chapel." Gawain turned to Father Baldwin. "Is it not said that the night of Samhain, when both Gods and Sidhe roam through the land of men, is followed by All Saints' Day in the church?" The cleric nodded his assent. "Then there's no better time to go to my fate," Gawain declared, full of drunken bravado.

When he sobered up the next day, he was somewhat abashed by what he'd done, but no amount of reasoning could get him to change his mind. "It's become a matter of honor," he declared, and I knew the die was cast.

But as Samhain approached, the King's Champion began to recognize the extent of his jeopardy. He took to collecting amulets and went about whispering charms, though still stoutly refusing to take even a squire with him.

As usual, we opened the Hall to all who wished to shelter with us on the night when all men stay indoors. Whole families began to arrive well before sundown, climbing the cobbled drive with a misty, red-tinged sunset setting the sky afire behind them. Noble and peasant, servant and freeman, all came gladly welcoming the safety of human company during the time when the borders between this world and the Other grow blurred. As I greeted them, I found they all had one concern—would Gawain be with us this night? Awe of the Champion's courage flickered among them like summer lightning in a cloudy sky.

By the time the barley soup had been dipped out of the hanging caldrons and platters of bread and pickles put on every table, the last light of day had faded. Once the fire was roaring and the double doors had been barred against the dark, Gawain took his place beside Arthur and called for attention.

"As you know, tomorrow I leave to go meet the Green Man," he announced, coming right to the point. "But tonight I am still among you and would be most cheered by the ring of laughter and the sound of songs. If you would honor me, make this a party I can remember, rather than an early dirge I would rather forget."

There was a moment of silence, then a Scottish lad with a bagpipe stepped forward, puffing up his instrument and bowing low to the Orkney Prince. The drone of the pipe began to fill the air, and soon the Hall was alive with skirls and flourishes. Someone put down a pair of crossed swords, and Gawain began to pick out his sword dance, starting slowly at first and gradually increasing in speed as each step brought him closer to the nexus of the blades. His face shone with sweat as he concentrated on this ritual display of a warrior's skill and stamina. As his toes flew deftly in and out of the quadrants, there was clapping and stamping and a fine hurrah, because he neither touched the sharp metal nor lost his energy, and it was the piper who slowed first.

After that the night became one long party, full of food and song and tales of past daring well spun by Riderich the Bard. No one celebrated more heartily than Gawain.

He left next morning at sunup. Arthur and I waited for him in the kitchen, and while my husband made him a present of a fine Welsh dagger, I shook out the new lamb's wool cloak I had intended to give Mordred. Gawain received our gifts solemnly, and gave each of us the kinsman's embrace. For a moment my eyes blurred with tears to see him in such peril, and I leaned against Arthur as the King's nephew turned at the door and gave us the thumbs up. Without a word, we returned the salute.

When he had gone, the household turned its attention to the chores of late autumn. Yet even as we went about our work, we worried for his safety. The beekeeper spent all one afternoon sitting by his hives, telling the drowsy honeymakers about the mission of the King's Champion. Bees must be kept informed of everything that happens in their master's lives—not to do so invites their death or desertion and brings bad luck to the master's house. I wondered if the keeper could explain not only the "what" of it but also the "why" of Gawain's trip.

Hunters, stopping by the Hall with braces of hares or pairs of red-shanked partridge, asked hopefully, "What news?" Dairy-maids nodded their heads and whispered about the hero's valor, and crones who remembered Gawain's more rakish days sniffled over their teapots and murmured that he always was a good boy, for all that he'd once been notorious among women.

"I never should have let him go," Arthur fretted one evening, suddenly looking up from his chess game.

"And how would you have stopped him, short of playing the tyrant and clapping him in chains?" Lance signaled to a page to take the board away, since neither man was able to concentrate on the game. We all knew whom Arthur spoke of, though he hadn't mentioned Gawain by name.

"Well, together perhaps we could have dissuaded him," my husband mused, chewing on his mustache. "Or gone with him. At the very least he should have had Gaheris and Gareth beside him. To face such an end without even kinfolk near. . . ."

"He has claimed it as his moira, M'lord—and must find his own solution to it." Lance stretched his feet toward the brazier and stared into the flames. "Every man's shadow contains the ghost of his worst fear, whether it's death or dishonor, cowardice or the dreaded exposure of a secret. We each do battle with our own nemesis. And considering how superstitious he is, I cannot imagine a more fitting trial for the King's Champion than actually confronting one of the Old Gods."

Lance's voice faded away, and in the silence that followed, each of us made our own separate prayer for Gawain's survival.

The days of December crawled slowly toward midwinter, and during the longest night we rang the bells and danced around the Yule log, clapping and singing and trying to make merry in order to lure the sun back from the north. But we only went through the ceremony for tradition's sake, not because of any gaiety of spirit.

When New Year's Day arrived, there was no pretense of pleasure, for all thoughts centered on Gawain and his ordeal. Camelot was as quiet as though wrapped in a shroud.

Slowly the days that followed crept by as we waited word of
his end. Then one morning as I was counting the beeswax candles
we had left between winter dark and the coming of summer, one
of Frieda's sons came pounding into the pantry, calling frantically
for me.

"Highness! Highness!" he hollered. "Come quick, M'lady—
Gawain's at the gate."

I dropped my tallying tablet and spun around to stare at the
youngster. His freckled face radiated joy, and grabbing my hand
in his, he pulled me toward the door. Together we went pelting
across the Hall and out to the porch, where half the household
had already gathered. The other half was escorting the redhead
up the drive, laughing and clapping and hugging each other in a
frenzy of relief and goodwill.

Lance and Mordred dashed up from the stables, Arthur and
Bedivere from the barn, all of them hot and sweaty and full of
hope. Lance came to stand by me, while Arthur and his foster
brother waited to greet their longtime friend.

The Prince of Orkney was haggard and dirty, his clothing mud-
stained, his new cape torn in several places. He dismounted at
the foot of the steps, pausing for a moment to speak to the young
man who accompanied him.

The youth was dressed in pelts and homespun, and had tied
back his long dark hair with a thong from which hung a clutch of
kingfisher feathers. He took charge of the warhorse while Gawain
turned to Arthur.

The High King's nephew went down on one knee as slowly and
stiffly as an old man, yet beneath the years of toil and turmoil, I
saw once more the impish youth who'd knelt at such a step and
handed up a bouquet of wildflowers when Arthur and I were wed.

"M'lord," he croaked, giving Arthur a lopsided grin, "the
Green Man sends greetings and compliments to Arthur Pendra-
gon, High King of Britain, and to the brave men of his Round
Table."

Arthur smiled broadly and, throwing his arms wide, bade his
Champion rise. A great cheer went up around us, and Arthur

asked Lucan to get out a keg of our finest beer and share it around as we listened to the Orcadian's tale.

In the Hall everyone gathered around Gawain, some finding chairs, others sitting on bolsters on the floor. The younger warriors pulled the benches from under the loft, and I saw Mordred, eyes bright with anticipation, rest his chin on his hand and stare admiringly at his brother.

Gawain stood in the middle of the circle, gazing around at his friends as though he could not believe he was safely home among them.

"I went from Camelot with a heavy heart," he began, "and made my way toward the Welsh coast, stopping to see old friends and mending fences I had once left broken. But mostly I wanted to talk with the hermit at Saint Govan's head."

He found the holy man perched on a ledge in the cliff face above the sea, contemplating the sky and clouds and wind. Gawain stayed with him through the whole of November, trying to prepare himself for the ordeal that lay ahead. The shadow of fear grew around him, but the hermit prayed with him every day, forgiving his past sins and calling down the Christian God's powers to protect him against the Pagan fiend. Finally, just before he left, Gawain asked to be baptized.

When he resumed his journey, he kept to the forest, avoiding both Roads and towns in order to remain pure in his resolve and not be tempted from his purpose. His only company was a lone wolf which followed his progress, skulking at the edges of his fire at night and howling at the moon when he tried to sleep.

At the northern coast of Gwynedd he turned east, riding along the coast beside the Straits of Menai. Beyond the narrow waterway lay the Isle of Mona, sacred center of the Druids before the Legions came. He was terrified that the Old Gods would reach out and reclaim him, so he made the Christian sign, praying that the power of the cross would keep the Pagan nature of his early life at bay.

When he reached the entrance to the region known as the Wirral, Gawain stopped at a crofter's hut to ask directions to the Perilous Chapel. The farmer blanched and clenched his teeth tight against incautious words as he nodded toward the verge where the dark, primal wildwood began. So, with a falling heart, Gawain turned his steed into the trackless forest.

* * *

"It was just as frightening within as without," the King's Champion reported, pausing to have his drinking horn refilled. "And compared with Logres, where grace and light and civilization make their home, it was a tangle of terrors."

His meeting with the Green Man was only three days away, and after so many weeks alone, Gawain ached for the company of other humans. Then, toward evening, he came upon a large meadow commanded by a roundhouse of wattle and daub topped by a heavy thatched roof, and his heart lifted with joy. The sound of children's laughter ran out to greet him as the leather curtain over the doorway was thrown open and the lord of the steading came out.

"He was short and sturdy," Gawain recalled, "with the dark look of the Ancient Ones, and his eyes were full of mischief. He capered on the edge of the green, gesturing me to come nearer, and when he spoke, it was in a language very much like that of the Prydn."

The lord's name was Bercilak, and his household was as fey and lively as he was. Nowhere in the roundhouse did Gawain see anything made of iron, for the "firstborn of the gods" distrust the metal used by "tall-folk," relying instead on stone and wood and bronze.

"And gold," the Orcadian added. "Everywhere you looked there were golden vessels and plates, boxes and jewelry, utensils and baubles. Like the Prydn, they seemed to have a treasure that they loved for beauty's sake alone."

I nodded silently, remembering the night Gawain had brought the Prydn Queen to our Court. Small, pert, and homely, Ragnell had altered a tunic of mine to fit her tiny frame, and on it she'd sewn coins from Roman times along with beads and bangles and woven bands of gold. She herself was adorned with armbands and amulets, torcs and diadems and dangling earrings, so that in the torchlight, she looked like a miniature Goddess covered with the precious metal. It had certainly increased the speculation that she was, indeed, one of the fey.

Gawain's voice cut across my reverie. "They gave me the seat of honor, and we sat around the fire-pit, dipping into the communal pot and tearing scraps of heavy bread from lumpy loaves."

He began to feel like one of their own, for they wrapped him in warmth and laughter, and took him to their hearts. After so many weeks of lonely fear, Gawain's soul filled with joy.

When the dining was over, the Champion of the Round Table explained the reason for his journey, and there was much buzzing and consultation before the host called for silence.

"You must be a very brave man," Bercilak said admiringly. "It's clear you know how forfeit your life will be before the Green Man. No one escapes his magic unless he himself wills it." There was a mumble of agreement around the circle, and the household eyed Gawain with a respect that verged on awe.

"The Perilous Chapel is not far from here," Bercilak's lady said impulsively. "Why don't you stay with us until the time of your ordeal?"

The woman was very young and proud, and she talked as much with her hands as with words, sometimes with neat, elegant gestures, sometimes flinging her arms about impetuously. As Gawain described her, she sounded very much like Ragnell herself.

Gawain accepted the invitation, glad of the chance to rest before going to confront his fate.

Bercilak was a fine host, and he put his entire household at the redhead's disposal. Since Gawain was stiff and sore from so many days in the saddle, on the first day Bercilak stayed home with his guest, showing him about the steading and telling him all he knew of the Green Man's activities—although few had seen him, the stories of his ferocity were legion.

As they moved about the holding, Gawain noticed they were accompanied by a young man, taller than the rest of the fey folk and more ruddy than dark. He was both attentive and courteous, and Bercilak treated him as a member of the family, though when Gawain asked him about the lad in private, the lord of the steading shrugged.

"That's just Gingalin. Comes from one of those nomadic branches of the clan in the north who still follow their animals from pasture to pasture. Judging from his look, I'd say he's a half-breed; perhaps his mother was raped by a Pict or flirted away midsummer's night with one of those Scottish lairds. No matter —he was sent to us to learn more civilized ways, and we've been pleased to make him honorary kin."

That night Bercilak asked if Gawain would join him on a hunting expedition the next morning, but the Orcadian was still worn out from his trip and mindful that it was his last day before he must go to the Chapel. So he asked to stay at the steading, and Bercilak announced that was a fine idea; he would commend the guest to the care of his wife.

"But, lest you think I've forgotten you," the burly warlord added with a grin, "I shall make you a gift in the evening of whatever I catch during the day, in return for your doing the same for me." His eyes sparkled with good nature, and he tugged absently on one ear as he watched his guest. "Whatever each of us encounters shall be forfeit to the other, eh?"

The Ancient Ones are famous for their love of games and tricks, so Gawain assumed it was a custom of the place and, bowing gallantly, agreed to the conditions.

He slept fitfully that night, and his dreams were haunted by the specter of the Green Man and the memory of the nomad queen he had lost so long ago. Between the one he sought to find and the one that stalked him, he raced through a nightmare landscape, sweating and tossing on his pallet until, with a cry, he sat bolt upright, trying to free himself from the dream.

"That's when I saw Bercilak's wife." The redhead paused and looked upward to the rafters, eyes shining, though I couldn't tell if it was with tears or memory.

"She was standing by the window in my sleeping niche, and when she pulled the heavy drapes aside, the bright light of morning filled the room.

" 'What a wonderful day,' she cried, running toward me with outstretched arms. She was all things glorious in life, all that I was so soon to lose, and I suddenly wanted desperately to take her in my arms and know that now, for this moment at least, I was still alive. Indeed, I had a hard time containing both our desires."

There was a long silence, then the Prince of Orkney finished off his ale with a sigh.

"It was a wretched predicament, for as a good Christian I could not make love to my host's wife. Yet when I refused her invitation, she chided me, saying I dishonored my oath to come to all women's aid. So I was deeply relieved when she laughed and made a jest of it, then turned to go."

But as she reached the door, she slipped off the girdle that bound her waist and gave it to Gawain as a gift. "It will keep its wearer from dying a violent death—and you can use it at the Green Man's Chapel tomorrow," she said, coming back to the bed and handing over the talisman.

Gawain took the thing in his hands. It was green and gold and worked with ornate symbols and spells that reeked of ancient magic. Perhaps, indeed, it could save him from certain death at the hands of the Old God.

He looked up at his hostess, hope for his own survival beginning to course through his blood. She stared down at him tenderly and, reaching out her hand, ran her small fingers along the scars on his cheek where Ragnell had scratched him when they parted. It touched him deeply and brought tears to his eyes.

That night there was much merriment when Bercilak came home, though the hunter confessed that the prey had eluded him during the day, and therefore he had no gift to exchange with Gawain.

"Nor I in kind," the Champion said, thinking of what a narrow escape he'd had in bed. For a moment he wondered if he should give over the green-and-gold girdle, but fearing he would die without it, he kept that gift a secret.

The last evening of Gawain's stay was spent in merrymaking, and after the feasting was done, Bercilak called Gingalin forward and presented him to the Champion. "He'll be your guide tomorrow, when you seek the Chapel," the warlord said, "and if you wish, he will act as your squire and bear your shield."

Gawain liked the boy's manner, so he handed over his armor and weapons to the youth, and when it was time for sleep, gave his host a farewell embrace. Bercilak wished him well and promised to ask the Goddess to temper the Green Man's rage when they met.

This night the Champion got no sleep at all, so long before daylight he tied the magic girdle under his tunic and set off with Gingalin for the elusive chapel of the Green Man.

It was a cold, misty morning, and the squire led Gawain into the vapors and fogs that wreathed the high ground. Dampness dripped from fern and brake while sharp, stony crags appeared and disappeared around them. Finally they came to the edge of a hidden valley where the forest drew back and an ancient, hoary barrow rose beside a spring which had frozen into feathery plumes of white ice, as though sculpted by the fey. The Prince of Orkney stared down on the scene with amazement.

The barrow was open at one end, and the eerie, keening wail of metal being sharpened on a grinding stone floated up from it. The sound screeched and skittered on the morning air and pulsed in Gawain's blood like the beat of his heart.

"It was more a heathen place than a chapel," Gawain recounted, crossing himself while various others in the Hall made the sign against blasphemy. "Grasses grew on its sides and over the top, and at one end was the dark hole of a doorway. I'd seen such barrows before, for the Prydn sometimes camp near them and go freely in and out of those Hollow Hills."

When his drinking horn was refilled, the redhead slaked his thirst, then continued his tale.

"That's when Gingalin suggested I give up my quest and return to Camelot without confronting the Green Man."

The squire promised he would not mention it if Gawain chose to save himself instead of meeting the ogre. The instructions had not been clear, the appointed day might have been missed. . . . "You know you don't have to go to your death," the boy added earnestly.

Gawain stared at the lad, who stared back at him from under a ledge of dark brows. There was something discomforting about the youngster's look, and Gawain wondered suddenly if he was a devil, sent to keep him from proving himself.

"I will not have it said that the Prince of Orkney lacks the courage to face an Old God now that he's found the new one," he answered brusquely as they circled the green sides of the burial mound and came to a halt before the narrow opening.

"Come forth," the Orcadian shouted, trying to make himself heard above the whine of the stone. "Come forth and see that Gawain of the Round Table accepts your challenge, in the name of King Arthur and the White Christ."

The whine of the stone stopped abruptly, but no one emerged, so after a bit Gingalin spoke up again. "You've met the conditions of the challenge, M'lord. Surely if the Green Man refuses to come out, you can go home."

But Gawain was not satisfied, and girding up his courage, he pushed his way between the two rough stones that formed the doorway slot.

"The inside was much bigger than I'd expected," the King's Champion recalled. "A torch guttered at the far end, casting shadows and gleamings across a scatter of gold on the floor. A skeleton was laid out in one corner, and several piles of bones near the doorway looked new enough to have come from recent encounters. But the thing that held my attention was the crouched form of a little man testing the edge of an ax against his thumb. He was as much covered with leaves and branches as he was with hair, and when he stood up, he grew in size until his head nearly touched the ceiling."

"Ah, you have come to face your death," the creature cried, his voice rumbling hollowly through the tomb while his shadow towered above Gawain. "For that I pay you honor."

In the guttering light the ogre bowed formally, seeming to shrink again to less than normal size. Gawain kept a firm grip on his sword hilt, reminding himself and the Christ that it was cast in the shape of a cross.

"The agreement was a return stroke on my part. I think," the Green Man said casually, "that altar will make a suitable block." Gawain's glance followed the little man's gesture toward an ancient stone that stood in a dark corner, its sides blackened by countless spillings of blood. "Please extend your neck."

For a moment a savage thought raced through the Champion's mind—Old God or no, when the Green Man was shrunken like this, anyone with a lick of sense and half a sword-arm could cleave him in two. Gawain's hand twitched to draw his blade, and his ears rang with the sound of laughter and relief.

"But the White Christ stopped me," the King's Champion said softly. "He reminded me that I was there on a matter of honor, so I knelt before that accursed altar and I stretched my neck out, waiting for the Green Man to deliver his blow. The Old God came to my side, and I could see his shadow cast against the barrow wall, flickering in the torchlight. He stretched and lengthened into gigantic form, his two-handed ax held aloft, and when the curved blade began to swing downward, I closed my eyes and gritted my teeth, praying the end would be quick."

Gawain let out a long sigh, but we held our breaths, waiting for him to go on.

"The giant checked his swing at the last second, and rocking back on his heels, hooted with laughter. 'You flinched,' he cried. 'I saw you—you flinched. Sir Gawain—you've a coward's heart, after all.' "

I gaped at the Orcadian, thinking that anyone would do the same. Arthur leaned toward his nephew and asked incredulously, "He *laughed?*"

"Aye, great, gusty bouts of demoniacal laughter, as though it was some fine joke. By then I thought I was as much in danger from a madman as from a giant of the Otherworld. But we went through the same ritual again, only this time I did not flinch, and the ax completed its fall. The blow came down beside my neck, not on it."

"That, my good sir," roared the Green Man, "is for not telling me my wife had given you her girdle."

The ogre had shrunk back to mere human size, and when Gawain slowly raised his head, it was Bercilak's gleeful laugh that filled the barrow. "Thought you'd protect yourself with a little Prydn magic, eh? Well, I can't blame you," he allowed, carefully checking the blade of the ax to make sure it had not been nicked when it hit the stone altar. "But by rights you should have given it to me last night, you know. Honor and all that stuff."

Amazement was turning into relieved laughter among the Companions, and Gawain stood shamefaced in the middle of it. "So in the end, I lost my honor by keeping the secret of the lady, even though I met the challenge of the lord."

"Nonsense," Arthur exploded. "You put too fine an edge on the matter."

The laughter was turning to a cheer, and Gaheris jumped to his feet to toast his brother. "To the bravest, and most courteous Companion of all," he cried as everyone joined in the merriment.

"But why would Bercilak set up such an ordeal?" I asked.

Gawain looked aside and answered slowly. "He said it was to fulfill the last wish of a Prydn queen who had died in childbirth. She had sent her mixed-blood infant to Bercilak with the request that he raise the youngster until he should be old enough to act as squire to his father . . . but only if the man proved courageous to the end. I'm not sure that I deserve the honor," the Orcadian concluded, "but the lad has taken the notion that I am his sire and begged me to bring him back to Camelot. May I present him now—Gingalin, whom I am pleased to call son."

I looked more closely at the dark-visaged youngster, thinking he might well be Ragnell's offspring. There was an impudent bravado in the way he answered the questioning stares of the Companions, and Gawain gave him a fond grin. "Besides, he's proved himself an excellent squire."

So there was more cheering and a toast for the newfound son, and our Hall was filled with joy for the better part of the night. To have the hero home again after such an encounter was miracle enough, but to have acquired a son as well was a pure wonder.

* * *

So you met the challenge, O Prince of Orkney, and the fame it has brought you is more than a little deserved. May your prayers help me meet mine on the morrow with an equal dignity.

18

The Next Generation

fter Gawain's confrontation with the Old God, a kind of sea-change occurred in the men of Camelot. Many who in the past had gone adventuring with cheerful mien and high spirits now began to talk of wanting quests that reflected noble purposes.

"Something that lasts, if you know what I mean, M'lady," Ironside explained as he escorted me across the springy turf to the sheep market at Priddy. "A cause with glory in it, that gives the bard something grand to sing about."

I suspected the old warrior was more interested in being immortalized in song than in noble causes, but there was no denying his fervor on the subject.

"Why," he allowed, "I might even get myself a new mail jerkin if something *really* important came up. . . ."

Nor was Ironside the only one; Gaheris, feeling that he'd been cheated of taking part in the adventure with the Green Man, began looking for more notable endeavors. And handsome, cold Agravain became more picky about his choice of quests, ranging farther afield and coming back with more grisly tales. Some of these adventures kept him away for quite a time, and I wondered if he weren't slipping in visits to Morgan le Fey.

News of the Lady of the Lake was moderately peaceful—her Sanctuary now served nothing but women, all the rest of the druids having left. She seemed to have no interest in life beyond being High Priestess and made no discernible effort to keep in touch with either her husband, Urien, or her exiled son, Uwain. In spite of that, when he returned to Britain, Uwain sought her out before coming to see us.

"The Prince of Northumbria, recently of Brittany," Lucan caroled at dinner one night, giving the title a deep, resonant sound. He'd have accompanied the announcement with a flourish on the trumpet, if one had been handy.

All eyes turned to the entrance of the Hall as both food and goblets were lowered, forgotten, to the table. It had been more than ten years since Arthur sent Uwain away, and many felt they'd waited overlong for the fellow's return.

The man who strode into the Hall was surrounded by a smartly turned-out entourage. Lieutenants, warriors and squires—in short, all the panoply of a bachelor noble—accompanied him as he moved forward to greet the High King.

Tall, elegant and supremely confident, Urien's son had grown into a striking man. His long hair and heavy, drooping mustaches were reminiscent of his father, though he had Morgan's sea-green eyes. Yet for all that the mixture of his parents was evident, there was about him a sense of his own identity shaped beyond—or in spite of—his heredity.

"Well come, nephew," Arthur intoned when the younger man bowed to us. "It is a pleasure to see you back in Logres again."

Uwain gave his uncle a diplomatic nod, but his face was taut. He might have accepted Arthur's apologies for having banished him, but he had not forgotten the unfairness of it. The smile of friendship was saved for me—a fine, open-hearted grin that made even his eyes twinkle.

"M'lady, I bring you greetings from across the Channel, where your name and reputation grow apace."

"How gracious of you," I murmured, wondering what they could possibly be saying. "What brings you back to Britain?"

"A matter of some concern to my father. New boatloads of Angles have landed on the Northumbrian coast. So far there is no armed conflict, but the people in the villages are getting nervous."

Startled, Lance looked up, and our eyes met. Joyous Gard lies in the northern reach of that windswept coast.

"We'll give you whatever support you need," Arthur immediately offered, but Uwain's response was cool.

"I have no doubt we can manage on our own."

For a moment I thought the King would take umbrage at the

snub, but instead he insisted that new trestles be set up and the kitchen find enough to serve both our guest and his followers. I blessed the fact that I'd had a dovecote built, as it assured a quick supply of birds when Cook needed to create extra meals in a hurry.

The evening went pleasantly enough, with Gawain and his brothers delighted to have their cousin in their midst again. He brought with him a young Frank he had befriended on the Continent, and once the Orcadians discovered that Colgrevance had several sisters in tow, there was much eagerness to get to know him.

The girls caused quite a flurry among the Companions. They had charming manners and brought a new sort of flirting to our squires and young warriors: the sweep of eyelashes as a demure little lady suddenly flashed up a very knowing look; an impudent shrug or long, slow smile full of half-hidden promises. Compared with the forthright lasses of Britain, these new damsels were like catnip to our boys.

"Silly fellows," Uwain noted when he came to sit next to me after the meal was over. "They could learn more from an older woman than from a pretty youngster."

My eyebrows went up, and the Prince of Northumbria laughed. "My first love was a woman well into her prime, and she taught me not only about trusting the heart and warming the bed, but many a military strategy as well."

"Military?" It used to aggravate me considerably that once the Romans came, British women ceased to be taught the arts of war. Perhaps on the Continent there were still a few Celtic queens who wielded the old power of leading armies.

"I'm afraid not, M'lady," Uwain hastened to explain. "But the Lady Automne was an unusual woman, who had done many remarkable things in her life. Ever since childhood she'd studied the arts of war—tactics, rather than brute force, of course—and when she came to the age of marrying, there wasn't a warrior among her father's men who wanted to make her his mate. Seems they were fearful she would outclass them in military knowledge. Then, too, I fancy none of them met her standards. Being high born, her father couldn't force her into an unwanted union, so she chose to remain single and keep control of her own life." He cast me an arch look, then added, "You know, I assume, that Christian wives are expected to view their husbands as their masters and play the servant to their whims?"

"No, really?" I'd never heard it stated so baldly before, though considering the way many of the clergy treated me, I should have guessed as much.

"Well, at least that's the way it is in the Roman Church," Uwain continued. "So I don't blame Automne for choosing not to marry. And it was to my good fortune, for by the time we met she'd had enough of the usual bumptious males and found me a lover eager to learn all that she could teach me. It made up, in part, for some of the things so long missing in my own life."

It was barely a passing comment, but the words brought up the whole of his childhood. How many times had I wondered what would happen to the lad, caught between warring parents who could not learn to tolerate each other? Perhaps Morgan's ignoring him in favor of pursuing political schemes was a blessing—her bitterness might have crippled him for life.

"What of your lion?" I asked, remembering the story of his healing the hurt animal.

"Ah, he is with me in spirit," Uwain replied with a smile. "I've learned a great deal about veterinary medicine, and commemorate the lion on my badge as well as my shield."

I followed his gesture toward the table where his men sat, happily exchanging news and toasts with the Companions. Every one of their tunics had the emblem of a lion sewn on the shoulder.

"We'll have the Smith use the pattern for your hanging lamp when you take your place at the Round Table," I promised.

Uwain spoke quickly, though still with a fine courtesy. "Oh, that won't be necessary, Your Highness. I have more to do up north than here with the Pendragon. Let me just visit occasionally, as my need arises."

"Are you that resentful?" I queried softly.

"Not resentful, just aware of where my own fate leads—and it is not currying favor with the High King. I shall probably spend my life serving at my father's side, and when he no longer leads his warriors, I will keep the Hall warm, give out the gold, and meet the challenge of the invaders. I don't foresee much time for noble causes or grand quests."

Perhaps you were the first of the realists, Uwain. The first of the sons grown to manhood who returned to question where our dream was leading, what we had become. I watched you that night with admiration and fear, and a certain sentimental fondness for the lad you had once been—it was easier than looking at the message you were now conveying.

"But though I cannot stay, I'll leave you an eager young fellow in my stead," Uwain told Arthur later. He gestured to his lieutenant, who fetched a dirty, wild-eyed boy from the pile of dogs by the hearth.

"Found him roaming in the forest, Your Highness," Uwain explained. "He ran right up to us, begging us to take him in. I shooed him away, assuming he was nothing more than a loony living in the wildwood, but he came back next day, riding a piebald nag and carrying a wooden spear. He claims he's destined for Camelot, so I brought him along."

Arthur was looking the boy up and down, and being openly assessed in return.

"What's your name, lad?" the High King inquired.

"Perceval. What's yours?"

My husband sat back, startled by the impertinence, and Uwain rolled his eyes upward. "He's a bit rough, Your Highness. But more untaught than unteachable, I'd say. Seems he was raised by a mother who feared for his life if he became a warrior, so she kept him in the forest, ignorant of the ways of men. Taught him nothing but bare survival and notions of heaven."

"Mum says the angels are made of light," Perceval declared, looking admiringly at the Prince of Northumbria. "When you wear your shiny hat, you look exactly like an angel."

A guffaw went up from the Companions, and the boy whirled around. One hand reached for the sling that hung from his belt.

As he moved, his tattered cloak flew back, and I saw for the first time the familiar gold-and-enamel brooch. "Would you be Pellinore's son?" I inquired, wondering if the crazed widow who had left the Wrekin had been unable to find refuge with King Pellam at Carbonek.

"Pellinore?" The boy savored the sound, as though it had a flavor he was trying to place.

"Pellinore of the Wrekin," I supplied. The lad was small and stocky, unlike the massive warlord, but there still might be a connection.

"Mayhap." The bumpkin shrugged his shoulders in unconcern. "Can't remember my da. Only Mum and the people who came to the fountain in the woods. Never been in a house before, either."

He stared in amazement at the Red Dragon on the tapestry behind us, then sent his feral glance to the shadows under the loft. The Companions held their breath, as though watching some strange, unpredictable animal, and in the silence Palomides's falcon ruffled its feathers and settled back to drowse on its perch. With a motion almost too fast to follow, Perceval had his sling out and hit the creature with his first stone. The hawk toppled to the floor, stunned.

Palomides's turbaned squire let out a shriek of outrage and drawing his dagger, leapt at the half-wild boy, who was intent on retrieving the bird. There was a moment of scuffling, during which a number of warriors converged on the two, trying to keep them apart while the girls from the Continent squealed excitedly.

Perceval managed to evade them all. Grabbing the bird, he wrung its neck for good measure and handed it to me. "Not much good for spitting," he noted. "But it will do in the soup pot."

The ruckus around him was turning into a brawl, and Cei began to pound on the table to restore order. Palomides was restraining his squire and finally had to lead him away as Perceval looked on without a trace of remorse.

"And why did you want to come to Camelot?" Arthur asked.

"This fellow here said that's where he was going." Perceval nodded toward Uwain. "Said that the King's men all wear metal helmets and carry bright shields . . . you that king?"

"I am," Arthur acknowledged, hard pressed not to smile at the boy's ingenuousness in spite of his atrocious behavior. "What would you do for me?"

"Catch your dinner, fight your wars, wear one of those shiny hats."

The remark brought a burst of laughter from Cei, and the boy crouched as he turned to glare at the Seneschal. "That will do," Arthur warned them both.

"Then tell the tall man not to laugh at me," Perceval responded, as prickly with pride as any Champion.

"What are you going to do with him?" I asked later that night.

"Send him to his Uncle Pellam at Carbonek," Arthur replied with a sigh. "The old, ailing King needs all the warriors he can get, and since there's a blood-tie there, he can be responsible for the boy. Whew—I warrant there'll be the devil to pay over that falcon!"

Surprisingly, Palomides was fairly calm about the loss of his most-prized possession, but the turbaned servant was inconsolable. The fact that no one in Britain knew how to train such birds didn't help, and in the long run the fellow's despair, along with his already noticeable homesickness, led Palomides to arrange for his passage on the next boat bound for Alexandria.

"He's a canny one, and can find his own way from there," the Arab allowed. "Perhaps it was arrogant of me to think he could adapt to this foggy little island just because I have."

So Palomides and his servant prepared to go to Exeter and wait for summer trading to commence. Arthur decided to accompany them, wanting to check further on how things were going with Gwynlliw.

"I'm sending Mordred out on his first assignment," my husband noted as he packed for the southern trip. "He's to check on the Bristol coast from Sea Mills down to the River Exe. The Irish haven't shown any signs of resuming their raids, but it doesn't hurt to be prepared."

"Oh dear, he had so wanted to go to Northumbria with Uwain," I mused, hoping my husband would reconsider his opposition to that plan. "Might do him good to get to know his cousin better."

"Uwain?" Arthur spit the name out. "I don't trust Morgan's son any more than he trusts me—don't want to give him a chance to turn Mordred against me." His tone was so contentious, I couldn't point out that it was he himself who was driving his son away. "The two of them plotting who-knows-what is the last thing I need," he added.

There was a rasp in his voice that made me stop and take a good look at him. He was glaring at the map case with an unconcealed fury. This was no momentary flare-up of anger, but the overflowing of a long-simmering rage.

"I know you wish I'd do more for Mordred—that I'd treat him

more like . . . kin. But Gwen, the very thought of him makes my skin crawl. I cannot stand the sight of the boy, can't even *look* at him, without remembering . . ."

Arthur's jaw clamped shut, and his muscles tensed, as though this most noble of kings was locked in physical combat with his own imperfect nature, and I understood for the first time the extent of his struggle. Since time began, a monarch must be without blemish, whole and strong and vital. But Arthur's soul carried the blot of incest, rendering him tainted, a man to be cast out of decent society. For all that he was the finest leader in Europe, his moira left him shadowed and at war within himself.

Suddenly he relaxed and, dropping the leather case, came over to me. Taking me firmly by the shoulders, he searched my face imploringly.

"Lass, I'm trying to do the best I can. I've sent the lad out on his own this time—he'll be in charge, without anyone else to oversee him. I *want* to be able to trust him. Maybe once he proves his loyalty, maybe then I can meet him man to man, without the other getting in the way."

"Most likely," I said. "He still wants so much to please you."

"Ah well," Arthur sighed, turning away again. "We all do the best we can. And I swear, if this assignment goes well, I'll promote him to a more important post."

I heard the promise and felt cheered by it. "That would be splendid, my dear—good for both of you, I think."

Thus Arthur went south with Palomides, and Mordred headed to Sea Mills, going first to Wells, then along the Mendips, while I kept the household at Camelot. And no one suspected the chaos that little trip would bring.

19

The Witch of Wookey

s was my wont, I began each day working in the garden, weeding and pinching, mulching and clipping. It gave me a chance to touch the earth again, to draw in strength and calm for the day. In particular, it provided an hour or two of inner communion that was hard to find elsewhere in a busy Court, and restored the balance that was always missing when Lance was gone. At such times my thoughts often went to Joyous Gard, where, I hoped, the Breton was safe. I liked to think of him working in his garden just as I was in mine.

"M'lady!"

The sound cut across my reverie as sharply as it clove the air. I sat back on my heels and blinked at the figure that came careening down the path. He moved like a drunken scarecrow, clothes flapping about raggedly and a dreadful grimace contorting his features.

"Mordred? Mordred, what is it?" I cried as he lurched to a stop in front of me.

The young man was gasping for air so hard his whole body shook. Goaded by who knew what demons, his face had become sunken and ravaged, while his eyes burned wildly in the shadows of their sockets. Even his beard, which he had a youthful vanity about, was tangled and dirty, and both his hands and face were badly scratched.

"Is it true?" he rasped.

A cold premonition slid over me, and I reached toward him. "Is what true?"

"That King Arthur is my father?"

The air went still around us and the very earth ceased to breathe. Even my hand stayed in the effort to find his, and I gawked at my stepson, horror-stricken. Not this way, I prayed; don't let it come out this way.

But my silence was confirmation enough, and he spun away, as though by not seeing me he could avoid the truth. Then, with a sudden swing of direction, he turned back, his manner veering from entreaty to accusation.

"You knew, didn't you?" he hissed, bearing down on me. "Answer, M'lady! You knew!"

The young, powerful hand grabbed my wrist as I bit my lip and nodded a silent admission. For one terrible moment we stared at each other before he loosed his grip and flung my hand away.

"Then why? Why in the name of all that's holy didn't you tell me?" The words welled up out of him, as scalding as milk overflowing a seething pot. "You knew, and yet you let me go on trying, day after day, to make the man like me. Trying to live up to impossible standards. Trying to earn some respect from the King, who himself carries a loathsome secret. At the least you should have told me it was hopeless. Why, M'lady . . . why didn't you?"

I shook my head in stunned disbelief. Why, indeed? It was the same cry I had made to his father all those years ago when I, too, had found out about Mordred's origins. How could I have let this boy, this child I thought of as my own, walk into the same horrifying discovery without giving him the protection of being forewarned?

"I . . ." My mouth opened and closed, yet no sound came out. Tears were filling my eyes. "There never seemed to be a right time . . . I tried. No, that's not true . . . not quite. I wanted you to know—I just had no way to tell you."

Mordred heard the words, but his face showed no understanding of their meaning. The truth had heaved him into a blind pit, and he stared through me to his own inner horror, like a man enmeshed in nightmare. When he spoke, despair had leached his voice of color.

"I wouldn't believe her, you know. Tried to kill her when she taunted me. Spent the whole night chasing through the woods—

each of us hiding in the dark, listening, darting away, jumping after—through bramble and thicket and holly shaws. Just before dawn she made it back to the cavern and hid beyond my grasp."

This time he let me take hold of his hands, which were growing cold as ice. "Who, Mordred? Who told you?"

"The Witch of Wookey Hole." His teeth started to chatter, and a long shiver ran through him. "Named the truth for me, the reason that the King finds me so hateful. Just a voice at first, coming from the woods but following as I went along the Road . . . 'He has been where he should not, you are the spawn that he begot. Unnatural child of an unspeakable union, that's what you are, and even the Gods despise you.' Unnatural—that's what she called me. Unnatural. . . ." The word hung on the air, sick with self-loathing.

Cursing the crone silently, I chafed Mordred's hands in an effort to warm them. The color was leaving his face, and he whimpered once as he slumped on the bench and I called frantically for help. After Enid and I got him wrapped in blankets, Griflet was summoned to carry him to my chamber.

When we'd put my son on the bed and bundled the comforter around him, the Kennel Master asked quietly, "Do you want me to stand guard?"

I shook my head, grateful that I could trust that neither he nor Enid would mention this to the household. "He's had a bad shock, but will be better for a sound sleep and some hot broth."

Mordred slept through much of the day, with me sitting beside him, seeing again the boy who loved to track the golden eagles in their flight, who cherished the stories of the Trojan War and had always dreaded the dark secrets of the woods. A bright child given into my care, born to run free into the promise of tomorrow, now tripped and forever caught in the dark snare of his father's secret.

Over and over I wondered how I could have handled it better. What could have been done or said to make Arthur see him as a boy in need of a father rather than the eternal reminder of a shameful act? Perhaps men never face their own humanity in the way that women do—and there was nothing anyone could have done to deflect the moira of this father and son.

By nightfall Mordred had slept through the worst of his exhaustion, and the restless tossing of nightmares gave way to calmer waking. He lay there looking at me, sad-eyed and empty, no longer wracked by the feverish horror of the morning.

"You'll be needing your chamber," he said softly, glancing out the window at the new moon that lay cradled in sunset clouds.

"You needn't go on my account." I spoke up quickly, unwilling to send him from the safety of this nest. "I use the royal bedroom even when Arthur's gone."

He grimaced as he raised himself on one elbow, though whether at the sound of his father's name or the bruises of his body, I couldn't tell. "No, M'lady . . . not on your account but my own. There are things I must learn to live with, and that's easiest done at a distance." Pulling himself upright, he smiled bleakly and reached for my hands. "We'll have no need to speak of this again . . . but before we leave the matter to the past, please know I don't blame you." His voice went gentle for a moment. "You gave me the best childhood one could ask for, have been the best mother one could want. Morgause . . ." he stumbled on the name, then gave a faint shrug. "The memory of her is far back and faded. Not even she saw fit to warn me."

His mouth firmed into a hard, cold line, and he tightened his grip on my hands. "I have but one request—that you not tell the High King. There is no reason for me to put into words what he has left unsaid. I will not bring it up myself; why should I? But I ask your promise to keep my secret as well as you kept his."

His dark eyes watched me intently. There was neither reproach nor anger in them, just a deep pleading. Out of sorrow and guilt, and without thought to the ramifications, I gave him my oath.

"Well now, 'tis done," he said, throwing off the covers and looking about for his boots. "I must be off to find Cynric before he decides the goblins caught me on the Road." There was a new brittleness to his voice that had not been there before.

I watched him stand and stretch, thinking how much he moved like his father. He turned at the door and gave me a sardonic smile. "After all, one must uphold the honor of King Arthur's Court."

O Mordred, would that we had bridged the chasm then, dragged the hidden anguish into the light and been done with silent wars. Neither

*you nor Arthur would have found it easy, but at least it would not
have come to this.*

*But I lacked the courage to refuse this one special favor, and made
a promise there was no way I could keep. By then I myself was
complicit in your betrayal, whether by silence or by speaking. . . . and
the Witch of Wookey laughed in her cave.*

Arthur returned from the south a fortnight later, coming in
tired but happy. A week on the Road had left him gritty from
head to foot.

"Bagdemagus's friend Gwynlliw has matters in Devon well in
hand," he reported as I scrubbed him down in the niche of the
garden I reserved for bathing. I used a fresh chunk of soap to work
up a full lather, and he sputtered when I poured a bucket of
rainwater over his head, then rose and shook himself like a dog.

"Those hill-forts are full of crusty old veterans and youngsters
eager to take on the devil himself! Good to see their spirits high,
in spite of Geraint's death. If anything, that battle gave them a
keener edge, made them more alert."

My husband groped for a towel and, wrapping it around his
loins, stepped dripping from the tin tub.

"How does that sit with the Federates?" I asked, thinking of
those settlers who had been loyal to the British crown all along.
"Don't they resent being treated with suspicion? We don't know
that they would have sided with the invaders, after all."

"True." Arthur turned his attention to drying himself. "I need
to establish better ties with them—show them we respect their
ways and want to live in peace, not just as overlords."

I watched him rubbing down his back—a fine, proud king in
the prime of his life. Only graying at the temples, not yet badly
weathered. He had no notion of what had transpired at Wookey
Hole, and for all that I ached to blurt out Mordred's story, I was
loath to shatter my husband's happiness. Besides, it would be
breaking my promise. So I, the woman whose tongue was always
running away with her, silenced the clamoring of my own common sense.

As it happened, Arthur didn't ask to hear Mordred's report for
several days, by which time the lad had returned from his private

journey. The High King scrutinized his scroll on the status of the settlements and forts along the Bristol coast, then began asking for further details. Mordred joined him at the map, and the two of them went over it together.

"The only real problem is the band of brigands that have holed up on Brent Knoll, that single hill to the south of Weston," Mordred noted. "They're nowhere near as destructive as the Irish raiders, but are causing the locals some concern. I'd suggest you send a group of four or five warriors to rout them out . . . it shouldn't require much more than that."

"You've done a more than competent job," Arthur said, raising his head to look his son fully in the face. My heart lifted, seeing the effort he was making to overcome his aversion.

"Thank you, Your Highness," the young man replied courteously enough, but he refused to hold his father's gaze.

"I've been thinking," Arthur went on, rising to pace about the room. "You and the Saxon hostage, Cynric, have become pretty good friends, haven't you?" He turned to catch Mordred's reaction, and when there was an assenting nod, Arthur smiled. "I need a representative to the Saxon Federates. If you think Cynric can be trusted, you could use him as a kind of liaison when you meet the individual leaders. That is, if you want to be my envoy to these people."

Mordred was staring at Arthur, summing him up for the first time with the knowledge of their kinship. Whatever thoughts or feelings lay behind those brown eyes remained hidden, unmoved and unmoving. At last he inclined his head. "I'm at your disposal, Your Highness, and willing to serve in any capacity you choose."

My eyes flicked to Arthur, wondering if he heard the cautious hope in his son's voice. But Britain's High King was already thinking of other business. "Fine. It's settled, then. We'll make the trip to the Saxon Shore this summer—visit the settlers and introduce you at the same time."

He was rummaging about, looking for a different report, the matter of Mordred having been dismissed. I saw the younger man's face before he bowed to his father's back and walked stiffly to the door. Whatever hope he had of recognition, of having earned the right to his father's candor, died in him. He was retreating, hurt but not yet harmed. That's when I realized that, promise or no, I must tell Arthur how things now stood.

"What!" The exclamation was so savage, my husband's voice cracked. "Who told him, and why?"

"The old crone at Wookey . . . seems she had some grudge against me."

His dear, familiar features were changing into those of a savage animal and a look of raw, primal hatred flashed across them. In the blink of an eye he'd gone from being the finest of kings to a beast confronted by the unendurable. I jumped to my feet as he whirled away from the long table, his fists doubled, shoulders shaking.

"How he found out isn't what matters!" I declared, following my husband across the room. He was moving with a cold, determined air, and I searched desperately for words to reach a man who was on the edge of blind violence. "Now's the chance, the time to make things right. Call him back, Arthur, *talk* to him. . . ."

But I pleaded in vain. Instead of sending for his son, Arthur Pendragon lifted Excalibur down from its position on the wall, his jaw set like granite, his eyes hard as iron.

"What are you doing?" My voice rose with a wail of fear as he buckled the baldric in place and settled the sword within hand's grasp. The gems in the hilt winked with a cold fire. "Arthur," I begged, "where are you going?"

Without a word he headed for the door, murderous rage writ across his face. I rushed after him, but he flung me to one side without even breaking stride—as much the wild, bloodthirsty Celt as Gawain had ever been.

I lay where I had fallen, awash with the memory of seeing the redhead dancing over his foe's body after a battle—a gleeful, giddy maniac whacking off the head and brandishing the wretched thing by the hair. It was terrifying to realize that Arthur, too, was capable of that kind of savagery.

"Dear Gods," I whimpered. "Protect him, as well as his son."

Arthur did not return at all that night. When it was clear that he'd left Camelot and that Mordred was still among the Queen's

Men at dinner, I relaxed a little. At least Arthur's vengeance was not focused on his own offspring.

Indeed, it was only next morning, while I was at my gardening, that I learned what my husband had done.

"Dead." The word fell flat in the morning air, followed by the thud of something dark and gruesome landing on the ground where I knelt. "And here's her head for proof."

I jumped back and stared up at Arthur. He was as worn and haggard as Mordred had been, and splattered with blood and gore besides. When he spoke, the words were wrenched out of him. "Bury it if you wish—or set it out for the carrion crows, it's of no mind to me."

He heaved a ragged sigh and turned to look out over the countryside like a fevered man reaching for a cup of water. Farmers were burning the stubble in their fields, creating the soft gray haze that always ushers in autumn's gold. High above, a skein of ducks was heading for the winter on Glastonbury's lake, their distant calls conjuring long nights and warm fires. Closer by, the hips on my rosebushes were beginning to ripen. Slowly, inevitably, Arthur's gaze came home to me, and when I opened my arms and took him into them, tears coursed down his cheeks.

"It's done," he whispered. "The old witch will never again preside over her stream of sorrows."

I've often wondered if he truly thought killing the hag had solved the problem of his son, any more than Lance's disappearance had made me cease to love him. Perhaps it was simply a matter of at last having someone to take action against, a clearly defined foe he could confront. In the months that followed, my husband acted as though the question of his relationship with Mordred did not exist, and we entered a time of irony, for each man knew—and knew the other knew—but weighted silence filled the space where understanding could have grown.

20

Winter

was confident that Arthur would not renege on his promise to make Mordred his envoy to the Federates and that Mordred would do a conscientious job. They met several times to discuss the problems of the Saxons, but there was no warmth or personal trust between them and each would be silent for some time afterward. When Lance came back from Joyous Gard, I told him about it, decrying the fact that being open and truthful hadn't made things any better.

"They're only open and truthful with you, Gwen, not with each other," the Breton pointed out. "Arthur is a long way from being able to acknowledge his son. But give him time. Now that Mordred's an adult, things may begin to change—fathers and sons have different relationships at different ages, I'm sure."

Then suddenly Arthur realized that his son had a keen interest in developing the law code. Before long Mordred was taking dictation, organizing information and making suggestions as they went along.

"He asked Cynric about the way the Saxons handle trials," Arthur mused one night. "Seems they choose a committee of men from the area—a jury of one's peers—and together they judge the case. It's an interesting idea . . . would take the pressure off the king to adjudicate everything."

I listened and nodded, pleased to see a working partnership developing between them; hopefully it would help heal the wounds in each.

Winter was a delight that year—crisp and cold, with days of

diamond brilliance and nights shimmering with sheets of color they call the Great Crown of the North. Since Mordred was so busy with the law, it fell to Lance to escort me on my morning rides, just as in the old days. We coursed the countryside, laughing and playing in the snow with a group of children, relaying messages from Gwyn about the training of our horses and taking baskets of food to those crofters less fortunate than the rest.

One morning I carried a joint of venison to a tanner's wife who was abed with childbirth. The hut was little more than a hovel. A single pot bubbled by the fire; there was but one chair to sit on; and a passel of children clambered in and out of my lap. The woman who was recently delivered lay on a pallet in the corner of the room, the swaddled babe in the crook of her arm.

"I've got a new brother," a young tyke announced, happily tugging on my sleeve. His little sister crowded in, caroling "He's mine, too," at which the boy made a face and pulled her hair. She ran to hide behind me, and soon both children were circling me as they swatted at each other until one of them hit the baby I was holding on my shoulder.

"No you don't," I admonished as their granny bore down on them, scolding everyone for inconveniencing the Queen.

"That's all right, Carwen, I understand," I assured her.

But afterward, as Lance helped me mount Etain, the Breton gave a short laugh. "Raising children makes managing a court look easy, doesn't it?"

"Probably not all that different," I allowed. "Just that the first are young in years while the second are childish by nature."

His marvelous full lips compressed in a secret smile, and his eyes began to sparkle. "You're the most amazing woman—running a country one moment, burping a baby the next. And beautiful . . . no matter what you're doing, you're so beautiful."

I looked down at him, dazzled by the outpouring of love and appreciation. Once I'd have leapt from my horse and flung myself into his arms with joy and tenderness and all the openness of my heart. But years of caution, of duty, of keeping a distance between us, held me in check, so I leaned down and putting my hand against his cheek, simply said, "Ah, love, I could not do the half of it without you by my side."

He caught my fingers and pressed them to his lips, a bright, fine laughter playing in his eyes. It was enough to sustain me through a myriad of duties, a month of conferences, half a year of boring routines. And I never, never took it for granted. That kind of soul-touching happens too rarely to be cavalier about.

When springtime came, Cei and I began the necessary preparations for the Court's progress through the Saxon Shore. I was in the midst of packing baskets and panniers, saddlebags and wicker trunks the day Dinadan returned from Brittany.

Dinadan—closest friend and cohort of the Cornish warrior Tristan, he was the sleek little terrier to Tris's wolfhound. For years, whenever Tristan blundered into love and combat, it was Dinadan who hauled him out, mopping up the mess and trying to mend the fences. In that sense, he was a shining example of what a best friend is.

"Nice to be back in the most civilized Court in Christendom," the Cornishman announced with a knowing smile. "Howell's a fine man, of course, and treats his warriors well, but it's just not the same as being with you two."

This last was directed at both Arthur and me, and I smiled at the compliment. Dinadan was best known for his droll and sometimes wry sense of humor, but I'd often thought he could have been a diplomat as well.

"What news from the Franks?" Arthur inquired.

"Ha! Each of the sons is chewing on the others, trying to wrest some larger portion of Clovis's kingdom for himself. Thank God, it keeps them out of other mischief."

"And Tristan?" Lance inquired.

"Quite the most effective warrior around—saving perhaps yourself," the little man added, nodding comfortably to Lance. "And well beloved for his music. He still plays the harp like an angel. It takes a bit of talent, you know—being able to whack off heads in the morning and sing ballads in the afternoon."

It was such an apt portrait of Tristan, we all burst out laughing.

Next day Dinadan accompanied me on my ride, for in spite of the piles of clouds skimming toward us, I needed to leave the treen-maker an order for the wooden bowls, trays and utensils I'd be wanting in the kitchen when we came back in the fall.

"Never knew a queen who took such a personal hand in running the Court," Dinadan commented. "Now Isolde of Cornwall, God bless her, let the housekeepers manage all that while she sat, pretty as a picture, working on her embroideries as Tristan played the harp for her."

"She's a far better needlewoman than I," I shrugged, remembering the many times I'd seen her deftly decorating some bit of cloth with bright flosses. "As good at that as Morgan le Fey, I think."

"And getting to be as famous a healer," Dinadan said. "Even in Brittany she's said to be one of the best. Of course," he added, "her mother was a famous shamaness in Ireland—a real wizard at curing illness and cleaning wounds."

Isolde's Pagan background had been one of the problems between her and Mark, but Dinadan now assured me she had become the model Christian. "And not just for show. She's really quite devout, they say."

The White Christ was popping up everywhere, it seemed, and as we talked, it became clear that Dinadan himself espoused the belief.

"What of Tristan?" I inquired. "Is he, too, bending the knee to Rome in spirit as well as body?"

"Ah, poor Tris. Sometimes I think the big lout doesn't know whom he wants, or what he believes. Take his marriage, for instance." The Cornishman scratched his chin and stared thoughtfully at the sky. "I suspected something wasn't right when he told me the bride's name was Isolde White Hands. After declaring a lifelong passion for Isolde of Cornwall, asking White Hands to be his wife seemed"—Dinadan cocked his head and squinted thoughtfully—"shall we say, a bit inconsistent?"

I grinned at the understatement. "We thought perhaps it was a political union. Isn't White Hands Howell's sister?"

"Aye, that she is," Tristan's friend nodded. "And a dear girl. But love is a very tricky business: catches you entirely off guard and makes you see only the things you want to."

"Is he that besotted on his bride?" I asked, wondering if Tris had truly forgotten his earlier love. The first drops of a summer shower were pattering around us, so we reined our horses into the protective shelter of a beechwood.

Dinadan shook his head. "Rather the contrary. Oh, I think he wanted to love White Hands; certainly he courted her assiduously and made all the usual protestations. But the wedding night didn't go well, if you get my drift, and it's gotten worse since. He blames his inability to function on his love for the Queen of Cornwall."

"You mean the marriage was never consummated?" Tris was a big, uncomplicated man, who saw both himself and life in purely physical terms. The idea of his becoming impotent was more than a little surprising.

"Ah, M'lady, it happens to the best of men at one time or another, and for some more often than not," Dinadan noted wryly as the rain pelted the leaves above us. "It's as unfair to judge a man by his randiness as it is to judge a woman by her looks."

I laughed at the astuteness of the comment. Lancelot might see me as beautiful, but he was looking considerably below the surface. I knew full well that any courtier who praised my looks was indulging in flattery for some design of his own. "But how does Tris's bride take his lack of interest?" I inquired. "Is she very upset?"

"The poor girl is totally devoted to him, trails around in his wake, sees to his every need—clean garments, mended hose, his favorite foods at every meal."

"Sounds like a servant," I quipped, remembering Uwain's assessment of Christian wives.

"And all this for love, M'lady. Does it all for love. I found her in tears one day, thinking there must be something wrong with her, that she isn't attractive enough. In the end, I told her about Tris and Isolde having drunk the love potion by mistake, and never being able to love another."

"What a dreadful thing for White Hands to live with," I blurted out. "Unfulfilled love is painful enough without knowing the person you love will *never* love you. That's plain cruel."

"I tell you, M'lady," Dinadan mused, craning his neck in an effort to see how soon the shower would pass, "the Greeks knew what they were talking about when they said love was devised by the Gods as a punishment for mortals, and no intelligent human goes looking for it."

"Has it never found you?" I cast my companion a sidewise look, suspecting he was not as impervious to romance as he would have us believe.

"I never said I was immune." Dinadan smiled crookedly, and blushed when he met my gaze. "It's precisely because I loved so much, I know how foolish it can make us. The lady, unfortunately, loved someone else, so I've never mentioned my feelings."

"Ah, friend." I reached over, putting my hand on his arm. "Surely you can find another?"

"Could you find another Arthur?"

"No, of course not," I laughed, caught once more by his cleverness.

"And I'm far from the only man whose love has never been expressed. There's Cei, for instance."

"Cei!" I was so astonished, the name leapt out of my mouth, sounding louder than I meant because the rain had suddenly stopped. I'd always assumed the Seneschal was uninterested in love, not that he cherished one who didn't return his feelings.

"I talk too much, and it seems to be clearing," the Cornishman announced, abruptly urging his horse back onto the Road. Patches of rainfall were still sheeting down on a nearby field, but my escort was determined to be moving. "I trust you'll forget my last comment, M'lady. . . . I'd hate to have the Seneschal mad at me."

"Of course." I laughed as a gust of wind sent a downpour over us, plastering my hair to my head. "Provided you leave the forecasting of weather to others."

The day before our journey to the Federates was to start, one of the Royal Messengers came loping up the hill, covered with mud and carrying the long pole such youngsters use to vault from tussock to tussock in the marshes of the Somerset Levels. He rushed past the sentry, crying out for the High King. I was just coming back from the stables and joined Arthur on the steps as he came out to see what all the fuss was about.

"It's Yder, Your Highness," the lad panted, his words tumbling out breathlessly. "Went to Brent Knoll alone, to get rid of the bandits. Hacked to pieces, he was."

"Alone, you say?" Arthur growled. "I told him to take a cadre of men with him."

"Why would he do such a foolish thing?" I asked, shocked at the news.

"Wanted to gain your admiration, M'lady." The messenger bobbed his head in deference to me. "At least, that's what his brother, Gwyn, said. Yder went off yesterday, and the bandits left his body where it fell. Gwyn went looking for him this morning, since he hadn't returned."

The realization of what had happened hit me like a punch in the stomach. The same miserable helplessness I'd felt when the bear died at Caerleon settled over me and I swayed unsteadily on my feet. "There was no reason . . . I never meant . . . so pointless. . . ."

"Here now!" Arthur exclaimed as I grabbed his arm to keep from falling. "It's not your fault, Gwen—by Jove, it isn't," he swore, catching me up and carrying me inside.

"Never meant to cause such death," I sobbed, clinging to my husband.

Arthur put me carefully on the cushion of a windowseat and called for Enid, then began to pace in front of me. "You know how the warriors are nowadays—bored with peacetime endeavors. Too little to keep them busy, so they get restless and go off doing foolish things. You mustn't blame yourself because the man wanted to look grander in your eyes."

I nodded, knowing in my head he was right—there are enough things to worry about that we are responsible for, without taking on those we can do nothing about. I hadn't any more encouraged Yder in this than I'd needed rescuing from the bear at Caerleon. Still, it hurt to know a good man's life was lost because of such foolishness.

"What if Gwyn holds me to blame?" I whispered, taking the cup of valerian tea Enid brought.

"He won't." Arthur was firm in his answer. "After all these years, I know Gwyn of Neath better than most. He doesn't place blame or look for scapegoats. Yder did what he felt he had to do; Gwyn will respect that, no matter how much he grieves the loss."

Sitting there, watching my husband through the steam from my cup, it occurred to me that, as Isolde was for me, Gwyn was the closest thing Arthur had to a peer. Bedivere and Cei were his foster brothers, and Lancelot his dearest friend, but these were men who looked to him as their monarch as well. The fey Welshman was just enough different to be set apart from other men, just as the High King was. Perhaps it explained the remarkable camaraderie that had grown between the two of them.

"I hope you're right," I ventured at last. "I'd hate to have the man think I brought about his brother's death."

As it turned out, Gwyn made a point of letting me know he considered his brother lucky to have met his end doing something he believed in so deeply. "Gave his death some meaning," the little man said solemnly. "I can't think of a finer end, even among the old heroes." I found his effort to make me feel better deeply touching.

We offered to delay our departure in order that Yder might have a proper funeral, but Gwyn preferred to take his brother back to their home in Neath and there perform the appropriate rites. I had a hunch they would be more fey than most, and not for the eyes of normal mortals.

"Yder and I don't need you on our journey, and you don't need me on yours," Gwyn confirmed in his odd, cryptic fashion. Squinting from Arthur to Mordred and back, he gave a little shrug. "Some moiras fulfill themselves no matter what we do."

I heard the prophecy and smiled. Over the winter months the High King and his new envoy to the Federates had worked diligently together—first on the law, now on what was to be expected from the Saxons. Surely, I told myself, the little man with Second Sight was referring to the growing rapprochement between father and son.

So we left Camelot on the first stage of a progress that would occupy us for the next six months. In retrospect, it ranged from early memories of our rule to the bright and terrible promise of the future, but at the time all I saw was the multihued present. Perhaps it was better that way.

21

The State of the Realm

ur itinerary took us to Winchester, and on the way we spent a night at the hill-fort of Sarum, the scene of Arthur's and my wedding.

While the High King met with the Dorset warlords, I went out and walked the ramparts of the ancient stronghold by myself. The sentries were young and had no reason to recognize me, and more than one challenged my right to be on the parapet. There were several stammered apologies, and someone hastened to explain, "We can't be too cautious, with Saxons living so close by."

I asked if there was any specific cause for concern and was told the measures were precautionary only—though the presence of the High King had led to a doubling of the guards. I was reassured that they took such measures, and disturbed that they were necessary.

As I rounded the far curve, past the grove of trees where Griflet had first met his Saxon dairymaid, Frieda, a solitary figure came into view, leaning against the parapet and gazing over the misty lands to the south.

"Ah, Gwen—takes you back a bit, doesn't it?" Bedivere commented as I came to stand beside him.

"Indeed," I answered, warming to the presence of my first true friend at Court. "One can almost imagine the woods and meadows full of tents again, with commons and nobles and kings all jumbled up together. Everyone trying out the stirrups Palomides brought to us, and sizing up the young High King and his bride. And you," I grinned up at the familiar, craggy face. "You, running across the Square at daybreak, trying to round up enough people to witness our very hasty wedding while the drums of war were beating—what a time that was!"

"Ah, yes," the one-handed lieutenant concurred. "That war was won, and the Irish never threatened again; those stirrups have given our cavalry the edge in every campaign; the people now know and love their monarchs; and the marriage has gone well for over two decades." Bedivere lifted one eyebrow. "No matter how chaotic the beginning, the structure has proved sound."

"Even the shadow over Arthur is lifting," I said, for it was Bedivere who referred to Mordred and his origins as a darkness that blighted Arthur's life. "Mordred knows, and Arthur no longer avoids him."

"I suspected as much." The lieutenant nodded thoughtfully. "It's an excellent idea, giving him a special post with the Federates. They need to be included as respected members of the realm; Arthur needs to understand and address their concerns; and Mordred needs a position that puts his energy to constructive use. I sometimes think Arthur doesn't realize how talented his son is. With any luck, this appointment will benefit everyone."

"Benefit everyone"—it was a phrase that came to mind over and over as we went through the Saxon territories. Both Mordred and Cynric sat beside the King when the local leaders came to pay their respects at Winchester. Once the walled city had been a bastion of Roman power, a stronghold against the incoming Saxons. Now it was an island of Britons surrounded by a sea of Federates, and their eyes moved ever and again to Cynric's prominence in our party. A rustle of whispers lapped about us.

"Did you notice the fellow beside the High King's envoy?"

"Aye, the son of Cerdic, who almost took the south away from the Pendragon. I wonder that Arthur trusts him enough to bring him back among his father's followers. . . ."

"Shows how confident the King is. Kept the boy as a peace-hostage, now uses him to build that peace. Whatever else you can say of the Pendragon, he's a man of his word."

It was the same everywhere—Federates looking cautiously at the unusual sight, noting the fair head and dark so often together —for Mordred and Cynric were well-nigh inseparable on this trip. In the marketplace, at the Council table, even at the feasts our hosts provided, the young Briton and German faced the world side by side.

The more warlike of our allies watched it too, shaking their heads as their hands drifted toward their sword hilts.

"Ain't natural having such close dealings with Saxons. A fox is still a fox, and can't be tamed."

"Maybe the High King's gone soft. Someone told me he's planning to become a Christian; you don't suppose he'll turn into a monk like some of those other converts, do you?"

"Not likely, with Merlin as his guide." This from Ironside, who was every bit as set in the Old Ways as Gawain had become in the ways of the White Christ. "They say the Archdruid still watches over his reign, even if he does speak through that doire who married Pelleas."

At this there was much nodding of heads and a surreptitious making of signs against evil, for Nimue commanded almost as much respect as Merlin had.

"We've a good man in Arthur—finest king Britain's seen in ages," someone averred, and a mutter of agreement ran round them. "Or for ages to come," someone else called out, remembering Merlin's prophecy of a timeless monarch. And before long there would be shouts and applause for the Pendragon as everyone rushed to align themselves with our reign.

Sometimes the Saxons themselves joined in, caught up by the hope of men who want to follow a just leader. But I noted how many of them were youngsters, boys not even born when Arthur had defeated their fathers at the Battle of Mount Badon. And part of me couldn't help wondering if they weren't just biding their time, waiting to find the soft underbelly of a king grown lax and careless. Unless we recruited them to our Cause, they might develop a separate one of their own.

As we moved deeper into Saxon territory, the changes in the landscape became more obvious. With their heavy, iron-tipped plows and great teams of oxen, the Federates were turning the heavy clay of the river valleys into rich farms. Steadings that were once isolated farms, as remote and lonely as Wehha's outpost, had now grown into villages where craftsmen displayed their wares around the edges of a common green; wooden buckets and barrels, clay pots and handsome baskets, well-turned wheels and iron-clad shovels that were wonderfully sturdy. Remarkable treasures from the Saxon homeland caught my eye: chip-carved brooches and beautiful goldwork, as well as glassware from the Rhineland factories. I marveled at the range of items and wished they were available to all our people. Perhaps Arthur could be encouraged to end the decree that kept Saxon boats from docking at the British ports.

Among the Federates I found no change in their notion that women had no place in government or matters of state, and High Queen or not, I was expected to follow our hosts' customs. Even in Canterbury my women and I had to stay in the kitchen area while the men boasted and caroused and drank themselves to sleep in the separate mead-hall.

"Do not fret, Good Lady," the Saxon Queen reassured me. "Ours is the finest Hall in the whole of Kent, as proud and comfortable as the famous Heorot built by Hrothgar. A fine hearth, with many sturdy tables and strong benches, and torches to keep the shadows away while the skalds sing of our great heroes —everything a man could want for comfort and ease. Your lord will be well cared for."

I stared at the woman, thinking her mind must be made of mush. How else could one explain a queen who presided over the kitchen and took no part in ruling the realm with her husband?

We stayed at Canterbury for three long days, during which the men talked and drank, went hunting, and played at games. On the last morning the Companions put on a display of cavalry maneuvers for our hosts.

Although the Saxons revere the white horse, they do not ride often, so there was much comment when the Companions took the field, mounted on the black horses which had become synonymous with our cavalry. Both animals and men were in splendid shape—vigorous, energetic, and lavishly turned out. Even the trappings were elegant—bronze bosses shone, bridle-bells rang, and on every headstall the red enameled rondels marked each as a member of Arthur's own corps. Seeing them in close drill and synchronized riding, I nodded with an inner satisfaction. It couldn't hurt to keep the Federates in awe of us.

Arthur had announced early on that Mordred would become their liaison with us, and would remain at Canterbury after we left. The Saxons were so pleased with the idea, they insisted on giving him a headband woven of golden threads. It was a handsome example of one of their most exacting arts, and when it circled Mordred's fair brow and black hair, it reflected the special status they accorded him.

On the last afternoon of our stay my stepson and I took a leisurely stroll through the market area, past stalls of local pottery, cages of chickens and piles of freshly harvested greens. Ironically, it was the only place we could say our goodbyes in private, away from the pressures of Court.

"I appreciate the opportunity to serve His Highness," Mordred began. I heard the carefulness of his tone and shot him a quick glance. His jaw was set as firmly as ever his father's had been, but when he caught my eye, he gave me a mischievous smile. "I don't have to ask how much you had to do with it . . . and I'm deeply grateful."

"It was his own idea, and his own decision," I interjected hastily. But he only gave me a skeptical look, then glanced away.

"Mordred—" I took his arm and guided him into the shadow of a Roman temple, away from the crowded market. "Whatever else you may think of King Arthur, he's a fair man. He was impressed by your evaluation of the Bristol coast; he'll be equally impressed by good, competent work here. Just keep your eyes and ears open, and report to him regularly. He's never been one to stint on recognition."

"Except for a son." Mordred stared at his feet, not even aware he'd spoken aloud, but his words had the sting of hornets.

"Look at me," I demanded, taking his chin in my hand. "Don't ask the impossible. And don't go around feeling sorry for yourself —there's much too much to be done in life to wallow in self-pity. Let him get to know you for the person you are, separate from the blood-tie—he'll respect you more and better that way. You can earn his admiration, I know you can."

The dark eyes burned with a sulky fire, half rebellion, half pain, but at last he gave a slight nod, followed by a boyish smile. "If *you* think I can, M'lady . . . then I guess I can."

"Of course you can," I teased as we ambled back into the stream of shoppers. "Why else would I have spent all those years raising you?"

Next morning, when our party was ready to leave, Mordred

and Cynric rode with our hosts as they accompanied us to the city gates. It was a grand procession, with the Banner of the Red Dragon unfurled, and the white-horsetail standards of the Saxons shining in the sunlight. There was the usual formal declaration of friendship and leave-taking, and Mordred was the first to salute our party as we turned to go. I gave him not only a royal nod but also a quick thumbs up, and every silent vote of confidence I could think of, though I was only vaguely aware of the remarkable future he would soon be offering all of us.

The rest of the summer was spent in travel. London was glad to see us, and we arrived in time to enjoy the fruits from the old cherry tree in the Park beside the Imperial Palace. On the way to Cambridge we stayed at a moldering mansion in Chelmsford, which was being renovated as a hostel for the Royal Messengers. The nearby temple was an ornate, octagonal building several stories high where we all paused to pay homage to the collection of Roman and British gods that had been worshiped there for centuries.

I looked down the Roman Road that leads to East Anglia and wondered how things were going at Wehha's settlement now that Wuffa was in charge. Unfortunately, he'd left on one of his regular trips back to the homeland, and so would not be able to host us this time.

Cambridge had not grown much over the years, but was still an army outpost—one of the many Uther Pendragon had set up to keep the Saxons within the agreed-upon boundaries. We camped on a nearby ridge and watched a whey-white moon rise out of the misty Fens on a soft night in July.

At Lincoln the troops assured us that all had been quiet in their area since each local Saxon had personally sworn fealty to the High King, following the Battle of Mount Badon. "They remember how you put them in chains and only released them when they bent the knee and made their oath," the captain of the outpost said. "Nothing like a good dose of authority to keep 'em in line."

"And a bit of humanity," Lancelot noted softly, remembering that if Arthur had not released those men, their crops would have gone unharvested and many a Saxon steading would have known famine that year.

York was considerably quieter since Urien had moved so many of his men north. Uwain kept the fort manned, however, and he took us to a room in one of the many-sided towers that overlooked the river Ouse. It was light and airy as tower rooms go, and held nothing but a table and some chairs, while a frame on the wall supported a stretched cowhide. A map of Urien's country had been drawn on the leather, from York all the way up to the river Tweed.

"My father's decided to make Yeavering his northern headquarters," Uwain explained, tapping the map with an ivory pointer. "It's an old hill-fort tucked into the hills above the river Glen. A bit off the track, but it commands a splendid view in all directions. There's been enough activity to warrant fortifying the area, keep out invaders and protect the villages along the northern coast. He's thinking about refurbishing the Roman signal towers, and the red-rock bluffs at Bamburgh are a natural spot for a seaside fortress."

Arthur stroked his mustaches and scowled, but it was Lance who spoke up. "What about the lands around Warkworth?"

"No trouble that I've heard of." Uwain put down his pointer and turned to the Breton. "That's where Joyous Gard is, isn't it? There in the loop of the river? You might consider putting up walls, if you haven't already."

"That likely to be attacked?"

Uwain lifted one shoulder noncommittally. "Considering what I've seen and heard on the Continent, I'd say Britain will be seeing an overflow of Saxons and Frisians, Angles and Jutes, for years to come. With the Goths having displaced so many of the tribes across Europe, these are the people who've been pushed to the water's edge. Naturally, if they can make it to Britain in a single day's journey across the sea, they're going to try."

Uwain's words made me think of Theodoric leading his hordes across the mountains into Italy—a wave of history that couldn't be stopped. It sent a shiver down my back.

"I don't want to turn Joyous Gard into a fortress," Lance noted as we walked back to the fancy terraced house Uwain had put at our disposal. "But perhaps something around the farmyard . . ."

Arthur agreed, so when we came to Portgate where the Roman Road known as Dere Street passes through the Wall, Lancelot bade us farewell and continued north to his Joyous Garden. He took some of his own men and Gareth as well, and as I watched them canter off down the broad pavement, I thought how fortunate it was that the boy he'd taken in as a squire had grown into such a close friend.

We turned west, traveling along the supply road that clings to the base of the Wall. According to Cathbad, it was some old Caesar who built the stone bulwark across the width of Britain, stretching from Newcastle to Carlisle. It rides the north-facing ridges and bristles with forts designed to keep the Pict and Scot from raiding the richer lands to the south. No doubt it has been successful; from base to parapet it rises to three times the height of a man. Certainly I wouldn't want to scale it.

The towers, which were built within shouting distance of each other, mostly stand empty and deserted. A few of the smaller forts are still used to shelter shepherds or farmers or the occasional traveler journeying to or from Carlisle. Villages had grown up outside the larger compounds such as Chester, and although they had dwindled in size after the Legions left, they still manned the Wall for local leaders.

The Romans were noted for moving men and goods in a straight line, rarely deviating for such things as rivers or gullies. Where these were too steep, they threw bridges across the canyons, as in the stretch of Dere Street north of the fort at Binchester. But along the Wall itself, bridges were used only for crossing major rivers, as the barrier had to hug the earth. Where the Wall followed the broad valley of the lower Tyne we rode comfortably enough, but as the land grew more rugged, the way became too steep for horses, and we had to dismount.

"Might as well climb to the parapet and walk along the top," Arthur suggested since we had to go by foot anyway. I thought it a splendid idea, so while squires took the horses down to the more level Road known as the Stone Gate, we strode along like Roman soldiers, surveying the land on either side of the Wall. A cleared area of trackways or ditches ran along its base, leaving few places where an enemy could hide, and I pitied anyone who tried to cross the thing by stealth.

"The Romans even fixed grates under the arches of the bridge," Arthur noted as the Wall took a huge, flying leap across the North Tyne at Chester. "They wanted to make sure no one could sneak through, either by swimming or using a boat."

We were standing outside the tower that protects the eastern abutment, where the guards were all in a dither to find the High King so suddenly in their midst. One of the sentries at the other end of the bridge dashed down the stairs to find someone who could welcome us officially.

While we waited for this little nicety—no Celtic ruler enters a town or fort without permission of the inhabitants, unless it is his own—I leaned over the railing of the bridge and stared down into the turbulent river. Stained dark as tea by the peat they seeped through, the waters leapt and tumbled along their rocky bed, and when I squinted, I could just make out the shadow of the grates Arthur had mentioned. Probably made of elm, I decided, since it is the wood that best survives years of submersion, and the Romans were nothing if not thorough in planning their defenses to last for lifetimes.

In every aspect the Tyne is a lovely river—broad and rambunctious as it flows toward the sea, bright and swirling in its upper branches where it foams over rocky rapids and drops into pools below fern-clad banks. Over the years I'd come to love the rivers of Logres and the Midlands, Caerleon and London and York, but none carries with it the clear, lovely music of an upland stream, or reminds me so much of my childhood. Now, with the sound of the Tyne in my ears, I looked at Arthur and laughed, just for the pleasure of it.

The people of Chester were a boisterous lot, rugged and vocal in their welcome, so we were fed and entertained in typical northern fashion. They might be proud and sometimes fractious, but their admiration for the Pendragon was beyond question.

We were greeted with equal enthusiasm at Carlisle, where the stuffy bishop delivered a welcoming speech in the name of the entire community. It seemed that the Christian leader had managed to convert a large number of the locals, and his cathedral was flourishing. Considering that, I should not have been surprised when the monk Gildas requested an audience with us at the big house by the river a week later.

When we were young, my father had turned down Gildas as a potential husband for me. I eyed the wispy little man with the haughty air and narrow eyes who now stood before us and was grateful to have escaped becoming his wife. The Church had proved the best place for him, and of late he'd been overseeing Maelgwn's stay at the monastery at Bangor. The notion he had come to report on my loathsome cousin brought a frown, but it seemed he had more pleasant things on his mind.

"A king of your stature needs someone to keep your archives," the monk told Arthur over dinner that night, setting his lips in a pinched fashion as he reached for a second helping of sea trout.

"Archives?" My husband hooted in surprise, and the cleric jerked his hand back guiltily. "What do I need archives for? I've a perfectly good bard to compose songs of my achievements—and a jester to remind anyone else who might forget."

"Besides," I interjected, gently pushing the platter of fishes toward our guest, "an old man at Oxford already asked to compile them."

"Yes, I know." Gildas gave me a smug smile. "I happened to be in Oxford when the fellow lay dying, and I gave him last rites. He was most upset at not having someone to carry on his task, so I promised to look into the matter. I have his scrolls in my luggage. If I came to live with you, I could catch up on whatever he hasn't already recorded. Besides"—this to Arthur with an ingratiating smile—"it seems to me your Court needs a holy man to round it out."

"Oh, we already have several," I assured him. "There's Cathbad the Druid, and Lionel, who officiates at the Mithraic rites. And, of course, Father Baldwin for the Christians. I think you'll find our household quite ecumenical."

The monk shot me a disapproving look and irritably pronged a trout.

"You're welcome to stay with us as long as you wish," Arthur interjected, giving me a nudge under the table. Clearly he felt it was important to have the Church's backing. "We'll be on the move much of the time. I don't expect to get back to Camelot until Samhain, but if you don't mind the traveling . . ."

Gildas gave the High King a gracious nod and studiously avoided my gaze.

So the prissy monk joined our entourage. At first I was sure he'd be a bother, but in truth I was so busy with other things, I hardly remembered he was there until his brother Hueil was hauled into Court on a charge of stealing cattle from a steading on this side of the Wall.

"I've been to your glens in the Trossachs," Arthur fumed, glaring at the Caledonian. "You've no reason to raid other people's livestock when your own lands abound with stag and boar and other game."

" 'Tis the way we entertain ourselves on nights with no moon," Hueil growled. He was a brutish man, with knotted muscles and a thick neck, and was clearly trying to decide if he could beat Arthur in a fight. I glanced at Gawain, who slid his hand down to his dagger.

"But it's my meat you'll be eating when winter comes," the aggrieved farmer replied hotly. "I demand the return of my cattle, reparations for my troubles, and justice in the King's name!"

Arthur was struggling to keep a straight face, for the farmer would never have been so belligerent if we hadn't been there. On the other hand, this was a perfect opportunity to try out the new legal system, so my husband convinced all involved to let the case be argued before a jury of peers, with the High King acting as moderator and judge.

The evidence went heavily against Hueil, who, in prideful folly, boasted of his acts. The jury of local farmers not only found the Scotsman guilty of stealing another man's food, they sentenced him to be beheaded. "Bloodthirsty lot, your subjects in Rheged," my husband opined that night.

The farmer and his neighbors thought the new system admirable and filled the Square on the day the public execution was held. But Arthur went hunting—"You don't think I'm going to stay and listen for that blade to fall, do you?" Gildas waited until he returned, then gave the High King a tongue-lashing before packing up and leaving. The man's personal hurt and anger were no doubt understandable, but I bridled at the idea that his alliance with the Christian God gave him the right to chastise monarchs. Later I discovered a pile of ashes where he'd burned the scrolls containing Arthur's history. I brushed them away with a broom and prayed the petty little man wouldn't cross our path again.

As the harvest drew to a close, we left Carlisle for the last stage of our progress, swinging over to Chester while Gawain and Gingalin went off to visit Bercilak in the Wirral. On the way down Watling Street we stayed in the new hunting lodge that Arthur had commissioned to be built beside the basilica wall in Wroxeter. It was a handsome building, but between the association with Maelgwn and the memory of Pelli's death nearby, I knew I would never be comfortable there.

And then at last we were home again, riding up the steep cobbled drive to our fortress on a nippy October evening that promised a night full of icy stars. Bedivere had taken the house staff on ahead, so the torches were lit, the smoke from the hearth climbed skyward and after a simple supper Arthur and I tumbled into bed with a huge sigh of relief. Neither of us had the energy for romping, but lay curled against each other, more than content to be back where we belonged.

"For all the rest of Britain's wonder, I don't think there's anywhere as splendid as Camelot," my husband sighed.

"Nor I," I whispered, sliding my hand into his. Long ago I'd realized Arthur would never be able to tell me that he loved me or willingly hear my words of love for him. But as we lay there on the verge of sleep, the fabric of our marriage, the interweave and overlay, occasional slubs and wonderful brocading of our years together, warmed us as much as the pelts we lay under. I might never know the fruition of a romantic love such as my parents had had, but still and all, I was content.

The soft, haunting sound of the curlew flying overhead stirred the night, and I smiled to myself, totally unaware of the clouds that were gathering on distant horizons.

22

New Dreams for Old

sometimes think that the young converse with the future much as we remember the past. Perhaps because their eyes have not seen all that ours have, they perceive a different world—one that can be frightening to their elders. Certainly there was a touch of fear in Arthur's reaction when Mordred, in his first report on the Federates, suggested that they be made part of the Round Table.

"What?" the High King's astonishment filled the office. "You ask me to give them a seat at my Council?"

"They've recognized you as overlord for twenty years, Your Highness. There's been no further western movement, no annexing of British farms or displacing of British subjects. What more proof of loyalty and peaceful intentions do you require?"

"Peaceful for the time, I grant you," Arthur replied, his shock beginning to subside. "But obeying my orders does not in itself give them the right to join the Round Table."

Mordred moved to the window where the white winter light played on the golden headband the Saxons had given him. After months of living among the Federates, he'd adopted a number of their fashions: his red tunic was trimmed with fancy braids and a polished crystal ball of the sort they term a life-stone hung from the scabbard of his sword. The sunlight glinted off the chip-carved pin at his shoulder as he turned and began to pace quietly back and forth across the room.

"It would bring them more fully into the fabric of your realm; encourage an exchange of ideas and philosophies—I've found some of them both interesting and useful."

Mordred's enthusiasm was evident, and he spoke with the controlled passion of a man who has found his cause. Just so had I heard Arthur speak when trying to ally the members of the Round Table, or advance the idea of a law code. "Listen to their request, Your Majesty—recognize their fundamental rights. Let this be the verification of your good faith."

"My good faith?" Arthur's surprise turned to anger and his fist hit the table so hard the ink pot jumped and threatened to spill. "Proof of my good faith? What kind of nonsense is that?"

Startled, Mordred paused in his pacing and looked directly at his father. "I promised them you are an honorable man and therefore would consider it."

"You overstep yourself, Mordred."

The cold fury in Arthur's face made his son drop his gaze. I watched him search for a way to move the discussion to a more reasonable footing.

"What would earn them the right of recognition?" he asked, carefully keeping his voice even.

"I haven't thought on the matter," Arthur growled, reining in his anger.

"Then I would like to encourage you to do so, Your Highness." It was a simple plea, open and honest and devoid of hidden stresses. I let out a sigh of maternal admiration; the boy had grown into a statesman of stature.

Arthur looked long and hard at Mordred, then nodded curtly. "We will take the matter under consideration. Otherwise your report has been satisfactory." With that he dismissed the subject, turning his attention to the new tax rolls before us.

"Don't say it, Gwen," he warned after Mordred had left the room. "I grant you the boy does a good job of representing us. But what does he know of Saxon treachery? Has he forgotten that they broke the treaties I made with them, forming secret alliances, rebelling against my rule? By Jove, are the lives of the men I lost in that war to be counted for naught, that I should now include their killers among the Fellowship?"

"He was barely a child then, growing up on the Orkney Islands, so far from the center of things. He may not understand what a betrayal that was." I spoke gently, not wanting to press the subject too hard. The lives of the men he'd lost always weighed heavily on Arthur's soul.

"Betrayal is still betrayal," he muttered darkly, pushing the subject away.

But Mordred brought it up again the next morning as he and I came back from a ride. We'd taken the wolfhounds with us and Augustus, who was still puppy enough to want to get Brutus to play, kept nipping at his sire's heels.

"Is there no way to reach the King?" Mordred queried, calling the younger dog into line. "Or am I asking something unreasonable?"

I glanced over at him, wondering how to explain Arthur's attitude. "No—at least *I* don't think it's unreasonable. But he's the one who had to lead his men against the Saxons, who saw the civilians they'd flayed alive for not joining their side; found his warriors scalped, mutilated, left to bleed to death. Those are hard memories for any leader to live with, Mordred. Your point is well taken, so let him think about it. It's likely he'll come round to seeing the value of what you say."

The young man appraised me carefully, as though trying to decide how much was my honest reaction and how much simply siding with my husband out of loyalty. The curtain had dropped behind his eyes, making it impossible for me to read his conclusion. At last, with a small smile, he agreed to drop the subject.

"But the Saxons aren't going to go away any more than I am, M'lady—and he'd do well to realize that."

Oh, Arthur, if only you'd been able to see the new dreams forming, the new realities around us! They were good dreams, solid ideas for the future. Yet you clung as much to the glory of the past as to your distrust of Uwain, and the energy we could have harnessed began to seek other outlets and flow into other channels. . . .

Later, in spring, Taliesin returned from Northumbria. He had become famous as Urien's chief bard, and his patron had rewarded him well with fine horses and golden bracelets, beautiful clothes and a splendid new harp. But although he arrived in splendor, his countenance was mournful, for he brought word that Urien, the Raven King of the north, was dead.

"Poisoned by a jealous ally who hoped to claim leadership of the north for himself," Taliesin reported with a shake of his head. "Uwain put a stop to that—tracked the man down and hacked him to pieces. Afterward the warbands elected Uwain to succeed his father, and he now bears the title of King in Northumbria."

The news sped through the household, and after dinner everyone gathered round, wanting to learn the details and curious to hear them told by Taliesin himself, who, as a child, was thought to be a changeling. Even I remembered how, in his youth, weird, wonderful words would pour from his mouth.

Taliesin was no more physically remarkable as an adult than he had been as a youth—of middle height and pudgy, with nondescript hair and a coarse mouth. But when he put fingers to strings, when his great bass-baritone filled the Hall, one felt the power of the Gods waiting within him.

This night it was the death song he sang, the eulogy that captures for all times the story of a slain leader, and he voiced the lament of a people lost and grieving for the lord who had sustained them through good times and bad.

> His memory I carry, close to my heart;
> The memory of Urien, generous leader of hosts.
> On his white breast, a black carrion crow now sits.
> The man I hold up, once upheld me.
> My arm is numb, my body trembles, my heart breaks;
> This one I cherish, who formerly cherished me.

The last line fell into silence, the faint echo of harp strings rippled on a pool of grief. Tears were running down the faces of the older Companions, and Gawain sobbed aloud at the loss of his uncle.

Putting his instrument aside, Taliesin spoke in his normal voice, proclaiming that life and kingship went on in Northumbria despite the passing of so great a leader. "Hail to his son and successor, Uwain of the Lion's Shield, as proud and generous as ever his father was—and loyal to Your Majesties."

"For which we are grateful," the Pendragon acknowledged, then asked if Taliesin would stay with us and be our bard, since Riderich had died more than a year before.

Taliesin looked about the Hall, his eyes lingering on the various Champions he'd known since childhood—Gawain and Gaheris, Agravain, Bedivere, Lancelot and Cei—and a smile that was part arrogance, part mischief played over his features as he answered. "I would be honored to serve the High King thus."

I wondered suddenly if we would regret the invitation, for a bard can ruin the reputation of king or hero as easily as a sword can shatter glass. But in the end, Taliesin did not so much destroy the old dream as sow the seeds of a new one at Caerleon, when we held the Round Table on the Christian feast of Pentecost.

As usual, the town was full of excitement and color. "Can't remember a time when things were better," Cei acknowledged as we made a last-minute check of provisions and accommodations. "Everyone in high spirits, and the locals setting up a market to take advantage of so many visitors."

Indeed, although they no longer boasted a dancing bear, there were games and mimes and musicians to charm the Round Table Fellowship. In the taverns young warriors bragged of their own deeds and boasted about friendships with older, more legendary heroes, while at various camps in the surrounding meadows and woods, squires kept watch over their sponsors' horse and armor, and dreamed of the days when they, too, would be asked to join the elite at Arthur's side.

At the praetorium, older kings and warlords reminisced while newer rulers listened, and Vortipor of Demetia—he of the arrogant attitude—condescended to thank me for the suite I'd put at his disposal. I resisted the temptation to say it was only because of his rank, not because he deserved it—compared with his uncle, Agricola, the man was an oppressive tyrant and a disgrace as a ruler.

Over the years Cei had worked wonders in the basilica. He'd managed to halt the ravages of ruin, repairing the corner of the roof that had fallen in, or replacing the missing flagstones in the floor. With its huge columns and incredibly high clerestory ceiling, it had become a majestic setting for the Round Table.

On the night of the first feast, the long nave was full of gaiety and laughter. We'd set the curved trestles in a full circle, each draped with white linen, each lit by the oil lamp in its standard. Urns of flowers flanked the doorways, and well-seasoned torches gave the huge room a clean and glowing light.

Throughout the Hall friend greeted friend, catching up on news of the months or years since their last encounter. They moved about like brightly colored leaves caught in a swirling wind, and in the center was Arthur. Wearing a new green tunic, arms laden with the golden bracelets he would bestow on his followers, he smiled and laughed, listened, nodded, frowned in concern, or extended a hand in sympathy to the various leaders who approached him.

Seeing him thus, like the sun in his element surrounded by lesser stars, I smiled to myself. If only Merlin could see how well it had all turned out!

There would be work enough at the next day's Council. Tonight friendship took precedence, with toasts to past allegiances, hints that Lamorak's youngest daughter was reaching marriageable age, even the introduction of Gwynlliw's brother, Petroc, recently arrived from Devon, where he was known as the finest spearman in the south. Colgrevance's sisters from the Continent had all married, but I noticed that didn't keep them from flirting outrageously, and even Pelleas, Nimue's quiet husband, was more outgoing than usual.

Seated next to me, Lance was full of droll observations about the different people who made up our Round Table family. And we toasted the new moon together, for I'd told him about Nimue's spell, and we took the crescent as the symbol of the love that was between us.

The food was superb, and I'd arranged to have the different courses brought in behind the pomp and majesty of a Highland piper. Trays and trenchers of meat were paraded—venison and boar, mutton and beef—roasted, boiled, stewed or braised. Whole poached salmon lay on beds of cress, while duck and goose and even swan made up the fowl course. There were puddings and aspics, pâtés and pickles—and spiced cakes full of raisins and dried figs, and that rarest of spices, ginger.

As the meal came to an end, our guests washed their fingers in rose-scented water and wiped their knives clean on linen towels before replacing them in their belts. I saw the gleam of lamplight on silver and gold, ivory and pewter, and smiled as the boy carrying the water pitcher refilled my beaker; he was using the Egyptian flagon with blue enamel designs around its lid which had been part of my dowry. It had once held the wine I'd poured for Arthur, the first time we met.

It occurred to me that all the treasures and toil of my life had come together at that great feast, and I reached up and touched the golden torc on my neck, feeling once more its timeless connection with great occasions, past and present, and was glad to add this one to its history.

The evening's entertainment was about to start when a fierce commotion erupted at the door, and Lucan the Gatekeeper ran into the center of the Round Table as though propelled by the stocky youth pounding at his heels.

"Perceval of Wales seeks admission," the butler panted, none too happily. Before Arthur had a chance to reply, the newcomer thrust Lucan to one side and, after a hasty bow in our direction, turned to survey the gathering.

Pellinore's youngest son had filled out since Arthur sent him to King Pellam to be civilized. He was still more sturdy than tall, more solid than lithe, and his chubby face had the open, childish look of one who has not dealt much with the world. This time his mane of curly brown hair was combed; he wore a coat of chain mail over a fine linen tunic and carried a spear instead of a sling. But his eyes were as restless as ever, and he sent his feral glance over every member of the Round Table. It never even flickered as it passed Palomides and I wondered if he'd forgotten having killed the Arab's falcon.

When he'd finished scanning the Fellowship, Perceval turned back to Arthur and planting his feet wide apart, folded his arms across his chest. Not even the fancy clothes could hide his loutish nature, and when he declared he'd come to take his place among the heroes of the Round Table, a snicker ran round the room.

"Have you gained some training in courtesy and the code of honor?" my husband asked with a gentle smile.

"Oh, absolutely." The youngster pulled himself to attention and bowed with an overblown flourish. "Lived with my Uncle Pellam and learned all manner of fine things. My poor mother never knew the half of it, hiding in the wildwoods, there by the holy well. But King Pellam, now there's a king what knows something, even if he is an invalid."

"And how is the King of Carbonek?" Arthur inquired.

"Not well, M'lord." Perceval's broad face became solemn: like a lake that reflects every cloud in the sky, his countenance mirrored his emotions immediately. "It's tragic, I'd say. Poor old man has been lying abed well over a score of years with that wound that won't heal. His lands are wasted by plague and draught for want of a vital leader, and his subjects grumble, yet he can neither live nor die."

There was a murmur of sympathy and fear from the household, and many among us made the sign against evil. Everyone knew the story of the king who was too badly maimed to recover, too weak to make the sacrifice demanded by the Royal Promise.

Perceval's voice softened and his eyes glistened with tears. "Unfair, Your Highness, that's what it is. Pellam is as willing as any other monarch to give up his life for his people, but the Old Gods won't take him. That's why he became a follower of the White Christ. At least the Father God sends down food and hope for him every day, and they are carried through the Hall in a grand procession. Why"—the lad's eyes began to sparkle and his voice filled with wonder—"I saw it once. It's the most amazing spectacle. There were harpers, and singers, and priests aplenty, all moving slowly across the room. And the girls!" For a moment I heard Pelli's admiration of women in his son's voice. "You wouldn't believe how many girls follow after, each bearing some kind of treasure—a spear that drips blood, a silver salver with a skull on it, a jeweled box that held a rock. Strange things, and holy. And in the center, a beautiful maiden carried the food for the ailing King under a cover of white samite. She was so splendid, I was dumbstruck when I saw her, M'lord—couldn't say a word."

It sounded as though Perceval was mixing some stately ceremony at Carbonek with the Thirteen Treasures of Britain. No doubt he'd heard a bard conjure that ancient story so well, the bumpkin with the poet's soul thought he saw them all around.

"Tried to find out that lass's name, but no one knew it," he went on. "She must live there, though—takes part in that ritual every night, according to Galahad."

Beside me Lance stiffened at the name, and I gasped with the realization it was his son.

"Galahad?" Arthur asked, immediately intrigued.

"My cousin." Perceval gestured to a lithe young man who emerged from the shadows under the loft. "May I present Galahad, son of Elaine of Carbonek and the Queen's Champion, Lancelot."

The boy was upward of fifteen or so; well built but not yet fully come to manhood. He had his mother's coloring and red hair rather than Lance's dark locks, and the features which formed such a fascinating whole in Lance's face were here more closely refined and balanced. He was far and away the prettiest of the men present but, I thought critically, he'll never be half as interesting to watch as his father is.

"I cannot tell you how pleased I am that you've come to Court," Lancelot said, rising to give the youth a kinsman's embrace. The son looked as uncertain as the father, for neither had seen each other since Elaine's precipitous visit when Galahad was only a babe in arms.

"Have I not done well," Perceval broke in eagerly, "bringing you the very flower of Carbonek? Why, if you knew how hard it was to get his mother to let him come with me . . ." He shook his head at the obdurateness of mothers.

Lance immediately left my side to go sit next to his son, and during the rest of the evening the two of them began to get acquainted. I watched them covertly and hoped it was going well.

But next morning Lance sighed and shook his head. "We're virtual strangers, Gwen." We were walking among the vendors' booths at the town market. With the Council not scheduled to start until noon, I was using the time to find gifts for some of the more notable members of the Round Table and had asked the Breton to accompany me. "After the first excitement of meeting," he added with a note of sadness, "we really didn't have much to say to each other."

"Maybe that's to be expected at the beginning—after all, he knows you only from the bard's tales, and whatever Elaine has told him."

Lancelot smiled ruefully. "It's the strangest thing. Here I am with a son . . . a son I want to get to know, and I think he wants to know me, too. But he credits me with achievements I've never even thought of. I haven't the slightest idea how those stories get started."

I grinned at that, having often marveled at how quickly noble adventures get embellished with the fantastic. "Happens to the best of us," I quipped, pausing to admire a handsome wool blanket. "There's probably a certain amount of hero worship he has to get over. But I've no doubt you'll understand each other in time, if you let it come naturally," I added. His eyes crinkled with a smile of appreciation for my confidence, and for a long moment we held each other's gaze, saying mutely all the things that would never be spoken aloud, before I turned my attention to the merchant.

At the tournament Galahad and Perceval were the source of much curiosity and there were many side wagers on how closely each boy would reflect his parentage. Like Pellinore, Perceval got rather carried away, and when he wrestled Cei to the ground, he accidentally broke the Seneschal's arm. He did offer an apology, which Cei was understandably surly in accepting. It seemed Perceval had not taken the measure of his own strength yet.

But it was Galahad who stole the people's hearts. As the day wore on, it became clear that he had the makings of an exceptional swordsman—might even become as good as his sire, eventually—and he was mannerly in all ways. By the time tournament came to an end, he was the darling of the Round Table.

"But there's still more formal respect than real affection between us," Lance noted later. "He's full of wild idealism, and prattles endlessly about Celtic honor and Christian purity."

"Christian?" My eyebrows went up at that. As I recalled, Elaine put as little faith in that religion as I did.

Lance nodded thoughtfully. "He got that from his grandfather, but it's all tangled up with Druid lore and Pagan rites; the Royal Promise and things like that."

Considering Pellam's state, it didn't surprise me that Galahad had such sacrifices on his mind, or that it made Lance uncomfortable.

His various relatives from Brittany—most notably Ector de Maris, and both Lionel and Bors—greeted Galahad with lively pleasure, seeing in him the next generation already come to fruition. No one could miss the family pride and happiness, particularly at the feast, when Galahad was feted for having taken the prize of the tournament. But in the midst of all the festivity I caught sight of Mordred watching Lance and Galahad with an envy so plain it clutched my heart. *I have loved you for many* things, Arthur Pendragon, I thought bitterly, but not for what you've done to your own child.

When the meal was completed and the trestles cleared, Dagonet came tumbling into the center of our attention, his piebald outfit wonderfully colorful, his jester's staff topped by a rattling bell. He posed some riddles, sang a song, and when all our guests were leaning back, full of wine and conviviality, he announced the presence of Taliesin, word-weaver of great renown. There was a murmur of excitement, for many had heard of the Bard's reputation, and in the flurry of comment that followed, someone called for the retelling of his trip to the Otherworld.

Bedivere and I exchanged glances, remembering the origin of that tale. It was the one-handed lieutenant who had rescued the changeling child from certain drowning when his coracle capsized in the waters of the Rough Firth. The boy had lain on the shingle, a forlorn, sodden corpse, while Bedivere struggled ferociously to squeeze the water from his lungs and drag him back to life. After he recovered, Taliesin swore he had been to Annwn and seen the Hall of the Otherworld King, boasting proudly to anyone who would listen. I learned forward now, curious to hear how the man would express the boy's experience.

"It was the first discovery of my moira," the Bard began. "Until then I was a child, knowing only the strange echoes of lives past, fleeting premonitions of a destiny I had no way to comprehend."

His eyelids dropped and his fingers moved deftly across the strings, evoking a haunting, melancholy glory as his voice began to spin its magic.

> I have been in many shapes,
> I have been the narrow blade of a sword.
> I have been a drop in the air.
> I have been a word in a book.
> I have been a light in a lantern.
> I have been the string of a child's swaddling clout.

Beside me the wolfhound Brutus leaned his massive head against my knee, as enthralled with the sound of Taliesin's voice as the assemblage was with his words. The Hall had gone silent, every ear atuned to the spell Taliesin was casting.

He told of bearing a banner before Alexander, of directing the work on Nimrod's tower, of being in India before Rome was built.

> I am a wonder whose origin is not known.
> I have obtained the muse from the Caldron of Ceridwen.

At the naming of the sacred source of inspiration and knowledge, many people crossed themselves or made the sign against evil. But Taliesin was well into the magic of his song, leading us into the realms of the Other, the realm of Annwn bounded by the heavy blue chain of the sea. Here was the gloomy grave, the revolving tower, the Glass Castle of the Perfect Ones where the Lord of the Dead assembled his Court. Here was the pot that would not cook the meat of those who were forsworn but, like Bran's drinking horn, gave every man the food he most desired, provided he was pure in heart and courage. By the breath of nine damsels it was warmed, and the purple rim was crusted with pearls.

Suddenly the spell of Taliesin's story was broken by a wracking sob, and Perceval jumped to his feet. "The grail! He sings of the grail," the lad called out. "My mum told me of it—the source of life, the provider of all sustenance. . . ."

Galahad hastened to pull his cousin back down to his seat as the Fellowship turned to stare at him, shocked by his outburst. A mutter of exasperation was flowing around the Table, and Galahad was quick to counter it.

"Forgive the country lad, good warriors. His mind has sent him to learn the ways of your Fellowship, but his heart still lives by his mother's well in the wildwood. It is love of what the great Bard has sung, not disrespect, which makes him burst out so."

Indeed, Perceval had gone into a kind of trance, his face lit with an inner glow, his eyes seeing things the rest of us could not. Taliesin, curious about the lad's Sight, put aside his harp as Perceval continued.

"Most holy of all the Treasures of Britain—most ancient, most sacred—it is the vessel of renewal and hope and Eternity."

Perceval's voice trembled with rapture. He had become a vessel himself, through which the Gods spilled their message, and we stared, awestruck and terrified, at the divine fool.

"It's been hid from men's sight all these years, waiting for the Pure Ones, the Brave Ones, to seek it out. My mum knew—she says it's here, someplace . . . in the wildwood, in the hermit's cell, in the Grail Castle it shall be found. That's what she said, back there by her fountain in the woods. But only the bravest, the purest of heart. . . ."

Uncertainty rippled through the Round Table as a fit of shaking brought the boy's words to a halt. But no sooner had Perceval collapsed in his cousin's arms than Gawain was on his feet.

"Hear, hear!" he cried, the fire of Perceval's madness blazing on his forehead. "Surely you must feel it—the presence of the Other, the naming of the hidden mystery? Perceval says it is one of the Thirteen Treasures and calls it a grail, a sacred object that can only be found by the bravest and most honorable of men. Truly, the search for such an object, the finding of that link with the Divine, would be the most important quest of a lifetime!" The Prince of Orkney solemnly pulled forth his dagger and held it hilt upward so that it made the symbol of Christianity. "By this cross I vow not to rest until I find the Grail, nor to turn aside from the least adventure until I have captured it and brought it back to Camelot, to be enshrined to the glory of the Round Table for all time."

"I'll be at your side, Father," Gingalin cried, rising to stand beside him. Not to be outdone, Gaheris and Agravain leapt up also, lifting their drinking horns and swearing to follow their brother. I gaped at the Orcadians, only just beginning to realize what was happening.

"You haven't said what you're looking for," Arthur noted uneasily. "So far no one has defined this thing. How can you tell if you've found it?"

"The soul will know." Galahad spoke for the first time, his quiet self-assurance a marked contrast to Gawain's burning zeal. "Each man knows his own level of purity, and the Divine will make itself manifest according to each man's worthiness."

A cheer went up at that, but I noticed that both Palomides and Lancelot remained silent. Only when the noise had abated did the Arab rise.

"I think you'd better decide what you're looking for, first," he said soberly. "If you are seeking a physical object, we can all take part in ferreting out this treasure. But if you are searching for something divine . . . that is an individual matter which requires thoughtful preparation. Spiritual quests aren't conducted like a fox hunt, you know."

There was a moment of silence as everyone weighed the alternatives, and one after another turned to look at Perceval.

"Spiritual," Pellinore's son announced, his face radiant. "A spiritual quest . . . that's what my mum said it must be."

With that a wave of ecstasy surged through the Hall, eddying around the Fellowship and lapping at the feet of even the most practical of Companions. "I'm with you," Bors pledged. "And I," averred his brother, Lionel. Old Ironside, thumping his mug on the tabletop, caroled, "I for one shall not return until the Grail has been won. Call the armorer, for this requires a new jerkin."

Cheers greeted each new declaration, and I glanced at Arthur. The High King of Britain watched as more and more of his men rose on a floodtide of excitement the likes of which we hadn't seen for years. Purpose, direction, and a noble cause had been carved out of the very air by a Bard's tale and a forest simpleton, unleashing a force not even the Pendragon could control.

The client kings and allied members of the Round Table looked on in fascination as my husband agreed, with some reluctance, to give his blessing to all who wished to embark on what came to be known as the Quest for the Holy Grail.

"Frankly, I think it's a dreadful idea," I exclaimed in the privacy of our chambers that night. "Who knows what divisions it will bring up, or how the Christians will react to a search for the Pagan Treasures? Won't they complain that you are sanctioning the Old Beliefs over their own?"

"Possibly—though perhaps they have some tale of a sacred vessel themselves. No one knows just what this 'grail' is, so it could prove to be anything."

"Mmmh," I sighed, not convinced.

"I'm more worried about the number of men who want to go on this quest," Arthur noted as he moved restlessly about the room. "If too many leave, the Saxons could see this as a good time for rebellion or outright attack."

He paused to study Excalibur, which hung on a stand by our bedside at night. The elegant gold-and-silver hilt glimmered in the lantern light, and he reached out to touch the deep purple amethyst that graced the pommel. The physical symbol of his power was gorgeous—as unique and special as he was. At last he turned away with a sigh.

"You can't fight a religious idea with physical means, no matter what enchantments are laid on the blade," he commented sadly. "I just pray that it strengthens the realm, rather than weakens it."

For once he was putting into words the very thing that I myself was feeling.

23

Preparation

he mystery of the Grail Quest held a kind of fascination for the members of the Round Table, and no
one went untouched by it. Although most of the
men who espoused the adventure were Arthur's
Companions, there was nothing to keep others from
joining the search. Some, like Lamorak and Vortipor, looked on
with admiration but felt they should stay home and take care of
more prosaic needs. Others not only decided to take up the cause
themselves, they recruited friends and allies as well. The crusty
warlord Bagdemagus of Dorset even agreed to take Melias, the
young scion of a Roman family in the south, as his squire. They
made a most peculiar pair—the warrior in heavy homespun and
leather, the youngster in elegant linen and silk.

Oddly enough, the Quest didn't appeal to Lancelot. "Oh, I
grant there is a magnificence to it—pure catnip to the Celtic
soul," he responded when I asked him about it. "Where else can
you find such a combination of glory and courage, mysticism and
the chance to touch the Divine? But with everyone rushing to be
part of it, it feels more like a circus than an honest effort at
reaching God. I don't doubt their sincerity, exactly. It's just not
the sort of thing I want to do."

Agravain made snide comments about Lance putting himself
above the common man, but the Breton ignored the jibes. It was
not uncommon for lesser warriors who were jealous of his fame to
attack him in petty ways.

Those who were taking part in the Quest decided they would
all leave together on Sunday, and most of the Fellowship stayed

to see them off. There was constant speculation as to what shape
the Grail would take. Perceval had said that it was one of the
Thirteen Treasures of Britain, so some thought they were looking
for the platter, while others were sure it was the caldron, or the
drinking horn, or even the spear. But all agreed that, as Galahad
had said, they would recognize it when they saw it.

Galahad himself was less vocal on the subject, quietly going
about his preparations for departure. Because of this, Lance made
a point of having a long talk with his son.

"He's consumed by the matter," the Breton reported as we
strolled past the parade grounds, following the main street of the
village that leads to the Roman quay at the bend of the river.
"He's convinced the Grail will cure his ailing grandfather, like
the Dagda's caldron that revives the dead. Elaine has taught him
that Pellam and the Waste Land can only be saved by returning
to the Old Ways, so he sees it as somehow connected to the
Royal Promise."

Oh Glory, I thought, human sacrifice not being one of the
ancient rites I wanted to see restored.

Lance sighed. "When I pointed out that that kind of ritual has
been outlawed for centuries, he countered that it's the same as
Christ's death on the cross . . . that He was a sacrificial victim
willing to die in order to save mankind. I couldn't make him see
the difference, and in spite of our discussion, he won't be swayed
from that belief."

We had come to the edge of the wharves, which were rarely
used since the Legions left. Like London or Chester, Caerleon
was situated at the upper end of the tidal reach, allowing the
ships to take advantage of the twice-daily ebb and flow. The tide
was high, making a quiet slap-slap of ripples against the pilings as
Lance brooded over his son. He was looking off toward the estuary, but I doubt he saw the birds rising or heard their calls, and
when he spoke, his voice was very soft.

"I'm afraid, Gwen . . . afraid for my son. What if he finds this
Grail and takes it to his grandfather? If it does restore life and
heal the sick, Pellam would no longer be an invalid. But he'd still
be an old man, feeble and doddering in his years. That's far from
the vital, vigorous leader the country needs to become healthy.
Traditionally only the sacrifice of the king can make a Waste

Land whole again . . . but such a sacrifice must be made freely by the monarch, as part of his pact with the people."

"Pellam's been a Christian for years," I mused. "It's why the High Priestess won't help cure his wound. Perhaps he can't be healed by a Pagan relic . . . or no longer believes in the Royal Promise."

Lance nodded. "Exactly. He may refuse to have anything to do with it, and if Galahad tries to convince him of its importance, he could be accused of plotting his grandfather's death. Apparently, the lad's quite popular in Carbonek, and likely to be made king after Pellam dies. So it wouldn't be hard to misconstrue his actions as nothing more than a personal grab for power. If he's successful, it might even be seen as murder." The word was little more than a whisper, but its threat chilled the air, and Lance shook his head sadly. "I tried to warn him, tried to point out there are always those who want to overthrow a favorite, but he thought I was questioning the purity of his motives and got very defensive. I can't tell him what to believe, but I'm frightened this will end badly."

There was little I could say to relieve his worry, but later I thought of Arthur, refusing even to enter into a dialogue with Mordred, and Lance trying so hard to reach a boy who wouldn't listen to him. I ached for both of them, but at least the Breton was making an effort.

Mordred and I took the horses out next morning, and once they'd run out their first high spirits, we settled to a more steady pace, talking about all manner of things, just as we used to when he was young.

He spoke enthusiastically about the Saxons, whom he found to be friendly, hardworking and reliable. Certainly they could not have asked for a more better envoy from the Pendragon. The fact that Mordred spoke their tongue and delighted in their games and riddles endeared him to them. For his part, it seemed he was truly beginning to find himself, now that he was away from Court. I'd noticed that on his return for the Round Table he was confident and relaxed, mixing easily with the men who were preparing for the Quest, chatting with his brothers and wishing everyone well, though he wasn't any more interested in searching for the Grail than Lamorak or Uwain were.

"Why not?" I asked as we stopped at a spring to let the horses drink. "I should have thought you'd want to be part of this adventure."

"*Me* go looking for something sacred, something that can only be attained by the pure?" There was a sudden sharpness to his tone, which was totally out of keeping with his earlier demeanor. I turned to look at him, surprised.

"Come now, M'lady—I'm the one the Witch of Wookey branded as unclean . . . born of a union so vile that even my father turns from me in disgust. Purity does not run in our family."

The very air was scathed by his words, and for a moment I saw a naked, brazen anger in his eyes. But as he spoke, his gaze drifted away. "The Gods did me no favor in my parentage—why provide another chance for divine snickering at my expense? Besides, if I call too much attention to myself, something terrible might happen . . . I sprang from a bedding far more forbidden than that of Lamorak and my mother, and she died for that little romp."

"Oh, Mordred," I cried, aghast at the depth of his bitterness. "Those are dreadful things to say. We make our own lives, my dear—surely you know that. There is no reason for the son to take on the guilt of the father." I closed the gap between our horses and put my hand on his arm. "You're a whole person, grown now, and free to walk out of the shadow. Or at least you could be, if you put aside the past. You cannot change it, child, so please, I beg you, let go of it."

"Are you saying moira doesn't count, M'lady?"

"What we do with it is what matters, Mordred—what we do with it."

The man I thought of as my son raised his dark eyes to mine and gave me a forlorn smile.

"Which is why I am becoming the best ambassador the Saxons have ever known. Let the dreamers go sniffing after the Grail. It's people such as Cynric and I who deal with the realities of the world and shape the future as best we can. Have you any complaint with that, M'lady?"

His tone had moved from sullen rage to a flat honesty, and I searched his face, trying desperately to read his heart. Instead I found the practiced, polished façade of a diplomat. Finally, with a sigh, I shook my head and agreed he was doing a fine job in the post his father had given him. It was the best I could say when faced with such despair.

As the day of the Grail Seekers' departure drew near, Arthur became more and more tense. The man who normally slept as soundly as a child tossed and turned endlessly during the night, making a mess of the covers and waking cross and cranky.

"There's far more practical matters to put your attention to, Your Highness," Mordred suggested one morning. "For instance, you might consider lifting the ban against Saxon ships docking at British ports. It would bring new and useful goods into our markets and improve relations with the tribes on the Continent."

"I suppose," Arthur said testily, "this is another of your ideas for making the Federates part of my realm?"

"Well, more or less. Trading across the Channel will happen eventually, so it seems reasonable to gain the benefits from it sooner rather than later. Just as they will eventually have leaders of their own, and if you began appointing them now, with local administrators who would still be responsible to you—through me . . ."

"And I suppose you have several in mind?" Arthur inquired abruptly.

Mordred was pacing slowly around the room, and his gaze swung my way as he opened his mouth to answer. I gave him the briefest shake of my head—this was not the day to pursue the matter. But he either didn't see it or ignored my warning.

"Cynric would be an excellent man for the Winchester area."

The name of his enemy's son flayed Arthur's already-raw nerves, and his response came out in a roar.

"Never! Never will I allow that to happen. Nor will I consider lifting the embargo. Or including the Saxons in the Round Table." His jaw had gone stiff, and he spoke between clenched teeth. "How many times must I tell you? I do not trust your precious Saxons now and never will. And that is the end of it, Mordred. The subject is closed!"

Mordred stopped dead still and a veil of ice dropped behind his eyes. For a long minute he stared at Arthur, as though unable to

believe what he had heard. And his father stared back, unflinch-
ing and unresponsive. Like two parts of a mountain split by a
narrow gorge, I thought . . . neither willing or able to move
closer, yet each defined by and defining the horizon of the other.
It was uncanny, immutable, and, perhaps, eternal.

I saw the stalemate and wanted to throw my hands in the air.
Of all the stupid stubbornness, devoid of empathy or willingness
to understand each other as human beings! Fathers locked into
keeping a grip on power, sons struggling to separate themselves
from the shadow of childhood and gain their progenitor's respect.
But instead of embracing each other in the warmth of kinship
and recognition, each prepared for defense or retaliation, fearful
of exposing his own vulnerability.

"This is beyond belief," I stormed suddenly, rising to my feet
and glaring at both men. "Absolute folly, and I will not be part
of it."

I caught only a glimpse of their surprise as I fled from the room.
In fury and frustration I headed for the stables, intending to take
Etain for a long, free run. Instead I ran into Lancelot, and came
a cropper of my own moira.

The barn was clean and well kept, smelling of fresh hay and
healthy horses. Sparrows twittered in the beams, flying in and out
of the light where honey-gold sunshine streamed through open
stall doors. One of the barn cats raised her head and blinked as I
passed her on the way to my mare.

But I stopped abruptly at the sight of Lance standing in the
middle of a free stall, surrounded by saddlebags and bedroll,
leather cape and fodder nets.

"What on earth are you doing?" I asked, suddenly forgetting
both Arthur and Mordred.

"Getting ready to go find the Grail."

He said it as though it was the most natural thing in the world,
but it caught me totally off guard. Considering his earlier doubts
about the Quest, it seemed a peculiar decision. A tiny rasp of fear
grated on my spine.

"Looks more like preparations for a war than a jaunt in the
wildwood." The remark was intentionally flip, tossed off as I came
in and perched on the edge of the manger. But in spite of my
effort at wit, a dreadful foreboding was creeping up on me.

Lance responded with a grin and went on with his work. I watched in silence, afraid to open my mouth lest something really frightful would come out.

Once his things were arranged in the saddlebag, he tied down the flap and came over to the manger. He was standing sideways to the sunshine, his face half in shadow, half in light—on the one hand open confidence, on the other brooding introspection.

He stared down at me as he used to in the past, with love and tenderness and all the magnificent caring of his soul.

"Don't go." The words jumped out without my volition. "Arthur needs you, and so do I. I'd be lost without you . . . we both would. With so many others searching for this thing, surely someone will find it and bring it back to share with the rest of us."

"That's not the point, Gwen." Slowly he put his hands on either side of my head, holding it gently while his thumbs wiped away the tears I didn't even know were on my cheeks. His voice came very low and sure.

"I have spent the better part of my life serving you and Arthur, both together and separately. He is the king I follow most gladly in the whole world. And you—you are my love, the only woman who touches me so deeply. It is for you I've done great things, sought out adventures, fought the enemies of Britain, shared the joys and sorrows of my heart. That can never change—it is captured in me like the fly in amber, and cannot be denied. But this matter of the Grail . . ."

His voice trailed off, and he looked away. "It's simply something I have to do. I want to find it before Galahad does, to keep him from making a terrible mistake."

He brought his gaze back to mine, a silent plea beseeching me to understand. And I stared back, remembering that this was the love I had turned away from in order to raise Arthur's son. The most basic law of the universe was being played out again: first you take care of the children.

"Then go with my blessing," I whispered.

He bent over me and softly, so softly, left a kiss on my forehead.

It was a dear and proper way to say goodbye, but something inside of me rebelled. Trembling fiercely, I threw my arms around his neck and pulled his face down to mine. Our lips met, brushed, and opened as he dropped his hands to my ribs and pulled me to my feet. Instinctively our bodies moved together, crushed and crushing as though to merge into one.

It all came back: the rush of passion, the flood of surprise that the love so long dormant could leap to life full-blown again. We had kissed less than half a dozen times in all our years together, yet always there was the same excitement, the wondering thrill of finding it was still magic, the promise of unexplored worlds that ached for discovery. We clung to each other, trembling like children lashed by a storm.

But he turned from me just as quickly as he'd reached out, and when he spoke, it was with his back to me.

"Go, now, love and let me get on with my life."

It was as much a request as a demand. Instinctively I put my hand out to touch him, but he was drawing away, beyond reach, and his shoulders were shaking with silent sobs. I dared not intrude further, so I turned and tiptoed out, leaving him in the sanctuary of the hay-sweet barn.

Had that kiss been expected? No. Was I being selfish, determined to mark him forever as mine before he embarked on this strange journey? In the light of what happened, some might say so. I do not have the luxury of hiding behind the Gods, claiming it was fated, as Tristan and Isolde were fated by their love potion. Yet that embrace was prompted by something far greater than my personal desire—something closer to the very nature of existence affirming itself through the two of us. And when we parted, I knew that no amount of soul-searching, of philosophizing and questing after the Divine, could ever gainsay the love we had been blessed with.

Once it was known that Lancelot was going in search of the Grail, many of his friends decided to join the Quest as well. Perceval and Galahad, Lionel and Bors, were already committed, but now Lamorak and Dinadan began packing also. Even Urr and Lavaine and Nerovens, who had been past protégés of the Breton, took up the cause. With the armorers working day and night— mending chain mail, honing blades, reinforcing helmets—Ironside began to fret that his own new jerkin would never be ready in time for the departure. But Nimue's husband, Pelleas, continued to eschew the Quest, though he kept his reasons to himself.

"Some things are better not sought for in this world," the doire replied when I asked her about it. We were gathering the herbs and flowers and birch-branches she would use in the blessing of the Grail Seekers before they left. "Merlin once said Arthur's greatest challenge would be keeping the Fellowship so busy they'd forget the corrosive feuds of old. As long as there was a cause—taming the Saxons, developing the Round Table, righting wrongs and redressing grievances—just so long would the Fellowship flourish."

The doire was staring down into the golden heart of a burnet rose. In the past the Goddess had spoken through her, making her eyes large and dark and her voice deepen to the sound of wind soughing through pine trees. I heard the change, felt the advent of the Great Mother, and hastily closed my eyes—one does not look on the naked face of a deity.

"But the Grail is different. . . ." Her voice was a roar and whisper all at once, filling my head with its presence. "It is a quest for the ineffable, for something beyond description. Although they don't realize it yet, each man is searching for what is inside himself, not something out in the world."

The Goddess was everywhere, humming in the air and making the ground beneath my feet tremble.

"Is that good or bad?" I asked fearfully.

She seemed to be amused, for I could feel laughter falling around me, pressing against my eyelids like coins of light. Frightened, I covered my face with my hands.

"Silly child, what do the Gods know of good or bad? Oh, the Grail will be found, but it will never be brought back to the Round Table, and whether that's 'good' or 'bad' depends entirely on your point of view, doesn't it? It could be the exquisite culmination of a lifetime or the unexpected discovery of the flaw that destroys a kingdom. Either way it is a journey of great risk."

"Yet the best and dearest of our men insist on undertaking it," I said suddenly, though whether I spoke the words aloud or only in my head, I had no way of knowing. It had never occurred to me to talk back to the Goddess before.

"That is why they are the best and dearest," She responded, still amused by what must have seemed self-evident.

"How utterly unfair," I railed, fear for Lance making me brave beyond the point of reason. "To leave the rest of us behind, helpless to aid those we love. Why, if it's such an important journey, I should be going too."

"Then why aren't you?" The question came from everywhere at once.

I recoiled in amazement, appalled by the realization that the Gods don't understand humans at all.

"A queen doesn't pick up and run off on personal adventures. It's my duty to stay with Arthur and my people. I can't just go looking for the Grail because I want to."

"Of course you can."

The Goddess was no longer amused, and an edge of exasperation sharpened her response. I could feel her shifting from the loving mother to the stern hag. "Haven't you heard what I said? Do you think you have to have a horse and wildwood to find the Grail?"

"No . . ." I answered tentatively, suddenly terrified at my own temerity. "But how would I know where to begin, what to do?"

"You'll know . . . you'll know, Gwenhwyvaer."

The ancient speaking of my name pulsed in the air, lifting me on wings so powerful, I had no way to resist. She gathered Herself into full majesty, an irresistible force that focused the entirety of the universe into me until I was drawn into a glorious freedom, billowing out and away from the limits of myself in endless wonder.

I floated in the early-morning light and stretched ecstatically along the wind. There was no place that I was not, no separation of me and Other. Suffused with a rapture beyond telling, I melted into the butterfly's wing; the night-shadow caught in the branches of the yew; the sweet, clear fragrance of the violet. Starlight flowed in my veins and thunder crashed in my heart even as I danced in the spindrift of the breakers below Tintagel's cliff. The vibrance of my joy echoed both within and without, then gradually, ever so slowly, coalesced into early-morning silence as my name distilled into birdsong and dew drops.

"Gwen," Nimue was saying, bending over me. "Gwen, it's all right, you're all right."

Drenched with sweat, I lay crumpled on the ground, sobbing for no knowable reason. My head hurt horribly, and I groaned as the doire pulled me upright.

"Is She gone?" I asked idiotically, as though I would be conscious if the Great Mother was still with us.

Nimue laughed gently. "As much gone as the Gods ever are. She spoke directly to you, didn't She? It was on your face, the light of Her presence. I had to close my eyes, it was so strong in you."

"In *me?*" I whispered, shaken anew by the thought. Always before She had spoken through Nimue.

"What did she say?" The doire was rubbing my temples, knowing from her own experience the headache such visits leave.

"She explained . . ." I blinked. The memory was absolutely clear, and I knew what it meant, but there was no way to explain. "She said . . . the Grail is for everyone," I finished lamely.

The doire nodded, though whether with comprehension of the message or mere resignation that I'd never be able to put it into words, I couldn't tell. She helped me to my feet, however, and gathering our basket of simples, we made our way back to Caerleon and the mundane world.

With the departure of the Grail Seekers set for the next day, I had neither time nor inclination to share my experience with anyone. Besides, since Lancelot was leaving and Nimue already knew, there was no one I could tell about it. It was not the sort of thing I would mention to Arthur.

On their last night at Court the Seekers were feted at a magnificent feast. We threw open the gates so that peasants and craftsmen, village artisans and local warlords mixed with the Round Table members in the great nave of the basilica. There was singing and dancing—though I noticed Lancelot abstained from the latter, preferring to spend the time in conversation with his son—and wonderful toasts to our heroes. Ironside loudly commended the armorer, who, although he had no time to make a new jerkin, had at least repaired the old one. Gawain drank only enough to pay honor to those being toasted; it would never do to start searching for the Grail with a hangover.

Cei sat next to me that night, watching the festivities with disdainful tolerance. I remembered Dinadan's mention of the Seneschal's unrequited love and wondered why the lady of this heart had not bothered to look beneath his acid bluff. In spite of his sharp tongue, he was a man of highest principles and great bravery.

"Do you realize," he mused, twisting one of the many rings with which he bedecked his fingers, "how many blessing and purification ceremonies will be performed throughout the night and morrow? Virtually every religious group is represented on this Quest."

"Really? I hadn't thought of it."

"Umhum," he averred. "Father Baldwin is providing confession and penance for Christians tonight and a Mass of the Angels in the morning. Lionel and the followers of Mithra will be off to their cellar chapel for a ceremony sometime between now and then—you know how secretive they are about their rites. I understand Cathbad and Gwyn of Neath have offered to lead some sort of communion with the Old Gods at moonrise, and Nimue plans to do a blessing at sunrise. One of the local priests will make sacrifice in Diana's temple as well, so you might say," he added with a twinkle, "that Arthur's Court is preternaturally sanctified tonight."

"You think we'll survive?" I queried.

The Seneschal gave me an exaggerated frown. "It will be up to Your Majesty to keep us from becoming entirely too holy," he responded, and we both laughed.

Indeed, the odor of holiness that filled the Court next morning was of a fine and ecumenical nature. Arthur and I sat on the raised platform in the curved apse of the basilica, hands resting on the carved arms of the special chairs Caerleon made available to us. To either side stood the new lamp holders the local smiths had worked into the shape of dragons. Each creature supported a plenitude of oil lamps caught in the curve of its tail, tucked into the body folds, captured in talons, or crowning the proud head. The clear flames played against the heavy crown that rested on Arthur's head and glimmered off my golden torc. Excalibur was strapped at Arthur's side, and the regal amethyst winked in the great sword's pommel.

Various friends of the Round Table were assembled on benches in the nave, with a wide aisle open down the middle. The sunlight that came in the clerestory played on a scene of bright color and rich texture—Celtic warlords, Roman aristocrats, the ruddy Cumbri of Wales and Cornwall, even a burly Caledonian chieftain. The Picts had not sent an envoy this year, being too busy defending themselves from Fergus of Dumbarton, and I wondered what the strange, dark people with the fine tattoos would make of the Grail Quest.

There was a rustling as everyone waited for the Seekers to arrive. The holy leaders were seated on the platform with us. Nimue smoothed her white robe and sat, hands folded and eyes downcast. Father Baldwin was likewise solemn, and even Cathbad wore a serious air, though the members of the audience murmured curiously among themselves.

At a sign from Arthur the trumpeter raised his battered instrument and played out a flourish both round and graceful. Two by two the Seekers made their entrance and moved silently down the length of the nave. Each had a garland of flowers around his neck and was escorted by a solemn, reverent child carrying a lighted taper. Dressed in fine linen tunics, new armor, polished helmets and creamy lamb's-wool capes, they looked like a congregation of ethereal spirits as they stood before us and bowed their heads. A kind of awe settled over participants and audience alike.

Father Baldwin gave a short prayer, Nimue dipped a birch branch into the bowl of herb water and sprinkled it over the congregation, and Cathbad called on the Old Gods to guide these searchers to the magic vessel that held the Essence of Being.

Looking at them assembled in all their odd, eccentric diversity, once more I wished Merlin were here. He had promised that men of all kinds would gather to Arthur's standard, and foretold that they would know eternal glory as members of the Round Table. No matter their origin, they would become part of a cause greater than themselves—brothers in a Fellowship whose name would echo down the length of time.

And now it had come to pass. One by one they knelt before us, splendid in their dedication, loving us in their own ways as much as we loved them. Together we had built a concept that would last forever, and when I extended my hand to each, I gave them gratitude as well as my blessing.

Once the ceremony was complete, the entire group turned slowly and, taking the tapers from the children who had guided them into the nave, made their way, still in pairs, through the audience. A quiet stole over the assemblage as they passed, as though the strange, unknown mystery these men had dedicated themselves to spread like a wake among all who were gathered there.

As Arthur helped me down off the dais—royal garments get no less heavy with age—I caught the furrow of concern that darkened his face. So I slipped my hand into his and gave it a reassuring squeeze while we moved down the aisle between hushed nobles. Once outside, we took our place on the steps and the rest of the Fellowship moved off to each side, spreading out along the covered walks of the colonnade that lined the plaza. Cei and Bedivere stood beside us, however; no matter what kind of adventure called, they remained with us if we needed them.

The Seekers had clustered in small groups, mounting their horses, bidding Godspeed to friends. They would each go their separate ways once they passed through the plaza's arch, but before they left, they filed past the steps, giving their monarchs a final salute.

Gawain and the Orcadian faction were first, outfitted in the richest of fabrics and jewels, and wearing the badge of the Red Dragon on their shoulders. They made a splendid showing and waved to us cheerfully, full of excitement and confidence.

Next came the various men who had no clan affiliation; they were an eclectic bunch, ranging from Palomides on his fine Arabian steed to Bagdemagus, riding what appeared to be a dray horse while his young squire, Melias, followed on a palfrey. Lamorak paused to say an official farewell, but Dinadan just smiled and gave us the thumbs up.

Last of all was Lancelot's contingent, with Galahad in the fore. The boy's face was radiant with hope and purpose, and he carried his white shield with the red cross as though it were his badge of honor. Behind him Perceval struggled to handle the new warhorse Arthur had given him as a gift, then came Lionel and Bors and finally, soberly dressed in black, was Lancelot. His big stallion, Invictus, pranced and pulled against the bit, but the Breton held him in check as he turned and nodded solemnly to Arthur and me.

At the sight of these men the crowd in the colonnades began

to murmur, sending up a soft chant of prayers, and I felt a lump of pride and fear fill my throat.

In spite of its holy purpose, this was a chancy adventure, and I wondered suddenly who among them might not return. *It was a dismal and frightening thought in the midst of so much glorious leave-taking, but one that would come back to haunt me in the days that followed.*

24

The Quest

hat *are* you doing?" I asked as Cook laid out a hodge-podge of flowers and leaves on the kitchen table. I was used to seeing her replace the bundle of oak, ash and thorn twigs over the door in order to keep the fairies away—though she put out a bowl of clean water each night so that those sprites that didn't leave could bathe their babies. And she waged a never-ending battle with the boggart who overturned the kailpot with laughter and high glee at her distress. But this was something new.

"My nephew Kanahins's gone on the Quest as Ironside's squire," the good woman confided. "The doire who watches over the spring in the elm grove taught me a charm to help him find the Grail . . . but it has to be made in secret, with no one watching."

She gave me such a pointed look, I offered to sit in the herb garden just beyond the door and keep others from interrupting her again, provided it didn't take too long.

"Oh, thank you, M'lady. It'll be finished quick on. And I'll include a word for Lancelot, too," she offered, glad to go back to her magic-making with impunity.

Charms and spells to help the Seekers were becoming commonplace among the household, for although no one had expected the Quest to end during the first week, it was going on a month now without any word, and people were beginning to ask the Gods to look after their loved ones.

I was not the only one who sometimes stood staring off into the green distance, wondering where particular friends were at the moment—Elyzabel, Bedivere, and even Arthur himself seemed distracted by the matter from time to time.

Once midsummer was well passed, we all trekked back to Camelot, still thinking the heroes would be returning soon. I formed the habit of walking along the top of the wall in the morning while Arthur and Bedivere made the rounds of the fortress and established their plans for the day. Looking out over the well-loved landscape, I let my spirit rove like a terrier snuffling for a scent, or a sight-hound scanning all quarters of the sky, trying to learn how Lancelot fared. But it was to no avail—I could no more discover where he was, or feel reassured about his safety, than I could predict how many toms would be in a litter of kittens.

Finally, when late summer was full upon us and the great wains of new-mown hay had finished trundling into Camelot's barn, Melias limped through the gates. He was tired, dirty and beaten down by misery—a very different sight from the aristocratic lad who had ridden out as Bagdemagus's squire.

Neither he nor the warlord had found anything that resembled the Grail, though they'd traveled steadily along the Roman Roads, sleeping at the edge of the woods by night and seeking adventures by day. One evening, outside of Cirencester, they set up their camp in a meadow by a crossroads. Suddenly an unknown warrior came riding down on them, screaming imprecations and making all manner of threats. There was a wild melee, during which Badgemagus was mortally wounded, and the stranger rode away, not even stopping to find out whom he had killed.

"It was all so quick," Melias said, his eyes dulled by the senseless violence. "We never even found out why . . ."

If that weren't disaster enough, while the squire was bringing his warlord's body back to Camelot, he was set on by bandits who stole both horses and dumped the corpse by the side of the Road. The young man buried the body and returned to Court, alone and on foot, not knowing what else to do. "And the adventure hardly even begun," he concluded with the lost, empty voice of hopelessness.

It hurt to see a young life scarred so early, and I was glad when Arthur suggested the lad report to Bedivere if he wished to stay on and train to become one of the Companions.

"Bandits on the Road outside of Cirencester, and I don't have enough men to send up there to take care of it!" Arthur fumed, striding across the reed-covered floor. "I knew this Quest would lead to trouble."

I agreed with him silently and made the sign against evil, wondering if this was an omen. Certainly it was a bad beginning for what was supposed to be the Companions' greatest achievement.

Several weeks later, on a night with a full moon, we were wakened by a guard who reported a man pounding on the gates, demanding entrance and an immediate audience with the King.

"At this hour?" Arthur mumbled.

"Yes, Your Highness. It's the Prince of Orkney, and he's very insistent."

"Good heavens, send him in," my husband exclaimed, sitting up suddenly and reaching for his clothes. I stayed under the covers, however, and drew the comforter up under my chin.

Gawain strode into our bedchamber with an explosion of questions. "Who is it? Mark of Cornwall? That Frankish fellow in Paris? I know—it's those insufferable Romans on the Continent!"

He came to a halt and began to look apprehensively around the room, as though startled to find us abed. When his gaze settled on me, he blushed and glanced hastily away. "Doesn't seem like you're mobilizing much."

"What *are* you talking about?" Arthur demanded with a yawn.

"The war! I rushed right back as soon as I heard you were going to war. Grail or no Grail, I'm still the King's Champion."

Arthur gave him a rueful grin and allowed there'd been some mistake; we had no war.

"No war?" Gawain gaped at his commander, repeating the words like a child who can't believe what he is hearing. "Do you mean I gave up my chance of finding the Grail for a war that doesn't exist?"

Arthur nodded, and the redhead sank down on the bench before my dressing table. "Neither honor for the Round Table nor glorious battles for posterity. . . . This is turning into a pretty poor summer season, if you ask me."

"Well, we're glad to have you back in one piece," Arthur assured him good-naturedly, no doubt thinking of Bagdemagus. "Now, tell us about your adventures."

So the King's Champion recounted apprehending two bandits, rescuing a woman who had been abducted from her family, and challenging an unknown warrior at a crossroads near Cirencester.

"Cirencester?" Suddenly I was the one thinking of Bagdemagus.

"Mmhum," the Orcadian affirmed. "Set up his tent in the meadow I was going to use. I warrant it's a lesson he'll long remember."

I looked at Arthur, who gave me a quick shake of the head; this was not the time to pursue the matter. No doubt he'd question Gawain more fully next day at the practice field, where they wouldn't be waking up the whole household if it came to a shouting match about the Orcadian's behavior.

"And the Grail?" I prompted.

Morgause's oldest son sighed heavily. "Ah, M'lady . . . it sounded grand at first, something that would bring immense prestige to the Champion who found it. But the longer I wandered in the wildwood, the less sure I became. It seems to me the true path of the hero is that of valor and conflict; only in battle are *all* the senses alive, when your muscles and mind and spirit are singing with power. That's when you touch the essence of life. And about the time I was wondering what the Grail has to do with that, the hermit of Saint Govan's cove came to me in a dream, saying that you'd be needing me when you went to war. So I broke camp and rushed back." He gave me a tired smile, gap-toothed and sincere. "Let the likes of Perceval go looking for the meaning of it all—I'll settle for a life of honor and courage, and a chance for single combat now and then."

Thus the King's Champion returned, having found the key to his own nature, if not the holy vessel itself.

From then on news of the Quest drifted into Camelot like the golden leaves that began to fall from the trees. Periodically miscreants of one kind or another showed up on our doorstep, men who were bested by Champions of the Round Table and came to pledge their fidelity to Arthur in the name of the hero who had beaten them. Most surprisingly, a good number were from Bors, who seemed to have given up killing his opponents outright in favor of sending them to us. Like Ironside, most of them preferred to stay on at Camelot, finding some niche for themselves in our household. Before the winter was over there would be any number of new men I barely knew by name.

Ironside returned in November, having concluded that the Grail was really the head of the Old God Bran. "I knew it all along—knew before I left that's what it would be. Wasn't it Bran's head that provided his followers with food and comfort for years after he died? The source of all sustenance, just like Perceval said." The old warrior spoke with the conviction of a man who is well pleased to have found exactly what he thought he would, then knit his brow in consternation. "But Bran's head is supposed to be buried on that knoll in London, to keep invaders out, and it wouldn't be right to go digging it up."

Ironside made the sign against evil, though his eyes slid surreptitiously toward Arthur. No doubt he'd heard that the Druids were still upset about the skull Arthur had uncovered when the Tower was being repaired; like the belief that Nimue captured Merlin with his own magic and holds him captive in a crystal cave, it is a rumor that has a life of its own, regardless of the truth.

Since both Arthur and I ignored Ironside's comment, he waxed cheerful and was obviously glad to be home again.

Agravain and Gaheris returned to Camelot in time for the midwinter festival. They each brought a new warrior they had met on the Road, men named Florence and Lovel, though I had trouble remembering which was which. We feted them all in the Hall, but they were tight-lipped and silent about their adventures, saying only that, like Gawain, they had decided the Quest was not to their liking.

Shortly afterward, word came that Lamorak had been killed, the victim of an ambush by unknown scoundrels. The Orcadians, long having held him responsible for their mother's death, showed no sorrow, and I fancied there was a cold smile of satisfaction on Agravain's face when the death was announced. But as was often the case, there was not enough proof against the man to warrant making accusations.

It was coming on February when Lionel showed up, glowering at the world in a mood as black as pitch.

"My own brother, with no more sense of loyalty than a stick of wood," he grumbled, sitting by the brazier in our office as I plied him with mulled wine and Arthur drew out his story.

"Bors and I've never been overly close, I know. Not like Gaheris and Agravain, who go everywhere together. But I always thought that was a measure of our respect for each other—can't fit two hands in one glove, after all. And I didn't berate him when he chose to become a Christian, though our whole family has worshiped Mithra since the days of the Legions. But now he's decided the Grail has a special Christian meaning . . . and he's gotten very stuffy about it."

The quiet, methodical warrior who was more noted for his physical strength than his mental abilities now struggled to put his experience into words.

"As a Pagan I said the Grail belongs to everyone, but Bors wouldn't allow that, and we got into a terrible row the very first day. So we each went our own way . . . but later, when I was in trouble and Bors came riding by, did he stop to help me? No, of course not."

The taciturn man stared into the fire as a large tear spilled over and ran down his cheek. "You'd think family loyalty would mean something, wouldn't you? Blood kin, raised together? If you can't count on family . . ." He blinked hard and tried to swallow around the ache in his heart. "It ought to mean something . . . I would have come to his aid if the situation had been reversed."

"Surely you can talk things out when he comes back," I suggested, but at the very notion Lionel's hand clenched into a ball.

"He'll be the one to beg for help next time. Left me as good as dead, without caring one little bit!" His fist landed on the table with such force, the wine in his mug slopped over. In the silence that followed I decided it best to hold my tongue.

Finally Arthur spoke. "Did you ever find the Grail?"

"Aye, that I did, and it's naught to do with those prickly Christians, either." Lionel nodded with silent satisfaction at the little lake of wetness on the tabletop. "No . . . not at all. But I'm not so sure I want to tell anyone—saving Your Graces, that is, if you'll keep it in confidence. Only another Mithraite can appreciate it fully."

He peered about to make sure no one else was within hearing, then leaned closer to us.

"I went off riding into the wildwood, thinking about the Grail . . . how some said it was a gold-and-silver chessboard, and some thought it was a casket covered with gems—fancy things, and fine wrought. And how could even the most splendid vessel be everything to everyone? I couldn't see the sense of it, though I thought about it a lot."

When Lionel lifted his mug and took a long draft, I caught Arthur's eye. This was more talking than the fellow had done in all his years at Camelot.

"Being alone in the greenwood gives a man a chance to remember what's important. Sleeping beside a stream where the singing trout leaps, watching an eagle circling in the high blue of the sky, snaring a hare for dinner . . . these are wonders enough for me. What would I do with a pearl-rimmed caldron or a fancy salver, anyway?"

He paused to finish off his wine, and without a word Arthur lifted the flagon that was warming on the brazier and with his own hand refilled the empty cup. Even a Bard could not ask a higher compliment, but Lionel was so enthralled by the memory of his adventure, he barely noticed.

"Then one morning I woke at the edge of a meadow where a little river broadens into pools. There was a mist rising up through the weeds—the sun hadn't come up yet—and I could hear the hooves and bellows of a wild bull bringing his herd of cows down to the water to drink. Lowing and roaring he was, looming up white in the ground fog, with his wide horns swinging this way and that as he checked the air for wolves and bears. Made me think of the bull the god Mithra sacrificed . . . the whole of creation came from its blood streaming into the ground. That's when I knew . . ."

The man shook his head in amazement, and his words came haltingly as he groped to phrase his discovery for us. "It's all the Grail, and everything is part of it: squirrel and bear, king and priest, sunrise and new moon . . . all of us, all growing out of the blood of the bull. But looking out across that meadow, that's when I knew . . . Mithra's bull itself was part of this Being-ness, if you follow. It's not something separate, this Grail. It is, and was, and will be . . . and before, as well as after."

Lionel was looking back and forth between us, hoping to see some glimmer of understanding, his dark brows beetled in concentration. "Ach, the words M'lady . . . words get in the way sometimes. I do know what I'm trying to tell you, honestly I do."

"I understand," I assured him quietly. After all, I hadn't been able to explain to Nimue what the Goddess had said.

Lionel put all his attention on me, peering into my face for confirmation that didn't need speech. Apparently he saw it, for with a great sigh he sat back and gave Arthur a curt nod.

"That's it, Your Highness . . . how I came to find the Grail," he concluded.

And that was it—as far as I know, he never told another soul, though he may have broached the subject with others who followed the soldiers' god, Mithra.

Later that night, when Arthur and I were talking after going to bed, I brought up my fear that this Quest might drive a wedge between followers of the various religions which had, heretofore, lived in peace in Britain. If two brothers as fond and loyal as Bors and Lionel could become estranged over it, what other damage might not result?

"None, if I can help it," my husband announced firmly. "There will be no religious intolerance while I'm High King."

He said it with such conviction and confidence, I put my arms around him in a hug and didn't ask just what he thought he could do to stop it.

If Lionel's experience with the Grail was profound but inarticulate, Palomides's response was both lucid and brilliant.

In the spring the Arab rode up to our gates without fanfare, waiting his turn behind a farmer's cart of pullets and the pack-train of a Scottish trader come to take orders for kippered herring. Fortunately I was on the parapet, wondering where Lance was, or I might have missed him altogether. It was his black cloak, edged with gold and embroidered with strange Eastern symbols, that caught my eye. From the look of him he'd been riding many a day and not stopped often for food, so I ran down to greet him and took him off to the kitchen.

"No, M'lady—I haven't seen the dark-haired Breton, though his blond cousin, Bors, spent some time in the forest with me," Palomides said as I served him a plate of cold meats and a ladle of soup.

"One evening Bors and Perceval and Galahad came into the

clearing where I'd set up my tent. Very polite and civil—unlike some of the other Companions." The Arab leaned forward to choose a drumstick, muttering darkly. "I think, M'lady, that if some of the Orcadians did not have a blood-tie to Arthur, and therefore the High King's protection, others would take steps to curb their arrogance. You might make sure the King knows there's those who like to cause trouble . . . ."

Such a simple comment, delivered by one who wished us well, for all that he held himself a little apart from the family; perhaps that very distance gave him a better perspective about what was happening. Did I remember to pass on his warning to Arthur? At this point, I can't recall, for when Palomides suggested it, all my thoughts were still on Lancelot and the Quest.

"It was a fascinating evening," the Arab went on in a normal tone. "Bors has always been the colorful one in Council—cheerful and outgoing. But now that it comes to spiritual matters, he's grown very quiet and is more likely to absorb the deeper lessons of the Grail than to expound on their meaning. So he sat silent, and I spent the evening listening to Galahad and the wild one, Perceval."

"What did they talk about?" I inquired, sitting down on the bench across the table from him, thinking this was probably as close as I would get to going on the Quest myself.

"A great many things, Your Highness. Their adventures on the Road, what they are looking for and how they go about it. Just the answers to those questions were immensely revealing."

The Arab lifted the chalice of wine I'd put out, and carefully sniffed the contents. His eyebrows went up and taking a sip, he rolled the liquid around in his mouth, sloshing it about and exhaling happily when he'd swallowed.

I was hard pressed to keep from laughing. It's a ritual Cei often performs, and one I've always thought amusing. Probably because I have no head for wine, I've never cultivated the finer points of enjoying it.

"Revealing what?" I asked, getting back to the Grail.

"Themselves. One learns a great deal about people by the way they approach a problem. Perceval now—there's a lad with two great goals in life: he wants to be accepted into the Round Table and to find the Grail. In a sense, those are conflicting goals, for the Round Table is the best of the world and the Grail is the highest achievement in the spiritual realm. The fact that these two goals may be in conflict hasn't occurred to him yet—he still thinks they are compatible."

Palomides paused to lick his fingers, and I slid a piece of cheese off the platter and sat back, nibbling it. "And Galahad?" I asked.

"Galahad is a pure spirit—narrow and intense in the worldly sense, totally focused on one thing: achieving the Grail. I think he is the one most likely to touch the heart of it."

"Really? What do you think he'll find?"

Palomides lifted his shoulders in an eloquent shrug that implied there was no way of knowing. But after a moment he cast his gaze upward to the rafters, as though the answer was hanging there among the hams and jerky and strings of onions.

"The story of a sacred vessel is common to all peoples, M'lady. The Sarmatians tell of the caldron Nartyamonga, which will endlessly feed those without fault, and among the Zoroastrians there is the Cup of Jamshyd, which contains all the mysteries of the world in its bowl. I believe the Grail is a mirror, reflecting the truth of each person's life—their nature, their commitment . . . their soul, if you will. I have no doubt that all who survive this adventure will be changed, some for good and some for ill, but all will be touched by what they discover on the Quest itself."

"Then you think the Grail is inside each of us?" I asked, remembering what the Goddess had tried to tell me.

For a moment the Arab searched my face, looking for some sign as to how much depth I brought to the question, before answering.

"Absolutely. It is the essence of each person's being. And because of that, each person will find a different thing. What they do with it depends on how truthful they are . . . truthful with the world and with themselves. The honest person's actions are a spontaneous reflection of their nature, just as the shadow is the reflection of its tree. In the end it is this link between the true nature of a man and how he lives out of his life that determines whether he 'achieves' the Grail. Unfortunately, we all have ways of deluding ourselves; we see the truth but call it by some other name. So in a sense," he concluded, his black eyes flashing with the fire of a falcon's gaze, "to know yourself is, without question, the first great challenge of Being . . . and not everyone is capable of it."

With that Palomides smiled graciously and lifted his goblet in a toast. "To all our quests . . . may we have the honesty to recognize what we find, and the courage to embrace it."

I smiled in response, grateful he'd shared his thoughts but, as always, a little confused by them. And I couldn't help thinking it was clear why monarchs are so rarely philosophers—with so many practical things on our minds, we've little room for the kind of complexities that Palomides enjoyed.

* * *

Yet even sitting here in the cell these last days, I haven't taken the time for philosophizing. Remembering, certainly. But not philosophizing the same way Palomides and Lancelot used to. Perhaps, like searching for the Grail, it is not part of everyone's moira . . .

"I often wondered why you didn't go on the Quest," I commented gently to my companion, and a small frown passed over Gareth's features.

"A part of me wanted to, M'lady. But with Lynette being due to deliver so soon, I was loath to leave her. And then, what with one thing and another, there never seemed to be time. Perhaps, in the long run, it was just as well." He sighed with the long, weighty sound of a man who wonders if he had, in fact, made the wrong choice. Then he sat up abruptly. "It seems the wood is almost gone. Shall I ask the guard for more?"

"Why not?" I answered, knowing there would be no sleep for the rest of the night anyway.

While the transaction at the door was carried on in muffled tones, I moved slowly to the window and folding back the shutters, stared upward into the sky of childhood . . . the great, high vault of the north.

It always seems so much richer—the blue darker, the black deeper—than that which covers the south. A clean wind had blown the clouds away, leaving the white fire of the stars sparkling with new brilliance now that the moon had set. Only an hour or so until sunrise. . . .

I shuddered violently and returned to the pallet on the ledge, tucking the edges of the comforter under my feet. Gareth was placing two new branches of applewood on the brazier. That someone should supply me, a queen convicted of treason and sentenced to the stake, with the most elegant and fragrant of firewoods was both touching and ironic. But then, that seems to be the very nature of human existence—poignant and wrenching, ludicrous and magnificent, all at the same time.

"Gareth, do you remember when Bors came back to Camelot, aflame with his news of the Grail . . . ?"

25

Bors

hile Palomides returned with quiet circumspection, Bors became the center of all attention when he led his horse up the cobbled drive one afternoon in May. The blond Breton moved slowly, like a man who is grateful that the aches and pains of winter are over, now that the buoyant new season has arrived. He turned into the stableyard just as Lionel emerged from the barn, and for a moment each brother stood transfixed by the sight of the other.

"God be praised," Bors cried joyfully. "I thought you were dead."

Lionel made no comment, but flew at his sibling with a shriek like a banshee. Bors dropped his reins and opened his arms for an embrace, only to find himself thrown to the ground by a whirling fury of cuffing and pummeling, clawing and biting. Within seconds a crowd of stable boys were cheering them on as they rolled about in the mud and horsepucky.

Bedivere came racing out of the barn at the racket, but as he told me later, there seemed no point in stopping the fight when it was clear the two men were as evenly matched as brothers could be. "And I figured it was better to let Lionel get it out of his system rather than have all that anger fester and turn poisonous. Besides, Bors seemed to be holding his own without much trouble."

When he joined the household for dinner that night, Bors had a bandage around his forehead, one black eye and numerous bruises. But he sat next to Lionel—who also bore visible signs of the fray—and both brothers seemed in good cheer.

"I didn't bring the Grail back with me," Bors replied to Arthur's question, his mood turning noticeably more solemn. "But I know what it is, and have even seen it."

The household erupted with excitement. "Tell us, tell us," someone urged, and Arthur said we would rather put off dinner than wait until afterward for the story.

So we formed a circle around Bors, as for any storyteller, and he moved into the center. It startled me to see this Champion, once among the most flamboyant of heroes, wearing only a humble peasant's smock and breeches, and a small wooden cross, which was suspended on a leather thong around his neck.

"Well," he began thoughtfully, "I was sure the monks at Glastonbury would know all there was to know about the Grail, so after Lionel and I parted, I headed there straight off. On the way I met a cleric who had just come from visiting Illtud in the monastery at Llantwit, and we ambled along together for a while. When I asked him about the holy relic, he said the only thing he'd heard of was a simple bowl of old workmanship that had caught the blood which flowed from Christ's body during the Crucifixion. Joseph of Arimathea had brought it to Britain after Christ's death, but no one had seen it for years. Since it had once held the blood of the Savior, the monk thought it would probably heal the sick and wounded, as well as bring food and good cheer to all honorable souls, just as the Grail was said to do."

Right then the youngster who was serving our table broke in to offer Bors a goblet of wine, but the blond Breton smiled at the lad and shook his head.

"That same holy man told me that only the purest will complete the Quest. He said I must attend Mass daily and abstain from both wine and meat until my Quest is complete—so I'll be taking only a little bread and water. I have also vowed to remain celibate, and not to take even my worst enemy's life."

That elicited surprised comment from the Companions, but the once-ferocious warrior looked slowly around the circle. "The shedding of blood once victory is assured achieves nothing," he said. There was a quiet certitude about him, and even Gawain nodded and looked away in the face of such a simple truth. I decided that perhaps Bors had more depth than I had given him credit for.

"In each case, when I bested a foe, I sent him back to Your

Highness—I trust four such men have come to you in my name?"
Arthur nodded in confirmation, so Bors continued his story.

"I went where my moira led me, never turning away from an
adventure but always keeping the inspiration of the Grail before
me. Once my path crossed that of my brother"—his glance slid
sidewise to Lionel—"and I had to choose between him and my
spiritual vows. No matter which decision I made, there would be
dishonor, and later, when I heard that Lionel was dead . . . dear
God, those were the saddest days of my life, for I thought he'd
perished because I didn't come to his aid."

"You should've thought of that at the time," Lionel grumbled.

"And the happiest day was discovering he's still alive!" Bors
added, disarming all of us, including Lionel, with the broadest of
smiles. "For that I thank the Heavenly Father, and his Son as
well."

"But the Grail—tell us about the Grail!" someone cried, and
the Breton nodded in reply.

"I'm a simple man, not a visionary like Perceval, and do not
understand the mysteries of such holy things. But I know what I
saw—and that I was blessed to spend time with Perceval and
Galahad. It is they who have found the holy cup."

"Galahad?" The name leapt off my lips abruptly. Hopefully
news of the son would include news of the father as well.

"Indeed, M'lady, but it was Perceval I encountered first—that
wild-child who was raised among the animals. Being pleased to
find another Seeker, we fell in together. He was full of high cheer
and good humor; you might say he enjoys the chase as much as
the dinner, and even though his ways are startling, I came to see
his heart is both pure and simple."

"And Galahad?" I prompted.

"He joined us on the shore of a northern lake, in the company
of a maid who had taken the veil of holy life. Amide, her name
was, and she turned out to be Perceval's half sister."

A ruffle of amusement filled the room, and I smiled inwardly
that another of Pellinore's progeny had turned up in such an
unlikely place. It seemed they were scattered all over Britain, no
doubt as a result of his insatiable search for the perfect woman.

"Amide accompanied our party from then on," Bors was saying, "regaling us with tales of ancient heroes and magic. I think
she and Galahad were falling in love, though it was a saintly,

spiritual kind of union and not carnal in nature," he added quickly.

"All that winter we traveled through the north, and by early spring were desperately cold and hungry when we finally came upon a hill-fort. But in spite of our condition, the warriors refused us entrance unless one among us was willing to provide a bowl of blood for the fertilization of the fields. It seems they still follow the Old Ways, but no longer expect the King to provide the blood if someone else will volunteer."

I felt a rabbit run over my grave, for it is this custom which lies at the root of the Royal Promise, but the blond Breton went on with his tale.

"Amide offered to give her blood, provided they gave us shelter, so we stood by and watched as her arm was extended over an antique bowl and the vein slit open. I was more interested in the carving on the sides of the krater than in the letting of her blood, and it was only when the bright red life of her spilled over the edge of the rim that I realized something was very wrong."

Bors's voice cracked with a sob, and he stared off into space as though still not believing what had happened. None of them thought the ceremony would kill her. But it was a sacrifice as surely as any monarch could make—as surely as Christ's himself —for she bled until that bowl overflowed. Afterward she lay in Galahad's arms, pale and shaking, and he wrapped his lamb's-wool cape around them both.

"To Carbonek," she whispered. "You must go back to Carbonek, for only you can make the Waste Land whole with the Grail. It is your destiny . . . your moira, as mine is to show you the way. . . ."

Just before she faded into death, she smiled up at the lad, calling him the fairest and purest of souls. It was heartbreaking, and when she was gone, Bors cried for her as though she had been his, though in truth the only man she ever loved was Galahad.

Bors stopped speaking and seemed to say a little prayer. Then, after crossing himself, he blinked back his tears and looked carefully around the circle of the household.

"They formed a solemn procession and poured her blood over

the land. Afterward Galahad begged for the bowl to keep in her memory. God sent a terrible storm that night, as if He were angry at so hapless a loss, and the next morning Perceval and Galahad set off for Carbonek in a little boat they found on the river. They laid Amide's body in state on the craft, and since there wasn't room enough for me as well, I agreed to go by horseback. Later, when we all met in the Waste Land, Perceval told me about their strange and marvelous voyage. . . ."

The boat traveled under its own power, guided by the spirit of Amide, whose body remained uncorrupted on its bier. All through the journey Perceval heard strange, airy voices berating him for his past thoughtlessness—for having deserted his mother in the woods to go to Camelot; for losing his sister, Amide, so soon after finding her; even for not realizing that the Grail might be among the treasures in Carbonek. He was deeply upset, and full of shame and guilt.

But Galahad sat wrapped in serenity next to Amide's body, the krater that had caught her blood cradled lovingly in his lap. Sometimes his fingers caressed its sides, tracing the designs over and over. And sometimes he prayed. But never once did he doubt what the results of the journey would be.

They arrived at Carbonek on the evening of the third day, and Galahad ran forward from the pier, without waiting for Perceval, who had to scramble to catch up. Carrying the antique vessel, he raced up the steps of the fortress and, after a quick greeting to the sentry, bounded into his grandfather's chamber. The old man lay on his bed in great pain, his face turned to the wall.

"Grandfather, I've found it," Galahad cried, throwing himself down by the bed and taking the old man's hand in his own. "Look, look what I've brought home for you. . . ."

King Pellam stirred at the sound of the young man's voice, rousing himself as though from far away. He turned his head so that his rheumy eyes made out the shape of his grandson kneeling next to him, and lifting his hands, he traced the outline of Galahad's cheek with frail fingers.

"A gift, I've brought you a gift," Galahad declared, propping the old fellow up among his pillows. "It's ancient, and sacred, and specially for you." With that he brought forth Amide's bowl and placed it carefully in the old man's grasp. "Do you know what it is?"

The ailing king ran his hands along the rim, then down over the swelling of its body, and his fingers found the carved design.

"Jesu Christi," he cried suddenly, his feeble voice quavering with excitement. "It's the cup of Joseph of Arimathea, which he used to catch the blood of Christ. . . ."

Pellam grew more excited as his hands clutched the treasure, and he broke into a sweat, all the while praising Galahad for having brought his salvation to him. Courtiers came running into the room, eager to see Galahad again and to learn what was making their king so joyful. By the time Bors reached the doorway, there was little space to enter.

"But I could see the tears of joy running down the aged monarch's face," Bors recounted. " 'You've found the Grail, my son, and brought it to heal me.' Those were his exact words—and his last ones, for the old man's head fell gently against Galahad's breast, and he died with all of us crying for happiness and sorrow mixed together."

The blond Breton stood silent in the center of the circle, wrapped in the mystery of his story. There was a stirring in the household, like a soft exhalation of joy. The Grail had been found at last. The fact that it was of Christian origin, although surprising, made it no less mystical. Father Baldwin's eyes glistened with tears, and the other Christians in our group began to pray. Several crossed themselves.

"What happened next?" Griflet asked.

"A great mood of jubilation swept over the land, as if the very first spring of creation came fresh across the hills. For a fortnight they celebrated the healing and dying of the old king and the saving of their land. Then, in the fullness of time, they prevailed on Galahad to be their new monarch. A Mass was said on the day of his crowning, with the Grail used as chalice—so that finally, once more, it was filled with the Holy Blood."

Bors's face was radiant with memory, and he lifted his hands toward the heavens. "Thus has the Quest been fulfilled, and the Grail found," he intoned. "Galahad is dedicated to helping the Waste Land recover, but he says that when time allows, he'll come to visit the Round Table again."

I let out a sigh of relief, thankful that Lance's fears for his son had not come true.

"For myself," Bors concluded, "I am returned to Camelot with a new dedication of my own. My whole life will be a quest, and it is more important that I carry the Grail in my heart than that I hold the reality of it in my hands. I am not ready for a monastery, but will live in the world, though not of it, doing good works and keeping the vows I made before the Grail was won."

"Hallelujah," someone cried, giving voice to the sentiments of the entire household. Arthur, assuming with the rest of us that the Quest was over, congratulated Bors roundly. As we all settled down to eat, there was a wonderful sense of elation.

But later that night, when Arthur had long been asleep, I went to the window and sat looking out. From a tree in my garden the call of a nightingale stirred the darkness, while no doubt below our hill the vixen prowled around the village chicken coops. The air was full of dreams, and somewhere out there Lance was still trying to protect Galahad. I stared hard at the Goddess-eye moon riding above the clouds and prayed that She tell him to come home—the Quest had been completed, and what Lance sought for with his mind had been found by his own son's heart.

26

Lancelot

hose who had left Caerleon for the Quest had been gone for a year now, and news about them filtered back to us piecemeal. Some had met with mischance, some with adventure, but no one else claimed to have found the Grail.

Stories about Lancelot's exploits abounded, passed from peddler to holy man to farmer to noble, but nothing indicated he had heard of Galahad's achievement or was heading for Carbonek. Bors maintained he would go there as soon as he learned that his son had become its new king, but I had my doubts. Elaine may have been silent all these years, but that didn't mean Lance wanted to see her again, even accidentally.

Word that the Grail had been part of the Christian sacrifice brought a sudden surge of interest in the Church. Father Baldwin was in great demand both at Court and in the nearby towns. Sometimes he had so many converts, he baptized them in groups, all standing in midstream or being dunked in a pond, or taking turns climbing into the tin tubs that were common in the village chapels. He even tried urging me, gently, in that direction. "It's a miracle, M'lady. A real miracle. Are you sure you don't want to be part of it?"

All I could do was shake my head. The White Christ might be an admirable and loving figure, but I'd ally myself with many another deity before I accepted the pompous dictates of his Father.

Many of the household members converted—Melias, who had been Bagdemagus's squire, and Cook's nephew, Kanahins, among them. Cook herself began incorporating Christian customs into her never-ending battle with the sprites and took to marking her cakes and biscuits with a cross on the top—"Keeps the fairies from dancing on them, and spoiling their tops with dimples, M'lady," she explained earnestly.

Before long a delegation came to Arthur asking permission to build a church at Camelot. They had already drawn up the plans for the little building and conferred long and hard with Bedivere and Cei about the feasibility of finding materials. I personally was much less concerned about where we would put it than about the effect its presence would have on the non-Christians in the Court.

"If His Highness isn't Christian, M'lady, why should he want a church?" Lynette looped a braid up to the top of my head and stood back to study the effect.

Gareth's wife was pregnant for the third time. Their first two children were girls—sober little Lora, who had her father's blond hair and gentle ways, and lively Megan, who was busy climbing into my lap at the moment. The girl was as much of a tomboy as I had ever been, and I took delight in playing with the child; it was possible she was as close as I would come to having a grand-child.

"Or is the High King planning to convert?" Lynette queried.

The idea was so preposterous, I laughed aloud before pointing out that both Arthur and I honored all the religions of our sub-jects. But neither marriage nor motherhood had mellowed Ly-nette's nature, and she harried the matter with the tenacity of a terrier.

"They're saying you were married in a church, instead of by the High Priestess."

"True, we were. We would have been prayed over first by the Lady of the Lake if Arthur hadn't been going off to war that afternoon! But that was close on to three decades ago, child. Stop and think—who slits the throat of the white bull every year at Samhain so that the blood flows into the caldron?"

"King Arthur."

"And who leads the fertility dance at Beltane?"

"You and King Arthur."

"And who starts all the bells ringing at midwinter, to call the sun back from the frozen north?"

By now Lynette was grinning from ear to ear. "You and King Arthur."

"I don't think you need fear for the King's spiritual health," I concluded, wishing I felt as confident as I sounded. The memory of the Frankish monarch who converted for political reasons had not diminished with time.

When I mentioned the matter to Arthur, he looked up from the horse-breeding chart and gave me a quizzical frown. "I thought we agreed to support whatever Gods our people choose. . . ." I nodded, and he gave a silent shrug. "There are more Christians at Court than all other beliefs combined, Gwen, and they say the Mother's Church at Glastonbury is too far to go to, particularly in bad weather."

"That many?" I exclaimed, startled by the notion so much had changed without my realizing it.

"Indeed. And not just among the Companions who are here. Gwyn tells me Lancelot has converted as well."

I turned on the little Welshman with a sharp inquiry to which he gave a laconic reply. "So the monks at Glastonbury tell me. Surely it comes as no surprise, M'lady?"

As usual Gwyn's expression was one of conspiracy, as though we shared a secret only he was privy to. But for once it didn't amuse me, and I turned on my heel with a few well-chosen invectives. I wouldn't believe such nonsense till I heard it from Lance himself.

The Queen's Champion presented himself to Arthur on a day when the hedge-sparrows were flitting happily through my garden. I was down in the winnowing room at the time, counting fleeces from the summer sheering. Word of his arrival raced through the barn and, dropping my tallying tablet, I ran headlong for the Hall.

"Of course I'm glad Galahad found it," he was saying as I burst through the door to the office, "and that everything is going smoothly in Carbonek."

I was halfway across the room when he turned to face me, and I froze on the spot. The finest warrior in the realm now stood before his king, a thin, lank shadow of the man he once was. If Bors lived on bread and water, Lance looked as if he partook of neither. And whereas he used to move with the fine, lithe grace of an athlete ready at any moment to leap to action, now every motion was constrained, though he bore no visible sign of wounds.

His angular face was drawn and gaunt, high cheekbones craggy over sunken cheeks, while the wide blue eyes that once held all the laughter in the world were as sober and guarded as Mordred's.

Our gaze met briefly, but instead of the expected joy, the trusted, silent pledge of love between us, I saw only the slightest flicker of recognition before he turned back to Arthur.

"I have learned much about pride, M'lord. There was never before a task I could not complete, a battle I could not win, a prize I could not attain. Blessed—or cursed—by the Gods, I've had fame and fortune and the highest of respect heaped on me all my life . . . until now. Perhaps I was overdue for a few strong lessons in humility."

"Oh, come now," Arthur replied lightly, "you've earned every accolade you've ever had. A braver, more loyal, absolutely trustworthy lieutenant doesn't exist, and I'll not have you discounting those qualities in yourself."

Lance's full lips gathered in a partial smile, but it never reached his eyes. "Those things are fine for worldly matters, but they don't help much in a spiritual Quest." He looked off into some unknown space, and I wondered what inner voices he was listening to.

Arthur was insisting that he tell us his adventures, so he settled into the guest's chair while I drew up a cushion and the High King perched on the table. Still the Breton kept a distant reserve, as though he were only half aware of our presence.

"I—I thought you didn't believe in the Quest—that you went seeking the Grail to protect Galahad. . . ." I stammered, and for the first time Lance looked at me fully.

"Indeed. Perhaps that was part of my arrogance—thinking I was above such an endeavor. But riding alone with only one's God and one's horse for company clarifies the mind, and I began to see the Grail as something much bigger than a bit of country magic. In the end, I discovered that it could become the heart of my life."

The Breton gave Arthur a sheepish look, suddenly embarrassed about putting such matters into words. Arthur was carefully avoiding his lieutenant's eyes, and Lance let a quick glance slide my way before continuing.

"After weeks alone—sometimes finding shelter with peasants, sometimes sleeping under the canopy of stars—I had formed the habit of spending a part of each day in silent communion with God . . . thinking, or praying, or slipping, trancelike, into some other state in which I hoped to approach the Divine. So when my path crossed that of Galahad, I was delighted to discover the lad meditates in much the same way every day. It became a kind of bridge for us, and before long we were sharing all sorts of ideas and feelings. I was amazed at how much we had to talk about, to catch up on after all the years of not knowing each other."

This time it was the Breton who avoided Arthur's eyes, knowing that talk of such closeness between father and son was not likely to set well with the High King. But in the end the man was too honest to gloss over the truth, regardless of Arthur's reaction.

"I'm proud to have a son like Galahad and I'm glad we had this chance to find out how much we mean to each other. It's only a beginning, but we've years still ahead of us, after he takes care of the problems in Carbonek."

"Are you going to visit him there?" Arthur queried.

"Carbonek is not my favorite place, M'lord," Lance answered evenly, without mentioning his desire to avoid Elaine. "Perceval joined us at a tiny hermitage, and as the lads were eager to go off on their own, I stayed there with the holy man. It was he who pointed out that all my achievements have been in the worldly vein. Things that brought glory to myself, honor to the Round Table, peace for you"—he nodded toward Arthur—"and admiration from the rest. But still, in all, I was not worthy to find the Grail . . . not then, maybe never."

The dark head bowed, sadly, and I wanted to put my arms about him and hold him close, telling him about the Goddess, about looking inside oneself. But Arthur's presence stopped me; that and the fact that Lance himself had begged me to leave him alone and let him get on with his own life. It was not a request made lightly, or easily forgotten.

Later that night, when Lance recounted his adventures to the whole of the household, Arthur made sure that everyone knew he did not consider the Breton's Quest to have been a failure.

The older Companions were thrilled to have him home again, and Arthur insisted that he return to the seat beside him as his lieutenant. Gawain, who sat there whenever Lance was not available, moved aside with a withering look. Some little instinct awakened in me; with Pellinore and Lamorak both dead, Gawain might shift the focus of his anger to Lancelot.

"Oh, I don't think so," the Breton reassured me when he found me on my knees in the garden next morning. "He's been a good friend and ally all these years, in spite of his roaring temper. I can't imagine him turning against me now."

"Maybe. But he was angry at being displaced from Arthur's side," I cautioned as I scrambled to my feet.

Lance nodded thoughtfully. "Well, it won't be a problem in the future. I've decided to go live in Joyous Gard, Gwen—permanently."

I heard the words, weighed their meaning, even took a step toward him before the full scope of what he'd said hit home. The idea of his leaving Camelot forever left me dumbstruck, and I stood for a moment with my mouth open and no words coming out. The Breton smiled gently and lifted my chin with his finger.

"So many things happened on the Quest—so much that I don't even know how to begin to tell you. But first I would like to sit down."

I watched anxiously as he lowered himself to the marble bench. There was still something stiff and uneasy about the way he moved, and I wondered if his ribs had been bandaged. A dozen questions rattled in my head but I was determined to keep silent lest harsh words drive him away again.

"Gwen, next to God I have loved you best of anything in the world—there, the word is said. I love you, have loved you, will love you . . ." The admission was quickly followed by a rueful smile. "Ah well, you knew that. Have known it for years. But you . . . whatever else there is between us, you are still my king's wife, and completely unattainable."

I looked away, not wanting to open old wounds. Ever since his near-death at the hands of the bear, I had kept my distance, never pressing for the expressions of love I had so long wanted. Now, when his very soul was drawn taut, I dared not touch upon the matter.

Instead, I leaned over and, picking one of the honeysuckle clusters from the vine beside the bench, silently handed it to him. He reached for it gingerly, but I let it drop just before his fingers closed on it so that it fluttered to the ground. When Lance bent to pick it up, I grabbed hold of his tunic and lifted the skirt well up above his waist since he was wearing no sword belt to hold it down.

There was no sign of bandaging, but under the linen outer garment was a short, coarse shirt made of hair.

"What on earth?" we both exploded, him in amazement at my boldness, me in horror at the sores abraded around his waist by the thing.

"Why?" I sputtered. "Why are you wearing that contraption?"

"Mortification of the flesh," he responded, carefully not meeting my eyes.

"But whatever for?" Heaven knew he hadn't indulged any of the fleshy delights I could have thought up.

"Because I am far more subject to loving you than I was willing to admit. What you've never known was how much I *wanted* you, or how deeply, or with what guilt. Gwen, it was the sin of that wanting that kept me from attaining the Grail. Because for all that we never consummated our love, my desire is as profane as adultery itself in the eyes of the Church."

"Church is it now?" I bridled, wondering which of us was the greater fool, him for his constant denial, or me for my constant loving.

"Aye, Church it is. I've become a Christian."

"So I heard." The words were tart, and I bit my tongue against the hundred other comments that came to mind. Instead, I turned to the subject of the Grail.

"Did you ever consider it might be inside yourself, not out in the world?" I queried. "Palomides thinks it's our own inmost spirit, and getting to know it is what the Quest is all about."

"I can accept that," Lance said with a sigh, then looked down at the flowers which were still in his grasp.

"After I left the hermitage, I rode all day through the woods, finally dismounting and leading Invictus when the trees grew thickest around us. Then, just past sunset, I came out into a clearing which contained the ruins of a chapel—or maybe it was what was left of a temple; in the dusk it was hard to tell. It seemed a good time to meditate before fixing camp for the night, so I tethered the stallion to a birch beside the steps. A new moon was caught in the branches of the tree, and I saluted it for you before walking slowly up the steps."

Lance's free hand slowly slid over to mine and, lifting it gently, he laid the flowers in my palm and closed my fingers over them.

"I was thinking about you—about woman as the holy vessel, the container of life, and how much I have wanted you. So much that tears came to my eyes. When I got to the door of the chapel, I found the inside ablaze with the light of nine wicks floating in a bowl of oil. It was an old lamp, patinaed with age and bearing who-knows-what inscriptions and faces on its side. From the look of it, I would guess it has done service to many Gods down through the ages, lighting this holy spot since time began. It was carefully placed on a cloth of fine white linen that covered the altar, and through my tears the golden flames splintered and flared and blinded my heart.

"It was the source of All; beauty and light, warmth and sustenance. I rushed to enter the sanctuary and kneel within the holy spot . . . but something stopped me. Something felled me to the ground suddenly, as if I'd been axed by a Saxon.

"I stayed there, stunned, waiting for my head to clear so that I could get back to my feet. But for some reason, I could not move. All night I lay motionless on those steps, watching in a half dream while others came and went, entering the chapel and adoring the Grail. All around me I felt their rapture, knew that they were moving out of themselves and into the presence of God, and longed for the experience of oneness with the deity. As much as ever I longed for you, that's how much I wanted to join that holy company.

"It didn't happen, Gwen—any more than your and my bedding can happen. And when I came to in the morning, I was back in the cell of the hermit, sobbing for the loss of what I had come so close to. I begged the old man for absolution, for help and understanding of why this was denied me, how I had failed in my love of God. He said it is because of my loving you."

Lance stroked my fingers softly, then looked long and hard into my eyes.

"I can never have you, for you belong to Arthur—but with some real dedication, some honest repentance, perhaps I can have the Grail. Something of my own, Gwen—a cause, a fulfillment, a reason for living. That's why I'm renouncing all claim on my place beside you and Arthur, in Court and in love, and will go live at Joyous Gard. There is nothing else to be done if I am to salvage anything of my own life now, my love. Do you understand? Does it make any sense to you? I know there is more to life than the mundane experience—know the Divine is there to be touched, if we only have courage enough. I want *more* out of life than the everyday things. . . . I want the breath-catching wonder, the Otherness, the rapture. . . ."

His voice trailed off, and he continued to search my face, desperately looking for some sign of understanding. I remembered my experience with the Goddess and nodded mutely, knowing what he longed for, hating that I must do without him in order that he find it.

"Once more I tell you good-bye," he whispered, carefully putting my hand in my lap and getting stiffly to his feet. "This time the best I can ask is God's blessings on you."

And with that he bowed formally and walked steadily away, leaving me as wordless as when the conversation began.

And so You won, You wretched, intractable Father God! And Lance moved as far away from me as geography and political reality allowed.

I have lived too long to cry piteously with pain any more, but I still feel the anger of it. Anger at Lance for taking what seemed to me the coward's way out, anger at the Goddess for letting him, but most of all, anger at the Christian God who denies all human frailty and, like difficult fathers everywhere, sits in stern, unbending judgment of His offspring.

27

Perceval

 was not the only one stunned by Lancelot's leaving Camelot. His decision to live henceforth at Joyous Gard cast a pall over those who had known him best—for all that he had spent so much time off on adventures, or plying between his two homes, he had still been one of the pillars of Arthur's Court. Now that it was no longer his central haven, some of Camelot's luster dimmed.

"If only Galahad had come back," Gareth said with a sigh. "Lance would have stayed if his son were here."

He paused, and I motioned for him to move the second caldron of water onto the coals. It was a hot day in high summer, and both of us were sweating as we worked in the outdoor kitchen, minding the fire.

I've never learned the arts of midwifery, having had no time for the training. But the specter of death which haunts the bearing of life can unnerve a husband as caring as Gareth, so over the years I've become adept at keeping expectant fathers occupied while the women got on with the birthing.

Gareth seemed well pleased with his daughters, playing gently with solemn Lora, and roughhousing with the fiery Megan. Still, neither girl could join him on the practice field, or carry his flag in tournaments or war. Like Bedivere and Lance, Gareth wasn't afraid to show his fondness for children, and I thought how lucky any boy would be to call him sire.

"You hoping for a son this time?" I inquired.

Gareth nodded in affirmation, then qualified it immediately, not wanting to rile the Gods unduly. "As long as Lynette and the bairn are healthy, I'll be grateful with whatever we get, but she and I've agreed, if this one is a boy, we're going to name him Lancelot."

It was a lovely idea that did them both honor, and I smiled fondly at him.

By eventide his gamin wife had produced a bonny boy, and there was much rejoicing in the household that night, with all the Orcadians toasting the next generation of warriors. Even Mordred, who had come with another report on the Federates, took part in the family festivities.

I was glad to have my stepson home and see him in better spirits than at the start of the Quest. Watching Mordred, I was struck by how much he was like his father—open, frank, generous with time and interest, quick to show his confidence in and appreciation of the men around him. He might have proved as good a leader as well, if his moira had been different. For all that kingship among the Celts is not hereditary, our people could do far worse than Mordred when Arthur's successor must be picked. They would doubtless consider him more seriously if Arthur recognized him as his son.

It was a thought that had crossed my mind more than once, but I dared not approach my husband with it until he himself acknowledged the blood-tie between them. Whenever they spent time together, each came away from the encounter wrapped in dark silence. Mordred no longer pressed for giving the Saxons more say in their governance or letting them join the Round Table, but the subject hovered over father and son like a kestrel —vital, unswerving, marking time until the moment to move came clear. It made each man uneasy with the other.

Mordred's brothers thought as well of him as I did, however, and now that he was grown, accepted him fully as an equal. Gawain praised him often for his skill with the sword, Gaheris and Agravain sought out his company, and Gareth frequently pointed out that Lance considered Mordred one of his best pupils. At least the Orcadian contingent at Court was whole and intact.

Not everyone fared so well, however. There had been no Round Table gathering since Caerleon, what with so many of the Fellowship off on the Quest. Some had returned to their own lands, discouraged and saddened by their inability to locate the Grail, only to find that their holdings had suffered from their absence—harvests not collected, taxes in arrears, outlawry on the rise. And the coming of a bitter winter didn't help matters.

Cold storms held the land in thrall, killing both animals and humans who were unlucky enough to be without shelter. Even when the clouds lifted, the sun provided only enough warmth to melt the surface of the snow, which often turned to treacherous ice before moonrise. Winter game grew scarce, firewood was used in great quantities, and before the feast of Imbolc, farmers and villagers alike began to straggle to our gate, asking help from their rulers when they could no longer help themselves. I talked Cei into allowing each family a ration of free wood, and Cook served more stew and soup than roast so that we could share the meat with those who had none of their own.

Then, as March came in without any promise of surcease, we received word that Dinadan had died while still looking for the Grail. The demise of Tristan's wiry little friend struck me closer than any of the others had. A man of wit and humor, deft at avoiding self-pity and pretension, he was never known to follow the well-trod paths toward fame and glory. Why his search had led him into the moors of Yorkshire no one knew, but both he and his horse had been found frozen out in the vast, empty hills, without even a tree for protection. The news brought an infinite sadness to my world, for I had known him since childhood.

"Ah, lass—it's the kind of thing I feared when this Quest began," Arthur commiserated as the tears ran down my cheeks that night. "Between men lost or gone . . . Cador dead of old age, Pellinore and Urien of treachery . . . Tristan in Brittany with that new wife of his . . . Lance living like a monk at Joyous Gard . . ." He shook his head as though unable to encompass the long, slow arc of it all. "And if that's not enough, there's Lamorak, Bagdemagus and now Dinadan killed while searching for the Grail."

My husband stood behind me, one hand on my shoulder, and I put down my brush in order to lay my fingers over his. Instinct still prompted me to turn toward him, wanting to rage against the cruelty of the human condition and, by sharing this moment of vulnerability, help blunt the anguish for both of us.

But Arthur gave me a reassuring pat and turned away. Just so had every poignant moment between us been deflected in the past. And just so did I take a deep breath and smile at the back of the husband I loved. I reminded myself that in his own way he loved me, he'd just never learned to express it. By now the words of caring had been silenced so often, he probably had no voice with which to phrase them.

" 'Tis all part of life, I suppose," he commented briskly. "And we'll no doubt come to know the new men and the youngsters as well as we did the old, given enough time."

Arthur was only partially right about that. He had a natural talent for making young men comfortable, and they sought his approval by the droves—an approval he seemed capable of giving everyone but his own son. I, on the other hand, found the new-comers not that easy to get to know. They gathered in their own groups, laughed at their own jokes, and showed little interest in having contact with their Queen. Before long, I simply lumped them all together as "those young people." *Perhaps, in that, I was as resistant to the new warriors as Arthur was to Mordred's new ideas.*

There was one, however, who caught my attention. Bagdema-gus's squire, Melias, had made a place for himself among the Companions and his pleasure at being included in the Round Table was wonderfully contagious. He had a deep admiration for Lancelot, but since the Breton was no longer with us, Melias attached himself to Gareth as a logical substitute for his idol. Gareth not only took him as his squire, but remained friends with him after the boy achieved warrior status. Watching the two of them striding up from the practice yard together, I was reminded of Lance and Arthur, in the early days of Camelot.

The thaws came late that year, and the priest who rode up to our gate in mid-April claimed that wolves had followed him boldly along the Road, barely retreating into the verge until he made the sign of the cross at them. No doubt the starving animals would have feasted well on the plump little man—he was one of those clerics with an appetite for food and wine, as well as dogma. I noticed he scowled when Father Baldwin asked Cathbad to lead the blessing at dinner.

"All manner of things happening to the west," the priest an-nounced, eyeing the brimming bowls of stew that were being carried from trestle to trestle. I wondered which would win out, his lust for food or the desire to be the important bearer of tidings from distant courts.

It was a dead heat between the two; eyes and hands concentrated on heaping all manner of edibles onto his plate while mouth and voice paid service to his news. Of primary concern was the death of Illtud, the founder of the monastery at Llantwit, who had helped train and manage our horses.

"He was a fine man, saintly and pious," the priest opined, grabbing up a handful of dried pears from the tray a servant brought round. "All of us in the Church will miss him. Of course, they say he was far too lenient with the Pagans in his area—even had dealings with a descendent of the Fairy King, Gwyn ap Nudd."

I choked at that, having myself once wondered about our horse breeder's lineage, until his brother Yder died a mortal's death. Still, it was a fine joke, one that both Illtud and Gwyn would have enjoyed. Just then Arthur shot me one of his "don't you dare" looks, so I swallowed my laughter, and on a more prosaic note, asked if Gwyn would take over the maintenance of our horses at the monastic stables now that Illtud was gone.

"Not likely, M'lady," the priest announced. "The Church won't tolerate such contact with heathens. Why," he went on, his voice trembling with indignation, "some Pagans are claiming there's a cup in Carbonek which once held the Savior's blood. When the Pope heard that, he was scandalized . . . says it just shows how the uninitiated corrupt our beliefs." By now the cleric was eating and talking at the same time, sucking the marrow out of the stew bones and popping fresh bits of bread into his mouth between each phrase. "Since the Church won't accept it, their 'holy relic' is obviously a fraud."

Many of our Christians bristled at the notion, and Father Baldwin was hard put not to call the man a liar. We held our tongues, however, and gave the guest his due in Celtic hospitality, but all were glad when he left the next morning.

"So much for the sacred vessel," Agravain sneered that afternoon. "Wouldn't you know that goody-goody spawn of Lancelot's would try to profit from a fake."

I was in the Hall closet, replenishing the supply of tapers when the Orcadian spoke up, apparently not realizing I was so near. Of all Morgause's sons, Agravain was the most difficult, being both cruel and cunning, and I'd never found a way to like him.

"I'd be more inclined to believe Bors than that cleric," Gawain noted. "Bors is scrupulously fair and not prone to slant things one way or the other."

"I don't know." Agravain was playing with his dagger, sliding it effortlessly in and out of his belt and making it spin nimbly through his fingers. Like most warriors he rarely sat still, but always kept honing some part of his skill. "He's a cousin of Lancelot's, isn't he? Bound to make that foppish boy look as good as possible, just to curry the father's favor. You know," he added under his breath, "I don't trust that Breton. Have you ever thought how much closer we would be to Arthur if it weren't for the Queen's Champion?"

"That's nonsense," Gareth declared, rising like a guard dog to his mentor's defense.

"Besides," Gawain cut in, "Lance has gone to live in Northumbria. It hardly speaks well of your honor to be attacking a man who isn't here. If I were you, I'd look to serving your King better instead of besmirching someone else's reputation."

Dear Gawain. I turned back to my work, glad to see him exert a steadying hand on his less reliable sibling.

During the next week the Roads opened more fully, and a spate of Royal Messengers came and went with reports from all over. There were no insurrections, few complaints, and here and there a spark of bright hope. Uwain had cleared the northern reaches of Northumbria of Saxon invaders and sent word he was adding buildings to Thirlings as well as Yeavering. He included an invitation for us to visit him this summer, if we could arrange it. Arthur read the communiqué aloud and raised an eyebrow.

"Perhaps this would be a good time to solidify our bond with the man," I noted, and Arthur nodded.

"Go see him in the summer, after we hold Court at Carlisle," he suggested. My heart rose at that, for it had been some time since I'd been home, and any year that contained a trip to Rheged was a good year. Besides, it was that much closer to Joyous Gard.

Then suddenly, three weeks into May, Perceval arrived from Carbonek. As usual, he came while the household was at dinner, and Lucan made a solemn occasion out of announcing his presence.

Pellinore's youngest son walked soberly across the circle and bent his knee to Arthur. His hair was still a riot of curls, and his eyes flashed with the same feverish fire as before the Quest, but otherwise his untamed energy was kept in check. I wondered if time itself had calmed the God that drove him so, or if his new demeanor stemmed from some other, more harrowing, experience.

"Up, up off your knees," Arthur called jovially, "and tell us how things are in Carbonek. We're eager for news."

A hush came over the Hall, all eyes and ears intent on Perceval. Even the faces peering through the carved foliage on the pillars seemed to pause in their mimicry of humans, and I fancied that the Red Dragon on the wall behind us held his steamy breath to hear what the holy fool would say.

"It is a sorrow, and a wonder both," Perceval replied cryptically. "There has been both a coming and a going, and it brings much awe."

A mutter of discontent flitted around the room. It was one thing to listen to Perceval weave one of his magical tales for entertainment's sake and quite something else to get such a fey response when what everyone wanted was news.

"Did you bring the Grail with you?" someone called out, to which Perceval replied with a shake of his head.

"Where is it now, then?" Griflet asked.

"Gone. Gone to heaven, it has . . ." A shadow crossed Perceval's face, but he began to beam as he mentioned Galahad. "Once he became King of Carbonek, the Waste Land came back to life—waters flowed in the streambeds and flowers bloomed in the meadows. Birds returned, horses foaled, the crops grew rich and ripe again, and for a whole year the earth blossomed. There was, as Galahad predicted, a returning to the Old Ways, for he saw the Grail as bridging the gulf between Christian and Pagan, so paeans of praise to both Christ and the Goddess filled the air. I've never seen Galahad happier. He would climb to the top of a ridge or sit on the topmost wall of a hill-fort, staring out over the land, marveling at its revival."

Perceval's voice began to go low and raspy, and he stared at the embers on the hearth when he spoke. I heard the change, and a cold dread crept into my heart as Perceval spun out the story of the boy who would not let the Royal Promise be.

"The people of Carbonek rejoiced in their new King, surrounding him with love and accolades, but Galahad was ever modest, saying it was the Grail which had saved them, not he himself.

"When Beltane came round, Galahad made me promise to help him with a secret ceremony, a rite he wanted to complete alone, while the people of Carbonek were busy dancing round the bonfires and coupling with the joy of returning summer. So, when the music and revelry were at their height, we slipped away into the shadows without being seen. He carried Amide's bowl and led me down from the hill-top and out to one of the further fields.

"A full moon was riding free and clear, and in her light the plowed ridges looked like furrows made by the Goddess's fingers caressing the curve of the earth. He came to a stop at the top of a rise and stood looking out over the land like a lover looking at his beloved. Finally, a long, slow smile came to his face, and he said a little prayer to the Mother. As though in answer, the strange call of a nightjar drifted through the air. Then, before I realized what he was going to do, he took his dagger and made a quick, deliberate slash across his wrist. In the moonlight the blood spurted out, thick and black, and he held his arm over Amide's bowl, letting his life pour into the Grail just as hers had."

There was a gasp from the household, and Perceval paused to dash a tear from his face. Bors sobbed in shocked disbelief, and I swallowed hard around the lump in my throat for the bright, lively boy we had all admired.

"At first Galahad walked across the fields, holding the krater so that his blood pooled into it, then spilled over onto the earth —a dark, steamy shower that smelled of salt and guaranteed the future of life in Carbonek. I wanted to stop it, to bind up the wound and make him lie down, but he met my protest with silence and a gentle shake of his head; Galahad was determined to fulfill a destiny greater than his own. So I walked beside him, holding the Grail when he grew too weak and supporting him when he begged me not to let him fall.

"Back and forth across the land we went, the first vigorous thrust of direction becoming a zigzag staggering as he grew more feeble. His skin was clammy and his mind was wandering as he called on the Christ and the Great Mother and sometimes Amide as well. Just as it seemed I could hold him up no longer, we stumbled on a ewe and lamb nestled together under the boughs of a hazel bush. I pushed them out and made Galahad as comfortable as possible, propped up in that warm sanctuary and looking out over the earth he'd given even his life for. His face was as white as the moon, but there was nothing but love in his eyes when he whispered his last words: 'It is finished. I have fulfilled the Promise.' "

Perceval had reached out, as though wanting to offer this miracle to the whole of humanity and all the Gods, but when his voice dropped into silence, he was left staring helplessly at his hands. No one moved. At last, with a heavy sigh, he let his arms fall. But he kept his eyes averted as he completed the story. Perhaps it was easier to bear his grief that way.

"I dug his grave on that very spot, burying him and the Holy Grail together. It seemed a fitting thing to do, and I didn't want to see the same sacrifice be made, year after year. This once was bad enough. I wished his grave could have been near my mother's well, where all the Old Gods have gathered since forever, but that would be too far from the plowed fields . . . I thought he should be where he could see the rich harvests his death ensures.

"That was almost a month ago. At first the people of Carbonek were distraught at the discovery of their young monarch's death. They mourned him deeply, then chose a new King in his place. I wandered about for a while, not sure where I should go, or whom I should be with. Finally I made my way back to my mother's well. It was while I sat there, in the bower of her shrine, that I heard the voice telling me to bring the story of the Grail to Camelot—to the most noble Court in the world, from which the Quest had started."

When Perceval finished, he stood stock-still before us. The retelling of Galahad's death had left him empty, and his usually quick eyes bore the soft, vacant look of a child newly wakened from a nap, who still half lingers in the dream state.

A murmur of sadness and sorrow stirred the Companions.

Some were openly crying for the lad we had known so briefly, while others quietly debated just what the Grail had been, and a few applauded Perceval for being a steadfast friend in both life and death. I myself thought of Lancelot and the anguish he would feel at the loss of the son he had so recently found.

"I'll send a courier to him—one of the Royal Messengers," Arthur said that night. "See if we can get him to come to Carlisle this summer. It would give him a chance to hear the details from Perceval, and afterward he can lead us back to Uwain's new headquarters in Northumbria."

I nodded my assent and crawled into Arthur's arms, grieving for the loss of Galahad, for Lance, and for all dreamers, everywhere.

28

The Trap

areth left for Joyous Gard two days later, having volunteered to take the news of Galahad's death to Lancelot.

"Lynette and the babes will be safe with you while I'm gone," he reckoned, sizing up the sky to the north. "And I'll bring the Breton to Carlisle, if he'll come."

I was glad it was arranged thus—in light of the bond between the two, Gareth could be counted on to break the news gently.

With the plans for a summer in Rheged looming large, I threw myself into packing with a passion, thankful that the uncertain days of the Grail Quest were over. The surviving Companions who didn't have commitments elsewhere were back with us, and the prospect of moving north pleased everyone.

So, on a lovely day in June, we made our way down the cobbled drive, harness bells jingling and banners whipping in the morning breeze. At the juncture with the Road, I turned to look back at Camelot, seeing the barn and stables, men's quarters and handsome Hall rising high and proud atop its massive hill. A white confection of summer clouds piled behind it, outlining the buildings which gleamed pale gold and gray, and the four towers that lifted majestically from the corners of the upper wall. A fierce joy swept through me at the sight. A wonderland, I thought; a place where dreams could still be realized.

Word of Galahad's death had swept across the land like a rainbow flitting over Scotland. Just as the glory of this spring was more delicious for being late in coming, so the end of the boy's Quest took on a unique splendor because of its strangeness, and people everywhere were talking about it.

The stories must have come piecemeal out of Carbonek, for they varied from place to place, as did the story of how the youth had died. Some said he had looked into the heart of the Grail and died of ecstasy, some that he and the Grail had suddenly been carried up to heaven by angels. None mentioned the Pagan nature of his sacrifice, however.

And instead of becoming the bridge between the Old Ways and the new as Galahad had hoped, the Grail had been co-opted by the Christians who claimed it was theirs, and theirs alone. This, in spite of the fact that they couldn't agree on what the Grail was.

"It's the pair of cruets that Joseph used to capture the blood and tears shed by the Pascal Lamb."

"Naw, it's a bowl. I heard it from my cousin, who got it from her brother-in-law in Gwynedd. It's a big old bowl what caught the blood and water that flowed from Him when He was sacrificed on the cross."

" 'T'ain't neither. I'm a Christian, and I ought to know; it's the chalice that held the wine our Lord consecrated at the Last Supper."

Yet no matter how much they argued over the relic, the very idea of it inspired a remarkable piety. Peasant and noble alike came to wayside chapels that not long ago had housed the Gods of the Old Ways, bringing flowers and ribbons and votive offerings with which to bedeck the tiny shrines. Where there were already churches, such as at Glastonbury and Cirencester, whole congregations turned out to greet us, making a grand occasion out of thanking their God for having allowed the Grail to be seen again by mortals, even if it was for a short while and then only by the best and purest of souls. I noticed that the Bishops' envoys refused to endorse the miracle, however.

The demands on Father Baldwin increased even more when people realized he had personally known Galahad. Finally the gentle cleric asked permission to leave our party and make his way into the Chiltern Hills, where he'd heard there was an untended chapel to which he could retreat. "All this notoriety can't possibly be good for the soul," he said quietly. I gave him my best wishes and a message for Brigit as well, since he'd be going near her convent. So while we continued north, he took the Road which leads to Silchester and the Goring Gap.

But if we lost one of our dearest that summer, we made up for it with Mordred's return. Arthur planned to hold a Round Table meeting at Carlisle, and after delivering his report on the Federates, my stepson agreed to accompany us on the progress to Carlisle and stay for the Council. As our procession made its way up through the Welsh Marches, he took to riding beside me, behind Arthur and Bedivere.

Naturally the subject of the Grail came up. "Perhaps I'm too much of a skeptic," Mordred said thoughtfully. "Or at least a realist. But I'm not about to accept a God who demands we remake ourselves in the name of what some priest defines as virtue. I much prefer the old-fashioned deities, who take us as we are."

I nodded my agreement, glancing over at my stepson's handsome face.

"The barbarians have a very direct relationship with their Gods," he went on, always glad to explain the people he had come to think of as his own. "Much more like the Celts than the Christians. For one thing, they have a very clear picture of Them —creatures with real shape, not invisible spirits wafting around everywhere. And there's all manner of Goddesses with power and strength—none of this looking at women as the work of the devil, designed to tempt men into sin."

He slid a sly look my way, knowing how I would react to that, and I snorted in reply.

"I'm sure my aunt would like to know more about the Saxon Gods as well," he continued, still watching me. "Since we're going past the Road to the Lakes, do you think His Highness would allow me to go visit her? It's been a long time since I've seen the High Priestess . . ."

For a moment I wondered if Mordred were using me, trying to get at—or around—Arthur by appealing to my good auspices. On the other hand, Arthur remained adamant in his distrust of the Lady of the Lake and was unlikely to give his son permission if he asked for it directly.

From the occasional bits of news I'd picked up over the years, I gathered that Morgan had sunk into a spiritual quagmire. As more and more people deserted the Sanctuary, she'd grown inturned and bitter, surrounding herself with acolytes who fluttered helplessly around her like wounded doves. Their greatest virtues seemed to lie in adoring Morgan and hating men. I thought it a blighted life, particularly for one who had once aspired to become High Queen of Britain. But although I had no intention of trying to establish a new rapport with the woman, that was no reason to deny Mordred the company of his kin. So I smiled and assured him I'd see what I could do.

Thus, ironically, I was the one who eased the way for his going to the Sanctuary, never thinking that Morgan le Fey might still hate me, in spite of the years of silence between us.

By now I'd come to love the Romanness of the big house in Carlisle, with its courtyard rooms and muraled walls. In a city that had grown cluttered with lean-tos and small huts scattered between Roman structures, the house and grounds were an oasis of civility.

It had been years since we'd stayed here, and the garden was a mess of weeds. I eyed it critically and set to work restoring order as soon as we'd settled into the house. It was no accident that all our major residences had gardens laid out around them. Even the hunting lodges at Wroxeter and Birdoswald had their little plots. In a life so circumscribed by matters of state, I jealously guarded the hours spent with my hands in the earth.

No doubt that's where I was on the day that Mordred returned, bringing with him a personal letter from Morgan to her half brother. Certainly the missive went directly to Arthur without my seeing it. When Arthur mentioned it, it was only to say she was complaining about having a church erected in Camelot. "Seems she sees it as a betrayal of her having helped to put me onto the throne," my husband said with a sigh.

The only other complaint we found was voiced in the local Councils, and was both military and political in nature. Some of the Caledonian chieftains had taken to making raids across the Wall in reprisal for Hueil's execution, and Arthur, feeling responsible for the situation, immediately ordered a full manning of the defenses along the Wall. He and Bedivere spent several weeks traveling from fort to fort, enlisting the men who lived in them and agreeing to send some of the Companions to augment their forces where necessary.

While he was gone, I began to notice a subtle shift of attitude in the men who remained in Carlisle. Conversations stopped abruptly when I came near, and some of the younger ones began eyeing me with unusual boldness. The most obnoxious among them was Gawain's son, Gingalin, for he developed a habit of covering his mouth with his hand and snickering whenever I appeared. Even after the High King returned, I had the distinct impression that something was wrong.

"Enid, does it seem to you that the Companions are acting different these days?" I asked Geraint's widow one morning while she was fixing my hair.

"A little, M'lady," she answered, carefully combing out a side-lock. "It's not like it used to be when we were young, with warriors and squires of all ages getting on well together. Now the newcomers keep to themselves and gather around Agravain—and Mordred, too, when he's with the household."

I nodded thoughtfully. Just two days before there had been a fight at one of the taverns, apparently instigated by Agravain. Mordred had come out of it unscathed, but a farmer's son had been hurt. For some time I had worried about Agravain's influence on my stepson, and decided this was a good time to talk to him about it.

So I asked Mordred to accompany me to the market in the Square that afternoon, and gave him a motherly lecture on the proper behavior of nobles.

We were standing beside a peddler's rug, on which were spread all manner of things the man had no doubt picked up in trade or barter as he wandered between the northern kingdoms. A Scottish bagpipe lay deflated in one corner, along with several pairs of sandals and a bronze handmirror, whose back was covered with swirling designs. In the center of the rug was an odd assortment of armor which Mordred eyed while I pointed out his responsibilities as a Companion.

"A drunken argument among your own . . . well, that happens in any group of warriors. But a public brawl where commoners are hurt—that's simply not acceptable," I concluded.

My stepson ducked his head and allowed that I was no doubt right. "But the fellow attacked Agravain first—took umbrage at something he said about Lancelot. Naturally I had to come to the aid of my brother."

He gave a small shrug of dismissal and turned his attention to a Roman baldric on the rug.

"What about Lancelot?" I demanded, mindful of the comments I had heard Agravain make in the past.

"Oh, just the usual things—that the Breton is arrogant and proud, and rash in his actions . . . always claiming to be best at everything, and terribly superior to the rest of us."

"Now, Mordred, that's unfair," I chided. But he was ignoring me, reaching casually to pick up the sword belt and examine the boiled oxhide for cracks. Stung by the insolence of his action, I spoke more curtly than I intended.

"Whatever have you got against Lancelot? You of all people know how generous he is. Didn't he make you his squire and protégé when Arthur was too busy to?"

"Ah, the Breton has a talent for such things," Mordred shot back, his voice rimmed with ice. "He seems to have made a career of stepping into the good King's shoes—raising his son, servicing his Queen . . ."

Appalled by the snideness of the comment, I rounded on my stepson without thought or warning, slapping him across the face with all the strength I could muster. The force of the blow caught him off guard, and he raised his hand to his cheek in surprise as he rocked back on his heels. My hand was throbbing painfully, but I glared at him with ill-controlled rage and thrust my face into his.

"Don't you ever sully your King or Lancelot with such slander again," I hissed.

The dark eyes were wide and startled, but as he stared at me, they narrowed briefly to slits before returning to the cool, guarded look he habitually affected.

"I shall remember, my Queen," he murmured.

Mordred's comment had unnerved me badly, and I stormed back to the house, shaking both inside and out. That Lance was my personal Champion, and the closest of the Companions to me, was recognized and accepted by all. But after all the years during which we had avoided bed—and that not always easily— it was both ironic and galling to have Mordred use the subject as a means of insulting Arthur.

I could understand Mordred's pain and anger at his father, and his desire to lash out at him. But it was dangerous to give vent to his feelings through such accusations, and I prayed it wouldn't happen again—that it was not a rumor being spread by all the Orcadians. No doubt Agravain had given Mordred the idea to begin with; the stomach-curdling innuendo, with its implication of incompetence on Arthur's part and sneaky deceit on Lance's, sounded like Agravain. Hopefully the matter would go no farther; the very thought of Lance's reaction to such gossip made me wince.

Gareth and the Breton rode into Carlisle that evening, having taken advantage of the long northern twilight to extend their hours on horseback.

The two of them came into the main room, where people lounged in various groups, some playing chess or dice, others listening to one of Ironside's interminable stories. Agravain looked up, then away, apparently not recognizing that the man in the long monk's robe was the Queen's Champion.

Life as a rural recluse seemed to agree with Lancelot, for he had regained some of the weight he had lost during his Quest for the Grail. He also moved more freely, so I suspected he no longer wore the hair shirt. But even though he held his sorrow in check with rigid self-control, the reason for his visit was written plain across his face.

"We hope you'll stay awhile," Arthur declared, hastily guiding him into the room we used as an office, away from the curious eyes of the household.

I nodded my concurrence. Time spent with Bors and Lionel had always cheered him in the past. Perhaps their company could now help him cope with his grief over Galahad.

"Mostly I just want to talk with Perceval," Lance said stiffly, his voice flat and stoic. "I understand he was there . . ."

"Of course. We've put aside a room facing the garden for you," I responded, but Lance shook his head without looking at me.

"I'd rather sleep in the barn. I may stay on, or maybe not, depending how I feel. But if I decide to leave early tomorrow, I want to be able to go without causing any fuss."

Or seeing me. From the careful way he spoke, and the fact that he never met my eyes, it was clear he intended to keep as much distance between us as possible. I wondered whether he was simply exhausted by his sadness or had been warned by the Church against turning to me for solace.

He spent that first night with Pellinore's son, but when I returned from my ride next morning, I noted that Invictus was still at the stable.

The day turned hot and sticky, and Arthur decided to take a hunting party out along the cool course of the Eden. "Maybe up to Armathwaite," he opined. "They say the greylings are biting, and if it doesn't rain, we may camp over. Do us 'elders' good to get out and about," he added wryly.

The notion that somehow, when no one was looking, we'd all become "elders" seemed preposterous. "Just don't get a summer cold," I admonished, then laughed in rueful recognition of how much I sounded like a nattering granny.

"I won't." Arthur was bundling up his leather cape and an extra blanket, and when he had the bedroll ready, he paused, suddenly awkward.

"You look out for yourself," he said, coming over and deliberately slipping his arms around me. "And be good," he added, staring down at me.

It was such an odd thing to say, I pulled back and searched his face carefully. But outside of looking tired, I saw nothing to explain it, so I reached up and tweaked his nose in an effort to lighten the mood. "Always," I assured him. "And you bring home a good catch."

And that was it. He went off with half the Companions, and I stayed in Carlisle, working in the garden until the heat drove me inside. Later I asked Enid to bring a cold dinner to my chamber. I had no idea where Lancelot was, and while I didn't want to avoid him, neither could I seek him out, under the circumstances. I figured he knew where to find me if he so desired.

The evening was muggy and still; even the warblers in the willows along the riverbank were quiet. I sat in the open window, staring out into the long twilight and thinking back over the years: the rowdy freedom of my childhood in the hidden valleys and high mountains of the Lake District; my delight at discovering that Arthur was a man to love as well as a husband to honor; the pain of losing the only child I was ever able to conceive; and how Lance had sat beside my bed for days when I lay ill in Brigit's convent after Maelgwn kidnapped and raped me. Tender and loving and dedicated . . . just as I had been at his side following his battle with the bear. Just as I should be now while he struggled to come to terms with Galahad's death.

The memory of his plans for a future with his son suddenly came to mind, and I railed silently at the irony of its loss. Lance might try to hold his anger and misery inside, but I held mine up to the Gods, wanting them to admit the unfairness of it all.

A figure moved at the base of the garden, tall and shadowy, wearing a monk's habit. It was Lancelot, pacing slowly along the river's edge, his head bent in meditation, or prayer.

Instinctively I raised my hand, meaning to call out his name, but uncertainty stayed my voice. Once I had dreamed him thus, clothed in the habits of a holy man. Then I had hated it; now I was not so sure. Christianity was something that filled his life as nothing else could—something he had chosen, had deliberately sought out. I could compete with another woman for his love, but there was no way I could win in a contest with God.

The greeting died on my lips. Perhaps his prayers would give him as much comfort as I could . . . at least I would respect his choice.

With a sigh I moved back into the room, and getting into the coolest nightshift I could find, sat down to comb out my hair. When it was done, I was still too wakeful for sleep, so I tossed the covers off the bed and stretched out on my stomach on the cool sheets, staring up at the stars beyond the casement.

The new moon had long since set, and the sky was finally darkening. Soon it would be netted with brilliants, a fine black velvet strewn with jewels of burning ice that whirl in majesty to music only bards can hear. I watched them dreamily, wondering what they might know of life and death, or what it was to love.

I must have dozed off, for when I realized someone was tapping at my door, the room was enveloped in darkness. The rush-light in its clip had burned out, and I hadn't thought to light my lantern before lying down, so there was nothing for it but to make my was across the floor in the pitch-black, not even pausing to search for a robe.

Whether by instinct or empathy, or some inner communication that needed no voice, I knew who it was even before I lifted the latch. Lance stood in the hall, still in his monk's robe, candle in hand. I stepped back before the halo of light, inviting him in without a word.

He put the taper on the bedside table as I closed and barred the door. I turned to look at him, seeing a man who stood un- moving and helpless in the face of tragedy. He was as defenseless against the despair of his heart as he was unarmed against the world. Tears began to run down his cheeks, and he slowly reached out to me in mute appeal.

A great, profound quiet had descended on the room, and I moved toward him as in a dream. Like the Great Mother, I opened my arms, gathering him in to my embrace as I would a child—comforting, holding, shielding him with a love that asks nothing, but simply is. At such moments one draws on the oldest power in the world, and it flowed through me as a spring flows up through rocks to slake the thirsty greensward.

I felt the long shudder that shook his frame as he bowed his head and let the aching of his heart pour out in silent tears.

How long we stood like that I have no idea—I would have stayed there all night if he had needed it. But suddenly there came a wild stamping in the hallway and someone pounding loudly on my door.

"Open. Open in the name of the King!"

Startled by such shattering of the night's peace, Lance and I jumped apart.

"Who disturbs the Queen?" he demanded, reaching for the candle.

"You there, Lancelot. We hear you in there! I demand you surrender, in the King's name."

There was no mistaking Agravain's voice, and realization of danger flashed through me as I whispered to Lance, "It's a trap to discredit us, and Arthur. Quick, out the window."

"Wretched woman, we've caught you with your lover. Open up, I say!"

The shouts were coming from different voices now, some I could identify, some I couldn't. Clearly there were a number of warriors intent on breaking down my door.

"Have you any weapons?" Lance asked, hastily scanning the room.

"None that would help. Go out the window, love, and let me deal with this."

"And leave you to face that mob alone?" Lance's question was a statement in itself, made as he pulled off his robe and wrapped it around his shield-arm. Wearing only his trews, he advanced on the door, which shivered in its jam under the onslaught of constant pounding. Putting his shoulder against the wood, he paused to look back at me. "Whatever happens, if we survive this, I'll not leave you again."

Before I had a chance to answer, he was easing the bar from its hasp and, bracing himself against the crush, opened the door just enough to allow a single person into the room.

It was Colgrevance who stumbled into the gloom as Lance forced the door closed again. The Frenchman stood staring at me, momentarily bewildered, until Lance leapt on him. There was a scuffle of bodies, silent and deadly, while bedlam continued in the hall, and suddenly Colgrevance slumped to the ground, his neck broken. Lance turned the body over and, grabbing his shield, tossed it on the bed while I fumbled for the baldric, being careful not to look at the fellow's face.

Fortunately he was wearing Roman armor rather than mail, so we had it off him in seconds. Retrieving both sword and shield, Lance motioned me to the window before he jerked open the door.

Caught off balance when it suddenly gave way, the howling intruders fell forward into the room. Lance used the door to protect his flank, hacking and swinging with a strength born of desperation. The clash of blade on blade was punctuated with occasional oaths, a hideous gurgle, and someone's scream of death or destruction. The sweet, sticky smell of blood filled my nostrils as I watched, horrified.

Slowly the flailing of arms and legs began to lessen. In the shadowy melee one figure turned to flee, leaving behind three bodies sprawled upon the floor, one more groaning beside the bed. Lance was still engaged, however, cornered by a silent, deadly opponent.

I lifted the heavy water pitcher from its ewer on the chest, hefting the weight with every intention of coming to Lance's aid if the chance arose. There were just the two of them now, moving away from the door, slashing and parrying. It was easy to pick out Lance, sweating and straining to keep the other fellow at a distance, but only when the dark head turned to profile did I see—and know—that the last of the attackers was Mordred.

What depth of bitterness and hate had turned him thus? Was it jealousy? Ambition? A feeling of betrayal, fed by his cruel, vicious brother? Or did it shadow a destiny delivered at birth, a moira from which there was no appeal?

In the midst of the blood-spattered present my mind hared off to the past, hounded by questions which had no answer: where had I failed, what could I have done differently? All the wrong decisions I'd made in raising the boy piled up around me as waves of riotous glee began to ricochet in my head, goading me past reason. Whatever help I might have brought to Lance was lost in peels of mirthless laughter.

Through the demonic veil of tears and hysterics, I saw Mordred break away, his arm squirting blood, his face smeared with hate. The rage that had driven his body forward now turned to fear, and he bolted for the door, leaving his comrades heaped at my feet. I stared at the carnage as the awful laughter continued.

"Stop it! Stop it, Gwen!" Lance was shouting at me, and when I continued to laugh idiotically, he took me by the shoulders and gave me a hard slap before demanding, "Are you all right?"

The laughter ended as abruptly as it started. I turned to stare at my savior, trying to blot out the pictures of the bodies strewn around the room, and nodded numbly. "And you?" I whispered, unable to control my voice.

"Only flesh wounds."

Footsteps were pounding down the hall, and lantern light swung wildly around the walls as people rushed to converge on my room.

"Whatever happens, I will not desert you," Lance said planting a hasty kiss on my forehead. "Remember that."

And then he was gone, grabbing up the monk's robe and leaping out the window. I stood there, cold and shaking, as members of the household poured through the door and came to encircle me. Some had friendly faces, many did not, but there was caution and fear on all of them.

"Arrest her!" Agravain demanded, pushing his way into the room. "We caught her in adultery, in plotting against her husband, in treasonous actions. She must be held for trial."

I stared at him without comprehension.

"See how she stands, near naked in the flimsiest of gowns? Not even wearing a robe to cover her shame! And the bed . . ." With a sweeping gesture he pointed to the covers that lay in a heap where I'd pushed them, then shrugged as though that were proof in itself. "Didn't the Lady of the Lake warn us of this woman's treachery? Didn't she tell us that Lancelot and Guinevere were lovers? Have been lovers for years? Now we've caught them in the act!" He was riding the crest of triumph now, his voice grown ominous as he brought home his point. "If Morgan le Fey was right about their adultery, is she not likely to be right about their plots—their treasonous plots to overthrow Arthur?"

Gradually, with the slow, ponderous weight of the inevitable, the truth came clear. It reeked of Morgan's determination to destroy me, and I looked slowly and carefully at the faces of my captors, hearing the mutter of their agreement, seeing the accusation in their eyes.

Aside from Ironside, who had declined to go on Arthur's hunting party, and Agravain, who strutted before me, the men were young or new to our domain. The women, with the exception of Enid and Lynette and Elyzabel, were equally unknown—girls whose names I might recall but whose hearts and natures I had not bothered to get acquainted with. Some of them bent to attend the warriors on the floor: Gingalin and Florence and Colgrevance dead at Lance's hand, Gaheris groaning in half consciousness.

In the center of it all I stood defenseless, wrapped in the tatters of royal dignity and wondering where Arthur was, if Lance had gotten away, and what would happen next.

Mordred appeared, having put a hasty bandage around his wound before going to fetch the manacles and chains from the dungeon. When I saw the irons, I stretched out my wrists with cold disdain while my eyes searched his face, trying to find some knowledge of his heart. But all I saw was the bruise from where I'd slapped him the day before.

Perhaps that was enough.

29

The Trial

nd so the nightmare began . . . noisy at first, with Arthur returning, ferocious as a bear routed out of hiber-
nation. . . .

"Yea Gods, Gwen!" He roared as he stamped furiously about the room. "Did you have to walk right
into their trap?"

"Me walk into a trap?" I shot back, lifting my hands as high as
the manacles allowed. "That trap was to discredit both of us,
fashioned by Morgan le Fey and set by the Orcadians, at her
suggestion."

"Only Agravain and Gaheris," he corrected me grimly. "Gareth was not privy to it, and Gawain refused to be involved. As
for Mordred . . ."

His voice trailed off, and I shied away from the implication,
still unwilling to reconcile my stepson's actions with my belief in
his worthiness.

"You should have told me there was more in Morgan's letter
than concern over the church at Camelot," I declared, coming
back to the bone of contention. "Why, Arthur—when she accused Lance and me of treason—why didn't you ask me?"

My husband abruptly stopped pacing and stared silently out the
window. He stood with one shoulder raised, as if prepared to deflect a blow, though the only thing stirring in the room was a breeze
that carried the sound of a bargeman poling his wares up the
river. Finally Arthur shrugged. "Maybe I didn't want to know."

"Of all the damned stupidity!" I howled, my own frustration
flaring out of control. "So you believed someone else's false ac-

cusations rather than ask your wife for the truth? I could have told you—do tell you now—that Lancelot and I have always been loyal to you . . . have never, could never, *will* never, plot against you."

"I believe you," he said softly, resuming his trek across the rushes.

"Then why on earth did you let them talk you into an over-night excursion, away from Carlisle, so they'd have a chance to catch Lance and me together?"

"They agreed to retract their claims if he didn't come to your chamber."

Oh, Glory, I thought, heaving a sigh. The only time in all our lives together he's crossed my threshold, and that for succor more basic and needed than bed would ever be. I was as angry at the Gods who let this happen as I was at the men who set it up.

"They have agreed to a trial by jury," Arthur was saying, trying to move away from arguing. "Your defense will be heard by a panel of your peers."

"And where are you going to find enough High Queens to sit on it?" I lashed back, wondering how anyone other than a ruling monarch could understand the principles involved.

But my husband just raised an eyebrow and ignored my jibe. "As for Lance—he and his followers have all left Carlisle. Ector, Bors, Lionel, Melias, the lot of them . . . gone into hiding in the woods, no doubt."

Or back to Joyous Gard, if they had any sense. No point in staying around to be picked off like Pellinore and Lamorak. The focus of my wrath was beginning to shift from Morgan to her nephews.

"Gaheris died this morning," Arthur continued. "Brings to four the men Lance killed before he escaped."

Well, at least something good came of it, I thought bitterly. One less viper to worry about.

"I . . . I have said I will not sit as judge." Arthur was speaking quietly, now. His ire having run its course, he was concentrating on the miserable details of salvaging my reputation from Morgan's attack. "Father Baldwin has suggested someone from the Church —maybe the monk Gildas—should take my place."

"No!" I hurled the word across the room. In no event would I consider letting that narrowminded prig sit in judgment of me. "There are reasons why he can't be impartial, Arthur. My father turned him down when he was suggested as a husband for me, back before you and I married."

"Wonder how *he'd* have coped with you as a wife?" my husband mused, then gave me a long, speculative look. "I'm glad he didn't get a chance to try."

The half-hidden compliment caught me off guard, making me smile in spite of everything, and I took a step toward him.

"Arthur," I said gently, "truly, it wasn't the way they make it sound. Lance and I have never even bedded."

"It would be none of my business if you had." His response was brusque, but he added softly, "Thank you for telling me . . . I'm glad to know."

I caught the unguarded moment of admission, the words that had slipped around his barrier of silence like the first trickle of water that begins to seep out a crack in a dam when the pool behind it becomes too great to contain. Now, I thought. Now is the chance I've been waiting all our marriage for. If I can just reassure him. . . . But even as I started to speak his name there was a loud knock at the door, and Agravain entered without being bidden.

"It's time, Your Highness," he announced, though which of us he was addressing wasn't clear. Arthur blanched and turned away and the Orcadian pushed me roughly toward the door. As I stumbled into the hall I caught one last glimpse of my husband. Arthur stood there, alone—an isolated man drawn in on himself, struggling with a dozen inner demons. I wanted desperately to go to him, to reach out and hold him and encourage him to give voice to the fears and dreads he had so long denied. But Agravain slammed the door between us and led me, sobbing, back to the room in the wine cellar they were using as a dungeon.

After that came silence as I languished in the cell, closed in, bereft of friend or freedom. . . .

It could have been worse: the guard didn't keep me chained, Cook sent a tray of hot food from the kitchen every day, and I could see both treetops and sky through the high window. Even the long days of inactivity were bearable. But what the days didn't bring in torture, the nights did.

Horrible dreams—dreadful, familiar nightmares that have haunted me in times of terror since childhood. There was the vision of my father, jigging and capering atop the Beltane blaze, only this time he wasn't thrusting the flaming brand into the center of the pyre. He danced in the heart of that inferno, not scrambling down as he had in reality but endlessly giving up his life for his people as I wailed disconsolately and woke sobbing.

Or Morgan's laughter, silky and gleeful, gloating over the loss of my only child. Anger and pitiful helplessness knotted my stomach, and I woke, retching.

But worst of all was the sight of Arthur in battle, slowly, inexorably run through by a spear when he fought Maelgwn in retribution for my having been kidnapped and raped. Fatally skewered, his death agony sent wave after wave of pain through my sleep as he reached out to me from the blood-blackened pool of disaster and I woke, screaming.

Just so the most awful fears of my life came back, parading grotesquely through the dark. In between, I prayed. As hard as I'd prayed for Lance when he was so close to death, now I prayed for his safety and that the trial might prove our innocence. . . .

By the time the trial was held, my eyes were sunken from lack of sleep, my spirit dampened by so much horror. I moved slowly into the big room with the mosaic floor and sank down on the chair Agravain gestured to—a plain, hard-backed piece of furniture that was a far cry from the carved chairs I had used for years as Queen. Those at least had cushions.

The position of judge was eliminated after Arthur stepped down, and since no one would accept the job of sitting on the jury, the entire household was enlisted. I looked slowly around the room, blinking at the sight of so many strangers. Here and there I found a familiar face—Enid and Elyzabel sitting together, Lynette with her newest babe at breast, Frieda holding a grandchild on her lap, Cook still wearing her apron. Nimue was present, but she kept herself separate from the rest, as befits a priestess.

Among the men, the Companions fidgeted—adjusting belts, studying their boots, playing with their daggers. Gareth and Griflet held my gaze and tried to smile encouragingly; Gawain stared at the ceiling; Cei sat beside Arthur with Palomides on the other side, offering whispered comments. Of the rest, not even Ironside met my eyes.

It was Agravain who presented the case against me, swaggering about the small open area in the center of the group, making his points with flair and dramatic gestures.

"Captured in her own chamber," he stressed. "As good as lying naked in her lover's arms. . . ."

"I wasn't naked, and we were standing," I interrupted, but my voice was too weak to carry, and he ignored my statement.

Holding up Morgan's letter, the handsome Orcadian declared that Arthur deserved better in a wife. Watching him, I wondered vaguely what drove the man to attack me so. His jealousy of Lancelot was well known, as was his devotion to the Lady who had absolved him of matricide. Still, to carry the charges from the two of us being lovers to that of treason was preposterous. I listened to his ravings and had trouble taking them seriously, so outlandish did they seem.

When Bedivere rose to defend me, he pointed out the flaws in Agravain's argument, the lack of evidence, and the fact that Morgan herself had once attempted to have Arthur killed by her lover, Accolon. "Is it not a bit of irony," he said dryly, "that the Lady of the Lake should now accuse the High King's wife of the very action she herself was guilty of?"

He went on to note the lack of proof in Agravain's case.

"But you have years of proof of loyalty, years of service to the King and Round Table—by both Lancelot and the Queen. The Breton brought honor and courtesy and courage, while M'lady brought the human touch that kept the Fellowship from being just another gathering of warriors. Has she not always been there to listen to your problems, cheer you when you were down, lead the celebrations when you triumphed?"

And, as his final argument, he reminded the Court that by ancient custom Celtic women have the right to choose their bed-partners on the basis of merit. If I had chosen to exercise that right, what would be more natural than that I turn to my personal Champion and finest warrior in the realm?

When Bedivere was finished, I breathed a sigh of relief. I had begged him to find a way to defend me without ever casting doubts on Arthur as a husband, and he had done it brilliantly.

It was a splendid and spirited defense. Every God I had petitioned, every spirit I had called forth guided Bedivere's rhetoric. At the end I would have applauded if I'd had more strength.

His words had their effect; the newcomers looked at me with curiosity, and possibly respect, while the rest nodded in agreement and reminded each other of this favor I had done or that trouble I had taken on their behalf. The hope that Arthur's hard-won legal system might produce justice after all gave me confidence. I sat up straighter in my chair and resolutely faced my accusers.

That's when the Bishop from Carlisle's cathedral stepped forth—the man Vinnie used to encourage me to entertain. Old and venerable now, with a long white beard, he looked kindly and wise as he leaned against his shepherd's crook and sealed my fate in a thunderous voice. . . .

"Can you say you are innocent of adultery in spirit as well as body?" he demanded.

"What right have you to judge my spirit?" I flashed back, stung by the old man's righteousness.

But the moment the words were out of my mouth, I wished desperately I could take them back. The patriarch turned from me to the household with the grace of a born orator.

"Thus you see clearly the dangers of a prideful Pagan monarch ruling a Christian Court, my children. Overweening pride invariably leads to other sins—unbridled lust, treason against her husband, all forms of arrogance and plotting for personal ends. I have heard that this Queen thwarted the true and rightful union of Lancelot and Elaine, and banished the girl from Court, simply to keep her lover close at hand. What was that but a misuse of power, a corruption of her position? And yet she continues to go among you with a total lack of shame."

He paused and turned back to me, making such a sweeping gesture with his arm that everyone's eyes traveled from his accusing finger to where I sat, transfixed, in my chair.

"Look at her now," he intoned. "Even now, defiant when her vile actions are exposed. Only if she confesses her sins, renounces her proud ways, and submits to the authority of God and her husband can she be saved."

It was then I knew the cause was lost. A cold chill reached my heart, and I lowered my head lest my judges see the despair in my eyes. The Bishop, naturally, took it as a sign of belated contrition.

I stayed in the cell while they all deliberated, and when Lucan came to escort me back for the verdict tears were running down his face. Elyzabel walked beside me, ostensibly to hold me up should I feel faint, though I noticed that it was she who clutched my hand. I avoided looking at Arthur, glancing only at those who had known me well; yet whether Christian or Pagan, their faces reflected a terrible doom, and not a few among them cried. For the rest, a bare few looked away in shame. The others stared me down, scornful of the monarch they were about to depose and send packing back to Rheged. Once more I bowed my head.

Standing there in the sandals and shift of a penitent, long since stripped of crown or robes, or even the golden torc I had so loved, I witnessed the indictment of Pagan Queenhood; the ending of co-ruling as an equal and respected partner. . . .

They had heeded their Bishop's demand, and I heard, rather than saw, their verdict. "Guilty." "Guilty." "Death at the stake come dawn."

It was only then that I raised my head, horror-struck by the sentence. Loss of my Queenhood, exile from Court, even banishment—these were the worst I had imagined. Not public execution.

My knees went weak, but I held my head high and walked out of the room with the greatest dignity years of practice could provide. They might take my life, but they would never find me crying over it.

And to think that wretched churchman wanted to see me afterward! I sent him packing with a well-invoked curse when he came to offer his pious consolations. Bravado can only last so long, however, and the moment Nimue stepped into the cell, I collapsed, sobbing, in her arms. She held me gently, reminded me of the Druidic teaching on death and reincarnation: "A new life, Gwen. A fresh beginning, a whole new start."

But I was not so much worried about Afterward as I was about the morrow. . . .

"I don't want to die," I whimpered, clinging to her frail form. "I love this life, I love Arthur and Lance and the Round Table, too. To be burned to death in public. . . ." A fit of shaking seized me, and the doire wrapped her cloak around me as the words tumbled out between sobs. "What if I can't face it? What if I can't make my feet work, or keep from screaming, or remember suddenly some little homely thing and sink down, bawling in despair before we even reach the pyre? I can't do it, I tell you—I can't do it."

"Of course you can." Her voice was normal and not that of the Mother, but with one simple phrase she called up every imperative of my life. How many times had it come down to this—moments of fear or uncertainty, times when I shied away from doing what must be done, only to have someone else give me the confidence that I needed?

"Of course you can." She said it a second time for good measure, lifting my tearstained face and looking hard into my eyes. "Don't forget, Gwen, I was Merlin's protégé and I have the Sight. You will face it well, you will come through the ordeal. I know. I have seen."

And so she poured her strength and belief into the leaky basket that held my courage. By the time she left, I was all cried out, and moderately able to face the dawn. When Enid came to spend the night praying for me, I was calm and poised. Even Gareth has found me at least coherent company this night. But still I wonder how it came to this . . . and where Mordred is.

The one face I did not see, either at the trial or sentencing, was his. Where did you go to, my son? Into the wildwoods to find your soul? Back to your Auntie to report on your success? Or simply away, as Lance has gone away, to be healed somewhere of the wounds life dealt you? I cannot say I wish to see you this morning, when the fire lights up the sky in bloody competition with the sun . . . but still I would like to know the truth of your motives.

"I think," Gareth said suddenly, "that Mordred is deeply distressed by what has happened. He ranted a good deal against Lancelot after he read the letter—became obsessed with outrage toward the Breton. But he's always spoken well of you, M'lady."

I managed a faint smile, hoping Gareth was right. Perhaps Mordred's resentment of the Breton reflected some kind of twisted loyalty to Arthur, hidden and unspoken though it might be. But the crack around the edge of the shutters was growing lighter, leaving me little time to ponder such matters. The best I could do was consign him to the Gods and know I'd done all that was in my power to give him a good childhood.

There was a mumbled exchange outside my cell, and Gareth rose when a key grated in the lock. In her corner, Enid stirred to wakefulness and hastily crossed herself as the door swung open.

Standing next to the torchbearer, looking gray and old as death, was Arthur Pendragon.

I scrambled off my pallet, startled by his visit and horrified at his condition. All thought for my own situation fled at the sight.

"Leave us," he said in a hoarse voice, and Gareth hastily led Enid out.

We stared at each other, he no doubt as shocked at my state as I was at his. Once before I had seen him thus—hollow-eyed and gaunt-faced, frail as an old man hunched against a storm. It was back before we'd wed: standing in the moonlight on the Wrekin, the night I'd realized that our moiras were entwined. Old and haggard, beaten by a crushing weight . . .

I'd thought then that there was something I could say, something that would heal the anguish I beheld. But what do youngsters know of visions? It had disappeared before I understood it. Now it was here in reality; the husband I loved and admired, racked with a need to hear—or say—some word of release.

"Ah, Gwen." He spoke in a raspy whisper, and the sound went creeping around the stone walls like a mouse looking for a way out.

I moved toward him, but as I reached up to put my arms around his neck, he stepped back and took me firmly by the shoulders. By sheer force of will he brought his voice under control.

"I've come to give you your freedom . . . thought of nothing else since the verdict, really. Gawain and some of the Companions are pressing for a pardon; Nimue says it is not time for you to die; and I—my life is over without you by my side. So I have decided. I will walk out with you before the entire Court and pardon you by Royal Decree."

"Arthur!" I gasped, shocked that he would even consider such a thing. Using the royal power to overturn the legal system he had himself worked so hard to establish was unthinkable. "You can't do that."

"No, lass. What I can't do is sit by silently and let them lead you to the stake."

Gritty-eyed and grimy, the High King of Britain and I confronted each other, my life hanging somewhere between us. To live, to laugh and love and dance again on the greensward . . . tears of hope and gratitude filled my eyes, and threatened to undermine the little hoard of bravery I'd collected these last hours. I stared at him, awash with tenderness and love—and the realization that everything we had lived for was about to be scattered in oblivion. Driven by the terror of such a thought, I pulled myself up to my full height and looked him levelly eye-to-eye.

"Of course you can," I said, my voice trembling only a little at the beginning. "If I can face it, you can face it. To do anything else is to make a mockery of all your life. What else have you striven for but the rule of law, where all people, noble or not, are held accountable for their actions? The trial was fair, the jury as impartial as could be gotten under the circumstances. If you overturn their verdict, the whole of our reign will end as a sham."

He was looking into my eyes, more open and vulnerable than I had ever before seen him.

"Gwen, without you, life would be a sham anyhow."

The words tore at me like eagle's claws. It broke my heart to realize that the man who had such difficulty admitting love was willing to throw the whole of his life away just to keep me alive. He was the King all Britain had prayed for during the days of the tyrants; the leader Merlin had created—by magic or otherwise; the one who was destined to keep the flickering light of civilization from being swept into darkness by the barbarians. His name, the Wizard had said, was writ in the stars, and would be remembered for all time. To this task Arthur had brought honor and wit, an appreciation of his men, a loyalty beyond question, an openness of personality and spirit that drew all to him. The dream might be the Sorcerer's; its accomplishment was the man's. I could not see it founder over me.

"I won't accept," I said curtly.

He gazed at me in silence, puzzled and hurt by my response. Thank goodness he still held me by the shoulders; a warm, protective embrace would have undone me entirely.

Tears began to fill his eyes, reflecting the things he'd never been able to say. I marshaled every scrap of resolve I had left and forced myself to smile. "It's been a splendid time, Arthur Pen-dragon. And I've been honored to be your wife. But the needs of the people come first, no matter the personal cost. They need you, need your law, need to believe in all you've done. I will not deny them that."

The muscles of his jaw tensed as though he meant to argue the point, and I rushed to head it off in a half-bullying way.

"Don't you dare start crying, you sentimental oaf. I've work to do, and I'll not have you getting the whole front of my dress sopping with tears."

My change in tone seemed to startle him, and he let go of my shoulders as the sound of marching men came to a stop outside the cell. I stepped back and took a deep breath. "Get on with you, man. I've still got to fix my hair."

The guard rapped on the door before opening it. My escort— all members of the Queen's Men, their white shields draped with the black of mourning—waited outside.

Arthur paused a single heartbeat more, still holding my eyes. For a moment I thought he was going to say something further, so I raised my chin defiantly and gave him the thumbs up. He turned his face away, blinking, but returned the salute before bolting out the door.

Fix my hair, indeed! What silly, mundane things we cling to in the face of chaos! I'm doing well to be on my feet, swaying like a sapling and unable to move, much less worry about my hair all hanging down. Well, buck up, girl. It's the last of your public appearances, and Nonny would never forgive you for making a botch of it.

The thought of my old nurse brought a wry smile. When Gareth came rushing to my side, I reached gratefully for the arm he extended. He started to speak, no doubt wanting to give me some word of understanding, but I interrupted, fearful that any delay would leave me unable to face my destiny.

"Don't blame yourself," I told him carefully. "Or let Lance fret over it. He broods too much as it is."

Gareth murmured some response but made no effort to move. In the hallway my escorts stood as still as stone, a terrifying lethargy holding them captive.

What was it Mama told me, just before she died? Once you know what you have to do, you just do it . . . no matter how hard it is or how much pain you feel. It's as simple as that, really.

Lifting the skirt of my shift with one hand, I gave Gareth's arm a squeeze with the other and urged him forward.

Time to get on with it, while I still can. One step at a time. Eyes on the ground, looking neither to left nor right, lest you find compassion in someone's face. Concentrate on not tripping—on what has to be done, for the people's sake. As a Celtic queen . . . as part of the Royal Promise.

30

The Stake

he sky overhead was gray when we made our way to the Square at the heart of Carlisle. A light fog had risen off the river, blurring the edges of the buildings and swirling around us as we came into the open space.

I looked up once and saw, half-hidden in the mists and shadows, a pile of logs and branches heaped up around a stake. It was tall, like the pyres they build at Beltane.

There were ghostly figures moving in the Square, and those nearest to us parted silently to let me through. Shoes and hems, and the edges of cloaks drew away. Many of them were near the fountain . . . the same fountain where I'd been drawing water the first time I saw Arthur.

Thought he was a country lad, as no doubt he thought I was a scullion, standing there barefoot with the bucket slopping over. Great Gods, was it almost thirty years ago? Seems more like yesterday. . . .

I stumbled suddenly and clutched Gareth's arm to keep from falling. A groan rose from the phalanx of men around me, but still I didn't look at them.

Stairs, not a ladder, leading up to the little platform. Thoughtful of them. An extra bit of work for the carpenter. If only he'd included a banister, to help me keep my balance.

Gareth was half supporting me now, guiding me across the boards to the post that rose, rough-hewn and sturdy, out of their center. I leaned back against it, grateful for its solidness, and raised my eyes to the Fair Unknown. I wished I could trust my voice enough to tell him how much I appreciated his help.

He leaned forward, as though to whisper something, but Agravain pushed him away, roughly slipping the rope around me—*a good thick rope, such as might hold a snorting bull. Or a fractious Queen, too prone to letting the words leap out unbidden.*

Someone began fussing with my hair, trying to tie it back before they slipped the hood over my head.

"No need for that," I snapped, turning to glare at the man. "At least let me look on the new day dawning."

He paused, uncertain as to what right of authority I—an about to be dead queen—might have to give orders, and I mustered a wan smile. "I promise I won't lay a curse on anyone, if you'll leave it off."

The man backed away, chastened.

As the mist began to clear, I could make out the crowd more easily: farmers and peasants, merchants and townspeople, all come early to get a good spot for seeing the spectacle. A herald with a drum was marching up and down, periodically disappearing into one of the adjacent streets, his booming instrument waking anyone who might be tempted to sleep through the event. When he came into the Square for the last time, he took up a position in front of the pyre, still beating out a steady cadence.

Across the paving stones the Smith was tending his forge, his helper making the flames leap up against the declining darkness as he clapped the bellows' handles together. A bevy of pages stood in place, each holding a resinous torch ready to be lit and brought to my feet.

I looked hastily away, seeing for the first time the members of the Court. They were coming from one side of the Square, some anxiously peering my way, others speaking in hushed tones among themselves.

On the other side of the plaza, the Bishop stood on the steps of his church, no doubt intoning prayers for my salvation in order to ease the conscience of the sizable crowd surrounding him. They were too far away to make out their faces, but judging from the bright colors they wore, a number of them were nobles.

And Arthur? I put the question aside with a shudder. *God help him, don't let him watch! We have shared too many good times to leave him with a last memory of this.*

Lifting my eyes to the sky, I stared at the high, small clouds that riffled toward the east like water foaming over rocks. They were beginning to hint at sunrise splendor. *Salmon it will be today, perhaps going to pink when the sun finally rises. At least it isn't red.*

Below me the drummer continued, and I thought grimly that on this day, at least, he was calling up the sun just as harpers do.

A sentry on the wall was watching for the first brilliant sliver of sun to break the horizon, and at his signal the great belling warhorns, whose call to death and duty make every warrior's blood run hot, roared out their challenge. The ancient sound echoed away down the alleyways as the people grew hushed. Someone from the town's Council—I did not know who—strode into the Square, signaling for attention.

In a terse, clipped voice he read the proclamation of my guilt. In spite of itself the mob let out a gasp when the man came to the sentence. "Death at the stake come dawn."

As the first wedges of sunlight sliced between the buildings and began to stripe the Square, the fellow declared it was time.

A low, moaning chant came from the throng, throbbing in time with the renewed beat of the drum. Out of the corner of my eye, I caught the motion of the boys dipping their torches into the forge-fire, then running with youthful eagerness to plunge the brands into the logs at my feet. I wanted to scream to them, to order them to go back, to ask why they were doing such a dreadful thing, but I had promised not to make a scene and was determined to hold my tongue as long as possible.

The morning breeze had risen, bringing the smell of burning pitch to my nose, making the Dragon Banner above our house flutter and unfurl. When I looked at them, the Queen's Men seemed to waver and shift in the smoke that began to rise between us.

I looked deliberately around the Square, doubt and fear and bitterness sweeping through me. *For the good of the people? For this you gave up a life of your own, and any promise of love and personal freedom? For what? To hear their every request? To listen to their complaints? To care about the rabble who are now waiting to see you burn?*

A sudden rage raced to my heart as my eyes filled with tears. I stifled a scream of denunciation and searched frantically for distraction.

The sky. Look at the sky. Forget your duty or who you've done it for. There is no more they can ask or you can give. Galahad knew that . . . sought out solitude, went among the fields, away from the throng he wanted to save. Forget the people, ignore the crowd. Hold on to the sky—the dear, wide vault of blue, arching deeper and darker here than anywhere else in the world.

High over the plain a golden eagle circled, lovely and clean in the first rays of light. The crackle of flaming twigs exploded in my ears, and the breeze wafted capriciously, sending waves of heat first from this side, then from that. I stared upward, refusing to be tethered to my panic.

Free—free as the eagle. Soon I shall soar above the valleys and fells of my own land, winging my way to the Isle of the Ever Young . . . and never again be born a queen!

I clung desperately to the thought, trying to ignore the pounding of my heart, the increasing heat from the flames, the storm of noise that washed over me.

Someone screamed—was it me?—and the platform beneath my feet began to shake. Perhaps the crowd had gone mad, was charging the bonfire in order to rip some poor part of me away as a souvenir, a memento of my service, my loyalty to them. Blinded by tears, I swore at this untidy ending with all the power at my command.

Suddenly my bonds loosened and the post no longer held me. I crumpled, sobbing, only to be grabbed roughly, dragged down the stairs, and thrust abruptly up onto the withers of a large horse. Someone's arms went around me, pulling me close in against his body, and I stared up, uncomprehending, at Lancelot's face.

Chaos was sweeping the Square—men pushing and shoving, the ring of iron on white shields, a bedlam of swearing and groaning interlaced with screams of surprise, of outrage, of deathblows raining.

Lance swung Invictus around, intent on getting away. As the animal whirled, bunched, and prepared to leap forward, I saw Gareth pause at the base of the stairs, smiling at us. Out of the smoke, a blade flashed red in the fireglow.

There was no warning. The blow caught him above his mail tunic, in the juncture of shoulder and neck, severing the jugular. A geyser of blood fountained upward, splattering Lance and me and the horse.

The moment froze in time. He did not even scream. A dreadful grimace of surprise and disbelief contorted his features as the gentlest of heroes raised his hands slowly to his face before sinking —first to his knees, then to the stones already slick with his life's liquor.

The snorting horse reared and plunged, then raced away as I let out a wail of despair and fainted.

Light . . . brilliant, shattering light and the thunder of hoof-beats pierced my head. Dimly I knew our lives depended on the speed and endurance of the stallion, and the drumming of his hooves, hard against the paving, clattered in and out of my consciousness. I heard the sound, felt the motion, was vaguely aware of the Breton's arms holding me firmly before him. Time and space had broken their bounds and I was tossed violently between them. Here I caught a glimpse of the present, there a flash of memory—everything and nothing tumbled in my head like leaves in a whirlwind, and I could no longer tell what was real and what was not.

The fire-bright sun lay directly ahead of us, but when I closed my eyes against the pain of it, a pall of smoke and blood engulfed me and the sight of Gareth's death's head rushed into view. With a strangled scream I opened my eyes, struggled to throw off the nightmare, and Lance leaned forward, his mouth barely inches from my ear.

"Don't think," he commanded, tightening his grip on me as I started to sob. "Don't think about anything."

We flew down the supply road at the base of the towering Wall. Guards were not posted at the quarter-mile towers so close to the city, and there was no one on the road, since most people had gone to Carlisle to witness their Queen's death. We might have been fleeing across an empty world.

The stallion was growing winded as we came to the ford of a small stream, and Lance turned off into the wooded watercourse that meandered between gentle hillocks. No sooner were we hidden from sight than a pack of riders went flying past. I began to shake.

"Bors and the others," Lance reassured me. "But I have no doubt the King's men will be close behind."

He dropped the reins and let Invictus pick his way slowly between the trees along the burn. When we reached the edge of a broad meadow, Lance drew the animal to a halt and helped me dismount, then spread his bedroll beneath a birch well back from the verge of the woods. He also tossed me his monk's habit with the admonition to put it on.

"Did you get any sleep last night?" he asked when I'd complied. I shook my head uncertainly, unable to remember what had happened the night before.

"I thought not. You rest—just lie here and rest—while I take care of the horse. We're going to need him for some days to come."

He leaned across me to tuck the blankets closer, and I looked up at him, too tired and confused to speak. For a moment he paused and stared down at me, his eyes crinkling in a weary smile. That we were both alive and here in this sylvan glade was almost beyond believing. How we had gotten here was of no more consequence than whether this was all a dream or not.

I let myself float in the beauty of the moment, disconnected from any reality but this. Above me a red squirrel frisked in the branches, while a thrush filled the morning with glory from the higher canopy.

Lying there, safe in the dappled shade of the grove, I watched as Lance unsaddled his mount and walked him long and thoroughly around the edge of the meadow. The lea was wild, full of both grass and flowers, and there was no sign of fences or buildings within sight. We might have been the only people in the world at that moment. It was a heavenly thought.

Seen from that distance, Lance looked like any horseman caring for his steed. Although he was wearing a mail tunic, both sword and shield had been left with me. There was a bandage on one arm from the night we were trapped together, but one might still think him simply a man of the land—a farmer, probably a horse breeder. All of his attention was directed to the needs of his animal, just as, when we were together, all of his attention focused on me. A good husbander, I thought softly. Definitely a man of the land.

When the stallion had cooled off, the Breton brought him back by the trees and rubbed him down with handfuls of grass.

"What he really likes is to roll after being ridden," Lance sighed, "but as long as we're in hiding, he's in hiding too."

Hiding. The word wandered slowly around my brain, devoid of meaning. Once Lance hobbled the horse and threw himself on the ground beside me, I shifted to rest my head in his lap, staring up into the leaves overhead.

"Hiding?" I murmured. "Whyever should we be in hiding? Didn't you save my life?"

"Aye, and that with the King's help. Arthur sent me a message before the trial, saying that if it came to the worst, he'd make sure your escort was unarmed. He begged me to save you if he could not. The Banner was our signal, and when I saw the Red Dragon flying over the house this morning, I knew he had not found a way to keep you alive. That's why I came."

"But if the Queen's Men were unarmed, why was there so much fighting?" I whispered, trying to make sense out of the disjointed memories that had begun to creep back to me.

"I don't know—I was concentrating on you and didn't see how it began. At a guess, I'd say it was likely to have been Agravain who broke the faith. It . . . it wasn't supposed to be that way. My men promised they wouldn't use their weapons unless they had to. Now, God knows how many have been maimed or killed."

"Besides Gareth?" I formed the name carefully, praying all the time it wasn't true. "He died, didn't he?"

"Umhum," Lance nodded miserably. He was silent for a long while, gently brushing my hair from my face. When he spoke, his voice was husky. "Gareth insisted on being next to the stairs, so as to be able to cut you down and bring you to my horse. It meant I didn't have to dismount. It was his choice, his moira."

The reality was even worse than I feared, and the realization that he had given his life for mine brought out a deep, aching moan.

Lance gathered me close in his arms, shushing me softly and crooning a little wordless lullaby just as he had when he'd carried me to safety after the rape all those years ago. That had been in the middle of the night, with stars flung all around us; now we were in the first flush of morning, with the peaceful flutter of a green bower overhead and a splashing brook nearby—a time fresh spun, separate and away from all the past.

"Sleep if you can," he whispered, rocking me gently. "We have to wait till evening before moving on anyhow. They'll be expecting us to use the Road, and patrolling along the Wall, so we'd best stick to the cover of streams and forest paths for a while. If necessary, we can follow them all the way to Northumbria, and make Joyous Gard in little more than a fortnight."

Joyous Gard—that memory of pleasure and delight, the haven in the midst of difficulty, the peaceful home untouched by violence. Like a child, I repeated the name over and over, until it became a murmur akin to the sound of the nearby stream, and I drifted into a heavy, dreamless sleep.

31

The Journey

 full day's rest and only moderate travel that evening did much to restore my strength. We talked little—perhaps both needing to come to terms with the devastation we'd left behind—but we touched often, in the simple, companionable way of partners facing hard times together: a hand on my shoulder when I bent to dip up water from the stream, a pat on the knee before rising from a meal. At night, fully clothed and sharing the single blanket, we cuddled together for warmth with the innocence of children. Both age and circumstances were bound to have banked the fires of passion, a fact I noted with only mild interest; no doubt exhaustion had something to do with it as well.

The stream we'd been following joined the South Tyne just before the waters of that rambunctious river went leaping through a gorge where soft gray cliffs rise above the water, their crests festooned by hanging forests. Above the high branches a flock of rooks filled the air with their raucous cries and endless acrobatics. The blue streak of a kingfisher skimmed above the water like a peacock jewel flashing amid the mossy, fern-clad steeps, and the serene majesty of the place filled me with a sudden, sharp joy.

Clearly death and fighting, intrigue and power were not the only definitions of life; the grandeur and simplicity of places such as this touched my soul more deeply than any fancy court ever could. I would have liked to stay there and let it heal my battered spirit, but Lancelot, ever mindful of the danger we were in, insisted we press on.

By then we'd developed a routine of sorts. Lance spent the early morning catching fish or fowl while I searched out wild turnips, greens, and whatever edible fungus was available. We moved our camp during midday if there was a cover of trees, or in the long evenings if the land was open, and took turns riding or walking the stallion.

Where the river opened out into a broad, grassy vale, I found a blackberry patch and we stopped to pick the sweet fruit with the glee of youngsters on a holiday. It was the first time in years that I'd seen Lancelot enjoy himself so thoroughly.

We lived simply for the moment, as much intent on finding food and shelter as on our travel, and both body and spirit grew stronger. The horror in Carlisle's Square began to fade, as though all that went before had happened to someone else.

When we reached the confluence of the North and South Tyne, we made a small camp and fire in the protection of a long-deserted hill-fort. "Do you suppose," I mused as I turned the salmon on its willow-wand spit and stared into the coals of our tiny fire, "that I am still Queen, for all that I'm living in the wilds like an outlaw?"

"Probably," Lance responded. "The people will not forget you so fast, nor will Arthur. And I'm quite sure they'll be wanting you back, sooner or later."

I groaned aloud at the thought. Lance had brought me a second chance, a new life over and above the one my moira had envisioned, and I wanted to reach out and take hold of it freely, without being tied to what used to be. The past was over and gone.

Except perhaps for Arthur . . . the picture of my husband standing alone as I was dragged back to the cell returned whenever I thought of him. Even now he was no doubt struggling through the turmoil following my rescue—alone, hemmed in, without anyone to break through his inner isolation. The idea brought a terrible pang, and I turned resolutely away from it. Once we reached Joyous Gard, I would send word that I was safe. Under the circumstances, there was nothing else I could do.

"We need to get across the Wall," Lance said, spearing a piece of salmon with his dagger. "We'd best follow the northern branch of the river up to Chester and see if we can slip across there."

"Chester? Yea Gods, that's a full-sized community. They'll have guards at every gate, for sure."

"I was thinking we'd swim under the bridge."

"Swim?" The word came out as a squeak. Lance made it sound like the most reasonable idea in the world, but I couldn't have been more shocked if he'd suggested we sprout wings and fly. "Have you ever seen how fast the river rushes through there? And there are grates between the piers that hold up the bridge. I've seen them—put up by Romans to keep people from doing just what you're suggesting."

"They've been untended for at least a hundred years then. Even elm is going to weaken somewhat in that time," Lance noted, not understanding my reticence.

"What if I can't manage the swimming part?" I inquired. "I haven't been in anything other than a calm pool since I was a child."

"You can always hang on to the horse's tail, if your royal dignity doesn't mind," Lance teased, and I made a very unroyal face, convinced we were courting disaster.

But Lance was not going to put aside the idea till he'd proved to himself it wasn't possible, so the next night we crept along the bank of the North Tyne until we came in sight of the fort.

It was in the heart of the night, with no moon above and most everyone asleep in the town. As we neared the ruins of the bathhouse, a dog set up a commotion, barking his challenge though we couldn't even see him. He must have been on a chain, for there was shortly an explosion of swearing, a whine from the beast, and a noticeable silence.

We stopped while I tore off a length from the bottom of my shift and Lance wrapped it around the horse's bridle to keep the jingling from alerting anyone else. Then we started forward again, the Breton walking at the animal's head, steadying him against nickering or snorting. And I trailed behind, my heart in my mouth as we came up to the walls of the fort.

By great fortune the guardroom at our end of the bridge was lit with only a feeble lantern, and there was no sign of shadow or silhouette in the window. Torchlight spilled from the tower on the other end of the bridge, and from the laughter and swearing that carried on the summer night, it would seem that the sentries were involved in a dice game whose stakes were high enough to hold everyone's attention.

After we crept under the bridge to the abutment, Lance slid

into the water and worked his way up stream to where the remnants of the grates slapped and pressed against the stone piers. It took some time, and a lot of strength, but he finally succeeded in tearing one away enough to allow us to get through.

Since it was high summer, the water was down, or we might not have made it. As it was, both Lance and the horse had to struggle against the current, while I clung to Invictus's tail and tried to keep from swallowing half the river. It was one of those wild, exhilarating experiences which could easily have turned to tragedy but in retrospect is called a fine adventure.

The caterpillar spins its cocoon and emerges forever changed. The Christians claim to be reborn after baptism. And for all that I misunderstood her at the time, Nimue had promised me a new beginning. By the time I clambered out on the far shore of the Tyne, soaked and bedraggled, the last remnants of my old life had been swept away like the ashes in Carlisle's Square. I was as clean and free-washed as the pebbles that tumble along the river's bed . . . and full of excitement.

"Didn't think I could do it," I declared, planting my hands on my hips like any country maid proud of her accomplishment.

"You?" Lance responded, wiping down the horse and grinning at me in the starlight. "There isn't anything you can't do. I could have told you that. Now, get on up on Invictus's back; there's a clear path ahead and we'll all dry off best at a brisk trot."

Later we tethered the stallion to a birch tree and bedded down on the woody slope that overlooks a curve in the river. For the first time since the entrapment I no longer went to sleep under a shadow of dread and sorrow.

At dawn the pretty little song of a linnet wakened me, and when I stretched slowly and opened my eyes, it was to find the Breton propped up on one elbow, watching me intently. The look on his face was so loving, I flushed in surprise, and he laughed softly.

"You snore, did you know that? Little, puffy snorts, as if you were muttering to yourself in your sleep."

"Hmmph," I responded, reaching up to trace the tantalizing line of his lips with one fingertip. "Do you know what I was saying?" He shook his head, and I whispered, "Where's Lancelot, where's Lancelot . . ."

"Right here, M'lady," he answered, bending his head until his lips were covering mine—full, rich, and trembling as much as mine were. A breathless flutter of desire leapt to life in me, and when he started to lift his head, I raised mine to follow, unwilling to be separated from the mouth that had fascinated me for so long.

Thus we embarked on our long-deferred idyll of loving. His hands moved over me like a sculptor's, forming and smoothing, defining the shape of my desire from rib to haunch to hip, and I responded to his touch like a cat arching its back to be petted.

Wave after wave of desire enfolded us, building slowly until all my limits began to melt, smudged and blending like the colors of a sunset. A fine, soft mist stole over us, making my skin both hot and cold—and still our lips touched, gliding, nibbling, sometimes breaking away, always plunging back like moths into a flame. Inside me the whole of existence trembled, rising, pulsing, turning toward his touch like a flower opening to the warmth of the sun.

And when I rose to gather him to me, pulling, plunging, drawing him downward to the heart of the stars, a deep, unconscious moan rose between us.

Afterward, dozing in the crook of his arm, I drifted as light and free as a butterfly wafting on the barest breeze. Isolde had once spoken of the indefinable wonder of being with Tristan, and I, jealous of such depth of intimacy, had not wanted to hear. Now I smiled to myself, saluting the Queen of Cornwall with full understanding. Lance and I might have lived all our lives without this coming together, but with the hindsight of experience, I would no longer call such a life complete.

"Happy?" I asked, turning to look at my love.

"Umhum," he confirmed, eyes closed but fingers playing with a lock of my hair. "And you?"

I nodded vigorously. "I didn't know . . ."

It was true, I didn't know it could be like this, but of a sudden I wished I hadn't said it. It was too much like comparing him with Arthur.

"Nor I," Lance sighed, his easy tone making me forget my embarrassment. "Perhaps," he teased, opening one eye but not moving his head, "we should try it again sometime."

"Sounds like a good idea," I agreed, sitting up and stretching my arms over my head. Yet even without seeing, I felt his eyes caressing me, and when I turned toward him, he was watching me intently.

"Put your clothes on, Lady," he grinned, "before I ravish you all over again."

I gave him a punch in the ribs, and then we were rolling and laughing like children half our ages, and when we came to a breathless stop, he looked down at me, slowly shaking his head. "It's remarkable to be able to say I love you without having to rely on words."

Who knows how long we would have stayed there if Invictus hadn't begun pawing the ground and reminding us that he, too, was awake. "It sounds," my lover noted with a sigh, "as though the old fellow thinks we'd best be on our way."

Whether because the constraints of the past were lifted or simply because we took such joy in being alive, the rest of the trip to Warkworth was more pleasurable than difficult. We followed the ever-changing Tyne past swirling pools, whiffling rapids, mossy crags and fringing woods. I loved its marvelous liquid song, and was sorry to leave it when we turned up the stream they call the Rede and headed for the high, heather-covered moors.

Soon the soft leafiness of the river valley was left behind. Instead of dappled shade and gentle zephyrs there was naught but wide skies and rolling, sweeping, wind-swept hills covered with rippling grasses. We made our way along tracks that followed the curve of the land, occasionally climbing to the high summits where the moors were bursting into purple splendor. Huge buzzards wheeled lazily overhead, while skylarks from the grassy slopes below hurled their tiny bodies upward, frantically fluttering higher and higher into the blue as they flung their song against the day.

Not since childhood had both body and spirit been so free, and I ran to the brow of a hill, arms extended to the wind that ruffled my hair as it combed the grass. Lance caught me from behind and, locking his arms around my waist, lifted me from the ground. I leaned my head back against his shoulder as we spun in gentle circles, there on the top of the world. I don't think either of us had ever been happier.

Signs of people were few and far between in this high, open land. Once I saw the hives of a beekeeper—brought, no doubt, to collect the special nectar of the heather—and occasionally Lance would point out the distant outline of a steading on a south-facing hill. By tacit agreement we avoided such places, me because I wanted no intrusion into this happiness, Lance for fear of recognition.

But when a summer storm came racing across the sky, we were forced to seek shelter at a crofter's home. The wind was whipping around us as I piled my hair under a cap Lance had, then hid the whole by drawing the monk's hood up as we approached the run-down steading.

A farm wife appraised us with silent thoroughness, eyes narrowing at the sight of the warhorse. Just then a gust of rain swept across the farmyard, so she gave a terse nod of welcome and ordered the boy by the barn to look after the horse.

"Kimmins's hunting," the woman allowed as she led the way into a farmhouse with drystone walls and a heavy thatched roof. "But I've enough pease porridge for supper, whether he brings home meat or not."

"We're much obliged," Lance answered as I drew close to the fire-pit, grateful to be inside while the rain pelted down.

A small girl was sitting by the cooking pot, carefully carding a hank of wool. She stared at us open-mouthed, and when her mother came to stir the porridge, the child asked in a hoarse whisper, "Why's he not wearing a kilt?"

"He's from the south, I presume," the woman answered, then gave her a dour look. "It's rude to ask questions, child."

So we sat in silence while the farm wife went about her chores. When she set out bowls and a chunk of thick barley bread, I asked what I might do to help, but received only a curt admonition to rest myself.

Luckily the storm drove Kimmins home early, a bag of young grouse slung over one shoulder. He was a weathered, hardy man, in all ways as outgoing as his wife was reticent. Both he and his two grown sons immediately made us welcome.

By the time the rains passed, we had feasted well and were

sitting cozy around the fire. The farm wife disappeared into some dark corner while the younger children bundled up in their box-bed, but the older boys hunkered on the dirt floor by their father, and I sat on a cushion at Lance's feet, my head resting against his knee. Kimmins searched through the firewood piled near the hearth, and finding a pine knot, drew his dagger and began to whittle on it.

"Two sets of visitors in barely a week—now that's remarkable," he noted casually, eyes intent on his woodwork. "Mayhap the two are connected?"

"Mayhap," Lance responded carefully. "The first wouldn't be someone from the High King's Court, would it?"

The crofter snorted as his knife sent a scatter of chips flying. "A fellow wearing the badge of Orkney—said he was Agravain's man. He was an arrogant sod, who searched the house in disbelief that we weren't hiding Lancelot and the Queen."

I sat very still, not making a sound, but looking back and forth between Kimmins and his sons.

Lancelot absorbed the news thoughtfully. "Did he say where he was headed? Further north, perhaps?"

"Doubt it." Kimmins had outlined a face around a knot in the wood and paused now to hold it to the light, appraising it critically. "Don't think Uwain would care for that. Urien was a good old King, but this son of his keeps a tight rein on his lands, even down here. He's not about to put up with strangers marching through his territory, giving orders to those of us as lives here."

"What sort of orders?" The words were out before I knew it.

Kimmins was bending over his work, intent on adding the last few touches, his blade flashing this way and that. "Demanded we send word if the couple showed up. Says they're wanted for treason."

At the word Lance put his hand on my head. But our host never looked up. "Such men'll whistle up a snowstorm in August before they hear from the likes of us; we don't take kindly to outlanders telling us what to do." He made one last nick in the carving, then held it up for my inspection. "There now, I do believe it's a bogey I found. Every piece of wood has its sprite, you know."

A funny, lopsided face with huge horse teeth peered out of the whorls of the pine knot, and I smiled at the humor of it, in spite of my fear.

"I'd be honored if you'd take it, M'lady. Might help lift your spirits," Kimmins allowed gruffly. "I think it's that Hedley Kow who loves to disrupt things in the kitchen and always vanishes laughing."

We slept that night in a bed—the children having been doubled up to make room for us—and, after a breakfast of porridge, prepared to continue on our way. The little wood carving was carefully packed in Lance's saddlebag.

Kimmins never asked our names, but insisted on giving me a pony to ride.

"And not to worry about returning it," he added, helping me up onto the beast's back. "If I need it, I fancy I'll find some way to let you know."

We left him with a wave and a prayer of thanksgiving, sure our safety would be well guarded.

From there on, Lance and I rode constantly, making our way down Coquetdale with the dark escarpments of the Simonside Hills guarding the south and the bright, playful river leading us from the high moors through cool green canyons and out onto the coastal plane.

There, in the broad, sweeping loop that swings past its rocky knoll, Coquet River brought us to Joyous Gard and home.

32

Bargains

here is much to love about the north—the hardy honesty of the people, the wild and untouched sweep of the land, the constant challenge of the weather. The south of Britain may be lush and poetic and pretty as a garden most of the year round; Northumbria is crisp apples in old orchards, and great huge clouds piling up over the North Sea, and the graying housekeeper who came running into the yard as we emerged from the forest track that leads to Joyous Gard.

" 'Tis Himself returned!" she exclaimed, arms flapping and face aglow. "And he's brought the Lady with him, safe and sound." A sudden frown dampened her exuberance when she saw the bandage on Lance's arm. "You aren't bad hurt, are you?" she queried, looking anxiously up at him.

"No, Mrs. Badger," he assured her as he swung down from Invictus. "Nothing that your good cooking and a little rest won't cure."

She reddened at the compliment and ducked her head bashfully; it always amused me how easily women of all ages were charmed by Lance. Then she turned her shrewd blue eyes my way, and I caught a moment of quick appraisal as she tried to assess how much trouble I was likely to be. Between the natural caution of the peasant confronted by royalty and her own fierce protectiveness of Lance, I had the bemusing thought the woman might run me off if she didn't like what she saw.

"Well come, Your Majesty," she said at last, essaying an awkward curtsey.

"Oh no, Mrs. Badger," I interjected quickly. "There's no need for that. I'm simply the Master's Lady here."

She flashed me another look, this one a bit warmer. But the voice remained stubbornly neutral. "We'll see about that," she declared, clearly reserving the right to restore my queenly status in the future, if she saw fit. "Now then, let's get you inside and into some fresh clothes."

Since her own garments would have gone around my lanky frame twice over, we settled for one of Lance's old tunics and a pair of breeches her youngest son had outgrown. They weren't fancy but were more convenient than either of the long-skirted garments I'd lived in for the last few weeks.

After I was dressed, she began trying to fix my hair, patiently undoing the braid and working out the snarls while she chattered on about Lancelot.

"What a relief it is to have him home. Been worried sick, those boys have, not knowing what had happened to him. Once they all met back here and discovered you and the Master hadn't got home safe and sound ahead of them, it was all Bors and Lionel could do to keep Ector from riding back to Carlisle trying to find you two. It's a good family, M'lady; one that stands together, and they all look to Lancelot as their leader. Would go anywhere for him, do anything he'd ask. They'll be so glad to see him safe and sound . . ."

Her words trailed off as she frowned at my hair, now lying long and heavy down my back. A note of consternation crept into her voice. "We're mostly simple folk at Warkworth—not much used to fancy things. How's about I just put it in a bun?"

I assured her that would do admirably, and once she had anchored the washerwoman's twist firmly to the top of my head, she went back to her chores, and I went out to join Lance in getting reacquainted with the place I always thought of as the most beautiful in the world.

Joyous Gard stands astride a ridge that swings around like a cocked arm extending out from the forested hills. High up, at the elbow, the house and barn and stables stand, while down below, at the base of the steep bluff and following the inner crook of the elbow, the Coquet doubles back on itself in a horseshoe curve before swinging wide around the fingers of the hand, where a small village had grown up since last I was here.

It was all much as I remembered: a world in miniature, subtly drawn in the browns and rusts and purples of the Cheviots, the billowing greens of the forests on its closer flanks; the golden sand and gray-green grasses along the dunes that formed a miniature estuary not more than a mile away. Only the village brought a new texture, adding to the palette an occasional glimpse of bright flowers blooming in the garden plots so dear to the British heart.

From Joyous Gard the eye beholds the best of wild and tilled, leafy and sea-swept, heart-lifting freedom and snug security, and my soul filled with gratitude that Lance and I had such a place in which to live and love for the rest of our days.

He took me on a tour of the steading, pointing out the kitchen plots tended by Mrs. Badger's husband, the herbs and flowers and medicinal plants carefully arranged to take advantage of a sunny aspect or shaded nook. Even the orchard that filled the space between farmyard and forest was well cared for and full of both apples and pears.

A scruffy goatherd wearing a bright red cap appeared on the path that skirts the steading, bringing his charges home from a day's browsing in the woods. He kept the nimble foragers moving lest they be tempted to jump the rail fences into the orchard, and only after the animals were safely headed down the hill to the village did he doff his hat in salute to us. I grinned and waved back, my heart as high-spirited as his goats.

News of our arrival spread as fast as the goatherd could run, and by evening not only Bors and Lionel and Ector shared our hearth, but also Palomides and Urr, Lavaine and Cook's nephew, Kanahins, who had run away after the massacre at Carlisle's Square. Even Gareth's protégé, Melias, had joined the group in Northumbria.

They made their way into the big old farmhouse, ducking under the low-linteled door and greeting us with hugs and tears and deep joy at finding us both alive and safely home.

Only after they'd settled down in the long room, lounging by the fire or sitting on the benches, did it dawn on me how many were Companions. While I was relieved to know they had escaped Carlisle with their lives, the realization that they'd all left the Court to follow Lance came as a shock. So many defections among his elite were bound to hurt Arthur.

Mrs. Badger brought out a fine pot of chowder, and we caught up on the news of who had fallen in the battle at the Square.

"At least Agravain won't poison any more lives," Ector de

Maris announced tersely. "I ran him through myself after he started the bloodshed. And I saw Mordred covered with blood, though whose it was, I'm not sure. Serves them all right for setting up such treachery."

The rest nodded in agreement, and talk moved on to the other known dead; Lovel and Patris among Arthur's men, Belliance and Nerovens in the group that came to rescue me.

And Gareth, of course. At the mention of the flaxen-haired Champion everyone paused to make some sign of protection or appeal to their individual deities. Lance swallowed hard, and I saw the tears in his eyes.

As to the present situation, Agravain's men were clearly not going to let their leader's death go unavenged, and though they had not ventured as far as Warkworth, Kimmins was not the only crofter in the Cheviots who had been contacted by strangers asking questions.

"That won't sit well with Uwain," Bors commented, stretching his feet toward the hearth. "What with his duties as King of Northumbria and Regent of Rheged, he has a full plate. I don't imagine he wants a war between us and Arthur flaring on his flank. He sent word that he's withdrawn his invitation to the High King for this summer's visit, but asks you to come in his stead, after you're well rested."

This last was directed to me, and I pursed my lips thoughtfully, wondering what such a request presaged. It began to dawn on me that I was not as free of the past as I had imagined.

The question of Uwain was still on my mind later that night, when I perched on the bench by the window preparing to undo my hair. "It's bound to be something politic," I grumbled, much as I would have to Arthur.

"Probably," Lance answered, coming to stand behind me. He put his hands on my shoulders as I reached for the comb Mrs. Badger had found for me, and suddenly, breathlessly, I knew what he would say. "Here, I want to do that."

Taking the pins out of the bun, he let the heavy strands of hair tumble down through his hands, hefting the weight of them as though they were treasure.

"You have no idea how many times I dreamed of this." He reached over my shoulder for the comb and began carefully drawing it through my tresses, making them soft and silky.

As though he were stroking a cat, or polishing fine metal, he combed out the whole of my mane while I blinked back tears of joy. Then, suddenly, lest I get too sentimental, I ducked away and tossed my head sideways. Most of my face was hidden by the sweep of hair, and I peered at him mischievously through the veil of it.

"Oh, really," he exclaimed, seeing the challenge and taking a step back in mock surprise. But when I laughed and let him go back to combing it, he scooped my hair up into a pile on the top of my head and, bending over, began to kiss the nape of my neck.

I gave a yip and turned to grab him around the waist, full of rowdy laughter and devilment. We tumbled onto the bed, and I knelt beside him, shaking out my locks and letting them trail across his body in long, light, languid strokes that were half teasing, half tender adoration.

And all the while, inside, I was asking the Gods to keep our new life safe and inviolate and let us live in peace, far from the pressures of the world that had been so willing to see us die.

I might as well have asked for the moon on a silver salver, for all the good those prayers did!

We left for Yeavering a week later, traveling up the coast with Palomides, Melias and a light escort. As we rode along the splendid dunes, the Arab, who had been living here for some time, regaled us with stories about the land he'd come to love.

"Once, after a storm, I came upon a sunken forest—ancient trees poking halfway up through the sand. I thought it was the entrance to the Otherworld, but try as I might, I couldn't find the pathway in. And next time I came to the same beach, the petrified forest was gone—vanished—as mysteriously as it had come."

He made a sign to one of his Eastern Gods, then went on with more practical matters. "There's no better land for farming than that between the Cheviots and the North Sea . . . grains and cattle and fruit in abundance. Even on Holy Isle one can produce a credible harvest of barley."

"Holy Isle?" I asked.

"Lindisfarne," Lance explained. "It's a spit of dune and rock extending into the waters beyond Bamburgh. When the tide's out, you can walk across the sands to it . . . then the tide comes in and it turns into an island, separate and apart from the world.

It's a natural place for hermits and holy men to go to meditate. I've occasionally gone there myself, in the past . . ."

Lance didn't say anything further, but I knew instinctively that some part of him wanted to be out there now, communing with the mystics. Later, after we'd spent an evening with the people of Bamburgh, I asked if he'd like to stay at Holy Isle while I met with Uwain.

He went right on combing my hair, following each stroke with his hand, and at last cleared his throat.

"You know how much I love you, Gwen. And how much I love God. I won't ever let that separate us again, but I need to make my peace over Gareth's death—if it weren't for me, he'd still be alive. Maybe a stay at Lindisfarne would ease my heart . . . if you don't need me at Yeavering."

Of course I need you at Yeavering, I thought, feeling the same wretched jealousy that used to plague me about Elaine. But I had learned that lesson well, so I tilted my head back and smiled up at him.

"Why don't you join us in a couple of days?" I suggested, and he bent forward to plant a kiss on my forehead.

We parted next morning, and I watched him riding off along the edge of Budle Bay, an elegant, dark man on a dark horse, silhouetted against the silvery morning sea. Then with a sigh I turned inland, following Palomides on an old track that led through the Kylo Hills.

I stayed that night in a cavern the Arab knew of. It is a shallow chamber, carved into the western face of a large gray sandstone outcrop that protrudes about halfway up the hillside. Its long ledge was high enough above the sloping approach to afford me privacy, and the men built a watch fire on the apron to discourage predators. In a small nook hidden away behind the fronting rock-form, I was snug and comfortable all night long.

Waking at first light, I clambered up through bracken and heather to the top of the hill, thinking to get the lay of the land as the sun rose. I had expected it to be a good vantage point, but the beauty of the world laid out below me was breathtaking, and I stared at it in amazement.

The ridge I stood on formed the barrier between night and day. In the west the valleys and hills leading inland to the Cheviots still lay in shadow, sleeping under a scatter of stars. But to the east the soft, golden light of dawn already lapped the shore that stretched from north to south as far as the eye could compass. Beyond that beach the North Sea spread out to the edge of the world, shimmering like gray-blue silk under the pale sky. Peach and apricot clouds tumbled on the horizon, growing brighter by the minute until, suddenly, the sun rose dripping from the sea. It was vibrant and fiery as a molten coal, and laid a path of gold across the rippling waters.

The tide had come in, cutting Holy Isle off from the shore, making it an unearthly ship riding upon fey waters. Cormorants and shearwaters coursed past it; mallards and wigeon, eider and godwit came and went along its shore, and on some hidden beach a colony of seals was coming awake. Their barking carried to me on the wind. Above, whole flocks of birds filled the sky, some banking and turning in the sunlight, some cutting through the air in ragged vees. All forms of life that lived in air or sea, unfettered by earth and roots, flowed around that little bit of sea wrack; ebbing, flowing, carrying the spirit out and away from petty cares and man-made strife. Just so the Goddess had once carried me far and away from myself; just so Lance now sought the same from the White Christ.

Knowing that if I stood between him and his God he would feel trapped and unhappy, I turned resolutely away from the shore. It doesn't mean he'll leave you, I told myself as I found a broad, flat lump of rock some distance from the bracken and the flies that love to live in it, and sitting down, stared out to the west.

This was a panorama I was more comfortable with. The hills and vales and broad, sweeping vistas were beginning to take on the colors of the day. How Arthur would have loved this view! If he were here, he'd be assessing the landscape, looking at the hill-forts and routes of access, picking out the likely spots to clear, measuring the promise for foresters and swineherds, hunters and ore-diggers. In short, he would see it as a world to shape, a future waiting to happen.

For me it held a different spell, a warmer, more poignant allure. In the shadow of the ragged ridges, along the brow of the constant moors—fragile as a candle flame on a windy night—came the procession of generations past. Who they were, how they were called, what stories were written on their faces I couldn't see, but the echoes of their lifetimes whispered from them like an ancient hymn. Building their houses in the face of storms, plowing the land with sweat and hope, husbanding their crops and livestock against a future that might never come—in the heart-breaking brevity of their hour they had loved this land, sheltered in its lee, and called it home.

The boisterous bragging of a rooster rose to meet the brightening morning light, and the lowing of cows waiting to be milked drifted up to me and brought a smile. Here was my world, full of the earth-bound dreams of priestesses and mothers.

The realization crept up on me unawares, and I clasped my arms around my knees and rested my chin on them, looking out over the land. No matter what had happened in the past, I was as bound to the people as Arthur was to his Cause . . . and when they called, I would respond.

Perhaps they won't call, I told myself, suddenly thinking of Lance. Or if they do, I'll be deaf. We can go on living at Joyous Gard's quiet steading like any other farming couple, and the people will have to find someone else to hear their demands.

But even as I clung to the idea, I knew it was a delusion. Sooner or later someone, something, would draw me back . . . and I would go, just as Lance goes to Holy Isle. The certainty of it stole all my joy away, and I clutched my knees tighter, trying to blot out the realization that what Lance and I had now was only a respite, a dream that might never last the night.

Suddenly a great wave of emotion rose in me—anger, determination, desperation, a force as powerful as that that had made me kiss Lancelot in the barn.

Not yet, I told the Gods silently. I will not give it up yet. You will have to wrench it from me, twist it out of my grasp, steal it when I am not looking . . . and even then I will fight and barter and bargain for every last second in this paradise.

Behind me the sun had topped the ridge and was warming my back. Down in the fold of land below the cave the men were stirring, and I got slowly to my feet. Gravely and deliberately I raised my balled fist against the sky, against the sun, against the new day.

"Do You hear me?" I demanded, turning defiantly to face each quadrant of the compass. "You will not take this chance away from me so easily. I, Gwynhwyvaer of Rheged, will fight to keep my new life until all hope is lost."

I was still standing there, staring toward the south and Camelot as the tears coursed down my cheeks, when Palomides came to get me for breakfast.

During the rest of the journey to Yeavering I thought about Uwain, wondering what Morgan's son wanted of me, and if he had been involved in the Carlisle plot. No matter who brought the subject up at Court, it was clear Morgan had instigated the accusations against Lance and me, and I came back—as so often in the past—to the question of why. What was it that drove my sister-in-law to attack me with such ferocity?

When I was young, I thought her hostility was personal and assumed it stemmed from something I had done or said that she took umbrage at. It was only later, after she'd tried to kill Arthur, that I realized how much she coveted power. Personal power, political power, religious power—these were the spurs that goaded her on, the hunger she couldn't satisfy, the treasure she plotted for. I thought it sad and ironic, for as the High Priestess she had long since been acknowledged as one of the most powerful women in the country. Yet nothing seemed enough.

It was said that she had grown fanatic in her worship of the Goddess, and I suddenly wondered if, living so long in isolation at the Sanctuary, she had convinced herself I was a threat to her new Paganism. Might she have concluded that I was drawing Arthur into Christian ways? The very notion was so preposterous, I smiled to myself; Arthur was far more tolerant of the Roman faith than I had ever been.

But Morgan had jumped to wrong conclusions about me many times before, and no other explanation made sense. Even my death at the stake would not have given her access to the High Throne of Britain or endeared her to her brother. So political gain was not the likely motive.

Except . . .

Years before, my father had signed a treaty—at Arthur's insistence—that would allow the King of Northumbria to stand for the Kingship of Rheged if I never had children or never returned there to rule. Morgan may have seen my death at the stake as a way of hastening Uwain's chance to become monarch of Rheged as well as Northumbria.

It seemed a silly, needless thing to do, since both he and his father before him had been my Regents there, collecting taxes, overseeing laws, governing as monarchs with all but the actual title. I had no intention of returning to Rheged, and even now thought of it only as a last resort, if Lance and I could not stay on at Joyous Gard for some reason.

Still, ambition has spawned more fantastic plots than this, and Morgan was nothing if not ambitious. So when Uwain and I sat down across from each other at the conference table, I kept my eyes open and my mouth shut, waiting to see where he fit into the puzzle.

"I have far more pleasant memories of dealing with you than with your husband, M'lady," he began. His mouth smiled, but there was no warmth in either his voice or his eyes.

Indeed, the brusqueness of his manner denied the years I had known him as a youth; one might think we were little more than strangers. I was struck by how much he had grown to look like Urien—less florid, perhaps, but with the same solid build, swaggering air, and drooping mustaches. When I stopped to count, it was a shock to reckon Uwain must be over forty.

Palomides sat next to me, silent and watchful. I reached for the ale mug a servant had provided and waited for Morgan's son to show his colors, still unsure if he was my enemy or my ally.

"There are many in the north who take your side in this dispute with Arthur, M'lady," Uwain noted, slowly turning his mug between his fingers. "They remember you are one of them—a daughter of the Cumbri—whereas the High King is a Romanized southerner. The warriors of Rheged would take up arms against him in your behalf if you but said the word. And others as well— Caledonians who aren't happy with the Pendragon, Fergus's people at Dumbarton. Of course, if you agreed to lead such an uprising, you'd need a partner—a man who knows the land from a military point of view and could bring his own troops to the battle."

The thought of my starting a civil war against Arthur was appalling, and I stared at Uwain blankly, too shocked by the idea to respond. Beside me, Palomides was still as stone, never flicking an eyelash as Uwain talked treason. I tried to make my face as unreadable as the Arab's.

"Then, too," Uwain went on carefully, "what with Rheged in the west and Northumbria in the east, between us you and I control a sizable portion of the realm. If we merged our holdings . . ."

In spite of myself, I choked on my ale. It didn't matter whether Uwain was speaking in political or personal terms, I wasn't in rebellion against my husband and I wouldn't consider an alliance with any usurper.

"There is no reason to plan for such an uprising," I sputtered, furious that my body had betrayed my outrage.

"Ah," the King of Northumbria noted, raising one eyebrow. "Perhaps you'd prefer to find a quiet niche and retreat from the world, leaving others to mind the dogs of war? Well, that too, might be arranged, though it will take some doing. The followers of Agravain are furious about his death, and they prowl the edges of Northumbria, looking for vengeance. They've begun killing my subjects—most recently a crofter named Kimmins and his sons, for supposedly harboring you and the Breton."

I caught my breath, and Uwain, looking up quickly, pinned me under his gaze. A slow, hard smile tugged at his mouth. "M'lady, you have too soft a heart to be a great monarch . . . it gives you away. But if the gentler concerns are what you're looking for . . ."

His voice trailed off, and he settled back against his chair and downed the rest of his ale, watching me casually across the rim of his mug. I tried to assess how much he was bargaining in good faith, and when he lowered his cup and licked the last of the brew from his mustaches, I leaned forward quietly and asked, "What would it take to arrange that?"

"The price, M'lady? In exchange for my letting you and your lover live safely in Northumbria? Your abdication of Rheged's throne in favor of me."

It didn't come as a total surprise, but one does not hand over the future of one's people lightly, and I groaned inwardly.

Uwain was taking a righteous stance. "As I recall, by treaty the country was to come to us in the event you had no child to stand for the throne. Surely," he added with sly malice, "you cannot expect the people of Rheged to accept Mordred as your son?"

It seemed Uwain's parentage had finally come to the fore—Morgan herself could not have delivered that barb with more skill. My instinct was to give him a royal tongue-lashing and walk out, but his next words stopped me cold.

"Unfortunately, since Lancelot never built those walls, it appears you *must* seek my protection. If I do not keep Agravain's forces out, you stand little chance of surviving."

Palomides's hand dropped to his dagger, but I was in no danger of physical assault; Uwain was doing well enough with words. He was also far more snide than I had expected. I tried to meet him with an equally caustic tone.

"My skin for my country, is that it?"

"If you wish to put it that way, M'lady. I was under the impression that you might consider it a bargain well made."

"Mayhap." I backed away a bit. "How can you assure my safety?"

"I'll tell Arthur that none of his men will be welcome in Northumbria—and I will kill anyone who presumes to disturb you in any way."

"I see." I reached for my ale and drained the last of it slowly and purposefully before answering. "In return for Rheged?"

"In return for Rheged."

"I need some time to think it over."

"Of course." Uwain sighed and, putting both hands on the table, heaved himself to his feet. Now that he'd made a bid for my kingdom, he was really quite cordial. "It will be good to see Lancelot again. He's done well at Joyous Gard, though he should have taken my advice on those walls!"

At a signal a page came scurrying into the room and was given the charge of taking us wherever Palomides and I might wish to go. After touring the windswept heights of the fort, admiring its forge and noting the sleek, fat cows in the fields, we climbed down the path to the clear waters of the river Glen. Since it was well within sight of the hill-fort, I sent our page packing and, sitting on the stump of a tree, took council with Palomides.

"He's as sly as any bazaar merchant," the Arab said, folding himself up to sit cross-legged on the grass. "For all we know the people of Rheged may be on the verge of revolt against him, which is why he needs to have you concede the title *now*. But we have no way to ascertain that, and he's clearly an opportunist who knows how much you need his help."

Slowly we went over the details of the situation—how vulnerable I was, how strong Uwain. We also discussed the fact that the people of Rheged considered him a good regent and he was familiar with their problems in ways that I was not.

"Besides, if you don't mind my saying it," the Arab concluded, carefully examining his fingers, "there is a kind of symmetry involved. Lance has given up his search for God in order to be with you; it's fitting you should give up something equally important for him."

I smiled wanly at the man who so often looked into the more subtle heart of things. There was a fairness and justice in what he said, in spite of the fact that deserting my people was unthinkable. But even though the alternatives seemed to involve war and bloodshed, I was not ready to give over the throne just yet. When Palomides and I returned to the Hall, I still had not come to terms with my choices. If only the Gods would send me some sign . . .

The evening came on quietly, as northern summer twilights do, but shortly after the sun dipped below the horizon, there was a flurry of activity in the courtyard. At first it was kitchen-women, then the servants from the barn and stable, and finally noble and warrior as well who flocked outside, climbing to the peak of the hill which the ancient hill-fort encircled and staring toward the west. I went out to join them, curious as to what had captured so much attention.

"An omen," someone said, making the sign against evil.

"Indeed," answered the smithy, crossing himself heavily.

"A gift from all the Gods," a little girl whispered, pointing toward the sky.

There, riding on the very edge of the sunset's splendor, was the first, wee slip of a moon. Pale ivory and slightly blurred in the misty light, the lower point of its delicate sickle seemed to be hung with the glittering diamond of the evening star. I caught my breath and stared at the rare and beautiful sight, seeing in it the symbol of Lance and I finally coming together. It was the sign I was looking for and I silently thanked the Gods. If Rheged was the price that must be paid to allow us to live our little moment in the rainbow's heart, so be it.

The next morning I drafted my letter of abdication from the throne of Rheged. There were a number of Christians in his Court, so we had no trouble finding a scribe, and once the words had been written, I took the Seal of State in my hands for the last time and pressed it to the colored wax at the bottom of the scroll, making the act official.

I did not tell Lance about it right away, however. When he arrived from Lindisfarne, there was dancing and gaming and much high cheer, and by the time we headed back to Joyous Gard, picking up the Roman Road they call the Devil's Causeway, I had decided not to mention it.

As long as Uwain could keep us safe, I wasn't going to count the cost.

33

The Idyll

ever do I remember a more glorious autumn, when the land went rust and cream and soft blue-gray, and morning mists hung, wraithlike, on meadows and trees. The afternoons were pure gold—honeyed and slow, turning burnished in the late-afternoon light as the fruits of the sun-season were safely gathered and stored against the winter's needs. The barns bulged with hay and grain; apples and pears from our orchard lay sliced and drying on the winnowing floor; and at the dairy the last of the butter was being salted for storage in the spring house.

Lance worked closely with Mr. Badger—an imperturbable man who went off fishing each day when the chores were done—and sometimes I joined them in the garden, harvesting and mulching and preparing the garden for the winter storms.

"They come in pretty fierce," Mrs. Badger explained, jabbing handfuls of fresh bed-straw into the mattress we were restuffing. "I've seen ice and sleet cover the trees with a sheath of crystal that breaks the limbs and freezes the roots. But at least it keeps the Saxon sea-wolves from marauding."

Lance gave me one of his horses, a handsome little bay mare named Flyaway, and on a fine, crisp day we returned the pony we had borrowed to Kimmins's widow. "Caught them out on the moors, they did," she told us in a voice as hard as the land on which she lived. "Left 'em to the raven and vulture. I built up a cairn over their bones, but it's not the same as a respectful grave near home." With that she turned bitterly away, not even re-sponding when Lance asked if there had been any further contact with men from the south. Without news of what was happening in Camelot, we had no idea what to expect.

When it came time for the harvest fair at Rothbury, we all trooped to it together. While Lance discussed weather and crops with the farmers and Lionel proved his prowess in the hay-toss, Bors sat among a small group of monks and told them his story of the Grail. I picked up several large fleeces and a sheepskin, this last to go beside our bed; a warm, soft pelt to step onto was the one touch of luxury I missed from my former life. And a bee-keeper gifted me with a batch of heather honey after I asked if it was his hives we'd seen on our trip over the Cheviots.

I still had not mentioned giving up Rheged, nor had Lance talked of his visit to Holy Isle. Sometimes he went off to pray and meditate in the cave on the Coquet's bank, where an old hermit had carved out a personal chapel. And sometimes, when I was riding along the uplands, my gaze would be drawn to the southern hills gone blue in the haze of distance, and I would wonder how matters stood with Arthur. But neither of us mentioned these things, and when we sat before the coals of an evening fire and stared at the shimmering, glowing pictures in the embers, it was of our present happiness we spoke.

Bits and pieces of news filtered in from the outside world. Arthur had canceled the Round Table meeting, much to the relief of the various members of the Fellowship. There were many who said he had become as short-tempered and difficult as ever his father, Uther Pendragon, had been. I prayed silently that Nimue and Bedivere were at his side, giving him some kind of balance.

About Mordred I heard nothing. Still not knowing what part he had played in the entrapment, I was loath to speculate from such a distance. I kept my concern for both of them to myself— there was more than enough to do on the steading to occupy both time and mind. Besides, it does no good to brood over what you can't change.

Before long the bracken on the hillsides flamed to copper, the lynx's fur grew thick and rich, and in Coquetdale the rutting stags filled the air with their belching, grunting bellows as they cried out their defiant challenges to each other.

Palomides came to visit often, as welcome a guest as one could

want, and frequently joined our hunting parties. He happily pro-
nounced the game of Northumbria to be the best in the world,
and delighted in showing us his favorite spots.

But for me the greatest wonder was the birds. We saw the black
grouse dancing on their lek like demented things, feathers ruffed
and wings bent as they jumped and bobbed about. Once the rooks
convened a parliament a thousand strong, with new flocks joining
them all day long, churning the air in their tumbling flight and
shattering the peace with their clamor. As the days shortened,
the summer birds gathered into enormous flocks, gorging themselves on berries and bugs before winging away to the south.
Swifts and swallows and sand martins were the first to go, followed by redstarts and turtledoves, and finally the whinchats.
Meadow pipits came down from the hills to winter around the
steading, while fieldfair and waxwing and the great white swans
from the north came to spend the winter. The whole sky seemed
full of birds, coming or going.

Early winter brought occasional light snow that turned the
upland landscape into a stark picture of black and white. On one
such day, as we rode home with a bag full of blue hares, Palomides
asked what we had heard of Isolde's lover, Tristan.

"Nothing to speak of," Lance responded, and the Arab sent an
inquiring glance toward me. Since Palomides had loved the beautiful Cornish queen with a long and unrequited passion, I suspected
his interest was as much in news of her as of Tris. So I recounted
my visit with Isolde at Castle Dore, when she had mentioned
Tris's marriage and his growing reputation as one of the great
warriors in Brittany. There was no chance he would return to
Britain, however, since Arthur had banished him because of his
wild, drunken behavior after Isolde had returned to Mark.

The Arab looked slowly back and forth between Lance and
me, then smiled softly. "Ah," he sighed, no doubt remembering
the months we had all spent together here at Joyous Gard in the
past. "You have no idea how lucky you two are—so many dreams
of love go unfulfilled. . . ."

It was a comment made all the more poignant when I realized
that to this day he adored the memory of Isolde. By now she had
assumed the stature of an icon in his life, and I wondered what
he would make of the woman in reality, if they ever met again.

The storms Mrs. Badger had predicted kept us indoors through much of January and February. With a full larder and good companionship it was not a trial, and on the nights when the wind howled down from the north, Lance and I burrowed under the pelts on our bed and set the world afire with our passion.

It was part of the magic of our being together . . . no matter how often we bedded, each time was different: tender, poignant, long and delicately drawn; wild, fierce-shaking and demanding; playful or sly or silently yielding; there was more range of mood in our communion than I would ever have thought possible. And I cherished every moment as a jewel to be held in memory against the times to come. . . .

In April the weather lightened. One morning when Melias and I went to the fisherman's village to see what the day's catch had been, I noticed primrose and sweet violets beside the path, and marsh marigold trailing along the streambank. An otter dove under the surface of the river as we approached; no doubt he was following the young fish down from their spawning grounds in the higher country. So in spite of the nippiness of the morning, there were signs of spring everywhere.

On reaching Joyous Gard, I found strange horses in the paddock, and a fancy litter that had been pushed out of the way, just inside the barn door. Leaving Melias to care for our mounts and bring in the fish, I ran through the barnyard, my breath streaming behind me like a cloud.

"Another Queen," Mrs. Badger informed me, bustling forward to take my cape and gloves. "The Cornish one. I've heard for years about her beauty, but she's as pleasant and polite as yourself. I took her up to the front bedroom, as she wanted to rest, but the monk who came with her is with the Master, by the hearth. The cleric said you'd know him, though I've forgotten his name." This last was half apology.

"It isn't Gildas, is it?" I asked, feeling my spirits drop.

"That's it exactly, M'lady." She beamed at me happily. "How nice for you to have old friends come visiting!"

Friend, my foot! I thought, bolting from the kitchen. I intended to see Isolde first, both to welcome her and find out what this visit was about, but as I passed the door to the main room, Gildas's voice came through the curtains. He was haranguing Lancelot in tones that were both strident and patronizing.

"But, my son, it is an adulterous relationship. She's led you into the most base and venial sin and this debauchery will bring the vengeance of God upon you. Hear me, there will be despair and disaster for you and your followers unless you renounce her once and for all."

"You presume upon my hospitality, Father," Lance responded. "I brought the Lady Guinevere here in part because she was in danger of her life. I cannot and will not cast her out among her enemies now."

"She must go back to her husband, where she belongs," Gildas declared, his voice trembling with righteousness.

"So I can be led to the stake all over again?" I demanded, pushing the curtains aside and marching into the room. "Isn't that really what you want to see, Gildas—me hopping hot-foot up on that platform while the clerics all pray piously over my incinerated remains?"

"Of course not, M'lady." The monk showed no surprise at my entrance, but pressed his thin lips into a snakelike smile. "What I want to see is your acceptance of the One God and the bowing of your arrogant head to Christ, His only Son. You need only renounce your Pagan ways and throw yourself on His mercy in the hope of being saved."

"I have no desire to be saved by your Father God," I flared. "Nor will I tolerate your meddling in my life this way. It's bad enough that you've sheltered my cousin Maelgwn in your holy house all these years, you don't have to come bringing trouble to Joyous Gard."

"I come not to bring trouble, but to spare you great heart-break," the puny little man responded, drawing himself up haughtily and speaking directly to Lance. "Unless you pack her back to her husband, King Arthur will lead an army against you."

I gaped at the monk in disbelief, and Lance's face went pale.

"He wouldn't," the Breton declared. "He asked me to rescue her. He wouldn't turn on us now."

"Oh yes he would. Word has gone out to all the members of the Round Table that Arthur will march on Joyous Gard come May. Of course, if M'lady obeys the Church and returns to her husband, much carnage could be averted." Gildas didn't actually smile as he made his pronouncement, but he sent a triumphant look my way. "So you see, M'lady, the lives and deaths of many men hang on how much you cling to your stubborn pride."

"I don't believe it," I raged, my voice rising with indignation. "Arthur would never do such a thing! You're just saying this to separate us, you despicable, wretched little toad!"

Gildas wreathed his face in a spiteful smirk while Lance stared first at him, then at me, shocked to see me so venomous. I wanted to go to my love, to tell him how long Gildas had harbored a hatred of me, how unfair all of this was. But the presence of the gloating monk held me back, so I turned and ran upstairs to Isolde, outrage and fear pounding close on my heels.

I burst into her room, full of all my own concerns, and stopped dead at the sight of her. Thin and pale, she sat by the window, a quilt wrapped around her frail form. The bones of her cheeks showed through the milk-white skin, and there were huge circles under her violet eyes.

"Yea Gods, Isolde, whatever is wrong?" I demanded, rushing across the room before she could gather herself to rise.

"You hadn't heard, then? It has been coming on for some time —bad coughing, clots of blood. I thought everyone knew the Queen of Cornwall was dying."

"Nimue," I said immediately. "Nimue can help. Or my foster sister, Brigit. She's almost as good a healer as Morgan le Fey." I was kneeling beside her, holding the cold, fragile hands in my own, trying to will life and energy back into her.

But Isolde just shook her head. "As a healer myself, I can read the symptoms. And frankly, I'm not sad to be leaving this life. . . . I'd like to see Tristan again, perhaps, and take care of a few loose ends, but in general, it's time for me to go."

"Fiddlesticks," I countered, unwilling to see her surrender so easily. "You have to take better care of yourself; stay warm, stay inside. Whatever possessed you to come all the way up here, and in the height of winter at that?"

"Arthur," she said simply, pressing a handkerchief to her lips as a fit of coughing overtook her.

"Arthur?" Gildas's warning came back to me then, and I took my friend by the arms. "Tell me the monk is lying, that Arthur isn't planning a war. . . ."

"I wish I could, but it's that very fact that brings me north.

They will march as soon as the grass is high enough to provide forage for their mounts." Isolde sighed while I stared at her, dumbfounded. "The loss of both you and so many Companions has left the High King quite unstrung. He rides out day and night across the south, racing around on his big black horse with only Gwyn the Welshman to keep up. It's quite as bad as when you were kidnapped by Maelgwn and he was helpless to do anything about it. Then he was in the midst of fighting Saxons—now he does battle with shadows. Bedivere tries his best to run the country, and Cei is in as black a mood as Gawain these days, but it was they who begged me to go see Arthur."

"You went to Camelot?" Such devotion on the part of the stay-at-home Queen was making me feel very humble.

Isolde nodded in response. "It was not only a favor for a friend, but also one of those loose ends I mentioned. I don't think I'd ever properly thanked Arthur for giving Tristan and me shelter when we ran away from Cornwall. I sat and talked with him for one whole afternoon—first time we've ever really conversed, I think. He's not a bad man, Gwen, just inarticulate and trapped in his own moira."

I smiled softly, bemused at the notion of anyone defending Arthur Pendragon to me. For all that had happened, I could not blame him, and would always love him.

"That's why I'm here. . . . He wants you to come back. He begged me to tell you that if you'll return, he'll call off the invasion of Northumbria and send an envoy to escort you home."

"And Lancelot? Can he come, too?" I asked, knowing it was an impossible request even as the words were said.

"No. Lance and his followers are to be banished to the Continent. Arthur doesn't hold him responsible for the deaths at Carlisle, but Gawain does, and it would not be wise—or safe—to have him return to Camelot."

"Brittany is a long way away," I whispered, tears starting to fill my eyes.

"I know. . . . " Tristan's mistress replied softly. "Of all people, I know. And now, of all people, you know what I went through when I gave up Tris, here at Joyous Gard, to return to Mark and Cornwall."

I caught my breath, not having seen the connection. In this

very room I had had to tell Isolde that Mark was threatening war against Arthur if she didn't go back to Cornwall. Now she was delivering much the same message, and I shook my head at the intertwining of our lives.

"Either way, there's heartbreak," the Cornish Queen said. "And no one can decide for you. But I saw Nimue while I was at Camelot, and she told me to remind you of the Grail—the Goddess and the Grail."

I nodded vaguely, too caught up in the demand for practical decisions to worry about spiritual matters. "How soon does Arthur need to know?"

"As soon as I can return to him, though I'm sure he'll understand your taking a few days to make up your mind."

"If only it were that easy," I muttered.

Isolde began to cough again, so I left her to rest. At first I had meant simply to retire to the bedchamber, but the presence of the four walls hemmed me in, making me restless and angry, and before long I went down to the barn, intent on going for a long, hard ride.

Flyaway had picked up a stone-bruise during the morning trip to the fisher village, so I put the saddle on Invictus and rode the warhorse out of the steading. Since the wind was coming in from the sea, I headed the stallion toward the west, up into the hills and out along the ridges where there was nothing but scudding clouds and blowing grasses. We raced against the emptiness of the land, leaping gullies, skidding down inclines, wheeling and dashing away when outcrops loomed suddenly before us.

Gradually, with the rushing of the wind and the lowering of the sun, the panic in me wore itself out, and I slowed the horse to a trot. By the time we'd returned to the forest on Joyous Gard's flank, the sky had filled with storm clouds and Invictus was content to walk quietly along the path between the trees. When we reached the verge of the woods and only the orchards lay between us and home, I brought the animal to a halt, wanting to collect my thoughts before returning to the house.

To the south was Arthur, wracked by conflict. To the north was Uwain, sitting in his hill-fort and promising to come to my aid if necessary. And in between was Joyous Gard, a steading without any means of defense.

I wasn't convinced that Uwain would honor his promise of protection. If he did, there would be massive bloodshed. If he didn't—and having already secured Rheged for himself, he might not—then Lance and his men were as good as dead. With a sickening of my stomach I realized that Arthur also might die if there were a pitched battle.

The sun broke from cover just before it set, staining the underside of the clouds a lurid red. The wind had quickened as well, but as I was turning to take the measure of the incoming storm, a bundle of feathers and fluff fell out of the sky, as though thrown down at my feet by the Gods.

Invictus snorted and shied sidewise, and when I looked up, the sky was full of birds—thousands of them, stretching across the water as far as the eye could see. They appeared to be redstarts, borne along on the front of the storm; a hapless flock returning for the spring, overtaken by the gale while they were still out to sea. The sun, catching them from below, splashed their underbellies and wings with crimson as though they were drenched in blood.

Small and light against the storm, they struggled to direct their course, to make this landfall before collapse. Within a minute they were landing all around me, clutching twigs and branches or plummeting to earth. Many were cheeping piteously, and some, too weak to cling to safety, slid, panting, from their perches and lay dying on the ground. All were too frightened or exhausted to move away from us, even though Invictus continued to snort and prance nervously. I held him firm with thigh and knee and stared with horror at the devastation taking place all around me.

A flock of gulls came wheeling over and, swooping down among the fallen migrants, began tearing them apart, often while they were still alive. A fox stole out of the trees and ran, brazen as you please, across my sight, her mouth full of feathers. Anger and indignation rose hot in me, and I shook my clenched fist at her, though I knew it did no good.

Wave after wave of new arrivals fluttered out of the sky until every tree was laden with this desperately panting fruit. Some had a small red drop of blood hanging from their beaks, like a jewel. Perhaps as many as half of them would survive, but while the tufted bodies piled up on the ground as thick as rushes in a Hall, the fox came back for another round, bringing her kits with her. In the same way, the screaming of the gulls brought others to gorge on the defenseless redstarts.

I sat in the midst of that death and destruction, sick at heart. Even though I had nothing to do with it, I was being splattered by its bloody end. The memory of the dancing bear leapt to mind —the bear and Arthur and these birds, all touched by disasters I could not control. Yet still they happened; mindlessly, piteously, they happened, and I wept for the sorrow of it. How much more horrible to face such carnage in a war I knew I could have stopped!

One of the redstarts hit against me, and I caught it before it dropped away. Light and fragile in my hand, it was still warm, though it lay with its head askew from a broken neck. Gently, hopelessly, I cradled it between my palms, wishing desperately I could bring it back to life.

Slowly, with an infinite sadness and full recognition of what must be done, I knew the time had come—my bargain with the Gods had been fulfilled. Lance's and my idyll was coming to an end, and I could not ask others to pay in blood for even one more day's continuation of it.

Under me Invictus was trembling, anxious to leave this rain of death. Still holding the dead bird, I slid down from the warhorse's back and, talking to him gently, led him out of the forest and along the path that skirts the orchard.

"I will return to Camelot," I said evenly, staring coldly at Gildas, "as soon as Arthur sends an escort for me. You and the Queen of Cornwall can tell him that when you return."

The despicable little man in the monk's robe had the sense to keep his satisfaction to himself, but Lance was looking at me in horror. "Come, love," I added, "we need to talk in private."

"You don't have to do this," he said as soon as the door to our chamber was closed. "We'll go to Rheged. They'll be glad to have you back, and there's more than enough forts there to keep us safe."

I couldn't look at him, couldn't admit I'd given my people over to someone else. "It's not just my return," I hedged. "Arthur has ordered your banishment as well. You must leave Britain entirely."

His gasp of surprise tore at my heart. "Then come with me," he pleaded. "We can go to Brittany. Bors would be for it, and I'm sure Palomides and Melias and the rest will join us. Howell can always use good men, and you'll be safer there than you are here."

He held me in his arms, talking about possible futures as the tears ran down my face. But I was on the ridge with the birds, vowing to stop an equal destruction among men while the power to do so still lay in my hands.

"We have had our time, my dearest," I said gently, my voice flat with resolution. "I could no more be the cause of a civil war any more than I could lead one. I cannot let Uwain and Arthur massacre each other, and would sooner die than see you and Arthur in combat. There will be no blood spilled over me."

By the time we went downstairs for dinner, he had accepted my decision.

The storm forced Gildas and Isolde to stay over, and, considering her health, I was just as glad. The monk and I avoided each other, and Isolde spent a good bit of time with Palomides, playing chess, listening to his adventures and travels, or just chatting by the fire.

The weather cleared toward evening three days later, and that night I sat with Isolde in her room while her serving girl packed her things.

"Odd that we don't necessarily love those who treat us best, isn't it?" the famous beauty mused. "Palomides is by far the sweetest courtier I have ever known, yet as long as Tristan was near, I had no interest in the Arab at all. When I was young, and still thought in Pagan terms, I truly believed Tris and I were fated to love forever because of the potion we drank. Now I am not so sure. Perhaps it was our own obsession, our own self-destructiveness. Oh, love we did—perhaps still do. But by the will of the Gods? I no longer know."

I looked at her fondly, the woman who had been ready to throw over everything to be with her lover. That I, who never intended such an action, should be confronted by the same miserable decision she had had to make seemed ironic indeed.

"Tell Arthur I will meet his men by the Lady's Well at Holystone in three weeks' time," I said firmly, determined not to slip into self-pity. "I do not want his men coming to Joyous Gard. In the meanwhile, I'll contact Uwain and ask him to arrange safe-conduct for whomever Arthur sends to escort me home."

Isolde was watching me with those great, dark-circled eyes, as though she were reading my very soul. With a sigh she reached out and laid her frail little hand over mine. "No one really dies of a broken heart," she murmured. "It just seems like it."

Next morning Palomides helped her get settled in the litter. When everything was arranged, he bent over and kissed her hand tenderly, thanking her for the time she had spent with him. "It is a memory to cherish," he said simply.

I smiled to myself, glad to know that in this case the reality had not shattered his belief in the dream.

During the next fortnight, life at Joyous Gard balanced precariously between chaos and commonplace. Bors and Ector left for Brittany to make arrangements there, while the rest of the men prepared to follow with Lancelot once I was safely on the Road to Camelot.

Mrs. Badger veered between certainty that the Gods would intervene to keep us from parting and wringing her hands in despair because there was nothing to be done. Her husband, however, went on with daily life in his usual, unruffled way, until the day before I was to leave.

"I've got it! I've got it!" he hollered that morning from the streamside, his voice carrying up the bluff to the henhouse, where I was collecting the first eggs of the year.

"Got what?" I called back, rushing to the edge of the cliff.

"For Himself," Mr. Badger responded, thrashing about in the water like a youngster taking a bath. He didn't sound alarmed, but considering his normal diffidence, I decided to find Lance.

By the time we returned to the bluff's edge, Mr. Badger was making his way up the switchbacks of the trail, huffing and puffing with every step. His cloak was wrapped around a bundle of twigs and leaves from which an occasional stick poked out.

"Call the missus," he demanded, once he reached the top of the bluff. "You, there, Lancelot—get to the table right proper now. Won't have you spoiling this for not knowing the custom."

By then we had reached the kitchen yard, and Mr. Badger

began ordering everyone else to accompany Lance to the main room. "You, too, M'lady—have to keep it right, you understand."

So we all gathered around the eating table, Lance still muddy from the garden, Kanahins with woodshavings in his hair, and me with a half-dozen eggs in the basket on my lap. Melias came pelting in from the stables and Palomides showed up just as the Badgers emerged from the kitchen, Mrs. Badger beating time on a hand drum while her husband carried a tray on which a fine fat salmon rested on a bed of cress.

" 'Tis the first of the season," the housekeeper announced as Mr. Badger went down on one knee and offered the prize to Lancelot. "It's known to bring good fortune to the one who catches it. But seeing as how the times are so trying, we thought to give you both the fish and its luck."

The two of them stood there before us, common and rustic in their simplicity, beaming with pride at contributing something to our beleaguered group.

"What a wonderful present," I cried, determined to hold on to the simple, earthy joys we had known until the last possible moment. Lance bent forward and took the platter from Mr. Badger's hands. "We'll have a party tonight, to celebrate, and make a custard as well," I added, lifting my basket triumphantly.

By then everyone was laughing and congratulating Mr. Badger, the shadow of the morrow's parting resolutely turned aside.

In the afternoon Uwain rode up the ridge with a small party of warriors, having come to personally take me to Holystone. "Just to make sure you're delivered safely, and they aren't playing any tricks," he growled.

That night we had a lovely party, with the salmon augmented by whatever Mrs. Badger could spare from the fowls in the barnyard. Not only were all the men present, but the villagers as well. The smith and his family came, and the tanner with his three daughters. A juggler who was stopping off at the tavern heard of the festivities and, bringing his colored balls, entertained us as well as any jester might. Two of the Badgers' three sons flirted outrageously with the tanner's girls, and when Palomides pulled out a little elder pipe and whistled up a tune, Melias asked the third girl to dance with him.

I looked around the room, thinking it not unlike the Round Table feasts, for family is family whether plain or fancy. Tears of love and despair welled into my eyes, and I turned away hastily, not wanting to spoil the revelry for the others.

Later that night Lance and I lay long in each other's arms, sometimes weeping, sometimes loving. That he must give up Joyous Gard because of me added one more loss to all the rest.

"Ah, love, I could not stay anyway, now that you are going," he said. "Your presence haunts every corner, and I would go crazy not having you here. There is no place else that I have been happier, so it's best to remember it that way."

The realization that he could never again come to Camelot—indeed, that we must never more see each other—was crushing me, and I began to sob again.

But by the time dawn came, all our tears were shed, and when everyone else was mounted, the big Breton helped me onto Flyaway.

"Kanahins will accompany you," he explained. "The boy's returning my shield to Camelot; I have used it always in defense of Britain and the Round Table, and do not wish to take it to my new life. Tell Arthur that I bear him nothing but love and gratitude for the years I was one of his Companions—and meant no dishonor in taking you away." He swallowed hard, then added softly, "I shall watch each month for the new moon."

A savage ache gripped my throat, and I nodded mutely as Uwain signaled we must leave. For one last heartbroken moment Lance and I stared deep into each other's eyes, until, with a sob, I turned the bay mare's head toward the gate and blindly joined the party, never looking back.

Even now I do not remember anything of the trip to Holystone.

34

The Return

hank God you're coming home!" Bedivere's smil
was as warm as his voice.

"Thank God you're the one to fetch me back," I
replied. Numb and empty as I was inside, it was a
relief to be under the protection of someone who
had always been a friend.

We were standing in the grove that surrounds the Lady's Well.
The Romans had captured the waters in a fine square pool, allowing thirsty men and tired horses to drink beside the Road. The
sound of their blowing and slurping mingled with the light trick-
ling of the runoff, making a mosaic of sounds like the changing
patterns of light and shade cast by the ivy-clad trees above us. I
stared at Arthur's foster brother and wondered what to say next.

"There's a separate tent for you, if you wish to rest." He gestured to the camp on the hillside below us. "We can even stay
over, if you would prefer to leave tomorrow morning."

"No," I said hastily. The last thing I wanted was to linger in
this limbo where my two lives overlapped.

So we walked down to the encampment. I kept my eyes lowered, not wanting to meet the curious stare of warriors sent to
bring a recalcitrant Queen back to the fold.

"I can't imagine it's easy for you," Bedivere commented as he
held open my tent flap. "But the world is unraveling around
Arthur, and you're the one source of stability he's always trusted."

"Does he still . . . trust me?"

"He still sees you as High Queen," the one-handed lieutenant
answered. A glance at the furnishing of the tent proved that.

There was a bronze brazier to warm the space, several thick sheep-skins to walk on, and a large wicker trunk at the foot of the bed. Bedivere undid the clasp on it with the hook of his gauntleted stump, and when he lifted the lid, a number of rich brocaded robes lay exposed.

"He had Enid pack them—wants the world to see that he holds no resentment . . . that you're not coming back as a penitent."

It was so like him, I had to smile. The fact I hated wearing them was beside the point; he would not make me grovel.

"How it will be between the two of you . . . " Bedivere's voice trailed off uncertainly. "That I can't presume to say. But I think, with any luck, you'll find your way together. Ah, here's Enid, herself." His tone lifted as Geraint's widow popped into the tent. She rushed forward to greet me with tears and hugs, telling me how everyone—including Arthur—was thankful that I had not died. She didn't mention the new factions that had carried the day at my sentencing, or Mordred—and I didn't ask. Perhaps, like Arthur, I didn't want to know.

Bedivere went off to oversee the striking of camp, and when I was fully attired in the robes of state, he came back leading a fine white mare that looked very much like the one Arthur had given me as a wedding present.

"Moonlight, the filly from Etain and Palomides's Arab stallion. Gwyn finished training her last summer," the lieutenant explained. "Arthur thought you might like to ride her home."

There were bells on her bridle and ribbons in her hair, and when she extended her nose to snuffle my hand, her small ears pricked forward and her big, dark eyes watched me intently. I had played with her when she was just a foal, but with so much else happening in the last three years, I had all but forgotten her. Now I ran my hand up along her jaw, scratched her behind the ears and down along the silken neck. It was the most magnificent peace-offering Arthur could have made, and one he was sure to know I would appreciate.

Thus I rode in splendor as our procession made its way down the Roman Road known as Dere Street. Both ahead and behind were a handful of scouts and guards, while in the middle Enid and I were surrounded by members of the houseguard, including Griflet, the Kennel Master. He had brought two of my Irish wolfhounds—the aging Brutus and his joyfully exuberant off-

spring, Augustus. Everyone smiled to see them greet me so affectionately, but once we were on the Road, they paced beside
Moonlight with all the dignity of their kind, looking like two gray
ghosts beside the white mare.

The Romans believed implicitly in engineering, and nothing
reflects it as much as one of their Roads. Dere Street lies like a
whip's lash over the curves of the Cheviots, as straight and un-
yielding as the will of the men who designed it. Broad enough to
carry eight legionnaires abreast, it now carried me inexorably
back to Queenhood.

Queenhood, and danger, I thought glumly. Morgan had
reached across years and miles to strike me down, and almost
succeeded at Carlisle. How quickly, I wondered, would she strike
again—and who would be her pawn next time?

Nor was that the only question I pondered. How would Arthur
receive me? Was he angry? Hurt? Likely to present a polite public
face and a cold personal rebuff? Or would we go back to our usual
partnership, friends as well as spouses? I stumbled on the last
word, wondering how he would feel about bed. Or how I would.

And then there was the matter of the people. Were they resentful that I had left them? Would those who had heard about
the trial believe Morgan's charge of treason and distrust me because of it? Or would they simply tolerate me, as the Cornish had
tolerated Isolde for so long, grudgingly accepting her as the consort of their King? That was an idea that cut to the quick.

I was so wrapped in these concerns that I barely noticed the
land had changed direction while Dere Street had not. The high,
grassy uplands along which we had begun the journey gradually
swung around until they became ridges cutting across the Road,
forcing us to breast them broadside. Here, just as at the Wall, the
Romans made no concession for the rugged terrain, and where
the crests and troughs became too steep to ride comfortably,
Bedivere had us get down and walk while the men led our
mounts.

"Sorry about that, Gwen," he said as I struggled up one of the
sharp inclines.

"Not your fault," I panted, holding the heavy skirts up and
wishing desperately for a pair of breeches. "At least we don't have
the heat of summer!"

For a fleeting moment I remembered the curved and sinuous

path Lance and I had traced last August—the green coolness of the North Tyne, and the open, wind-free joy of the Cheviot heights. The difference between that trip and this struck like a blow, and I thrust the memory aside immediately.

We were mounted again by the time we passed through the Wall at Portgate, and began the last long sweep into Corbridge, where the world rose up around me. Someone sounded a trumpet as we approached, and the whole town erupted. Sentries on the walls saluted while people crowded together in the streets, chanting my name and reaching toward me. "Hail the Queen, Hail Guinevere!" they cried, filling the sky with my name. I stared at them in amazement, and Bedivere gave me a quizzical look.

"You didn't know they swore to revolt if Arthur didn't bring you back?"

"No! We heard rumors of unrest in Rheged, but nothing like this. How long have they been this way?"

"Threatening to leave Arthur? Since the news of Carlisle reached them."

Nor was it just in the north. In every city, and most hamlets, the refrain was the same. At York they danced in the streets when I stayed over, and at Lincoln they lined the steep hill to the fort. People from the Fens poled their shallow skiffs along the waterways to come as close to my route as possible, and when we reached London, a great delegation greeted me at the gate and escorted us to the Imperial Palace. No matter how I felt about coming back, the people saw it as a triumphant return.

While we rested in London, I asked Bedivere if we could go by Brigit's convent in the Chiltern Hills.

"I don't see why not," came the reply. "I think she'd be more than pleased to see you again."

So we made a detour into the ancient beechwoods, riding between the silvery trunks of the trees that rise, straight and elegant, like columns in a natural cathedral. The ground was carpeted with the last of the bluebells, and I thought it a lovely place for a convent, if you wanted to retreat from the world.

"Bless my soul," Brigit cried as she ran across the courtyard to throw her arms around me. "Ever since I heard about the trouble at Carlisle, I've been waiting for you to come tapping on my door!" She stood back to examine me, concern furrowing her brow, then nodded in apparent satisfaction and looked up at Bedivere. "And it's good to see you, too, sir . . . both of you safe, after a year of troubles."

The lieutenant flushed under her praise, and then we were being directed to the guest quarters, and the quiet of the cloister settled around us.

That night Brigit and I talked for hours, catching up on everything. She was anxious to hear about the Grail Quest, and I was glad to know Father Baldwin often visited the holy house. But when all the worldly information had been exchanged, she leaned forward and studied my face closely.

"Most of all, I want to know how you are, Missy," she announced, calling me by my childhood name.

"Tired. Confused. Worried about meeting Arthur again. . . ."

"As I recall, you tried to run away rather than marry that young man, all those years ago in Rheged," Brigit mused. "That turned out better than you thought; I'll wager this will, too."

"Perhaps." I smiled ruefully at the memory of the red-headed Irish girl bullying me into compliance with the marriage agreement I had not wanted. "And I suppose we shall muddle through, one way or another—Arthur and I always have, somehow."

There was a momentary silence, and Brigit's green eyes searched my face. "You say the Mother told you to look for the Grail yourself but you've never done so? What sort of response is that?"

"A Queen's," I answered with a sigh. "When on earth have I had time to get involved with soul-searching?"

"Perhaps," she said thoughtfully, "it isn't so much a matter of time as of attention."

"Ah, Brigit, you ought to sit down and talk with Palomides. The two of you would get on famously, exploring all manner of philosophical questions! Here I am, facing God knows what, and you want to talk about spiritual Quests."

The Irish nun's cheeks dimpled, and she laid a gentle hand on mine. "Just the same, keep it in mind. You might be closer to your Grail than you realize. Ah, there's the bell for midnight prayers, so I must be off to chapel. Now, you just get into bed and don't fret so much about things. What the White Christ doesn't look out for, His Mother will."

Lying on the simple pallet after she left, I thought how much Brigit had brought to my life and thanked all the Gods I could remember for her friendship. And next morning I was glad to learn that Father Baldwin would be joining our party on the way to Camelot.

We crossed the Thames at the Goring Gap, making for Silchester, with its fine old mansions and strong earthworks. Even here, in Arthur's own kingdom of Logres, the people gathered at crossroads, lined the roadside, waved to me from their fields, all crying out their pleasure at having me home. I wondered, suddenly, if Arthur would be as glad to see me as our subjects were . . . or if he had invited me back out of political necessity rather than personal desire.

"He plans to meet us on the Road," Bedivere announced the next morning as we left Silchester. I shot him a quick glance, wondering what that meant, but the lieutenant gave me a wry smile. "He's never been one for patience when he knew what he wanted. As I recall, he came to meet you outside Sarum before the wedding as well."

Riding proud and tall, wearing his Kingship like the laurels of an athlete! Perhaps that was when I knew how much I could love him . . . back then, when we came together with the hope of all our lives ahead, not yet tasting disappointment, never having known defeat. Now we were meeting at the other end of our union, and I had no idea what to expect. . . .

I saw the Banner of the Red Dragon lifting against the sky before the horses came into view over the top of a ridge. It was a large party—probably everyone from Camelot and the nearby villages—and they came on at a brisk trot. Cei was in the van, resplendent in his best silk and brocade tunic, followed by Nimue and Cathbad, wearing their white robes of worship.

And then came Arthur, mounted on his black stallion. From a distance he was an immensely imposing figure—solid, powerful, still the consummate ruler—and my heart lifted at the sight.

Cei and Bedivere saluted each other, while the holy leaders fanned out around us as Arthur and I each moved slowly forward. The stallion tossed his head and nickered, but Arthur held him on a short rein, keeping the pace stately and majestic. Both Moonlight and I were trembling, and I drew her in sharply, following my husband's lead. Slowly and precisely we closed the distance. Before me was the middle-aged monarch of power and justice, the aged King grown worn and wise, the proud young man who'd been my groom—even a fleeting shadow of the boy he must have been, lively and impetuous. The whole of our lives together shimmered like a bridge across the years. And out of the light, the flow of color, the substance of vision, emerged the present man.

His hair and mustaches were now completely gray; still long and thick, but gray nonetheless. And his face was furrowed with lines of worry and concern. I saw the toll the splintering of the Round Table had exacted, and ached for the part I had unwittingly played.

My gaze sought his, and as the two horses came to a stop, nose to nose, exchanging breaths as horses do, my husband and I slowly searched each other's face. At last, with great solemnity, he raised his hand, and I realized he was holding Igraine's golden torc aloft for everyone to see. "It seems to me," he said softly, "you should be wearing this."

Urging the stallion forward until we were knee to knee, he waited while I lifted aside my traveling veil, then carefully put the golden circlet around my neck. Pitching his voice to carry to our audience, he settled back in his saddle and said, "Well come home, my Queen."

The riders who had crowded around us let out a cheer, and Arthur swung his steed around so that we could ride side by side. "Thought you'd never get here," he continued as the people made way for us and both Cei and Bedivere pushed ahead to form an escort with the standard bearer. "It's been a long year."

"For me as well," I replied.

This was neither the time nor place for private conversation, so we rode in silence for a while.

"Who stayed at Camelot?" I inquired at last, since the other face I had looked for was not in the welcoming party.

"Gawain and his men. He's my lieutenant now."

"Not Bedivere?" I was mildly surprised, having assumed Arthur's foster brother would have been given the same position he had when we were young. One-handed or no, he had a cooler head and wiser counsel than the Orcadian.

Arthur shook his head. "As my sister's son, Gawain stands closest to the throne. It's only natural he would be among those considered for the Kingship if something happened to me." The stallion was excited by Moonlight's presence, swinging his head toward her, lips extended, teeth bared. Arthur gave him a quick rebuke and swung his head to one side. "You ought to know, Gwen . . . Gawain was one of your staunchest supporters in Carlisle, outraged at what his son and brothers perpetrated and eager to have you back. He wanted to come greet you, but I couldn't leave Camelot empty."

"And Mordred?" I asked finally, half frightened of what I'd hear.

"Still at Winchester, with the Federates." Arthur's tone was cool and neutral, leaving nothing more to be said on the subject, so I let the matter drop and simply enjoyed my homecoming.

People of all sorts lined our way: farmers, swineherds, smiths and wainwrights, who left their work to watch our cavalcade move past; peddlers, merchants and messengers; monks and druids, nobles going courting, beekeepers taking their hives to new orchards—all those for whom travel was a fact of life swung off to the verge in order to let us pass. For the most part they were silent as the Banner went past, but when they saw me beside their King, a roar of welcome would burst forth.

Realization of how much the common people had missed me took my breath away, and tears of gratitude blurred my sight.

Not the nobles and the warriors, mired in politics and playing their courtly games, but the people. The people of the land—offering up their joy and dreams, their hopes and pleasure at my return. It was the thing I'd touched on after the night in the cave, the earth-dreams of humanity. Their song echoed in me like wind haunting a harp. It was this that gave me purpose, reflecting in my actions the very nature of my soul. It was this that balanced Arthur's capabilities—this that made us what we were together. And while it might not be holy and sublime, I could no more deny it than Lance could deny his need to seek the spiritual life or Arthur turn away from his beloved Cause.

As Camelot's hill came into view, a great wave of gladness surged through me. I had found my Grail, both within and without, and knew how blessedly lucky we were.

Life at Court began to return to normal for the first time since the events at Carlisle. Arthur and I moved gingerly into a reunion —when I tried to tell him about Joyous Gard, he stopped me abruptly, not wishing to hear—and though we bedded only occasionally, our teamwork in ruling had never been better.

There'd been some difficulties in getting salt delivered to the inland regions on a reliable basis, so we reassessed the system and sent Cei to Droitwich to make sure our changes were implemented. The Royal Messenger service had declined for lack of new recruits, but with a new proclamation reducing the taxes of any family who had a member willing and able to perform the arduous service, we were inundated with applicants.

Finally, there was the matter of the horse farms at the monastery in south Wales. Since Illtud's death, the monks had begun demanding payment for working with the horses, to which Arthur replied that as long as it was his cavalry that kept their barns safe, they could jolly well contribute to the upkeep of the mounts. The clerics ranted and raved at such a notion, so Arthur had Gwyn start bringing the animals to his pastures outside of Glastonbury, in the hope of putting an end to the bickering.

I took pains to get to know the new men better and spent more time with the ladies-in-waiting. And I tried not to think about those who were no longer part of the Fellowship—the men in Brittany; Perceval, who had stayed less than a year at Court before deciding to make a pilgrimage to the Holy Land; and those who had died on the Quest.

Most painful of all was the memory of Gareth. As at Joyous Gard, everyone missed the gentle warrior, and once I was settled in, I sought out Lynette, who had remained at Court, helping Enid run the household in my absence.

She was seated in the doorway of her hut, taking advantage of the sunlight to do some sewing while the toddler played at her feet. After an exchange of greetings I told her how deeply sorry Lance and the others had been, and that I hoped she didn't blame them for her husband's death.

Gareth's widow looked up at me slowly, her eyes as hard as Kimmins's wife's had been. "Frankly, M'lady, there's plenty enough blame to go around: the King for ordering your escort to go unarmed, Lancelot and his men for saving you by force, Agravain for starting the melee against them. No one knows who dealt the blow . . . so I lay it at the Gods' feet. I've no time for recriminations, not with three children to raise and household work to do." She shook out the little smock she'd been making and let her glance stray toward the boy. A softness came over her features. "I still cry for him, you know—silent, at night, so as not to wake the youngsters. But we'll make it through somehow. The one who won't let go of it is Gawain. Someone has to help him with his grief, M'lady, for it is eating him alive, like a poison in the blood."

Her assessment proved all too true. The red-headed Prince of Orkney carried a brooding anger everywhere he went, and even the most casual remark would send him into fits of rage, as though his own pain required him to flay anyone who came within range.

"I'm right glad to see you," he allowed the first time we met in private, "but I wish that wretched Breton had had the courage to come back as well. He'll not get away so easily, you know. He'll pay; someday I'll make him pay for cutting down the very lad who idolized him."

"Oh no, Gawain," I exclaimed, horrified to realize he believed Lance had personally delivered the fatal stroke. "Lancelot was on his horse, with me in front of him. He never even drew his sword."

"I might have known you'd defend him, Your Highness." Morgause's son looked at me coldly. "Not even the King will admit it, but I know . . . I know in my heart the coward turned on him. Gaheris and Agravain—even my son, Gingalin—had the chance to fight before they died. But to strike down my brother who was unarmed was a despicable act, an insult to the honor of my family . . . and I'll not rest till I have vengeance!"

Not only would Gawain not listen to reason, his mood seemed to darken further as the summer days lengthened.

"I don't know what to do," Arthur sighed one night in June, moving slowly about the room as I undid my hair. "He's been bullying me for months to go after Lance in reprisal for Gareth's death."

"Maybe with time he'll listen to reason. . . ."

"Not likely. It's coming up to a year now, and the grievance just grows deeper. I was hoping Father Baldwin could calm him some, but even the Church can't quell his thirst for blood."

I thought of the Orcadians' vendetta against Pellinore and Lamorak and knew that Arthur was right. The family feud—that
nemesis of the old Celts—was running full tide in Gawain.

"Worse yet, he's gathering others to his side, the followers of
Agravain and the like," my husband went on, sitting disconsolately on the edge of the bed. "They're the strongest faction left
in the Round Table, and I'm in danger of losing my hold on them
unless something is done."

I turned to stare at him, shocked by the idea that all he'd
accomplished was so close to dissolution.

"Come here, girl, and give us a kiss," he said with a sad,
hopeless smile. "I could use a little holding."

Never, in all our lives together, had Arthur asked me for anything. The simple admission of a need had always been beyond
him, and I turned to take him in my arms with a newfound
warmth of love and affection.

It was Mordred who suggested a solution to Gawain's demands
when he came to make his summer report on the Federates. I
watched him ride up the cobbled drive, a man of grace and
bearing, with a face as unreadable as stone. He greeted me po-
litely enough in public, and I invited him to join me in my garden
for a chat, wanting to see for myself where we stood with each
other.

"I am very glad you are safely home," he said in his smooth,
unruffled way. "I never meant to harm you, M'lady. It was Lancelot I wanted to bring down."

His voice was earnest and his manner contrite enough. I
watched him carefully, trying to find contradictions between
what his mouth said and what his body showed, but the façade
was seamless. So we talked of inconsequential matters and parted
amiably enough, though I knew that thenceforth I would be as
guarded with him as he was with the world. The mother in me,
remembering the child I had loved and raised, cried out to see
him walk away a stranger . . . but perhaps there are times when
that is what a parent must do.

Later, when Arthur mentioned how set Gawain seemed to be
on vengeance, Mordred spoke up quickly.

"*Wergild*," he announced. "It's the price of a man's worth. Among the Saxons, if someone is held accountable for another person's death, he can give the survivors the amount of the man's worth, and all blood debts are considered paid. It keeps grievances from becoming vendettas. Why don't you see if Gawain will accept that from Lancelot? Use it to balance the books of honor, so to speak."

It was an intriguing idea, and one that Gawain allowed he would consider, provided that Lancelot himself pay over the price in person.

"He's not to come back here," Arthur said hastily, wanting to stop that idea before it took root. "Let Bedivere carry the message and return with the payment."

"No!" Gawain's face flushed to crimson, and his voice was steel. "I will accept it only with a personal apology, and if it means tracking him down in Brittany, so be it. We of King Lot's clan have spent our lives in your service, Arthur Pendragon. And as my King you owe me something for all those years. The chance to reestablish my family's honor is what I request. Come with me to Brittany and help me redress this insult."

The demand was outrageous, but no amount of arguing could change the Orcadian's stand, so by mid-July the boatmen of London were making ready to take Arthur and a party of warriors across the Channel—not so many as to cause the Franks concern that we were invading but certainly more than a personal bodyguard.

"I don't like it, Arthur," I fussed as the day of departure grew close. "I don't trust Gawain to stay within the bounds of diplomacy. You know how hotheaded he can be. Besides, there's too much that needs attending here at home for you to go away just now."

"And too much at risk among the Companions if I don't," he answered, turning away from the work that lay strewn on our table and going to stand by the window, looking out. When he didn't say anything more, I ventured a comment of my own.

"Surely you don't *want* a confrontation with Lancelot. . . ." We had not spoken of the Breton since my first attempt was rebuffed, and now I was feeling my way along the subject like a person tiptoeing across a bog.

"Don't say it, Gwen! Don't beg for his life, no matter how much we both loved him." The words leapt from him—angry, pleading, full of bafflement. The force of his response startled me, and I instinctively took a step back. "You see," he went on grimly, "there's something else, love—a need of my own, if you will."

So the crack in the dam was still there, the feelings still trying to find a way out. I sat down and stayed very still, hardly daring to breathe, praying that at last he would open his heart.

"Do you remember when you returned from Brigit's convent?"

"After being kidnapped by Maelgwn?"

"Aye." Arthur spoke without looking at me. "I wanted vengeance—as any man would, whose wife was raped. Wanted a chance to even the score, to prove to the world I was strong enough to protect you and punish anyone who hurt you. But you begged for his life . . . and I listened. I swallowed my pride and my instincts, and I heeded your wish. This time I'm not after my rival's blood—the tangle of our lives is too thick a knot to untie with a sword. But I must take action of some kind, and not be dissuaded by you as I was when you sought to protect Maelgwn."

"*Protect* Maelgwn?" The very idea lifted me to my feet and sent me prowling across the room. "You thought I was protecting him? That scum? That toad? Oh, love, it was you I was scared for, you I wanted to save!"

I had come to my husband's side. Though he continued to stare out the window, I put my hand on his arm with full confidence that he wouldn't shrug it away. And I spoke aloud, for the first time, the fear that had consumed me in the convent.

"Arthur, I was beset by dreams—by nightmares in which I saw your death. Night after night, over and over. It terrified me. It still does. To be the cause of your death . . ." I paused, swallowing down the panic that rose with the idea, and picked my words very carefully. There was no need to explain Lancelot when the door was finally open to express my feelings for Arthur. "I plighted my troth to you on a chilly night at the Wrekin, and have never since regretted it. You are both my husband and my King . . . and even in Northumbria you were in my thoughts. In the odd moments, when I pondered what had happened, it was to the south I turned. To Camelot and you."

Blindly, without looking at me, Arthur reached out and, putting his arm around my shoulder, crushed me to him. Without a
word he buried his face in my hair, and I felt the sobs that
overtook him, long and hard and wracking.

"There are so many things I should have done differently," he
said at last, still holding me too close to look at him. "Mordred
—yea Gods, don't you think I know I've failed him as a father?
And you . . . oh, Gwen, every time I tried to tell you, tried to
say it out open and clear, the words disappeared or came out
wrong . . . or something got between us. So I ended up telling
myself you knew . . . you must know, how much I loved you,
how much I cared.

"And then, after you pleaded for Maelgwn's life so eloquently,
I thought he must have given you all the things I couldn't. And
those rumors that you had wanted to be with him didn't help."

"Rumors from Morgan," I reminded him, and heard him sigh.

"Yes, back before I realized how untrustworthy she was. I tried
to tell myself it wasn't true, that you were glad to be with me,
happy as my wife. And when you insisted on taking in Mordred
. . . well, it seemed like proof enough that you'd made peace
with our lot. I just never realized how hard it would be to face
the boy . . . or how much worse it would make things."

He pulled away from me and stared down at my face. "I didn't
believe you'd come back from Joyous Gard . . . didn't think
you'd leave Lance to return to me. Ah, lass, I've seen the look
on your face, watched the spark that leaps between the two of
you—who hasn't, over the years? And if I couldn't give you that
myself, well, at least I didn't want to take it away from you."

My arms slid around him, and I buried my face in his chest,
unable to hold his gaze. Tears of my own—for happiness, for
sorrow, I couldn't tell which—were dampening his tunic.

"I'd have left things be if it weren't for Gawain constantly
nagging at the matter of honor. I've no wish to go to war with
the Breton, no desire to do more than make a quiet peace with
him—he may have your love, but in the end, I have you. . . ."

"Oh, Arthur," I cried, "you have my love as well. Surely you
must know that?" The words burst out, as much for my own need
to affirm it as for his need to be reassured. "Good glory, do you
think I'd come back to Camelot's throne if there weren't *some*
loving involved?"

My outburst took him by surprise, and after a moment he lifted an eyebrow and gave me a wry smile. "No, come to think on it, I don't suppose anyone in their right mind would."

I caught the shift of mood and grinned up at him. "I'm here, we are together, there is the whole future still before us. We can't go back and do things over, but maybe we can make a better job of it in the days to come."

Arthur sighed, and lifted his head to look out upon the world. "After the trip to Brittany. I won't fight Lance, you know; to do battle with him would be to war against the best part of myself. But reparations must be made to Gawain for honor's sake. The *Wergild*—the *Wergild* and an apology will put an end to it. Once that is done . . ." He glanced down at me. "I, too, can come home. Come back to Camelot. And together we'll begin to rebuild."

The flush of excitement was bringing color back to his cheeks and a sparkle to his eyes. "We can do it, love—I know we can. Once we get the Round Table back on its feet . . ."

Just as when he was younger, his enthusiasm filled the room, and I hugged him fiercely, feeling the life course through him, believing there were still dreams to be fulfilled.

"When I come back," he was saying, "we'll begin all over again . . . make up for the things left undone—or unsaid—before. Think you can manage that?"

"Of course I can," I averred, raising my chin and giving him a sidewise glance.

It was the closest Arthur and I had ever been, and when he left to set sail for Brittany, I stood on the steps of the Hall while he and his men mounted their horses, filled with love and pride and excitement for him. The trumpet sounded, and he paused to look down on me, the smile of his youth lighting his face.

Smiling back, I gave him the thumbs up and watched as he wheeled his stallion around and went to face his destiny. With so much hope flowing between us, there wasn't room for fear.

35

Rebellion

lthough I knew Arthur had no intention of going to war with Lancelot, Gawain and the rest of his co-horts had convinced the courtiers that battle be-tween them was a forgone conclusion. I found the prospect so horrific, I simply would not admit to it, and spent my time assuring everyone at Court that it would never happen.

Arthur had left the State Seal with me, but as rumor of the potential conflict in Brittany spread, there was little need to use it; everyone's attention was focused on the Continent. So I settled for living day by day and prayed that Lance would pay the *Wergild* and Gawain would be satisfied.

By the end of a fortnight I was taut as a bowstring. "You'd think they'd have sent some kind of word," I fretted.

"It's possible they're on their way home," Cei pointed out. Arthur's foster brother had stayed at Camelot to command the houseguards while the King was gone—not that there were that many, most of the seasoned men being with Arthur or off on typical summer errands.

Over the years of working together, I'd grown used to the Seneschal's sharp tongue, but now it seemed his manner was less caustic. Whatever the cause for the change, I was grateful for it. "They'd probably get here as fast as a messenger," he added, turning his attention to the list of supplies he was laying in for the winter.

Three more days went by before a messenger climbed Camelot's hill, bringing a brief letter penned in Bedivere's hand. I rushed to open it but, after reading the first sentence, let out a howl of disbelief.

"Single combat!" I dropped the missive on the long table and stalked to the window. "Even though Lance has paid the *Wergild* and sent the Orcadian an apology, Gawain claims family honor demands the Breton meet him in single combat."

The Seneschal studied the message more closely. "Apparently the men are goading Gawain on, so they won't be leaving there till Arthur can talk some sense into his nephew—or Lance comes out of his fortress to do battle."

"Drat!" I wrapped my arms around my shoulders and shivered. Gawain could be stubborn beyond reason. When the Irish Champion Marhaus issued a challenge to single combat, Gawain had fought him for hours on end—until their comrades had to drag them both, bleeding and exhausted, off the field. Even so, Morgause's son had demanded more. Now he was not only pitting Arthur and Lance against each other, he was holding everyone hostage to his own outrageous pride. Indignation boiled within me.

Cei leaned across the table. "M'lady, you're going to wear yourself out with so much worry. I'm taking some men over to that villa near Weston-Super-Mare tomorrow to pick up a new supply of wine from the Mediterranean. There probably won't be further news from Brittany again for days—maybe weeks. Why don't you come with us? The ride would do you good."

It was a pleasant suggestion, so after a moment's thought, I agreed to go. Both Moonlight and I had been cooped up within Camelot's walls far too long.

"I can't imagine how nuns survive in a convent," I commented as Enid helped me pack a change of clothes. "Living forever behind four high walls would drive me crazy."

"I think most of them want the security," she answered. "I thought about joining one after Geraint died—you know they take in widows and women with nowhere else to go."

"Hmmm," I responded. No doubt they provided a needed service, but I preferred to limit my contact with such places to an occasional visit with Brigit.

The trip to Weston-Super-Mare was lovely. We followed the old track along the base of the Mendip Hills, stopping at Wells to leave a prayer ribbon on the Sacred Oak for Arthur's safety, and carefully skirted the edge of Wookey Hole. Memory of Mordred's experience and Arthur's revenge slunk around the edges of my mind, and I was glad we made camp farther on, at the base of Cheddar Gorge.

"Do you remember," I asked Cei as we sat by the fire that night, "when we visited Gwyn in his hunting lodge at the top of the Gorge?"

"Indeed. And the splendid cheeses he gave us," Camelot's gourmet affirmed.

"I've heard his hall at Glastonbury is empty," Enid noted. "Has he decided to move away?" There was a note of hopefulness in her voice. Like most Christians, she looked askance at those who were too close to the Old Ways.

"No, he's just gone to get the last of the horses from Llantwit," I explained. "He'll be bringing them back before harvest time, I'm sure."

Next morning, while Cei conducted his business at the villa, Enid and I strolled along the beach. The tide was out, leaving a long, golden strand between the high, rocky horns that flank the cove. I stared out over the wet, shining sand, as empty and clean-swept as the beach itself. The love and loss of Lance lay quiet against my heart, and I concentrated on my last sight of Arthur —flushed, excited, full of confidence that all would come well in the end. Hurry home, husband, I thought . . . hurry home so we can begin to build anew.

That afternoon Cei was actually lighthearted as we started back to Camelot. The many amphorae of wine made the ox-drawn wagon even slower and more cumbersome than usual, but the Seneschal rode beside me, cheerfully going over all the things he and Arthur and Bedivere were planning to do come the fall.

"With such good times ahead," I asked, "why don't you find yourself a wife to share them with?"

Cei's countenance darkened, but the look he shot me was more one of confusion than anger. "What do I need a wife for?" he blustered. "Bound to be more bother than she'd be worth."

"Haven't you ever wanted to marry?"

"I would have, but she was wed to another, so I put the thought aside." The words were flat and devoid of feeling, like a shield held up to protect a bruise that won't heal. But his manner became more blithe as he went on. "Besides, taking care of the kingdom keeps me more than busy."

When we reached the bottom of Camelot's hill, Cei signaled for a halt. "Something strange, M'lady—I don't recognize the sentry on the lower gate."

I gave the Seneschal an inquiring look, thinking he was being unduly cautious, but he rode up and challenged the stranger, then came back with a puzzled frown.

"Says he's the cousin of that new fellow, Martyn. The two of them were out carousing last night; Martyn's not feeling too well today and his cousin's taking his place. Sounds plausible enough, though I'll make sure it doesn't happen again."

So we made our way up the steep track that swings around the fortress's base and ends in the staging area outside our upper wall. Here, however, there was clearly something amiss: the guards at the double gates and in the tower were all big, blond and heavily armed. When Cei demanded an explanation, his voice was drowned out by the sounds of mounted warriors closing in behind the oxcart, making escape down the hill impossible. I glared at the strangers who opened the gate and swarmed around us, but they gave no heed to my protestations as they dragged our party into the courtyard and hustled me off to the Great Hall.

There was a chill silence when I entered the room, though my mind raced feverishly to make sense of what I saw. Mordred was sitting in his father's chair, elbows propped on the arms, fingers steepled under his chin. He watched me without moving as I was brought before him, then dismissed my guard and, rising, came down off the dais. With a smile he reached out to take my hand.

"Well come, Your Highness."

"What is this?" I snapped, struggling to keep my voice steady. If the boy thought I would let him stretch his wings so arrogantly while his father was gone, I intended to put a quick stop to it.

"This," my stepson replied, "is the new order of things." He led me to my own carved chair and after I was seated, retook his place in Arthur's. "His Highness is so concerned with honor and such in Brittany, he seems to have forgotten his poor subjects here at home. So we've decided to take matters into our own hands."

"*Your* hands?" I bridled. So many Saxons on Camelot's walls suggested a palace coup, and I had to remind myself to temper anger with caution.

Seeing my wariness, Mordred shifted to a more diplomatic approach. "We've talked before, you and I, and agreed that it's imperative to bring the Saxons and Britons together in peace. The Round Table is the perfect forum for it—or at least it could have been. But Arthur stunted it, turned it into a living relic—a haven for dreamers and posturing warlords out of the past. You and I both know it needs new blood, new ideas, the inclusion of the Federates—"

"So you've taken over the throne and are going to rectify all those wrongs?" I interrupted, trying to keep my tone inquisitive, not sarcastic, though outrage ran in my veins. "No doubt you've had help from the Federates?"

"Of course, through Cynric. I left him in charge of Winchester, by the way. Gave it to him as my first official act."

First official act—the inevitable statement of a conqueror. The seriousness of Mordred's intent came home to me with a cold certainty, and I suddenly wondered if this was another of Morgan's plots.

Mordred rose from the King's chair and walked slowly back and forth across the dais. His head was bent in thought, as though he were trying to decide just how much to tell me.

The setting sun bathed the Hall with a final golden sheen before slipping beyond the horizon. I wished we could have the lamps lit so I could at least see my opponent clearly, but Mordred appeared to be balancing on the edge of decision, and I didn't want to force his hand by calling in a servant; better he arrive at his own conclusions in his own time. With any luck, he'd take me into his confidence. So I folded my hands and waited.

"If only you'd spoken up more forcefully," he said at last, coming to a stop and looking at me earnestly. "I know you understood the problem, know you held more sway over the High King than I ever could. I was counting on your good sense to soften him." He turned away with a sigh and a shake of his head. "Well, you can make up for that lack now, M'lady." He went back to pacing again. "I have the Federates behind me, totally committed. But I need you to bring the Cumbri into line—the men of Rheged, the

Wrekin, the various countries in Wales. It was clear they'd follow you against Arthur, and if you'll recognize me as the new High King, they'll no doubt follow suit. Naturally, you can remain at Court as the Dowager Queen." He gestured from the tapestry of the Red Dragon to the stairs at the far end of the Hall. "All kept the same. Even your own carved chair. Just promise me you'll back my bid for Kingship and encourage the Fellowship to accept me."

So this wasn't just a local rebellion; Mordred was intent on ruling the whole of Britain as High King. And he was heeding the old maxim that he who controls the Queen controls the people.

"How do I know this isn't just a bluff?" I queried, playing for time and information. "Who among the Saxons are sworn to you?"

Mordred raised an eyebrow at my question. "All of them. Cissa of Sussex, Aesc's sons in Kent, Cynric in Winchester. And a number of others 'Good King Arthur' never bothered to recognize, any more than he recognized me."

The bitterness of his last words laid bare the grief that had driven him to this, and for a moment my heart was touched.

"And you trust them, Mordred? You trust *them*? Have you never thought they may be using you? Undermining the British rule from within, getting you to do their dirty work? What makes you think they'll let you live to sit in the High King's chair?"

"Haven't you noticed; I am already in the High King's chair." He smiled with cold satisfaction. "The rebellion has already taken place. All that's left is to secure my position."

All that's left! How blind the arrogance of youth can be! With a snap of the fingers he discounted Arthur, dismissed him as a force already overthrown, an old man who had grown blind to the realities of the day. Ah Mordred, you, too, suffered from lack of vision, the blindness of your hatred making you underestimate the very man who sired you!

Seeing that there was no way to reach him with reason, I sighed and put my hands on the arms of my chair preparatory to rising. "Let me think about it," I temporized. "Give me until tomorrow to consider the matter. By then I'll have some idea as to how to help you."

Again the cold smile, but this time I caught a hint of warmth in his eyes—not triumph as in a political matter but relief, as though having my approval still mattered to him. It might not be of any use to me, but I was grateful that he had not totally discounted all the years I'd cared for him.

Back in my room, I took my jewels from the treasure chest and slipped them into traveling pouches. Arthur had once told me they might be handy for bartering. Then I had Enid go in search of Cei and ask him to bring my dinner to my chamber, providing he was not under arrest with the rest of our houseguard.

Fortunately the Saxons had heard so much about the fine food at Camelot, they were demanding proof of the Seneschal's culinary skill. So while the rest of our men were in chains, Cei moved freely between kitchen and larder and Hall. Later, while the enemy were gorging themselves at their feast, he and I conferred in hasty whispers, making plans for escape.

I gave him various spices from the cupboard, explaining which herbs bring on sleep, and after the strangers had had their fill of mulled wine and sat nodding by the fire, I crept down the back stairs and joined the Seneschal in the kitchen courtyard. We dared not confront the sentries on the wall, but slipped silently through the postern gate and, keeping well to the shadows on the edge of the track, made our way to the nearest steading. Here Cei found a pair of horses, which he appropriated without even waking the farmer. I told myself we'd repay the man when this was over.

It was a chancy trip, as we had no idea how far the insurrection had spread and whether the more integrated Federates of the Thames valley would give us shelter in Arthur's name or take us captive in Mordred's. We rode at night and slept in ruined villas or hidden thickets during the day. Cei stole bits of food, his years as a tax collector having sharpened his eye for what was or wasn't available at every steading.

With luck and desperation we reached London before Mordred's men found us. Lynette's family let me stay with them in the Grounds Keeper's quarters at the Imperial Palace until we could secure Caesar's Tower. With its thick walls and square rooms set one on top of the other, it was the best defensive position around and would be a suitable headquarters from which to conduct Arthur's business until he returned.

While Cei went about finding an adequate food supply and Lynette's family rounded up a ragtag houseguard for my protection, I tried to determine how much Morgan was involved in this. That she wouldn't scruple to use Mordred was clear, but if she had initiated this uprising, he would not have turned to me for help in bringing the northerners to his cause. For once I decided my sister-in-law had nothing to do with the present disaster.

On our first night in the Tower Cei and I held a council to consider what to do next. Sitting on camp stools around a fire built on the dirt floor on the ground level, we might as well have been in the field. That's when I fully realized we were at war with Mordred.

"I must get word to Arthur," I declared. "He has to know what's happening."

Cei had already spoken with the Harbor Master. "There's a ship sailing on tomorrow's tide. One of the Royal Messengers will be aboard when she pulls out."

"What do you mean, Royal Messenger?" Surprise made my voice sharp. "You must go in person."

"And who's to take care of you in the meantime? That bunch of gangling boys?" He gestured toward the noisy group of youngsters playing dice just beyond the door. It was true that my houseguard was made up more of eager boys than seasoned warriors. "Well meaning, but not much for experience."

"We'll just have to chance it." I shrugged.

"No, M'lady. Years back I took an oath to defend you with my life if necessary, and that's not going to change now." He bent to add another branch to the coals. The Tower was as chill as the cell in Carlisle had been, and the fire would be my only heat throughout the night.

"I appreciate the sentiment," I said with a sigh, touched by his loyalty. "But truly, I'll be fine."

"I don't think you understand." The Seneschal continued to poke at the coals, not looking at me. "You asked why I've never married. . . . let's just say the lady I wanted was also my Queen —and my foster brother's wife. So I kept to myself and concentrated on my duties. Not that it was easy, watching Lancelot become your Champion, seeing the Breton come and go, disappearing for months at a time and leaving you unprotected. The man didn't half appreciate his position, in my opinion." He frowned at the new flame licking along the bark of the branch and shook his head as though wishing he hadn't said so much. "But now that it's me you need, I intend to be here."

I stared at him, speechless. It was the last thing in the world I expected to hear.

"Not that I would try to replace the Breton in your affections," he went on hastily. "Nor do I ask any favors in return—just the chance to take care of you properly until Arthur gets back." He lifted his head and looked at me worriedly, the firelight making his cheeks ruddy and his eyes shadowed. "I hope I haven't spoken out of turn, Your Highness, but you should know my reasons for not going."

"Well, um . . ." I stammered, unable to think of what to say. It was my turn to avert my eyes. "I deeply appreciate your . . . honesty. But it's desperately important that Arthur have as much information as possible—the names of Mordred's allies, a rough idea of their numbers, and the fact that he doesn't think he can count on the men of the north without my support. Who knows what Uwain's position will be. Now that I've given up Rheged, we've precious little leverage where he's concerned. Those are details Arthur will need to know, and even if I commit them to writing, he'll be wanting your assessment as well."

I looked up then to find the Seneschal still watching me. Our eyes held for a long moment, and at last he smiled—a wry, lopsided smile such as I had never seen before.

"If that's what you command, M'lady, that's what I'll do. We both know the risks of leaving you alone here, and I'd rather stay. But I've had my say, and having served both you and Arthur nigh on thirty years, I'm not about to go against you now." He rose to his feet, gathering his dignity with him. "I'll go pack some things for traveling while you write down those names. . . ."

I stared into the fire for a long bit after he left the room, puzzling that a man could carry such a secret for so long, and that I had never guessed. All things considered, I was glad he'd never mentioned it before.

Cei left on the boat early the next morning, and later that afternoon both Lynette and Enid slipped into the Tower, having managed to depart from Camelot without arousing Mordred's suspicions. He was, by all accounts, too busy raising his rebel army and scouring the nearby countryside for me to notice the departure of two widows and three children.

"The men of Devon *must* be loyal," Enid declared when we gathered around the fire after the children were abed. "You should send a message to Petroc and Gwynlliw assuring them Arthur is returning."

"The more allies we can muster before the High King arrives, the better the chances of winning," I agreed, glad to have her help.

We spent the next two days sending out word to our allies. Messengers went everywhere, from Vortipor in Demetia to the Scottish chieftains in Strathclyde and Stirling; from Constantine in Cornwall—King Mark being far too old for battle—to Wuffa in East Anglia. I even sent word to London's Bishop asking what help the church could provide, and to Cathbad in the hope that the druids would come to the Pendragon's aid.

And then we waited. During the day I paced the rooms in the Tower, climbing to the ruined parapet to stare out over the Thames and wonder where Arthur would land when he did come back. London was more secure, but the Channel at Dover was narrower, though it was possible the Federates who controlled the area had joined with Mordred. Then, too, he could make for the Wash to the north, where the Saxons might or might not prove loyal. Or he could swing around Cornwall and up the Bristol Channel, disembarking at Glastonbury and possibly taking Mordred from the rear. There was one consolation: if I could see so many possibilities, Mordred could also. It meant he would have to spread his forces thin.

In the evenings I took little Lora and Megan on my lap and told them stories. By one of those oddities of fate the pine knot carving Kimmins had given me was among my jewels, so I brought it out and showed the girls, delighting them with tales of how the invisible Hedley Kow used to plague poor Cook by overturning pots and upsetting churns before scampering away on his bandy legs, laughing his great horse laugh. I wove in stories of the heroes their father had known, and memories of our early days at Camelot. It helped to pass the time and raised our spirits as well.

And in the long, dark hours on my cot, I scrambled mentally from one corner of the realm to another, desperately dredging my memory for every political favor owed us, every small warlord and local chieftain who might come to our aid. My own men of Rheged were now under Uwain's rule: how they and the other northerners would react, I had no idea. All I could do was pray.

The Bishop of London sent a terse note allowing that certain "irregularities" in my domestic arrangements had come to his attention, and he could not condone any actions I might seek to initiate. I saw the Latin letters on the wax tablet, but heard the voice of Gildas behind them, and cursing roundly, hurled the tablet against the stone wall.

Nor was the druids' answer any better. Since they avoid writing things down, their answer was delivered in person by one of their representatives. He was a little man who wouldn't look me in the eye. "We notice that you are inhabiting the tower the Romans built over the sacred mound containing Bran's head. First your husband digs up the skull in an unconscionable fashion, and now you hold Court on the holy ground without even asking our permission. It does not seem that you or your husband have much use for us, except when you need our help to maintain your own status," he concluded nervously.

I couldn't throw him against the wall, but I stared at him coldly, and he scuttled out of sight without a backward glance.

Among the politicians who responded, there were some, such as Petroc of Devon and Constantine of Cornwall, who swore constant loyalty, and some, such as Vortipor, who wanted to hedge their bets, inquiring who else was aligned with us and asking various favors. Gwyn, however, promised to have whatever fresh horses Arthur needed available after he landed.

Wuffa's answer was curt and belligerent. He sent a caustic note making it clear that the Britons need not look to the Swedish settlers for any sort of alliance. He also announced that his father's name had been expunged from the tribal records because of his association with us, and in the future the tribe would be known as the Wuffings, not the Wehhings. I thought of the fierce old barbarian with the high pride and deep loyalty, and was sorry that the dynasty would not even carry his name.

I kept a tally as the replies came in, leaving a question mark beside those who didn't bother to reply. Perhaps, I told myself, they had not received the message.

It was going on the second week when Nimue arrived, coming unannounced into the upper room as though materializing out of thin air.

"Thought you'd want to know," the doire began as she slipped off her dark cloak. "Arthur is on his way. Lancelot finally agreed to do battle with Gawain, but then only defended himself—wouldn't follow up with blows of his own. In the end I don't know if Gawain dodged into it, or Lance simply lost his control, but the Breton felled him with a blow to the head."

"Dead?" I asked, too numbed by recent events to be shocked.

"Not that I could see." Merlin's apprentice accepted a cup of valerian tea and, after taking a sip, continued. "There are times when my Sight is blurred—like watching the reflection in a mill pond where the mists are rising. Merlin said it was often this way —when even he didn't know for sure what he looked on."

"Have you seen anything of the future?" I asked, hoping for some kind of reassurance.

Nimue drained her cup, then put it down on the camp table with great deliberation. "I see much death and sorrow, Gwen—an agonizing battle between Mordred and Arthur, with awful bloodshed. Gore and screams and the death throes of all Britain, if it can't be averted . . . at least until the stars are better. Another month, perhaps another outcome. If they do battle now . . ." She lifted her pale hands in despair.

"We need to find someone to talk to them . . . someone to mediate between them," I announced, willing to clutch at any straw that floated by. "Arthur would listen to you. Who would Mordred take council from?"

"Maybe the High Priestess. She's the most logical choice, being his aunt."

The suggestion hit me in the pit of the stomach. The very idea of trusting Morgan in any way brought a bilious taste to my mouth. "How do we know she won't try to kill Arthur during the negotiations?"

The doire got to her feet and walked over to the window, where she stood staring out over the Thames for a long time. At last she sighed and, coming back, sat down across from me.

"I can see nothing of her motives, or her hand in the matter—only the terrible destruction to come if we stand by and do nothing. How trustworthy she'll be depends on what she stands to gain. The recognition and prestige she'd get by being a peacemaker might be enough, but you'd be wise to have something else to offer—something that only you can give her. What would that be?"

"Good Glory, you're asking me? After all these years I still don't know what Morgan wants, besides power!"

The doire tapped her finger against her teeth before replying. "Then that may be your solution. I know it's hard for you, Gwen, but if there is a battle, she should be present for her healing talents alone."

I groaned at the realization that one way or another, I needed to ask Morgan for help. "How can I get a message to her?"

"The Ancient Ones tell me she's already left the Sanctuary at the Black Lake and seems to be heading for London. It's possible she'll seek you out with a bargain of her own."

"At least if she comes looking for me, I'll be in a stronger position than if I have to make the request of her," I muttered. "And how do you plan to get Arthur to accept this, after all she's done to him?"

The doire smiled softly. "I think he'll listen to reason, Gwen. Negotiation, even through someone you don't like, is still preferable to killing your own child."

Caught up in my own fear and worry for my husband, I had not thought what it would mean for him to have go to war against Mordred. Dismay knotted my stomach, and Nimue came over and put her arms around me.

"It's not of your doing," she said. "It is theirs . . . their moira, their choices. Has been since the day of the boy's conception. The best we can do is try to keep it from ending in a bloodbath." I stared up at her, and she gave me a gentle blessing and laid her fingertips on my eyelids. "Now, you just concentrate on Morgan. I'm off to join Arthur when he lands." She moved away to the door, then turned and gave me a smile. "Pelleas wants you to know, he'll be at Arthur's side as well."

With that she was gone.

During the next few days I thought constantly about what I

could offer Morgan, weighing the matter over and over, even after I heard that the High Priestess had arrived in London. She made no effort to contact me, however, and on the second day, fearful that she would leave to go to Mordred's side, I sent a message to her. She answered that she would come to the Tower the next morning.

In the afternoon a runner arrived with word of Arthur's landing and his first pitched battle with Mordred's troops. "Blood all over," the man panted, "and nothing decided. Mordred's withdrawn, but the High King is following, sure as death."

The news turned London into a madhouse. Always a polyglot city of Saxon, Briton, Celt, and Roman, its peoples now reacted in wildly divergent ways. Everywhere was speculation and rumor: that Saxon partisans were taking over the city in Mordred's name; the druids were offering sanctuary to any who wished to accompany them to the sacred groves; Merlin himself was seen flying over the city Wall near Bishopsgate, where he ran into an elm tree and settled down to roost in its branches.

Some of the stories were funny, others unnerving, and all of them without any shred of truth, though the people seemed to swallow them whole.

And if that wasn't enough, no sooner had the night darkened to the point where torches must be lit than the sentries on the walls sent out a horrendous cry. There, in the West, was a giant comet, plowing across the sky and leaving a furrow of sparks and fire in its wake. I stood and gaped at it, along with everyone else.

What had been confusion quickly turned to terror. Believing it signaled the end of everything, people ran screaming through the streets, hid in attics, and growled like mad dogs at friends and relatives. Some got roaring drunk, others became suddenly devout, but all filled the night with their fear, making sleep impossible.

I heard the commotion, saw the chaos, and wondered if they were right. Perhaps the world was coming to an end, at least as we knew it. "If so," I prayed, "let it happen now, so that I can avoid meeting Morgan on the morrow."

But dawn came as usual, and with it the need to rise and dress for the occasion. Though I'd left Camelot with only my traveling dress and cape, I'd found one of my old silk dresses left behind in a cupboard in the Imperial Palace. It was the color of green apples and had been made for me from a garment my mother had owned.

Enid helped me brush out my hair and pinned it into a simple bun at the back of my head, then held the bronze mirror while I slid Ingraine's torc around my neck. The end result, I decided, looked regal without being fussy, authoritative without being harsh.

With luck, I told myself, Morgan and I can discuss this matter calmly, in a statesmanlike way—two monarchs negotiating rationally, in a climate of diplomatic propriety. One doesn't have to like one's counterpart to see the need for rational agreement when the life and death of a country are at stake.

Finally, with a heavy heart, I thanked my women for their attendance, and taking a deep breath, went to the upper room to wait for the woman I feared most in the whole of Britain.

36

Morgan le Fey

organ's dwarf strode across the floor and planted himself directly in front of me. He was dressed in Kendal green, in a well-cut battle jacket that was padded and studded with brass bosses, and his stunted legs were covered by specially fitted boots. Just as in all our past meetings, he managed to look right through me, as though I didn't exist.

"Her Royal Highness, Morgan le Fey, Lady of the Lake and High Priestess of the Goddess," he announced in stentorian tones.

There was a rustle from the shadows beyond the door, and Morgan swept into the room, her cape flowing around her like a swirl of dark smoke. She was still petite and beautiful, with only a trace of gray threading through her black hair, and her green eyes were as compelling as ever.

Once I had been intimidated by Morgan: by her beauty, her power, and her immense presence. Now I just felt ragged and worn down—a tired Queen too used to wielding power of my own to be overawed by a beautiful woman. Not that I underestimated my sister-in-law; clever and determined, she would drive a hard bargain—if, in fact, I could tempt her to negotiate. But her physical elegance no longer impressed me.

When she came to a stop, I scanned her face, noting that age had not softened the vixen sharpness of her features. There were no overt signs of weakness that might give me an advantage: no petulant pout, no hint of overblown appetites. Over the years she had maintained the same purity of energy and dedication that had marked her as a young woman, though I noticed her mouth turned down in a perpetual frown. It was not a visage to inspire confidence in anything but her determination to get her own way. Still, I told myself, there were a few things I held the key to, and with careful bartering, we might reach a suitable agreement.

"Well come, Sister," I said, but I neither rose nor offered her the kinsman's embrace. Instead I motioned to the camp chair on the other side of the small table. "Won't you sit down? I was about to have tea served."

"I have little time," the High Priestess snapped, looking at my Spartan living arrangements with obvious distaste. "If there is something you want from me, I suggest you name it."

"That you help stop this war between Arthur and Mordred."

My directness didn't seem to disconcert her, though her eyebrows lifted.

"Why should I? As I recall, as long as my brother is King, I am banished from Logres on pain of death . . ."

"I'll have that revoked," I promised, hoping Arthur would honor it once the rebellion was quashed.

She looked me up and down thoughtfully. "Can you do that?"

"I can try, if you make peace between them."

So far our dialogue had been clear and to the point, and I began to hope the matter could be quickly settled.

But my optimism was short-lived. Some center of gravity shifted in Morgan, so that she sank down in the chair and began slowly and deliberately taking off her gloves, as though she'd suddenly found all the time in the world.

"What exactly did you have in mind?"

"Negotiations between them. If each of them has a mediator and is willing and able to make a truce on the promise that the concerns of each side be addressed . . . Mordred will surely listen to you, and Nimue has said she'd represent Arthur."

"Nimue!" The name whipped out of Morgan's mouth, and she jerked to her feet. "Merlin's little darling? Have you forgotten I had to expel her from the Sanctuary for arrogance and insubordination?" My sister-in-law suddenly glared at me with the malevolence of a hoody crow.

Drat, I thought, dimly remembering that back before Arthur and I married, Morgan had been jealous of Nimue's powers.

Apparently the High Priestess never relinquished a grievance, but guarded them like a miser hoarding gold.

"Perhaps you need not deal with her," I hedged. "Perhaps I can arrange for you to meet directly with Arthur."

It was a gamble, and one I felt very unsure of, but the idea caught her fancy, and Morgan sat down again and scanned my face with her green cat's eyes.

"How unfortunate that two men of such close kinship should be at each other's throats," she purred. "It is truly a pity when father and son set out to kill each other."

"So you knew. . . ." The words came out involuntarily, and she smiled at my surprise.

"And you wonder why I never made it public?" Morgan lifted her shoulders with an exasperated sigh and looked off into a space of her own. "My poor, foolish sister . . . Morgause was never very bright, you know. Big and lusty, she was the one to inherit Mother's passion for men. Not that she was besotted in the ways Mother was—never prattled on about love and always saw bed for the path to power that it is. But she didn't think things out very clearly. I remember how proud she was . . . so proud of having seduced Arthur, bragging to me that she would bind him to her by producing his child, as if it would make any difference to him!"

Morgan shook her head sadly, still seemingly distressed by her sister's naïveté.

"Men walk away from bed with a shrug and a laugh, but a woman is branded, sniggered at, seen as a whore or tawdry plaything and tossed aside. That was something Morgause never understood, anymore than Mother did. Oh, I suppose the guilty secret of incest could have given her some leverage over Arthur, if she hadn't let Merlin drive her away from Court. But as it was, she was driven out, left to bear the child and raise it by herself. Arthur took no heed of it at all . . . or of her, for that matter. Never once sent to inquire how she was, if she lacked for anything, what she might need or want. He'd taken his pleasure, and that was that."

I winced at the insult to my husband and had to bite my lip to keep from blurting out a rebuttal. But Morgan was caught in the grip of some inner fury and didn't see my response.

Anger and vindictiveness filled her face, twisting her mouth awry. "That for the power men take to themselves!" she snarled, spitting furiously on the floor.

I gasped at the vehemence of her action, but she quickly regained her composure, sitting back in the chair and carefully arranging the folds of her garment across her lap. By the time she spoke again, both her voice and manner had returned to normal.

"When I realized Morgause had died without even telling the boy, I saw no reason to broadcast what had happened. A secret loses its power if it becomes common knowledge, and I suppose I thought someday I'd find a use for the information. In the meantime, why ruin Morgause's reputation? She may have spent entirely too much time stumbling in and out of bed, but she was still my sister, after all."

I stared at Morgan with bemused surprise. Who would have thought that familial loyalty to her sister would override Morgan's desire for revenge against Arthur? As for myself, I was too exhausted from too many nights without sleep to worry about who knew or didn't know about the incest.

The Lady of the Lake suddenly changed both mood and subject, leaning toward me and speaking in a most patronizing way. "Mordred and I are very close, you know. He's asked me to become the Dowager Queen if I join his rebellion against your husband. We'll be discussing the matter shortly."

So that was why she'd left the Sanctuary. I nodded slowly, glad to know that Mordred had appealed to her political vanity.

"Does he also promise to support your religious crusade?" I inquired. "Build new temples, honor your rites with his presence, help spread the new teaching?" It was the one thing I felt confident she could not get from him.

Morgan's green eyes narrowed, but not before a gleam of interest flashed through them. I followed my advantage immediately.

"As I recall, Mordred has little use for any deity, much less the Goddess. He'd be an odd one to champion your cause—and not nearly as effective as I could be."

"In return for my helping Arthur?"

I nodded in affirmation as Enid appeared at the doorway, bringing the teapot and biscuits on a tray. With great deliberateness I turned my attention to the tea things, giving my sister-in-law time to weigh my offer.

When the herbal brew had been poured and Enid retreated, I looked over at Morgan and saw a cool, calculating smile on her face. Clearly she was intrigued by my proposal. It was then I backed away from the subject, hoping to force her to reach for the bait, to commit to wanting it.

"Such a nice tradition," I said casually, handing her a cup of tea. "I learned it from Igraine."

"Ah yes, Mother's famous tea parties." Morgan's attention wavered for a moment, then slid away from the negotiations. When she spoke, her voice was both wistful and sharp. "She was always great for manners and nice behavior. And handsome things."

The High Priestess was studying me with a cold contempt, and I realized too late that statesmanship had been forgotten and I was close to losing control of the entire meeting.

Morgan's gaze had gone to my throat. "She, too, wore that torc whenever possible. You're very like her, you know . . . smug, complacent pussycats, constantly preening yourselves in the belief you can wrap men around your little fingers. Though my mother, of course, was quite foolish about it. She thought those men *loved* her, when she was nothing more than the pitiful receptacle for their stupid rutting."

Shocked by the ferocity of her attack on Igraine, my already frayed nerves gave way and I lashed back.

"How dare you speak of your mother that way! What do you know of her life, you who never bothered to talk with her, who never came to visit? Why, you weren't even there when she died. It's no wonder Igraine considered me the daughter of her heart when you and Morgause cared so little."

"Cared?" Morgan's laughter had a hollow ring, as though it came from the sad, embittered core of her. "Don't talk to me of caring. Have you forgotten she sent both her daughters away the moment Uther Pendragon entered her bed, and farmed Arthur out to Merlin as soon as he was born? Such a singular lack of maternal instinct does little to inspire a sense of caring."

The High Priestess's face was hard as flint, and she flung herself from the chair. I blinked in consternation, realizing there'd be no chance to deal with truces and treaties until she'd given vent to the years of anger she'd compiled. So I settled back in my chair and watched the Lady of the Lake throw herself about the room like a wild animal trotting frantically back and forth at the end of a tether.

"All her life Mother was a pawn, a stupid, silly pawn, too proud to admit what a dupe she had been. Sold as a child bride to a man old enough to be her grandfather and kept like a pretty toy in the fortress at Tintagel. Tales of her beauty stirred up the jack-a-napes throughout the realm until the High King murdered my father, just to see for himself. Uther Pendragon"—Morgan's voice dripped venom—"raped my mother and placed her on the High Throne of Britain like a trophy, all to satisfy his own lust. And she let herself be gulled into thinking it was an honor to be so used. By the Goddess, I call such self-delusions criminal!"

Morgan stopped abruptly in front of the window and, folding her arms, glared out at the river Thames. Her shoulders were shaking, though whether with rage or tears, I couldn't tell. As the silence lengthened, I judged the worst of the outburst was over, and slowly, as if dealing with a fractious horse, I began to talk to her, quietly and calmly.

"There now, that's but one way of looking at it. I was with Igraine when she died, heard her last confession and know how she, herself, saw her life, Morgan. Igraine honored your father highly. Yes, he was much older, and yes he had raised her after her family was killed during the Time of Troubles. But that's hardly the same as purchasing her for prurient reasons, and she was proud to be his wife and bear you and Morgause for him."

Morgan kept her back to me, but her shoulders no longer shook, so I went on. Perhaps, in some benighted way, I thought that hearing the truth might help her let go of the anger she had nurtured for so long.

"As for Uther Pendragon—he did not murder your father. And she lay with him of her own free will, and with full knowledge and desire. Neither Arthur nor the marriage that followed was the result of rape, and neither your mother nor Uther had any idea that your father would die that night."

"Not true!" The Priestess whirled from the window, spewing denials in all directions. "Lies, all of it lies!"

Her face was contorted with fury and her hands balled into fists. The green eyes held a glassy malevolence as she stalked across the room, advancing on me with the intent of stopping my words at all cost. It was as though by physically closing my throat she could wipe out the reality she would never admit to. I shrank before the force of her onslaught and threw up my arms in defense just as the dwarf stepped forward and intercepted his mistress.

Carefully and firmly the little man took her hands in his own, staring up at her and murmuring some kind of private message. When her eyes began to fill with tears, he led her gently to the chair across from me. He was as tender with her as a mother with a frail child, and after she was settled, he gave her a courtly bow and resumed his post by the door. At no time did either one of them look at me, and I suddenly felt like an intruder in a very private partnership.

Once Morgan had her emotions under control, she reached for her gloves as though preparing to leave. "I really must get on to see Mordred, you know," she announced with a brittle smile, though she didn't look at me.

"But what about my offer?" I spoke hastily, jolted by the realization that because statesmanship had been forgotten, the chance of averting war had been lost.

"Can you *guarantee* Arthur will support my cause? That he will make worship of the Goddess mandatory throughout the realm and tear down the churches?"

"I will do my best," I pledged, knowing I could only commit myself, not my husband, to her demand. "I will work tirelessly for you."

"Not good enough." She got to her feet. "There's no way to hold Arthur accountable for your pledges."

It was obvious her outburst had wakened resentments more important to her than either political or religious ambitions. With dread tugging at my soul, I pressed on.

"What would satisfy you?"

Morgan gathered her cloak around her shoulders and stared down at me like the Goddess in Her hag aspect. Our eyes met, and I saw scorn turn to curiosity, then real interest. No doubt she saw, for the first time, just how desperate I was.

"You want my help *that* much?" A half-smile crossed her features, and she sat back down with a graceful gesture. Lifting her teacup from the table, she stared at me over its rim, dark brows knit in contemplation.

"There may, in fact, be something I can do," she said at last, her rich voice going low and thoughtful. "Mordred is counting on me to raise an army in the north for him. If he realizes I could just as easily take it to Arthur's side . . . perhaps he could be convinced to negotiate."

A long silence followed while Morgan continued to study me. She was now completely in control of the situation, and I waited, fascinated, wondering what the price would be. "And in return?" I finally prompted, my voice barely above a whisper.

"Something only you can give." She held the teacup in one hand and let the fingers of the other rub slowly around the rim. "Yes, an agreement we can make between us—one that doesn't need Arthur's approval—in return for my coming to his aid."

I held my breath while she continued to play with the cup. At last, quite certain of herself, she nodded and looked at me pleasantly.

"I swear to protect Arthur in every way I can; to attempt to dissuade Mordred from battle, or act as his mediator; even to bring my healing arts to Arthur's side if he needs them . . . all this I promise to do, once you abdicate as High Queen of Britain."

"What!" Disbelief shattered my reserve, and Morgan smiled outright.

"Of course not," I exclaimed, shock ricocheting through me. "I can't just up and leave my people."

"Oh, I think you can. You abandoned them when you fled from Carlisle, and later you abdicated your position in Rheged for Lancelot. Of course, it may be you secretly want this war—if Arthur dies, Lancelot could return to Britain. That is, if Mordred doesn't kill him as well." Painting such grotesque futures seemed to amuse her, and she shrugged eloquently as she put the cup on the table. "In the end, I suppose it all depends on how much you want any of them to live."

Outraged at her proposal, infuriated by her jibes, utterly powerless to deflect the demands she was making, I glared at her like a cornered animal.

"There is nowhere for me to go," I temporized, "unless Uwain will let me come back to Rheged."

"A popular Queen who has only recently given over her crown? No, my dear. Uwain may be awfully like his father, but he's not so dumb as to allow that." Morgan's voice turned to silk. "I'll make sure that Arthur doesn't die, provided you write out a statement saying you are renouncing your position at Court . . . in order to go live in a convent."

"Convent?" A wave of panic engulfed me, and I said the first thing that popped into my head. "I'm not even Christian."

"Oh, I think something can be arranged, as long as you promise to stay there for the rest of your life. Until you die. Otherwise Arthur's life will be forfeit."

Terrible carnage, Nimue had said. Blood and gore and all the horror of civil war that I had so long tried to avoid. No matter what I did, the specter rose again, spattering me with death and the knowledge I could have averted it.

Yet the concept of knowingly, willingly entombing myself behind walls for the rest of my life was worse than facing the stake. My mind darted frantically here and there, trying to find a way out of the predicament.

And all the while Morgan sat in silence, watching me wrestle with my love of freedom and my love for Arthur. No doubt she knew what the end would be.

"If I agree to this, how do I know you'll do as you say?" I asked finally, hoping to gain some last advantage in the bargain.

The Lady of the Lake drew her head back and gave me a haughty look. "I am a Celt, and I do not lie," she intoned, sounding exactly like Gawain.

"Of course," she added, getting to her feet again, "if you are unwilling, I must be on my way—Mordred is waiting for my answer."

It took every ounce of strength and dignity I could muster, but I rose and looked my sister-in-law in the face. For a long moment we stared at each other, the fear and loathing lying naked between us until I finally bowed my head.

"I will go to the convent in the Chiltern Hills," I said slowly and distinctly as the world constricted around me.

"Good. You'll write out your abdication now and leave for the holy house immediately thereafter," the High Priestess ordered. "My lieutenant will escort you, to make sure you arrive . . .

safely." She paused a moment more, eyes on the golden torc around my neck. "By rights that should be mine."

"Igraine gave it to me as a wedding present," I objected, instinctively reaching up to touch it.

But Morgan was too quick for me. Grabbing the lovely rope of gold that had been the badge of freedom since time began, she jerked it off my neck, springing it out of shape and abrading my skin at the same time.

Without another word she turned on her heel and left, while I stood there, a woman bereft of both past and future.

So it was done. What I had treated as a matter of diplomatic barter had turned into personal revenge for the Lady. And the bargain I struck to save Arthur's life became the agreement that destroyed my own.

I wondered if he would ever know the final gift of love I'd given him.

37

Camlann

stood in front of the only entrance in the convent wall and waited, dry-eyed, while Morgan's lieutenant used his sword hilt to reach the knocker.

It was a stout oaken door, banded with iron straps. A small square panel was set into the wood at head height so that visitors could be identified without compromising the barrier of the door itself. The novice who peeped through the panel in response to our knock was young and timid, and lacked the authority to let us in, so we waited while she ran off to find an older nun. Security here was nothing if not thorough.

When it was decided we posed no threat, there was much scraping of wood against metal as the door was unbarred from inside.

"Ah, you wish to see the Abbess," the sister responded when I asked for Brigit. "Whom should I tell her is here?"

"Gwenhwyvaer of Rheged," I answered. "Tell her Gwenhwyvaer is here."

The nun looked at me critically, noting my fur-trimmed cloak and soft leather boots. But these were no more than any noble lady might wear, and if she recognized me, she kept it to herself. There was no point in upsetting the peace of the holy house by announcing who I was—or rather, who I used to be.

I waited, my heart in my throat, while the novice went off to fetch my foster sister. Morgan's dwarf pointedly took up a position between me and the door and began flicking his riding crop against his palm. At last there was a commotion at the end of a far corridor and the sound of footsteps running toward us.

Brigit burst into the room, veil flying and wisps of red hair escaping from her coif. "Holy Mother be praised, it *is* you!" she exclaimed, enveloping me in a joyful hug, as though she'd expected never to see me again.

I leaned against her, grateful for the support and welcome. Suddenly, with nowhere else to go, nothing left to be done, I felt utterly and completely drained.

"Enid's waiting in the courtyard," I murmured, ". . . the one who married Geraint."

"Both you and your company are always welcome," Brigit said gently, but I felt her stiffen as her eye fell on Morgan's lieutenant.

"I'm here to make sure your new charge is settled properly," the man announced. "I'll be returning to London once you agree to accept her lifetime pledge to stay in your house."

"Lifetime?" Brigit pulled back to look at me, incredulity written all over her freckled face.

"Aye, I've come to seek asylum. I have promised to spend the rest of my days with you." The words came out in measured cadence, though I had no volition to say them.

Brigit stared at me long and hard, then turned to the dwarf. "You may tell your mistress that we will take care of her," she said firmly.

So she remembered, and knew who was driving me to this. I looked at her gratefully.

"Come, let us get you settled." Brigit sent a novice out to fetch Enid, then gave Morgan's lieutenant a curt dismissal before leading me down the hall to a guest room. "There's been rumors of all kinds that you were dead and buried already! I can't tell you how glad I am to have you here, safe and sound!"

When we reached the guest room, she offered to have a tray of food brought, but I was so weak and tired, all I could do was shake my head.

"You just rest—rest and sleep now, Missy," my foster sister said, taking off my boots and handing me a sleeping robe. "There will be plenty of time to talk tomorrow."

So I crawled under the simple wool blanket and, pulling the covers up over my head, slid into the deep, dreamless sleep of exhaustion.

The next fortnight was a time without measure, a waking dream in which real and unreal blurred into a kind of trancelike blur. The nuns might live behind stout walls, but events in the outside world filtered through to them. Refugees streaming north for fear of the battles to come, worried holy men and busy clerics, even the farmer's wife who delivered milk and cheese—all brought bits and pieces of news, and I hung on their words as though they were messages from the Gods.

Arthur's landing at Dover was much spoken of, along with the death of Gawain. The very audacity of landing in Federate territory seemed to have worked to the High King's advantage, for Mordred had not bothered to reinforce the troops along the Saxon Shore, and among the Federate commoners there were as many for Arthur as against him. It was said that the initial skirmish had put Mordred's troops to flight, though no one knew what would happen next.

"We always remember him in our prayers," Brigit consoled me, "and now we're including you and Enid as well."

"And Mordred," I said. "Ask your Father God to make him change his mind."

"Perhaps the Son would be more appropriate," the Irish lass quipped, and I smiled wanly, warmed by the wit which had sustained me all through childhood. If I had to be imprisoned, I was glad it was here.

Like one in a trance waiting for the release that might never come, I moved through each day, taking part in the pattern of work and worship that makes up convent life. Since I had not been baptized, I was not expected to join the sisters in chapel for the midnight prayers, though I was often awake when the bell rang to summon them from their beds.

My sleep was fitful at best, and beset by nightmares—the old, familiar terrors now shifting from known fear to unpredictable grotesquery. When I dreamt of my father dancing in the flames of Beltane, it was myself I saw, though nowhere could I find Lancelot and safety. Sometimes Gareth's dying face rose to haunt me, or Morgan came to call, her voice high and cold as she laughed at my heartache. But by far the worst—and most common—was the nightmare of Arthur dying in battle. It was this vision that haunted me every night.

I'd been at the convent for almost two weeks when the farmer's daughter, coming in her mother's place, stopped by the kitchen, full of news about the warriors gathering near the bend of the river on the Plain. "Camlann, we calls it. Dog-leg, you might say. Proud men on proud horses, with shields and helmets, and swords all shining in the light. Thousands strong, they say."

"What insignias?" I asked eagerly.

The girl shrugged slightly. "White horsetail standards swishing in the breeze . . . Saxon, someone said. And the High King's Dragon." She frowned, trying to remember. "And maybe a White Boar, from Cornwall."

"Constantine," I whispered thankfully, my mind seeing rank after rank of men spread out across the Plain, as in my dream.

"Dear God," I prayed, suddenly going weak in the knees, "give Morgan a tongue of gold. Give Arthur all the strength and courage he needs. And Mordred . . . give him some sense to see the futility of what he's doing."

That afternoon the first of the autumn storms passed through, soaking the woods and making the streams and rivulets spring to life. Come night, I lay on my cot, listening to the distant honking of geese moving down from the north, and wondered if the redstarts had left Northumbria for the winter. High in the dark sky a curlew's call fell to earth, wrapping me in dreams.

I was on a high, mossy upland, wide and free under the sky, standing beneath its blue dome with my arms held out like the crucifix I saw each day above the altar. Far away there was a tramping sound, at first a mere vibration that grew to thunder in my head. Eight abreast the warriors came, all unknowing that I lay beneath their feet, crying out like the earth herself against the death of her children. Only when the great auroch's horns boomed, their deep voices moaning over the land, did I dissolve and fall onto the shadowy edges of the Plain . . . onto the known, familiar place of death I visited nightly now.

Here were the two armies drawn up, horses pawing impatiently, carrion crows and wolves waiting for the carnage to begin. Here the future—death and life—and in the center, locked in silent, ghostly combat, a pair of Champions struggled.

"No!" I screamed, hearing my own voice break away as I ran, dodged, flung myself toward them in a long, desperate effort to cross the rolling land.

My lungs were bursting and my muscles ached, as though I both dealt and received each blow, while slowly, with infinite grace, the two combatants went through their ghoulish dance.

"Stop," I cried, though the words carried no sound. "No more, I beg you, no more!"

Deaf to all but the beat of their moira, drawn to each other in deadly embrace, the warriors moved in and out of my sight as in the past. But this time the sky turned red, my vision blurred, a gale whipped my hair into my eyes—and when I shook it free, the ground was littered with bodies. Dead, dying, moaning with the pitiful voices of lost children, screaming against the savagery of their slaying, I saw the messy wake of war, the tangle of guts and limbs and twitching hands, the red drop of blood hanging from each mouth like a jewel.

The scene went slack, sliding into repose, and my sight narrowed to the two in the center. Bloodied, hacked and weary to the point of blindness, one slumped morosely against the trunk of a nearby tree, the other on a pile of fallen friends.

"This time," I cried, "this time it must be different!"

But even as I willed it otherwise, the warrior with the sword stirred and rose from the shelter of his dead comrades. Like a hound that has just found the scent, his aching body responded to the enemy presence, collecting all faculties, centering on the exhausted man beside the tree.

After a long moment's scrutiny, the swordsman began the slow, inevitable advance toward his opponent.

"Leave be!" I cried, feeling the panic, knowing already the result, begging my love to turn aside from this last, fatal encounter. But there might as well have been a wall of glass between us, for he heard me not at all, and I was powerless to sway one little moment of the confrontation.

The warrior at the tree tensed, sensing danger, and straightened slowly. He moved his head from side to side, as if he could not see clearly, and without taking his eyes from the threat, reached for the spear shaft that stood upright not an arm's distance away. Wrenching the spearhead free of the corpse, he hefted the weapon for balance and crouched as he faced his opponent.

It was then I knew, as I knew every night, there was only one ending to the tale; only one victor over us all, regardless of the many forms I saw him take.

Usually, in the past, the man with the spear had been Maelgwn, grinning at Arthur with the same cold triumph as when he had raped me. Sometimes he wore a masking helmet, such as Accolon had when he almost killed the High King for Morgan. Once I thought it was Lance standing there, poised to kill my husband, and I had sobbed hysterically at the thought.

This time both figures were in silhouette against the crimson sky, and I saw neither face, though the dance was horribly familiar.

Closer and closer the swordsman came, slashing and feinting with a growing vigor. The spearman, however, moved like a man worn thin, hoarding his energy, using the length of his weapon to keep the flashing blade of his foe at a distance. Yet in spite of the spearman's longer reach, the swordsman would not be deterred. Risking all things mortal for the chance—the one last chance—of felling his nemesis, he made a ghastly dash toward the heart of the matter. I saw him leap forward and screamed as the cold iron spearhead plunged through armor and warm flesh.

The thrust I had seen so often before pierced my body as well as my dream, pinning me in helpless horror as I watched the warrior begin to die. But this was a new, a different dance, and I stared at the tableau, sickened to the soul, yet unable to look away.

Writhing in agony, shape against shadow, black against bloody heaven, I saw the impaled man lean forward and, using his free hand, pull himself along the ashwood spearshaft. His lungs gurgled; his hands were covered with sweat, and where it had come out his back, the spearhead took blood and entrails with it. Yet hand-hold by hand-hold, he drew his own death closer. The whole of his life's purpose was brutally, horribly focused in that one act, and when he had sufficiently narrowed the space between himself and the slayer, he lifted his sword in both hands, high above his head.

A light suffused his face, as cold as marsh-fire, as burning as lightning. It leapt eerily between the two men, casting first one and then the other in relief, and I gasped in that terrible heartbeat when I realized that this time the man on the spear was not my husband.

Arthur crouched beside the tree, his face twisted with anguish and disbelief as he gaped at the opponent who had clawed his way close enough to strike.

"Say it, damn you!" the skewered man begged, his upraised blade wavering as his life ebbed. He was glaring at the High King with every passion known to humankind, but Arthur was struck dumb by knowledge and despair.

"The word is *son*," the dying man sobbed, bringing the blade crashing down on his father.

"Mordred! Oh, Mordred!" I screamed, flinging myself upright on the pallet. I was drenched with sweat and horror and nausea.

"There, there now," Enid cried, rushing to my bedside from her room across the hall. "It's all right, M'lady, it's all right. It's only a bad dream."

"No," I whimpered as she wrapped her arms around me. "Not this time. This time it was real."And I began to shake uncontrollably with the sad, miserable certainty of it.

So we played out our eternal dance—fathers and sons, mothers and daughters. There was no way I could have changed the patterns of those fates any more than I could undo Camelot, or will the Breton to never cross my path, or kept from loving Igraine, or make Morgan less needful of power and revenge.

It took awhile to realize that, but by the time Bedivere requested permission to see me at the convent, I was beginning to come to terms with it.

I met him in a private room, away from the discreet but curious eyes of the nuns, and when the door was closed behind us, he immediately came to my side.

"Ah, Gwen, I do not know how to tell you . . ." His voice broke, and he took my hand and put it to his cheek. I felt the tears against my skin, and gently raised the other hand so as to hold his face between my palms.

"I saw it, Bedivere—I saw them kill each other in my dream."

The craggy lieutenant stared down at me, his face furrowed with sorrow.

"And I heard of Gawain's death at Dover," I added, leading Arthur's foster brother to the bench beneath the window. "Was it from Lance's blow?"

"Aye, I'm afraid it was." Bedivere sighed heavily. "But at the end the Prince of Orkney regretted all the trouble he'd caused.

When it was clear that Mordred was close to claiming the whole of Britain for his own, and the Orcadian knew he was dying, he dictated a letter to Lancelot, begging the Breton's forgiveness and asking him to come to Arthur's aid."

How like Gawain—impetuous, hotheaded, quick to love and hate, laugh and cry. I remembered the gap-toothed redhead and smiled.

"Who else, Bedivere? Who else was lost?"

"Almost everyone, M'lady. It looked to be working out well enough at first, when the armies were drawn up. Morgan le Fey and several of the druids stepped into the space between the men and demanded, in the Old Way, that there be no fighting until the matter had been negotiated. Many of the warriors were un-certain—Saxons don't have a tradition of priests who can stop wars, and the Christians weren't sure they could trust the Lady. But she and Nimue convinced Mordred and Arthur to meet in the middle, so the armies stood down, with the warning that if a single sword was drawn, the battle would commence."

Bedivere paused, as though reliving the scene in his mind. "I was at Arthur's side, just as I had been when he won his first battle, and again when he was crowned. And yet I cannot tell you what was said. He and Mordred stared at each other, neither blinking, neither giving way. Morgan tried to talk with them, tried to find some common ground, but they only sat there, still as stone. Perhaps she could have softened them if there had been more time. But the day grew warm, as autumn days occasionally do, and somewhere in the grasses an adder stretched and crawled across a warrior's boot. Without thinking the man drew his weapon to cut its head off—and all other warriors drew as well. So it began . . . and ended . . . that wicked, wicked day!"

"And Cei?" I asked, seeing the lopsided grin the Seneschal had favored me with during our last meeting in the Tower. "Where is he?"

"Long dead and buried in Brittany, lost in a melee with Lance's men. But Griflet still lived at Camlann, M'lady. It was he and Lucan the Gatekeeper who helped me carry Arthur from the field."

"From the field?" For a moment the smallest of hopes flickered before me. "Then he wasn't killed by Mordred's stroke?"

"Not outright." Bedivere swallowed hard and looked away.

"When the day was done and there was nothing left but broken bodies strewn about, I wandered through them, trying to find the King. I came upon him, propped against a tree, his hand resting on Mordred's forehead as though in blessing, or maybe apology. But already he had grown weak, Gwen—pale and clammy with loss of blood, unable even to stand. I was trying to make some kind of litter when Lucan stumbled up, and Griflet as well.

"Together the three of us moved Arthur away from that awful place, taking him, at his request, down to the riverbank. Griflet wasn't able to complete the trip; he staggered and fell before we reached the water. His tunic was hanging in shreds, and only after he collapsed did I realize his belly had been slit open. The wound was bad enough, but the exertion of carrying his King killed him. Before he died, he asked to be remembered to you."

Tears filled my eyes for the Kennel Master. A quiet, self-effacing man, he'd been but a boy sent to accompany me south to marry Arthur, a boy who fell in love with a Saxon maid, and gave us all a lifetime of service, a full measure of devotion. It was men like him who had made Camelot possible.

"But Arthur—where is he now?"

"Gone, Gwen. Taken away by the Lady of the Lake. He sent me to hide Excalibur, not wanting it to fall into Saxon hands, and when I returned, I saw a small boat riding on the river current. The King was lying in the prow, with his head in Morgan's lap, and it seemed they were drifting off toward Glastonbury —to Avalon, or the Isle of Glass. Whether he was dead or still living, I couldn't tell, but his sister has care of him now, and if anyone can heal him, she can."

So she kept her promise, and somewhere Arthur may or may not be alive. I smiled bleakly in the face of such uncertainty while Bedivere stood up and moved stiffly toward a table by the door. For the first time I realized he was limping, no doubt from wounds he himself had taken at Camlann.

"I have two reasons to come see you," he said, reaching for a package that lay on the table. "Although Mordred died, the Saxons were swarming all over the area, and I was afraid they might find Excalibur. Nothing proves the death of a leader so much as having his sword captured by the enemy, so I retrieved it from its hiding place."

He opened the oiled leather coverings of the bundle and lifted the sword and scabbard from the folds. Even in the dim light of the convent room it shone like a treasure from legend. Going down on one knee, he held it out to me, the hilt on his good hand, the tip supported by the hook on his gauntlet.

"There are some few of us left. Constantine of Cornwall survived, as did Gwyn of Neath, for all that he went coursing everywhere over that battlefield, like his namesake God who escorts the war-dead off to glory! He'd be willing to lead the Welsh, of that I'm sure. And Uwain in Northumbria, who refrained from coming to Camlann, would surely make common cause with us against the Saxons. If you would sanction such a coalition, and raise Excalibur as Arthur's Queen . . ."

His voice trailed off when I shook my head, slowly and sadly. "Even if I wanted to pursue the warpath, I cannot, my friend. Arthur's life, if he lives, is forfeit to my remaining in the convent. I dare not take the risk, unless it was absolutely certain he was dead. And even then, I have it on good authority I have too soft a heart to be a 'great' monarch . . ."

I reached out and ran my fingers along the sheathed sword, beginning at the chape. The designs on the scabbard were as elegant and mysterious as when Morgan first embroidered them, back before she turned against us. The gold-and-silver hilt was as bright as the first day I'd seen it, and I traced the intricate patterns with love and respect. Only the fire of the amethyst was gone; it lay cradled in its mounting like any other lump of stone, as though the spirit that had suffused its owner had now departed from it as well.

Knowing this was as close as I might come to saying farewell to my husband, I bent slowly and placed a kiss on the hilt so often held in his hand.

"If Arthur lives, he will need it again," I said slowly. "If he doesn't . . . I think you should cast it into a lake, as an offering to the Goddess who gave it to him to begin with. There is a kind of symmetry in that, since Morgan raised it for him by the waters of the Black Lake."

Bedivere nodded silently and rose with a sigh to return Excalibur to its coverings. Then he came back to the bench, and sitting beside me again, he took my hand in his.

"There is one more thing you should know. Lancelot did come

to Arthur's aid, though he arrived too late. There were a few minor battles with various bands of Federates, but most of his warriors have gone back to Brittany without him. He is with me now—waiting in the courtyard—in the hope that you'll see him."

I heard the words as from a long way away, like the echo of the wind across the grassy hills, and my response was a bare whisper. "How is he, Bedivere? Is he whole? Sane? As shattered by this as the rest of us?"

Bedivere ducked his head and swallowed hard. "Aye, all of that. Some days he blames himself unmercifully for what has happened. Other days he spends in prayer, lapsing into the kind of trance the mystics seek. Arthur may have found his end, but Lance is still questing. I think that's why he's sought you out."

Sitting very still, remembering the days and nights and years we'd shared, I reached out and covered Bedivere's hand with my free one.

"Tell him," I said softly, "that I can never take the place of God. I will always love him, as I have always loved Arthur. But he must find his Grail, just as I must honor my bargain with Morgan." A single tear slid down my cheek and fell on the back of my hand. "Say I will not see him, but release him from all past promises."

And so it came to an end, that fine, free dream of love that had raced against the clouds and leapt the rivers of time. Neither one of us, I knew, would cease to care, but each must stay apart from the other for the rest of our lives.

I said goodbye to Bedivere, but not before asking if he wished to see Brigit, whom he had loved as a girl, before she chose the holy life.

"I've already spoken to her, when I first arrived. She's a fine lass, still—and I'm glad she's by your side again."

With a last craggy smile Arthur's foster brother gathered up Excalibur and opened the door. Behind him the quiet of the convent stretched away down the corridors, and he turned to give me a last, final salute.

Only after the door closed behind him did I turn my face to the wall and begin to cry.

Epilogue

ow many years ago that was! Hard to believe that I, Sister Gwenhwyvaer of Rheged, have spent as many years in this holy house as I did on the High Throne of Britain! It is as puzzling as the fact that I, who used to run through the morning of my life, am now grown old and frail, content to shuffle quietly from the crones' bench in the garden to the back pew in the chapel. And where I once railed at the fate that shattered Camelot and limited my world to these four walls, I now look back and smile. *My horizons may have grown smaller, but not my heart.*

Over the years bits and snippets of news fell by, winging their way through the beechwood like the hedge sparrows that return to the garden every spring. Arthur was said to have been buried at Glastonbury; to be sleeping in a cave; to be living in Avalon with Morgan. Everyone and no one knew where he was, or even if he was still alive. But if he lives, I dare not leave the convent, for I'm sure Morgan will never forget my promise.

It's odd how, in the first half of my life, I always knew where Arthur was, and it was Lance who was off wandering. Now it is Arthur I pray for and wonder about, while Lance lives quietly at the hermitage in Glastonbury, with Bors and Bedivere.

They seem to have settled in there, telling their beads at the base of the Tor, in the shadow of Gwyn's pagan fortlet. Someone said that Palomides was with them for a while, before setting off for the Holy Land in search of Perceval, with whom he plans to pursue the Grail. *It is not as unlikely an alliance as one might think —the worldly philosopher and the holy fool. Between the two of them, they ought to apprehend some kind of deity.*

There has been other news as well, of Saxon victories and British loss. When London fell, both of Lynette's daughters made their way here, though only Lora stayed. Megan was too full of life and the deeds of heroes to take the veil, so she left to join her brother, Lancelot, who had gone to fight at the side of Duke Constantine in Cornwall.

In the years after Father Baldwin came to live with us, we passed more than one wintery evening remembering the days of glory . . . laughing over this adventure, smiling gently at that. Sometimes I tried to make sense of it, to find the shadow of a God's hand, or trace the moira through it all: Gawain pursuing honor until it became an all-consuming obsession; Lancelot questing for a God forever beyond reach; Galahad dedicated to his Grail while Arthur was salvaging some semblance of civilization from the dark threat of chaos and anarchy. And me—busy from dawn to dusk, living and laughing and loving every moment of it.

No doubt there is a pattern there, someplace, though I've never been able to say what it was. Of those that could be called the tragic aspects, the only ones I truly understand are Morgan's little-girl heartbreak and the aching betrayal Mordred found in his father's coldness.

One year Taliesin stopped to visit on his way north to become bard to Maelgwn's son, Rhun. It seems my cousin left the monastery as soon as he learned Arthur was no longer on the High Throne, and returned to rule Gwynedd, where he went back to being a despot. But when the plague swept the land, he sought to avoid the disease by having himself walled up inside a small country chapel with a year's supply of food. Unfortunately the servants, who were supposed to wait outside until the pestilence was gone, took sick and died, and when his food ran out, there was no one to unbrick the doors and windows. *Thus, ironically, he who had kidnapped me and kept me prisoner died as one himself. Perhaps there is some justice out there after all.*

When he left, Taliesin gave me a tract written by the monk, Gildas. Writing in the most dreadful Latin, he scathes all Britons with his acid tongue and claims the Saxon victories are God's punishment for our non-Christian ways. But nowhere does he mention Arthur—or me. *Petty, spiteful little man . . . did he think he could expunge us from history by pretending we didn't exist?*

If so, he's wrong. There was a beekeeper came last night,

asking room in the guest house in return for a comb of his thick, sweet treasure. For all that he was unlettered, he had a way with words, so after dinner we stayed on listening to his stories, while the fire flared up and the room grew warm and golden, almost like the Hall at Camelot.

There is, he said, a wild man who lives alone in the Caledonian Woods, making poems and magic and talking with a striped pig. Merlin, it is—Merlin come back, Merlin the King's Enchanter, weaving his spells all over again. He didn't die, the man said . . . didn't die any more than Arthur did. Why, everyone knows Morgan le Fey healed the Pendragon's wounds, and now he slumbers in a cave, waiting to return when Britain needs him most.

And if any proof is needed, one has only to go to South Cadbury, where the ruins of fabled Camelot stand. The locals, Saxon and Briton alike, will tell you that on any night when the wind has scoured the stars from the sky, 'tis Arthur and Gwyn of Neath who come riding out of the hollow hill, leading the Wild Hunt on their great black horses.

"It's him," the beekeeper swore. "King Arthur himself, with all the finest Champions of his Fellowship, racing to join the Queen who waits for them in the meadow, with May-flowers in her hair and joy in her heart."

The beekeeper didn't notice an old, old lady sitting in the granny-nook, smiling at his words. Why should he? I've become no more than the shadow of a time long gone.

But I heard the tale, and knew that Merlin's promise that we would live forever was a true-spoke prophecy. The people need us, and they will not let us die. Because of them, Camelot still lives, where a Sorcerer's dream became reality, and the Fellowship of the Round Table flowered. Camelot, where men of honor strive for noble causes, and a just king rules in a land of wonder . . . where love lasts forever, and I still watch Arthur and Lancelot come tramping across the courtyard from their morning rounds, heads bent in consultation . . . splendid men they were, for splendid times. . . .

So I smile, knowing the truth of it, loving the humans at the heart of the myth.

Yes, it was magnificent, and no, it was never easy . . . yet, still in all . . . I'd do it all over again, tomorrow.